Collector's Library

THE RETURN OF
SHERLOCK HOLMES
and
HIS LAST BOW

THE RETURN OF SHERLOCK HOLMES

and

HIS LAST BOW

Sir Arthur Conan Doyle

with an Afterword by
DAVID STUART DAVIES

Collector's Library

The Return of Sherlock Holmes was first published
in 1905 and *His Last Bow* in 1917
This edition first published in 2005 by
CRW Publishing Limited
69 Gloucester Crescent, London NW1 7EG
under the *Collector's Library* imprint

ISBN   978 1 904919 71 1

10 9

Typeset in Great Britain by Antony Gray
Printed and bound in China by Imago

CONTENTS

The Return of Sherlock Holmes

His Last Bow

THE RETURN OF
SHERLOCK HOLMES

I

The Empty House

It was in the spring of the year 1894 that all London was interested, and the fashionable world dismayed, by the murder of the Honourable Ronald Adair under most unusual and inexplicable circumstances. The public has already learned those particulars of the crime which came out in the police investigation; but a good deal was suppressed upon that occasion, since the case for the prosecution was so overwhelmingly strong that it was not necessary to bring forward all the facts. Only now, at the end of nearly ten years, am I allowed to supply those missing links which make up the whole of that remarkable chain. The crime was of interest in itself, but that interest was as nothing to me compared to the inconceivable sequel, which afforded me the greatest shock and surprise of any event in my adventurous life. Even now, after this long interval, I find myself thrilling as I think of it, and feeling once more that sudden flood of joy, amazement, and incredulity which utterly submerged my mind. Let me say to that public which has shown some interest in those glimpses which I have occasionally given them of the thoughts and actions of a very remarkable man that they are not to blame me if I have not shared my knowledge with them, for I should have considered it my first duty to have done so had I not been barred by a positive prohibition from his own lips, which was only withdrawn upon the third of last month.

It can be imagined that my close intimacy with Sherlock Holmes had interested me deeply in crime, and that after his disappearance I never failed to read with care the various problems which came before the public, and I even attempted more than once for my own private satisfaction to employ his methods in their solution, though with indifferent success. There was none, however, which appealed to me like this tragedy of Ronald Adair. As I read the evidence at the inquest, which led up to a verdict of wilful murder against some person or persons unknown, I realised more clearly than I had ever done the loss which the community had sustained by the death of Sherlock Holmes. There were points about this strange business which would, I was sure, have specially appealed to him, and the efforts of the police would have been supplemented, or more probably anticipated, by the trained observation and the alert mind of the first criminal agent in Europe. All day as I drove upon my round I turned over the case in my mind, and found no explanation which appeared to me to be adequate. At the risk of telling a twice-told tale I will recapitulate the facts as they were known to the public at the conclusion of the inquest.

The Honourable Ronald Adair was the second son of the Earl of Maynooth, at that time Governor of one of the Australian Colonies. Adair's mother had returned from Australia to undergo an operation for cataract, and she, her son Ronald, and her daughter Hilda were living together at 427 Park Lane. The youth moved in the best society, had, so far as was known, no enemies, and no particular vices. He had been engaged to Miss Edith Woodley, of Carstairs, but the engagement had been broken off by mutual consent some months before, and there was no sign that it had left any very profound feeling behind it. For the rest the man's life moved in a narrow and conventional circle, for his habits were quiet and his nature unemotional. Yet it was upon this easy-going young aristocrat that death came in most strange and unexpected form between the hours of ten and eleven-twenty on the night of March 30, 1894.

Ronald Adair was fond of cards, playing continually, but never for such stakes as would hurt him. He was a member of the Baldwin, the Cavendish, and the Bagatelle card clubs. It was shown that after dinner on the day of his death he had played a rubber of whist at the latter club. He had also played there in the afternoon. The evidence of those who had played with him – Mr Murray, Sir John Hardy, and Colonel Moran – showed that the game was whist, and that there was a fairly equal fall of the cards. Adair might have lost five pounds, but not more. His fortune was a considerable one, and such a loss could not in any way affect him. He had played nearly every day at one club or other, but he was a cautious player, and usually rose a winner. It came out in evidence that in partnership with Colonel Moran he had actually won as much as four hundred and twenty pounds in a sitting some weeks before from Godfrey Milner and Lord Balmoral. So much for his recent history, as it came out at the inquest.

On the evening of the crime he returned from the club exactly at ten. His mother and sister were out spending the evening with a relation. The servant deposed that she heard him enter the front room on the second floor, generally used as his sitting-room. She had lit a fire there, and as it smoked she had opened the window. No sound was heard from the room until eleven-twenty, the hour of the return of Lady Maynooth and her daughter. Desiring to say good-night, she had attempted to enter her son's room. The door was locked on the inside, and no answer could be got to their cries and knocking. Help was obtained and the door forced. The unfortunate young man was found lying near the table. His head had been horribly mutilated by an expanding revolver bullet, but no weapon of any sort was to be found in the room. On the table lay two bank-notes for ten pounds each and seventeen pounds ten in silver and gold, the money arranged in little piles of varying amount. There were some figures also upon a sheet of paper with the names of some club friends opposite to them, from which it was conjectured that before his death he was endeavouring to make out his losses or winnings at cards.

A minute examination of the circumstances served only to make the case more complex. In the first place, no reason could be given why the young man should have fastened the door upon the inside. There was the possibility that the murderer had done this and had afterwards escaped by the window. The drop was at least twenty feet, however, and a bed of crocuses in full bloom lay beneath. Neither the flowers nor the earth showed any sign of having been disturbed, nor were there any marks upon the narrow strip of grass which separated the house from the road. Apparently, there-fore, it was the young man himself who had fastened the door. But how did he come by his death? No one could have climbed up to the window without leaving traces. Suppose a man had fired through the window, it would indeed be a remarkable shot who could with a revolver inflict so deadly a wound. Again, Park Lane is a frequented thoroughfare, and there is a cab-stand within a hundred yards of the house. No one had heard a shot. And yet there was the dead man, and there the revolver bullet, which had mushroomed out, as soft-nosed bullets will, and so inflicted a wound which must have caused instantaneous death. Such were the circumstances of the Park Lane Mystery, which were further complicated by entire absence of motive, since, as I have said, young Adair was not known to have any enemy, and no attempt had been made to remove the money or valuables in the room.

All day I turned these facts over in my mind, endeavouring to hit upon some theory which could reconcile them all, and to find that line of least resistance which my poor friend had declared to be the starting-point of every investigation. I confess that I made little progress. In the evening I strolled across the Park, and found myself about six o'clock at the Oxford Street end of Park Lane. A group of loafers upon the pavements, all staring up at a particular window, directed me to the house which I had come to see. A tall, thin man with coloured glasses, whom I strongly suspected of being a plain-clothes detective, was pointing out some theory of his own, while the others crowded round to listen to what he said. I got as near him as I could, but his observations seemed to me to be absurd, so I withdrew again in some disgust. As I did so I struck against an elderly deformed man, who had been behind me, and I knocked down several books which he was carrying. I remember that as I picked them up I observed the title of one of them, *The Origin of Tree Worship*, and it struck me that the fellow must be some poor bibliophile who, either as a trade or as a hobby, was a collector of obscure volumes. I endeavoured to apologise for the accident, but it was evident that these books which I had so unfortunately maltreated were very precious objects in the eyes of their owner. With a snarl of contempt he turned upon his heel, and I saw his curved back and white side-whiskers disappear among the throng.

My observations of 427 Park Lane did little to clear up the problem in which I was interested. The house was separated from the street by a low wall and railing, the whole not more than five feet high. It was perfectly easy, therefore, for anyone to get into the garden, but the window was entirely inaccessible, since there was no water-pipe or anything which could help the most active man to climb it. More puzzled than ever, I retraced my steps to Kensington. I had not been in my study five minutes when the maid entered to say that a person desired to see me. To my astonishment it was none other than my strange old book-collector, his sharp, wizened face peering out from a frame of white hair, and his precious volumes, a dozen of them at least, wedged under his right arm.

'You're surprised to see me, sir,' said he, in a strange, croaking voice.

I acknowledged that I was.

'Well, I've a conscience, sir, and when I chanced to see you go into this house, as I came hobbling after you, I thought to myself, I'll just step in and see that kind gentleman, and tell him that if I was a bit gruff in my manner there was not any harm meant, and that I am much obliged to him for picking up my books.'

'You make too much of a trifle,' said I. 'May I ask how you knew who I was?'

'Well, sir, if it isn't too great a liberty, I am a neighbour of yours, for you'll find my little bookshop at the corner of Church Street, and very happy to see you, I am sure. Maybe you collect yourself, sir; here's *British Birds* and *Catullus* and *The Holy War* – a bargain every one of them. With five volumes you could just fill that gap on that second shelf. It looks untidy, does it not, sir?'

I moved my head to look at the cabinet behind me. When I turned again Sherlock Holmes was standing smiling at me across my study table. I rose to my feet, stared at him for some seconds in utter amazement, and then it appears that I must have fainted for the first and the last time in my life. Certainly a grey mist swirled before my eyes, and when it cleared I found my collar-ends undone and the tingling aftertaste of brandy upon my lips. Holmes was bending over my chair, his flask in his hand.

'My dear Watson,' said the well-remembered voice, 'I owe you a thousand apologies. I had no idea that you would be so affected.'

I gripped him by the arm.

'Holmes!' I cried. 'Is it really you? Can it indeed be that you are alive? Is it possible that you succeeded in climbing out of that awful abyss?'

'Wait a moment,' said he. 'Are you sure that you are really fit to discuss things? I have given you a serious shock by my unnecessarily dramatic reappearance.'

'I am all right, but indeed, Holmes, I can hardly believe my eyes. Good heavens, to think that you – you of all men – should be standing in my study!' Again I gripped him by the sleeve and felt the thin, sinewy arm beneath it. 'Well, you're not a spirit, anyhow,' said I. 'My dear chap, I am overjoyed to see you. Sit down and tell me how you came alive out of that dreadful chasm.'

He sat opposite to me and lit a cigarette in his old nonchalant manner. He was dressed in the seedy frock-coat of the book merchant, but the rest of that individual lay in a pile of white hair and old books upon the table. Holmes looked even thinner and keener than of old, but there was a dead-white tinge in his aquiline face which told me that his life recently had not been a healthy one.

'I am glad to stretch myself, Watson,' said he. 'It is no joke when a tall man has to take a foot off his stature for several hours on end. Now, my dear fellow, in the matter of these explanations we have, if I may ask for your co-operation, a hard and dangerous night's work in front of us. Perhaps it would be better if I gave you an account of the whole situation when that work is finished.'

'I am full of curiosity. I should much prefer to hear now.'

'You'll come with me tonight?'

'When you like and where you like.'

'This is indeed like the old days. We shall have time for a mouthful of dinner before we need go. Well, then, about that chasm. I had no serious difficulty in getting out of it, for the very simple reason that I never was in it.'

'You never were in it?'

'No, Watson, I never was in it. My note to you was absolutely genuine. I had little doubt that I had come to the end of my career when I perceived the somewhat sinister figure of the late Professor Moriarty standing upon the narrow pathway which led to safety. I read an inexorable purpose in his grey eyes. I exchanged some remarks with him, therefore, and obtained his courteous permission to write the short note which you afterwards received. I left it with my cigarette-box and my stick and I walked along the pathway, Moriarty still at my heels. When I reached the end I stood at bay. He drew no weapon, but he rushed at me and threw his long arms around me. He knew that his own game was up, and was only anxious to revenge himself upon me. We tottered together upon the brink of the fall. I have some knowledge, however, of baritsu, or the Japanese system of wrestling, which has more than once been very useful to me. I slipped through his grip, and he with a horrible scream kicked madly for a few seconds and clawed the air with both his hands. But for all his efforts he could not get his balance, and over he went. With my face over the brink I saw him fall for a long way. Then he struck a rock, bounded off, and splashed into the water.'

I listened with amazement to this explanation, which Holmes delivered between the puffs of his cigarette.

'But the tracks!' I cried. 'I saw with my own eyes that two went down the path and none returned.'

'It came about in this way. The instant that the Professor had disappeared it struck me what a really extraordinarily lucky chance Fate had placed in my way. I knew that Moriarty was not the only man who had sworn my death. There were at least three others whose desire for vengeance upon me would only be increased by the death of their leader. They were all most dangerous men. One or other would certainly get me. On the other hand, if all the world was convinced that I was dead they would take liberties, these men, they would lay themselves open, and sooner or later I could destroy them. Then it would be time for me to announce that I was still in the land of the living. So rapidly does the brain act that I believe I had thought this all out before Professor Moriarty had reached the bottom of the Reichenbach Fall.

'I stood up and examined the rocky wall behind me. In your picturesque account of the matter, which I read with great interest some months later, you assert that the wall was sheer. This was not literally true. A few small footholds presented themselves, and there was some indication of a ledge. The cliff is so high that to climb it all was an obvious impossibility, and it was equally impossible to make my way along the wet path without leaving some tracks. I might, it is true, have reversed my boots, as I have done on similar occasions, but the sight of three sets of tracks in one direction would certainly have suggested a deception. On the whole, then, it was best that I should risk the climb. It was not a pleasant business, Watson. The fall roared beneath me. I am not a fanciful person, but I give you my word that I seemed to hear Moriarty's voice screaming at me out of the abyss. A mistake would have been fatal. More than once, as tufts of grass came out in my hand or my foot slipped in the wet notches of the rock, I thought that I was gone. But I struggled upwards, and at last I reached a ledge several feet deep and covered with soft green moss, where I could lie unseen in the most perfect comfort. There I was stretched when you, my dear Watson, and all your following were investigating in the most sympathetic and inefficient manner the circumstances of my death.

'At last, when you had all formed your inevitable and totally erroneous conclusions, you departed for the hotel and I was left alone. I had imagined that I had reached the end of my adventures, but a very unexpected occurrence showed me that there were surprises still in store for me. A huge rock, falling from above, boomed past me, struck the path, and bounded over into the chasm. For an instant I thought that it was an accident; but a moment later, looking up, I saw a man's head against the darkening sky, and another stone struck the very ledge upon which I was stretched, within a foot of my head. Of course, the meaning of this was obvious. Moriarty had not been alone. A confederate – and even that one glance had told me how dangerous a man that confederate was – had kept guard while the Professor had attacked me. From a distance, unseen by me, he had been a witness of his friend's death and of my escape. He had waited, and then, making his way round to the top of the cliff, he had endeavoured to succeed where his comrade had failed.

'I did not take long to think about it, Watson. Again I saw that grim face look over the cliff, and I knew that it was the precursor of another stone. I scrambled down on to the path. I don't think I could have done it in cold blood. It was a hundred times more difficult than getting up. But I had no time to think of the danger, for another stone sang past me as I hung by my hands from the edge of the ledge. Halfway down I slipped, but by the blessing of God I landed, torn and bleeding, upon the path. I took to my heels, did ten miles over the mountains in the darkness, and a week later I found myself in Florence with the certainty that no one in the world knew what had become of me.

'I had only one confidant – my brother Mycroft. I owe you many apologies, my dear Watson, but it was all-important that it should be thought I was dead, and it is quite certain that you would not have written so convincing an account of my unhappy end had you not yourself thought that it was true. Several times during the last three years I have taken up my pen to write to you, but always I feared lest your affectionate regard for me should tempt you to some indiscretion which would betray my secret. For that reason I turned away from you this evening when you upset my books, for I was in danger at the time, and any show of surprise and emotion upon your part might have drawn attention to my identity and led to the most deplorable and irreparable results. As to Mycroft, I had to confide in him in order to obtain the money which I needed. The course of events in London did not run so well as I had hoped, for the trial of the Moriarty gang left two of its most dangerous members, my own most vindictive enemies, at liberty. I travelled for two years in Tibet, therefore, and amused myself by visiting Lhassa and spending some days with the head Llama. You may have read of the remarkable explorations of a Norwegian named Sigerson, but I am sure that it never occurred to you that you were receiving news of your friend. I then passed through Persia, looked in at Mecca, and paid a short but interesting visit to the Khalifa at Khartoum, the results of which I have communicated to the Foreign Office. Returning to France I spent some months in a research into the coal-tar derivatives, which I conducted in a laboratory at Montpelier, in the south of France. Having concluded this to my satisfaction, and learning that only one of my enemies was now left in London, I was about to return when my movements were hastened by the news of this very remarkable Park Lane Mystery, which not only appealed to me by its own merits, but which seemed to offer some most peculiar personal opportunities. I came over at once to

London, called in my own person at Baker Street, threw Mrs Hudson into violent hysterics, and found that Mycroft had preserved my rooms and my papers exactly as they had always been. So it was, my dear Watson, that at two o'clock today I found myself in my old armchair in my own old room, and only wishing that I could have seen my old friend Watson in the other chair which he has so often adorned.'

Such was the remarkable narrative to which I listened on that April evening – a narrative which would have been utterly incredible to me had it not been confirmed by the actual sight of the tall, spare figure and the keen, eager face, which I had never thought to see again. In some manner he had learned of my own sad bereavement, and his sympathy was shown in his manner rather than in his words. 'Work is the best antidote to sorrow, my dear Watson,' said he, 'and I have a piece of work for us both tonight which, if we can bring it to a successful conclusion, will in itself justify a man's life on this planet.' In vain I begged him to tell me more. 'You will hear and see enough before morning,' he answered. 'We have three years of the past to discuss. Let that suffice until half-past nine, when we start upon the notable adventure of the empty house.'

It was indeed like old times when, at that hour, I found myself seated beside him in a hansom, my revolver in my pocket and the thrill of adventure in my heart. Holmes was cold and stern and silent. As the gleam of the street-lamps flashed upon his austere features I saw that his brows were drawn down in thought and his thin lips compressed. I knew not what wild beast we were about to hunt down in the dark jungle of criminal London, but I was well assured from the bearing of this master huntsman that the adventure was a most grave one, while the sardonic smile which occasionally broke through his ascetic gloom boded little good for the object of our quest.

I had imagined that we were bound for Baker Street, but Holmes stopped the cab at the corner of Cavendish Square. I observed that as he stepped out he gave a most searching glance to right and left, and at every subsequent street corner he took the utmost pains to assure that he was not followed. Our route was certainly a singular one. Holmes's knowledge of the byways of London was extraordinary, and on this occasion he passed rapidly, and with an assured step, through a network of mews and stables the very existence of which I had never known. We emerged at last into a small road, lined with old, gloomy houses, which led us into Manchester Street, and so to Blandford Street. Here he turned swiftly down a narrow passage, passed through a wooden gate into a deserted yard, and then opened with a key the back door of a house. We entered together and he closed it behind us.

The place was pitch-dark, but it was evident to me that it was an empty house. Our feet creaked and crackled over the bare planking, and my outstretched hand touched a wall from which the paper was hanging in ribbons. Holmes's cold, thin fingers closed round my wrist and led me forwards down a long hall, until I dimly saw the murky fanlight over the door. Here Holmes turned suddenly to the right, and we found ourselves in a large, square, empty room, heavily shadowed in the corners, but faintly lit in the centre from the lights of the street beyond. There was no lamp near and the window was thick with dust, so that we could only just discern each other's figures within. My companion put his hand upon my shoulder and his lips close to my ear.

'Do you know where we are?' he whispered.

'Surely that is Baker Street,' I answered, staring through the dim window.

'Exactly. We are in Camden House, which stands opposite to our own old quarters.'

'But why are we here?'

'Because it commands so excellent a view of that picturesque pile. Might I trouble you, my dear Watson, to draw a little nearer to the window, taking every precaution not to show yourself, and then to look up at our old rooms – the starting-point of so many of our little adventures? We will see if my three years of absence have entirely taken away my power to surprise you.'

I crept forward and looked across at the familiar window. As my eyes fell upon it I gave a gasp and a cry of amazement. The blind was down and a strong light was burning in the room. The shadow of a man who was seated in a chair within was thrown in hard, black outline upon the luminous screen of the window. There was no mistaking the poise of the head, the squareness of the shoulders, the sharpness of the features. The face was turned half-round, and the effect was that of one of those black silhouettes which our grandparents loved to frame. It was a perfect reproduction of Holmes. So amazed was I that I threw out my hand to make sure that the man himself was standing beside me. He was quivering with silent laughter.

'Well?' said he.

'Good heavens!' I cried. 'It is marvellous.'

'I trust that age doth not wither nor custom stale my

infinite variety,' said he, and I recognised in his voice the joy and pride which the artist takes in his own creation. 'It really is rather like me, is it not?'

'I should be prepared to swear that it was you.'

'The credit of the execution is due to Monsieur Oscar Meunier, of Grenoble, who spent some days in doing the moulding. It is a bust in wax. The rest I arranged myself during my visit to Baker Street this afternoon.'

'But why?'

'Because, my dear Watson, I had the strongest possible reason for wishing certain people to think that I was there when I was really elsewhere.'

'And you thought the rooms were watched?'

'I *knew* that they were watched.'

'By whom?'

'By my old enemies, Watson. By the charming society whose leader lies in the Reichenbach Fall. You must remember that they knew, and only they knew, that I was still alive. Sooner or later they believed that I should come back to my rooms. They watched them continuously, and this morning they saw me arrive.'

'How do you know?'

'Because I recognised their sentinel when I glanced out of my window. He is a harmless enough fellow, Parker by name, a garrotter by trade, and a remarkable performer upon the Jew's harp. I cared nothing for him. But I cared a great deal for the much more formidable person who was behind him, the bosom friend of Moriarty, the man who dropped the rocks over the cliff, the most cunning and dangerous criminal in London. That is the man who is after me tonight, Watson, and that is the man who is quite unaware that we are after *him*.'

My friend's plans were gradually revealing themselves. From this convenient retreat the watchers were
being watched and the trackers tracked. That angular
shadow up yonder was the bait and we were the
hunters. In silence we stood together in the darkness
and watched the hurrying figures who passed and
repassed in front of us. Holmes was silent and motionless; but I could tell that he was keenly alert, and that
his eyes were fixed intently upon the stream of passers-
by. It was a bleak and boisterous night, and the wind
whistled shrilly down the long street. Many people
were moving to and fro, most of them muffled in their
coats and cravats. Once or twice it seemed to me that
I had seen the same figure before, and I especially
noticed two men who appeared to be sheltering
themselves from the wind in the doorway of a house
some distance up the street. I tried to draw my
companion's attention to them, but he gave a little
ejaculation of impatience and continued to stare into
the street. More than once he fidgeted with his feet
and tapped rapidly with his fingers upon the wall. It
was evident to me that he was becoming uneasy and
that his plans were not working out altogether as he
had hoped. At last, as midnight approached and the
street gradually cleared, he paced up and down the
room in uncontrollable agitation. I was about to make
some remark to him when I raised my eyes to the
lighted window and again experienced almost as great
a surprise as before. I clutched Holmes's arm and
pointed upwards.

'The shadow has moved!' I cried.

It was, indeed, no longer the profile, but the back,
which was turned towards us.

Three years had certainly not smoothed the

asperities of his temper or his impatience with a less active intelligence than his own.

'Of course it has moved,' said he. 'Am I such a farcical bungler, Watson, that I should erect an obvious dummy and expect that some of the sharpest men in Europe would be deceived by it? We have been in this room two hours, and Mrs Hudson has made some change in that figure eight times, or once in every quarter of an hour. She works it from the front so that her shadow may never be seen. Ah!' He drew in his breath with a shrill, excited intake. In the dim light I saw his head thrown forward, his whole attitude rigid with attention. Outside, the street was absolutely deserted. Those two men might still be crouching in the doorway, but I could no longer see them. All was still and dark, save only that brilliant yellow screen in front of us with the black figure outlined upon its centre. Again in the utter silence I heard that thin, sibilant note which spoke of intense suppressed excitement. An instant later he pulled me back into the blackest corner of the room, and I felt his warning hand upon my lips. The fingers which clutched me were quivering. Never had I known my friend more moved, and yet the dark street still stretched lonely and motionless before us.

But suddenly I was aware of that which his keener senses had already distinguished. A low, stealthy sound came to my ears, not from the direction of Baker Street, but from the back of the very house in which we lay concealed. A door opened and shut. An instant later steps crept down the passage – steps which were meant to be silent, but which reverberated harshly through the empty house. Holmes crouched back against the wall and I did the same, my hand closing upon the handle of my revolver. Peering through the gloom, I saw the vague outline of a man, a shade blacker than the blackness of the open door. He stood for an instant, and then he crept forward, crouching, menacing, into the room. He was within three yards of us, this sinister figure, and I had braced myself to meet his spring, before I realised that he had no idea of our presence. He passed close beside us, stole over to the window, and very softly and noiselessly raised it for half a foot. As he sank to the level of this opening the light of the street, no longer dimmed by the dusty glass, fell full upon his face. The man seemed to be beside himself with excitement. His two eyes shone like stars and his features were working convulsively. He was an elderly man, with a thin, projecting nose, a high, bald forehead, and a huge grizzled moustache. An opera-hat was pushed to the back of his head, and an evening dress shirt-front gleamed out through his open overcoat. His face was gaunt and swarthy, scored with deep, savage lines. In his hand he carried what appeared to be a stick, but as he laid it down upon the floor it gave a metallic clang. Then from the pocket of his overcoat he drew a bulky object, and he busied himself in some task which ended with a loud, sharp click, as if a spring or bolt had fallen into its place. Still kneeling upon the floor, he bent forward and threw all his weight and strength upon some lever, with the result that there came a long, whirling, grinding noise, ending once more in a powerful click. He straightened himself then, and I saw that what he held in his hand was a sort of gun, with a curiously misshapen butt. He opened it at the breech, put something in, and snapped the breechblock. Then, crouching down, he rested the end of the barrel upon the ledge of the open window, and I saw his long moustache droop over the stock and his eye gleam as it peered along the sights. I heard a little sigh of satisfaction as he cuddled the butt into his shoulder, and saw that amazing target, the black man on the yellow ground, standing clear at the end of his fore sight. For an instant he was rigid and motionless. Then his finger tightened on the trigger. There was a strange, loud whiz and a long, silvery tinkle of broken glass. At that instant Holmes sprang like a tiger on to the marksman's back and hurled him flat upon his face. He was up again in a moment, and with convulsive strength he seized Holmes by the throat; but I struck him on the head with the butt of my revolver and he dropped again upon the floor. I fell upon him, and as I held him my comrade blew a shrill call upon a whistle. There was the clatter of running feet upon the pavement, and two policemen in uniform, with one plain-clothes detective, rushed through the front entrance and into the room.

'That you, Lestrade?' said Holmes.

'Yes, Mr Holmes. I took the job myself. It's good to see you back in London, sir.'

'I think you want a little unofficial help. Three undetected murders in one year won't do, Lestrade. But you handled the Molesey Mystery with less than your usual – that's to say, you handled it fairly well.'

We had all risen to our feet, our prisoner breathing hard, with a stalwart constable on each side of him. Already a few loiterers had begun to collect in the street. Holmes stepped up to the window, closed it, and dropped the blinds. Lestrade had produced two candles and the policemen had uncovered their lanterns. I was able at last to have a good look at our prisoner.

It was a tremendously virile and yet sinister face which was turned towards us. With the brow of a philosopher above and the jaw of a sensualist below, the man must have started with great capacities for good or for evil. But one could not look upon his cruel blue eyes, with their drooping, cynical lids, or upon the fierce, aggressive nose and the threatening, deep-lined brow, without reading Nature's plainest danger-signals. He took no heed of any of us, but his eyes were fixed upon Holmes's face with an expression in which hatred and amazement were equally blended. 'You fiend!' he kept on muttering. 'You clever, clever fiend!'

'Ah, Colonel!' said Holmes, arranging his rumpled collar; ' "journeys end in lovers' meetings," as the old play says. I don't think I have had the pleasure of seeing you since you favoured me with those attentions as I lay on the ledge above the Reichenbach Fall.'

The Colonel still stared at my friend like a man in a trance. 'You cunning, cunning fiend!' was all that he could say.

'I have not introduced you yet,' said Holmes. 'This, gentlemen, is Colonel Sebastian Moran, once of Her Majesty's Indian Army, and the best heavy game shot that our Eastern Empire has ever produced. I believe I am correct, Colonel, in saying that your bag of tigers still remains unrivalled?'

The fierce old man said nothing, but still glared at my companion; with his savage eyes and bristling moustache he was wonderfully like a tiger himself.

'I wonder that my very simple stratagem could deceive so old a shikari,' said Holmes. 'It must be very familiar to you. Have you not tethered a young kid under a tree, lain above it with your rifle, and waited for the bait to bring up your tiger? This empty house is my tree and you are my tiger. You have possibly had other guns in reserve in case there should be several tigers, or in the unlikely supposition of your own aim failing you. These,' he pointed around, 'are my other guns. The parallel is exact.'

Colonel Moran sprang forward, with a snarl of rage, but the constables dragged him back. The fury upon his face was terrible to look at.

'I confess that you had one small surprise for me,' said Holmes. 'I did not anticipate that you would yourself make use of this empty house and this convenient front window. I had imagined you as operating from the street, where my friend Lestrade and his merry men were awaiting you. With that exception all has gone as I expected.'

Colonel Moran turned to the official detective.

'You may or may not have just cause for arresting me,' said he, 'but at least there can be no reason why I should submit to the gibes of this person. If I am in the hands of the law let things be done in a legal way.'

'Well, that's reasonable enough,' said Lestrade. 'Nothing further you have to say, Mr Holmes, before we go?'

Holmes had picked up the powerful air-gun from the floor and was examining its mechanism.

'An admirable and unique weapon,' said he, 'noiseless and of tremendous power. I knew Von Herder, the blind German mechanic, who constructed it to the order of the late Professor Moriarty. For years I have been aware of its existence, though I have never before had the opportunity of handling it. I commend it very specially to your attention, Lestrade, and also the bullets which fit it.'

'You can trust us to look after that, Mr Holmes,' said Lestrade, as the whole party moved towards the door. 'Anything further to say?'

'Only to ask what charge you intend to prefer?'

'What charge, sir? Why, of course, the attempted murder of Mr Sherlock Holmes.'

'Not so, Lestrade. I do not propose to appear in the matter at all. To you, and to you only, belongs the credit of the remarkable arrest which you have effected. Yes, Lestrade, I congratulate you! With your usual happy mixture of cunning and audacity you have got him.'

'Got him! Got whom, Mr Holmes?'

'The man that the whole force has been seeking in vain – Colonel Sebastian Moran, who shot the Honourable Ronald Adair with an expanding bullet from an air-gun through the open window of the second-floor front of 427 Park Lane, upon the 30th of last month. That's the charge, Lestrade. And now, Watson, if you can endure the draught from a broken window, I think that half an hour in my study over a cigar may afford you some profitable amusement.'

Our old chambers had been left unchanged through the supervision of Mycroft Holmes and the immediate care of Mrs Hudson. As I entered I saw, it is true, an unwonted tidiness, but the old landmarks were all in their place. There were the chemical corner and the acid-stained, deal-topped table. There upon a shelf was the row of formidable scrapbooks and books of reference which many of our fellow-citizens would have been so glad to burn. The diagrams, the violin-case, and the pipe-rack – even the Persian slipper which contained the tobacco – all met my eyes as I glanced round me. There were two occupants of the room – one Mrs Hudson, who beamed upon us both as we entered; the other the strange dummy which had played so important a part in the evening's adventures. It was a wax-coloured model of my friend, so admirably done that it was a perfect facsimile. It stood on a small pedestal table with an old dressing-gown of Holmes's so draped round it that the illusion from the street was absolutely perfect.

'I hope you preserved all precautions, Mrs Hudson?' said Holmes.

'I went to it on my knees, sir, just as you told me.'

'Excellent. You carried the thing out very well. Did you observe where the bullet went?'

'Yes, sir. I'm afraid it has spoilt your beautiful bust, for it passed right through the head and flattened itself on the wall. I picked it up from the carpet. Here it is!'

Holmes held it out to me. 'A soft revolver bullet, as you perceive, Watson. There's genius in that, for who would expect to find such a thing fired from an air-gun? All right, Mrs Hudson, I am much obliged for your assistance. And now, Watson, let me see you in your old seat once more, for there are several points which I should like to discuss with you.'

He had thrown off the seedy frock-coat, and now he was the Holmes of old in the mouse-coloured dressing-gown which he took from his effigy.

'The old shikari's nerves have not lost their steadiness nor his eyes their keenness,' said he, with a laugh, as he inspected the shattered forehead of his bust.

'Plumb in the middle of the back of the head and smack through the brain. He was the best shot in

India, and I expect that there are few better in London. Have you heard the name?'

'No, I have not.'

'Well, well, such is fame! But, then, if I remember aright, you had not heard the name of Professor James Moriarty, who had one of the great brains of the century. Just give me down my index of biographies from the shelf.'

He turned over the pages lazily, leaning back in his chair and blowing great clouds from his cigar.

'My collection of M's is a fine one,' said he. 'Moriarty himself is enough to make any letter illustrious, and here is Morgan the poisoner, and Merridew of abominable memory, and Mathews, who knocked out my left canine in the waiting-room at Charing Cross, and, finally, here is our friend of tonight.'

He handed over the book, and I read: 'MORAN, SEBASTIAN, COLONEL. Unemployed. Formerly 1st Bengalore Pioneers. Born London, 1840. Son of Sir Augustus Moran, C.B., once British Minister to Persia. Educated Eton and Oxford. Served in Jowaki Campaign, Afghan Campaign, Charasiab (despatches), Sherpur, and Cabul. Author of *Heavy Game of the Western Himalayas*, 1881; *Three Months in the Jungle*, 1884. Address: Conduit Street. Clubs: The Anglo-Indian, the Tankerville, the Bagatelle Card Club.'

On the margin was written, in Holmes's precise hand: 'The second most dangerous man in London.'

'This is astonishing,' said I, as I handed back the volume. 'The man's career is that of an honourable soldier.'

'It is true,' Holmes answered. 'Up to a certain point he did well. He was always a man of iron nerve, and the story is still told in India how he crawled down a drain

33

after a wounded man-eating tiger. There are some trees, Watson, which grow to a certain height and then suddenly develop some unsightly eccentricity. You will see it often in humans. I have a theory that the individual represents in his development the whole procession of his ancestors, and that such a sudden turn to good or evil stands for some strong influence which came into the line of his pedigree. The person becomes, as it were, the epitome of the history of his own family.'

'It is surely rather fanciful.'

'Well, I don't insist upon it. Whatever the cause, Colonel Moran began to go wrong. Without any open scandal he still made India too hot to hold him. He retired, came to London, and again acquired an evil name. It was at this time that he was sought out by Professor Moriarty, to whom for a time he was chief of the staff. Moriarty supplied him liberally with money and used him only in one or two very high-class jobs which no ordinary criminal could have undertaken. You may have some recollection of the death of Mrs Stewart, of Lauder, in 1887. No? Well, I am sure Moran was at the bottom of it; but nothing could be proved. So cleverly was the Colonel concealed that even when the Moriarty gang was broken up we could not incriminate him. You remember at that date, when I called upon you in your rooms, how I put up the shutters for fear of air-guns? No doubt you thought me fanciful. I knew exactly what I was doing, for I knew of the existence of this remarkable gun, and I knew also that one of the best shots in the world would be behind it. When we were in Switzerland he followed us with Moriarty, and it was undoubtedly he who gave me that evil five minutes on the Reichenbach ledge.

'You may think that I read the papers with some attention during my sojourn in France, on the lookout for any chance of laying him by the heels. So long as he was free in London my life would really not have been worth living. Night and day the shadow would have been over me, and sooner or later his chance must have come. What could I do? I could not shoot him at sight, or I should myself be in the dock. There was no use appealing to a magistrate. They cannot interfere on the strength of what would appear to them to be a wild suspicion. So I could do nothing. But I watched the criminal news, knowing that sooner or later I should get him. Then came the death of this Ronald Adair. My chance had come at last! Knowing what I did, was it not certain that Colonel Moran had done it? He had played cards with the lad; he had followed him home from the club; he had shot him through the open window. There was not a doubt of it. The bullets alone are enough to put his head in a noose. I came over at once. I was seen by the sentinel, who would, I knew, direct the Colonel's attention to my presence. He could not fail to connect my sudden return with his crime and to be terribly alarmed. I was sure that he would make an attempt to get me out of the way *at once*, and would bring round his murderous weapon for that purpose. I left him an excellent mark in the window, and, having warned the police that they might be needed – by the way, Watson, you spotted their presence in that doorway with unerring accuracy – I took up what seemed to me to be a judicious post for observation, never dreaming that he would choose the same spot for his attack. Now, my dear Watson, does anything remain for me to explain?'

'Yes,' said I. 'You have not made it clear what was Colonel Moran's motive in murdering the Honourable Ronald Adair.'

'Ah! my dear Watson, there we come into those realms of conjecture where the most logical mind may be at fault. Each may form his own hypothesis upon the present evidence, and yours is as likely to be correct as mine.'

'You have formed one, then?'

'I think that it is not difficult to explain the facts. It came out in evidence that Colonel Moran and young Adair had between them won a considerable amount of money. Now, Moran undoubtedly played foul – of that I have long been aware. I believe that on the day of the murder Adair had discovered that Moran was cheating. Very likely he had spoken to him privately, and had threatened to expose him unless he voluntarily resigned his membership of the club and promised not to play cards again. It is unlikely that a youngster like Adair would at once make a hideous scandal by exposing a well-known man so much older than himself. Probably he acted as I suggest. The exclusion from his clubs would mean ruin to Moran, who lived by his ill-gotten card gains. He therefore murdered Adair, who at the time was endeavouring to work out how much money he should himself return, since he could not profit by his partner's foul play. He locked the door lest the ladies should surprise him and insist upon knowing what he was doing with these names and coins. Will it pass?'

'I have no doubt that you have hit upon the truth.'

'It will be verified or disproved at the trial. Meanwhile, come what may, Colonel Moran will trouble us no more, the famous air-gun of Von Herder will embellish the Scotland Yard Museum, and once again Mr Sherlock Holmes is free to devote his life to examining those interesting little problems which the complex life of London so plentifully presents.'

2

The Norwood Builder

'From the point of view of the criminal expert,' said Mr Sherlock Holmes, 'London has become a singularly uninteresting city since the death of the late lamented Professor Moriarty.'

'I can hardly think that you would find many decent citizens to agree with you,' I answered.

'Well, well, I must not be selfish,' said he, with a smile, as he pushed back his chair from the breakfast-table. 'The community is certainly the gainer, and no one the loser, save the poor out-of-work specialist, whose occupation has gone. With that man in the field one's morning paper presented infinite possibilities. Often it was only the smallest trace, Watson, the faintest indication, and yet it was enough to tell me that the great malignant brain was there, as the gentlest tremors of the edges of the web remind one of the foul spider which lurks in the centre. Petty thefts, wanton assaults, purposeless outrage – to the man who held the clue all could be worked into one connected whole. To the scientific student of the higher criminal world no capital in Europe offered the advantages which London then possessed. But now – ' He shrugged his shoulders in humorous deprecation of the state of things which he had himself done so much to produce.

At the time of which I speak Holmes had been back for some months, and I, at his request, had sold my practice and returned to share the old quarters in Baker Street. A young doctor, named Verner, had purchased my small Kensington practice, and given with astonishingly little demur the highest price that I ventured to ask – an incident which only explained itself some years later when I found that Verner was a distant relation of Holmes's, and that it was my friend who had really found the money.

Our months of partnership had not been so un-eventful as he had stated, for I find, on looking over my notes, that this period includes the case of the papers of ex-President Murillo, and also the shocking affair of the Dutch steamship *Friesland*, which so nearly cost us both our lives. His cold and proud nature was always averse, however, to anything in the shape of public applause, and he bound me in the most stringent terms to say no further word of himself, his methods, or his successes – a prohibition which, as I have explained, has only now been removed.

Mr Sherlock Holmes was leaning back in his chair after his whimsical protest, and was unfolding his morning paper in a leisurely fashion, when our attention was arrested by a tremendous ring at the bell, followed immediately by a hollow drumming sound, as if someone were beating on the outer door with his fist. As it opened there came a tumultuous rush into the hall, rapid feet clattered up the stair, and an instant later a wild-eyed and frantic young man, pale, dishevelled, and palpitating, burst into the room. He looked from one to the other of us, and under our gaze of enquiry he became conscious that some apology was needed for this unceremonious entry.

'I'm sorry, Mr Holmes,' he cried. 'You mustn't

blame me. I am nearly mad. Mr Holmes, I am the unhappy John Hector McFarlane.'

He made the announcement as if the name alone would explain both his visit and its manner; but I could see by my companion's unresponsive face that it meant no more to him than to me.

'Have a cigarette, Mr McFarlane,' said he, pushing his case across. 'I am sure that with your symptoms my friend Dr Watson here would prescribe a sedative. The weather has been so very warm these last few days. Now, if you feel a little more composed, I should be glad if you would sit down in that chair and tell us very slowly and quietly who you are and what it is that you want. You mentioned your name as if I should recognise it, but I assure you that, beyond the obvious facts that you are a bachelor, a solicitor, a Freemason, and an asthmatic, I know nothing whatever about you.'

Familiar as I was with my friend's methods, it was not difficult for me to follow his deductions, and to observe the untidiness of attire, the sheaf of legal papers, the watch-charm, and the breathing which had prompted them. Our client, however, stared in amazement.

'Yes, I am all that, Mr Holmes, and in addition I am the most unfortunate man at this moment in London. For Heaven's sake don't abandon me, Mr Holmes! If they come to arrest me before I have finished my story, make them give me time so that I may tell you the whole truth. I could go to gaol happy if I knew that you were working for me outside.'

'Arrest you!' said Holmes. 'This is really most grati – , most interesting. On what charge do you expect to be arrested?'

'Upon the charge of murdering Mr Jonas Oldacre, of Lower Norwood.'

My companion's expressive face showed a sympathy which was not, I am afraid, entirely unmixed with satisfaction.

'Dear me,' said he; 'it was only this moment at breakfast that I was saying to my friend, Dr Watson, that sensational cases had disappeared out of our papers.'

Our visitor stretched forward a quivering hand and picked up the *Daily Telegraph*, which still lay upon Holmes's knee.

'If you had looked at it, sir, you would have seen at a glance what the errand is on which I have come to you this morning. I feel as if my name and my misfortune must be in every man's mouth.' He turned it over to expose the central page. 'Here it is, and with your permission I will read it to you. Listen to this, Mr Holmes. The headlines are: "Mysterious Affair at Lower Norwood. Disappearance of a Well-known Builder. Suspicion of Murder and Arson. A Clue to the Criminal." That is the clue which they are already following, Mr Holmes, and I know that it leads infallibly to me. I have been followed from London Bridge Station, and I am sure that they are only waiting for the warrant to arrest me. It will break my mother's heart – it will break her heart!' He wrung his hands in an agony of apprehension, and swayed backwards and forwards in his chair.

I looked with interest upon this man, who was accused of being the perpetrator of a crime of violence. He was flaxen-haired and handsome in a washed-out negative fashion, with frightened blue eyes and a clean-shaven face, with a weak, sensitive mouth. His age may have been about twenty-seven; his dress and bearing that of a gentleman. From the pocket of his light summer overcoat protruded the bundle of endorsed papers which proclaimed his profession.

'We must use what time we have,' said Holmes. 'Watson, would you have the kindness to take the paper and to read me the paragraph in question?'

Underneath the vigorous headlines which our client had quoted I read the following suggestive narrative:

Late last night, or early this morning, an incident occurred at Lower Norwood which points, it is feared, to a serious crime. Mr Jonas Oldacre is a well-known resident of that suburb, where he has carried on his business as a builder for many years. Mr Oldacre is a bachelor, fifty-two years of age, and lives in Deep Dene House, at the Sydenham end of the road of that name. He has had the reputation of being a man of eccentric habits, secretive and retiring. For some years he has practically withdrawn from the business, in which he is said to have amassed considerable wealth. A small timberyard still exists, however, at the back of the house, and last night, about twelve o'clock, an alarm was given that one of the stacks was on fire. The engines were soon upon the spot, but the dry wood burned with great fury, and it was impossible to arrest the conflagration until the stack had been entirely consumed. Up to this point the incident bore the appearance of an ordinary accident, but fresh indications seem to point to serious crime. Surprise was expressed at the absence of the master of the establishment from the scene of the fire, and an enquiry followed, which showed that he had disappeared from the house. An examination of his room revealed that the bed had not been slept in, that a safe which stood in it was open, that a number of important papers were scattered about the room, and, finally, that there were signs of a murderous struggle, slight traces of blood being found within the room, and an oaken walking-stick, which also showed stains of blood upon the handle. It is known that Mr Jonas Oldacre had received a late visitor in his bedroom upon that night, and the stick found has been identified as the property of this person, who is a young London solicitor named John Hector McFarlane, junior partner of Graham and McFarlane, of 426 Gresham Buildings, E.C. The police believe that they have evidence in their possession which supplies a very convincing motive for the crime, and altogether it cannot be doubted that sensational developments will follow.

LATER – It is rumoured as we go to press that Mr John Hector McFarlane has actually been arrested on the charge of the murder of Mr Jonas Oldacre. It is at least certain that a warrant has been issued. There have been further and sinister developments in the investigation at Norwood. Besides the signs of a struggle in the room of the unfortunate builder it is now known that the French windows of his bedroom (which is on the ground floor) were found to be open, that there were marks as if some bulky object had been dragged across to the wood-pile, and, finally, it is asserted that charred remains have been found among the charcoal ashes of the fire. The police theory is that a most sensational crime has been committed, that the victim was clubbed to death in his own bedroom, his papers rifled, and his dead body dragged across to the wood-stack, which was then ignited so as to hide all traces of the crime. The conduct of the criminal investigation has been left in the experienced hands of Inspector Lestrade, of Scotland Yard, who is following up the clues with his accustomed energy and sagacity.

Sherlock Holmes listened with closed eyes and fingertips together to this remarkable account.

'The case has certainly some points of interest,' said he, in his languid fashion. 'May I ask, in the first place, Mr McFarlane, how it is that you are still at liberty, since there appears to be enough evidence to justify your arrest?'

'I live at Torrington Lodge, Blackheath, with my parents, Mr Holmes; but last night, having to do business very late with Mr Jonas Oldacre, I stayed at an hotel in Norwood, and came to my business from there. I knew nothing of this affair until I was in the train, when I read what you have just heard. I at once saw the horrible danger of my position, and I hurried to put the case into your hands. I have no doubt that I should have been arrested either at my City office or at my home. A man followed me from London Bridge Station, and I have no doubt – Great Heaven, what is that?'

It was a clang of the bell, followed instantly by heavy steps upon the stair. A moment later our old friend Lestrade appeared in the doorway. Over his shoulder I caught a glimpse of one or two uniformed policemen outside.

'Mr John Hector McFarlane?' said Lestrade.

Our unfortunate client rose with a ghastly face.

'I arrest you for the wilful murder of Mr Jonas Oldacre, of Lower Norwood.'

McFarlane turned to us with a gesture of despair, and sank into his chair once more like one who is crushed.

'One moment, Lestrade,' said Holmes. 'Half an hour more or less can make no difference to you, and the gentleman was about to give us an account of this very interesting affair, which might aid us in clearing it up.'

'I think there will be no difficulty in clearing it up,' said Lestrade, grimly.

'None the less, with your permission, I should be much interested to hear his account.'

'Well, Mr Holmes, it is difficult for me to refuse you anything, for you have been of use to the force once or twice in the past, and we owe you a good turn at Scotland Yard,' said Lestrade. 'At the same time I must remain with my prisoner, and I am bound to warn him that anything he may say will appear in evidence against him.'

'I wish nothing better,' said our client. 'All I ask is that you should hear and recognise the absolute truth.'

Lestrade looked at his watch. 'I'll give you half an hour,' said he.

'I must explain first,' said McFarlane, 'that I knew nothing of Mr Jonas Oldacre. His name was familiar to me, for many years ago my parents were acquainted with him, but they drifted apart. I was very much surprised, therefore, when yesterday, about three o'clock in the afternoon, he walked into my office in the City. But I was still more astonished when he told me the object of his visit. He had in his hand several sheets of a notebook, covered with scribbled writing – here they are – and he laid them on my table.

' "Here is my will," said he. "I want you, Mr McFarlane, to cast it into proper legal shape. I will sit here while you do so."

'I set myself to copy it, and you can imagine my astonishment when I found that, with some reservations, he had left all his property to me. He was a strange little, ferret-like man, with white eyelashes, and when I looked up at him I found his keen grey eyes fixed upon me with an amused expression. I could hardly believe my own senses as I read the terms of the will; but he explained that he was a bachelor with hardly any living relation, that he had known my parents in his youth, and that he had always heard of me as a very deserving young man, and was assured that his money would be in worthy hands. Of course, I could only stammer out my thanks. The will was duly finished, signed, and witnessed by my clerk. This is it on the blue paper, and these slips, as I have explained, are the rough draft. Mr Jonas Oldacre then informed me that there were a number of documents – building leases, title-deeds, mortgages, scrip, and so forth – which it was necessary that I should see and understand. He said that his mind would not be easy until the whole thing was settled, and he begged me to come out to his house at Norwood that night, bringing the will with me, and to arrange matters. "Remember, my boy, not one word to your parents about the affair until everything is settled. We will keep it as a little surprise for them." He was very insistent upon this point, and made me promise it faithfully.

'You can imagine, Mr Holmes, that I was not in a humour to refuse him anything that he might ask. He was my benefactor, and all my desire was to carry out his wishes in every particular. I sent a telegram home, therefore, to say that I had important business on hand, and that it was impossible for me to say how late I might be. Mr Oldacre had told me that he would like me to have supper with him at nine, as he might not be home before that hour. I had some difficulty in finding his house, however, and it was nearly half-past before I reached it. I found him – '

'One moment!' said Holmes. 'Who opened the door?'

'A middle-aged woman, who was, I suppose, his housekeeper.'

'And it was she, I presume, who mentioned your name?'

'Exactly,' said McFarlane.

'Pray proceed.'

McFarlane wiped his damp brow and then continued his narrative.

'I was shown by this woman into a sitting-room, where a frugal supper was laid out. Afterwards Mr Jonas Oldacre led me into his bedroom, in which there stood a heavy safe. This he opened and took out a mass of documents, which we went over together. It was between eleven and twelve when we finished. He remarked that we must not disturb the housekeeper. He showed me out through his own French window, which had been open all this time.'

'Was the blind down?' asked Holmes.

'I will not be sure, but I believe that it was only half down. Yes, I remember how he pulled it up in order to swing open the window. I could not find my stick, and he said, "Never mind, my boy; I shall see a good deal of you now, I hope, and I will keep your stick until you come back to claim it." I left him there, the safe open, and the papers made up in packets upon the table. It was so late that I could not get back to Blackheath, so

I spent the night at the Anerley Arms, and I knew nothing more until I read of this horrible affair in the morning.'

'Anything more that you would like to ask, Mr Holmes?' said Lestrade, whose eyebrows had gone up once or twice during this remarkable explanation.

'Not until I have been to Blackheath.'

'You mean to Norwood,' said Lestrade.

'Oh, yes; no doubt that is what I must have meant,' said Holmes, with his enigmatical smile. Lestrade had learned by more experiences than he would care to acknowledge that that razor-like brain could cut through that which was impenetrable to him. I saw him look curiously at my companion.

'I think I should like to have a word with you presently, Mr Sherlock Holmes,' said he. 'Now, Mr McFarlane, two of my constables are at the door and there is a four-wheeler waiting.' The wretched young man arose, and with a last beseeching glance at us walked from the room. The officers conducted him to the cab, but Lestrade remained.

Holmes had picked up the pages which formed the rough draft of the will, and was looking at them with the keenest interest upon his face.

'There are some points about that document, Lestrade, are there not?' said he, pushing them over.

The official looked at them with a puzzled expression.

'I can read the first few lines, and these in the middle of the second page, and one or two at the end. Those are as clear as print,' said he; 'but the writing in between is very bad, and there are three places where I cannot read it at all.'

'What do you make of that?' said Holmes.

'Well, what do *you* make of it?'

'That it was written in a train; the good writing represents stations, the bad writing movement, and the very bad writing passing over points. A scientific expert would pronounce at once that this was drawn up on a suburban line, since nowhere save in the immediate vicinity of a great city could there be so quick a succession of points. Granting that his whole journey was occupied in drawing up the will, then the train was an express, only stopping once between Norwood and London Bridge.'

Lestrade began to laugh.

'You are too many for me when you begin to get on your theories, Mr Holmes,' said he. 'How does this bear on the case?'

'Well, it corroborates the young man's story to the extent that the will was drawn up by Jonas Oldacre in his journey yesterday. It is curious – is it not? – that a man should draw up so important a document in so haphazard a fashion. It suggests that he did not think it was going to be of much practical importance. If a man drew up a will which he did not intend ever to be effective he might do it so.'

'Well, he drew up his own death-warrant at the same time,' said Lestrade.

'Oh, you think so?'

'Don't you?'

'Well, it is quite possible; but the case is not clear to me yet.'

'Not clear? Well, if that isn't clear, what *could* be clear? Here is a young man who learns suddenly that if a certain older man dies he will succeed to a fortune. What does he do? He says nothing to anyone, but he arranges that he shall go out on some pretext to see his client that night; he waits until the only other person in the house is in bed, and then in the solitude of a man's room he murders him, burns his body in the wood-pile, and departs to a neighbouring hotel. The bloodstains in the room and also on the stick are very slight. It is probable that he imagined his crime to be a bloodless one, and hoped that if the body were consumed it would hide all traces of the method of his death – traces which for some reason must have pointed to him. Is all this not obvious?'

'It strikes me, my good Lestrade, as being just a trifle too obvious,' said Holmes. 'You do not add imagination to your other great qualities; but if you could for one moment put yourself in the place of this young man, would you choose the very night after the will had been made to commit your crime? Would it not seem dangerous to you to make so very close a relation between the two incidents? Again, would you choose an occasion when you are known to be in the house, when a servant has let you in? And, finally, would you take the great pains to conceal the body and yet leave your own stick as a sign that you were the criminal? Confess, Lestrade, that all this is very unlikely.'

'As to the stick, Mr Holmes, you know as well as I do that a criminal is often flurried and does things which a cool man would avoid. He was very likely afraid to go back to the room. Give me another theory that would fit the facts.'

'I could very easily give you half a dozen,' said Holmes. 'Here, for example, is a very possible and even probable one. I make you a free present of it. The older man is showing documents which are of evident value. A passing tramp sees them through the window, the blind of which is only half down. Exit the solicitor. Enter the tramp! He seizes a stick, which he observes there, kills Oldacre, and departs after burning the body.'

'Why should the tramp burn the body?'

'For the matter of that why should McFarlane?'

'To hide some evidence.'

'Possibly the tramp wanted to hide that any murder at all had been committed.'

'And why did the tramp take nothing?'

'Because they were papers that he could not negotiate.'

Lestrade shook his head, though it seemed to me that his manner was less absolutely assured than before.

'Well, Mr Sherlock Holmes, you may look for your tramp, and while you are finding him we will hold on to our man. The future will show which is right. Just notice this point, Mr Holmes: that so far as we know none of the papers were removed, and that the prisoner is the one man in the world who had no reason for removing them, since he was heir-at-law and would come into them in any case.'

My friend seemed struck by this remark.

'I don't mean to deny that the evidence is in some ways very strongly in favour of your theory,' said he. 'I only wish to point out that there are other theories possible. As you say, the future will decide. Good morning! I dare say that in the course of the day I shall drop in at Norwood and see how you are getting on.'

When the detective departed my friend rose and made his preparations for the day's work with the alert air of a man who has a congenial task before him.

'My first movement, Watson,' said he, as he bustled

into his frock-coat, 'must, as I said, be in the direction of Blackheath.'

'And why not Norwood?'

'Because we have in this case one singular incident coming close to the heels of another singular incident. The police are making the mistake of concentrating their attention upon the second, because it happens to be the one which is actually criminal. But it is evident to me that the logical way to approach the case is to begin by trying to throw some light upon the first incident – the curious will, so suddenly made, and to so unexpected an heir. It may do something to simplify what followed. No, my dear fellow, I don't think you can help me. There is no prospect of danger, or I should not dream of stirring out without you. I trust that when I see you in the evening I will be able to report that I have been able to do something for this unfortunate youngster who has thrown himself upon my protection.'

It was late when my friend returned, and I could see by a glance at his haggard and anxious face that the high hopes with which he had started had not been fulfilled. For an hour he droned away upon his violin, endeavouring to soothe his own ruffled spirits. At last he flung down the instrument and plunged into a detailed account of his misadventures.

'It's all going wrong, Watson – all as wrong as it can go. I kept a bold face before Lestrade, but, upon my soul, I believe that for once the fellow is on the right track and we are on the wrong. All my instincts are one way and all the facts are the other, and I much fear that British juries have not yet attained that pitch of intelligence when they will give the preference to my theories over Lestrade's facts.'

'Did you go to Blackheath?'

'Yes, Watson, I went there, and I found very quickly that the late lamented Oldacre was a pretty considerable blackguard. The father was away in search of his son. The mother was at home – a little, fluffy, blue-eyed person, in a tremor of fear and indignation. Of course, she would not admit even the possibility of his guilt. But she would not express either surprise or regret over the fate of Oldacre. On the contrary, she spoke of him with such bitterness that she was unconsciously considerably strengthening the case of the police, for, of course, if her son had heard her speak of the man in this fashion it would predispose him towards hatred and violence. "He was more like a malignant and cunning ape than a human being," said she, "and he always was, ever since he was a young man."

' "You knew him at that time?" said I.

' "Yes, I knew him well; in fact, he was an old suitor of mine. Thank Heaven that I had the sense to turn away from him and to marry a better, if a poorer, man. I was engaged to him, Mr Holmes, when I heard a shocking story of how he had turned a cat loose in an aviary, and I was so horrified at his brutal cruelty that I would have nothing more to do with him." She rummaged in a bureau, and presently she produced a photograph of a woman, shamefully defaced and mutilated with a knife. "That is my own photograph," she said. "He sent it to me in that state, with his curse, upon my wedding morning."

' "Well," said I, "at least he has forgiven you now, since he has left all his property to your son."

' "Neither my son nor I want anything from Jonas Oldacre, dead or alive," she cried, with a proper spirit. "There is a God in Heaven, Mr Holmes, and that same God who has punished that wicked man will show in His own good time that my son's hands are guiltless of his blood."

'Well, I tried one or two leads, but could get at nothing which would help our hypothesis, and several points which would make against it. I gave it up at last and off I went to Norwood.

'This place, Deep Dene House, is a big modern villa of staring brick, standing back in its own grounds, with a laurel-clumped lawn in front of it. To the right and some distance back from the road was the timberyard which had been the scene of the fire. Here's a rough plan on a leaf of my notebook. This window on the left is the one which opens into Oldacre's room. You can look into it from the road, you see. That is about the only bit of consolation I have had today. Lestrade was not there, but his head constable did the honours. They had just made a great treasure-trove. They had spent the morning raking among the ashes of the burned wood-pile, and besides the charred organic remains they had secured several discoloured metal discs. I examined them with care, and there was no doubt that they were trouser buttons. I even distinguished that one of them was marked with the name of "Hyams", who was Oldacre's tailor. I then worked the lawn very carefully for signs and traces, but this drought has made everything as hard as iron. Nothing was to be seen save that some body or bundle had been dragged through a low privet hedge which is in a line with the wood-pile. All that, of course, fits in with the official theory. I crawled about the lawn with an August sun on my back, but I got up at the end of an hour no wiser than before.

'Well, after this fiasco I went into the bedroom and

examined that also. The bloodstains were very slight, mere smears and discolorations, but undoubtedly fresh. The stick had been removed, but there also the marks were slight. There is no doubt about the stick belonging to our client. He admits it. Footmarks of both men could be made out on the carpet, but none of any third person, which again is a trick for the other side. They were piling up their score all the time and we were at a standstill.

'Only one little gleam of hope did I get – and yet it amounted to nothing. I examined the contents of the safe, most of which had been taken out and left on the table. The papers had been made up into sealed envelopes, one or two of which had been opened by the police. They were not, so far as I could judge, of any great value, nor did the bankbook show that Mr Oldacre was in such very affluent circumstances. But it seemed to me that all the papers were not there. There were allusions to some deeds – possibly the more valuable – which I could not find. This, of course, if we could definitely prove it, would turn Lestrade's argument against himself, for who would steal a thing if he knew that he would shortly inherit it?

'Finally, having drawn every other cover and picked up no scent, I tried my luck with the housekeeper. Mrs Lexington is her name, a little, dark, silent person, with suspicious and sidelong eyes. She could tell us something if she would – I am convinced of it. But she was as close as wax. Yes, she had let Mr McFarlane in at half-past nine. She wished her hand had withered before she had done so. She had gone to bed at half-past ten. Her room was at the other end of the house, and she could hear nothing of what passed. Mr McFarlane had left his hat, and to the best of her belief his stick, in the hall. She had been awakened by the alarm of fire. Her poor, dear master had certainly been murdered. Had he any enemies? Well, every man had enemies, but Mr Oldacre kept himself very much to himself, and only met people in the way of business. She had seen the buttons, and was sure that they belonged to the clothes which he had worn last night. The wood-pile was very dry, for it had not rained for a month. It burned like tinder, and by the time she reached the spot nothing could be seen but flames. She and all the firemen smelled the burned flesh from inside it. She knew nothing of the papers, nor of Mr Oldacre's private affairs.

'So, my dear Watson, there's my report of a failure. And yet – and yet' – he clenched his thin hands in a paroxysm of conviction – 'I *know* it's all wrong. I feel it in my bones. There is something that has not come out, and that housekeeper knows it. There was a sort of sulky defiance in her eyes, which only goes with guilty knowledge. However, there's no good talking any more about it, Watson; but unless some lucky chance comes our way I fear that the Norwood Disappearance Case will not figure in that chronicle of our successes which I foresee that a patient public will sooner or later have to endure.'

'Surely,' said I, 'the man's appearance would go far with any jury?'

'That is a dangerous argument, my dear Watson. You remember that terrible murderer, Bert Stevens, who wanted us to get him off in 1887? Was there ever a more mild-mannered, Sunday-school young man?'

'It is true.'

'Unless we succeed in establishing an alternative theory this man is lost. You can hardly find a flaw in the case which can now be presented against him, and all further investigation has served to strengthen it. By the way, there is one curious little point about those papers which may serve us as the starting-point for an enquiry. On looking over the bankbook I found that the low state of the balance was principally due to large cheques which have been made out during the last year to Mr Cornelius. I confess that I should be interested to know who this Mr Cornelius may be with whom a retired builder has such very large transactions. Is it possible that he has had a hand in the affair? Cornelius might be a broker, but we have found no scrip to correspond with these large payments. Failing any other indication my researches must now take the direction of an enquiry at the bank for the gentleman who has cashed these cheques. But I fear, my dear fellow, that our case will end ingloriously by Lestrade hanging our client, which will certainly be a triumph for Scotland Yard.'

I do not know how far Sherlock Holmes took any sleep that night, but when I came down to breakfast I found him pale and harassed, his bright eyes the brighter for the dark shadows round them. The carpet round his chair was littered with cigarette-ends and with the early editions of the morning papers. An open telegram lay upon the table.

'What do you think of this, Watson?' he asked, tossing it across.

It was from Norwood, and ran as follows:

Important fresh evidence to hand. McFarlane's guilt definitely established. Advise you to abandon case.

LESTRADE.

'This sounds serious,' said I.

'It is Lestrade's little cock-a-doodle of victory,' Holmes answered, with a bitter smile. 'And yet it may be premature to abandon the case. After all, important fresh evidence is a two-edged thing, and may possibly cut in a very different direction to that which Lestrade imagines. Take your breakfast, Watson, and we will go out together and see what we can do. I feel as if I shall need your company and your moral support today.'

My friend had no breakfast himself, for it was one of his peculiarities that in his more intense moments he would permit himself no food, and I have known him presume upon his iron strength until he has fainted from pure inanition. 'At present I cannot spare energy and nerve force for digestion,' he would say in answer to my medical remonstrances. I was not surprised, therefore, when this morning he left his untouched meal behind him and started with me for Norwood. A crowd of morbid sightseers were still gathered round Deep Dene House, which was just such a suburban villa as I had pictured. Within the gates Lestrade met us, his face flushed with victory, his manner grossly triumphant.

'Well, Mr Holmes, have you proved us to be wrong yet? Have you found your tramp?' he cried.

'I have formed no conclusion whatever,' my companion answered.

'But we formed ours yesterday, and now it proves to be correct; so you must acknowledge that we have been a little in front of you this time, Mr Holmes.'

'You certainly have the air of something unusual having occurred,' said Holmes.

Lestrade laughed loudly.

'You don't like being beaten any more than the rest of us do,' said he. 'A man can't expect always to have it his own way, can he, Dr Watson? Step this way, if you please, gentlemen, and I think I can convince you once for all that it was John McFarlane who did this crime.'

He led us through the passage and out into a dark hall beyond.

'This is where young McFarlane must have come out to get his hat after the crime was done,' said he. 'Now, look at this.' With dramatic suddenness he struck a match and by its light exposed a stain of blood upon the whitewashed wall. As he held the match nearer I saw that it was more than a stain. It was the well-marked print of a thumb.

'Look at that with your magnifying glass, Mr Holmes.'

'Yes, I am doing so.'

'You are aware that no two thumb marks are alike?'

'I have heard something of the kind.'

'Well, then, will you please compare that print with this wax impression of young McFarlane's right thumb, taken by my orders this morning?'

As he held the waxen print close to the bloodstain it did not take a magnifying glass to see that the two were undoubtedly from the same thumb. It was evident to me that our unfortunate client was lost.

'That is final,' said Lestrade.

'Yes, that is final,' I involuntarily echoed.

'It is final,' said Holmes.

Something in his tone caught my ear, and I turned to look at him. An extraordinary change had come over his face. It was writhing with inward merriment. His two eyes were shining like stars. It seemed to me that he was making desperate efforts to restrain a convulsive attack of laughter.

'Dear me! Dear me!' he said at last. 'Well, now, who would have thought it? And how deceptive appearances may be, to be sure! Such a nice young man to look at! It is a lesson to us not to trust our own judgment, is it not, Lestrade?'

'Yes, some of us are a little too much inclined to be cocksure, Mr Holmes,' said Lestrade. The man's insolence was maddening, but we could not resent it.

'What a providential thing that this young man should press his right thumb against the wall in taking his hat from the peg! Such a very natural action, too, if you come to think of it.' Holmes was outwardly calm, but his whole body gave a wriggle of suppressed excitement as he spoke. 'By the way, Lestrade, who made this remarkable discovery?'

'It was the housekeeper, Mrs Lexington, who drew the night constable's attention to it.'

'Where was the night constable?'

'He remained on guard in the bedroom where the crime was committed, so as to see that nothing was touched.'

'But why didn't the police see this mark yesterday?'

'Well, we had no particular reason to make a careful examination of the hall. Besides, it's not in a very prominent place, as you see.'

'No, no, of course not. I suppose there is no doubt that the mark was there yesterday?'

Lestrade looked at Holmes as if he thought he was going out of his mind. I confess that I was myself surprised both at his hilarious manner and at his rather wild observation.

'I don't know whether you think that McFarlane came out of gaol in the dead of the night in order to strengthen the evidence against himself,' said Lestrade.

'I leave it to any expert in the world whether that is not the mark of his thumb.'

'It is unquestionably the mark of his thumb.'

'There, that's enough,' said Lestrade. 'I am a practical man, Mr Holmes, and when I have got my evidence I come to my conclusions. If you have anything to say you will find me writing my report in the sitting-room.'

Holmes had recovered his equanimity, though I still seemed to detect gleams of amusement in his expression.

'Dear me, this is a very sad development, Watson, is it not?' said he. 'And yet there are singular points about it which hold out some hopes for our client.'

'I am delighted to hear it,' said I, heartily. 'I was afraid it was all up with him.'

'I would hardly go so far as to say that, my dear Watson. The fact is that there is one really serious flaw in this evidence to which our friend attaches so much importance.'

'Indeed, Holmes! What is it?'

'Only this: that I *know* that that mark was not there when I examined the hall yesterday. And now, Watson, let us have a little stroll round in the sunshine.'

With a confused brain, but with a heart into which some warmth of hope was returning, I accompanied my friend in a walk round the garden. Holmes took each face of the house in turn and examined it with great interest. He then led the way inside and went over the whole building from basement to attics. Most of the rooms were unfurnished, but none the less Holmes inspected them all minutely. Finally, on the top corridor, which ran outside three untenanted bedrooms, he again was seized with a spasm of merriment.

'There are really some very unique features about this case, Watson,' said he. 'I think it is time now that we took our friend Lestrade into our confidence. He has had his little smile at our expense, and perhaps we may do as much by him if my reading of this problem proves to be correct. Yes, yes; I think I see how we should approach it.'

The Scotland Yard inspector was still writing in the parlour when Holmes interrupted him.

'I understood that you were writing a report of this case,' said he.

'So I am.'

'Don't you think it may be a little premature? I can't help thinking that your evidence is not complete.'

Lestrade knew my friend too well to disregard his words. He laid down his pen and looked curiously at him.

'What do you mean, Mr Holmes?'

'Only that there is an important witness whom you have not seen.'

'Can you produce him?'

'I think I can.'

'Then do so.'

'I will do my best. How many constables have you?'

'There are three within call.'

'Excellent!' said Holmes. 'May I ask if they are all large, able-bodied men with powerful voices?'

'I have no doubt they are, though I fail to see what their voices have to do with it.'

'Perhaps I can help you to see that and one or two other things as well,' said Holmes. 'Kindly summon your men, and I will try.'

Five minutes later three policemen had assembled in the hall.

'In the outhouse you will find a considerable quantity of straw,' said Holmes. 'I will ask you to carry in two bundles of it. I think it will be of the greatest assistance in producing the witness whom I require. Thank you very much. I believe you have some matches in your pocket, Watson. Now, Mr Lestrade, I will ask you all to accompany me to the top landing.'

As I have said, there was a broad corridor there, which ran outside three empty bedrooms. At one end of the corridor we were all marshalled by Sherlock Holmes, the constables grinning and Lestrade staring at my friend with amazement, expectation, and derision chasing each other across his features. Holmes stood before us with the air of a conjurer who is performing a trick.

'Would you kindly send one of your constables for two buckets of water? Put the straw on the floor here, free from the wall on either side. Now I think that we are all ready.'

Lestrade's face had begun to grow red and angry.

'I don't know whether you are playing a game with us, Mr Sherlock Holmes,' said he. 'If you know anything, you can surely say it without all this tom-foolery.'

'I assure you, my good Lestrade, that I have an excellent reason for everything that I do. You may possibly remember that you chaffed me a little some hours ago, when the sun seemed on your side of the hedge, so you must not grudge me a little pomp and ceremony now. Might I ask you, Watson, to open that window, and then to put a match to the edge of the straw?'

I did so, and, driven by the draught, a coil of grey smoke swirled down the corridor, while the dry straw crackled and flamed.

'Now we must see if we can find this witness for you, Lestrade. Might I ask you all to join in the cry of "Fire!"? Now, then; one, two, three – '

'Fire!' we all yelled.

'Thank you. I will trouble you once again.'

'Fire!'

'Just once more, gentlemen, and all together.'

'Fire!' The shout must have rung over Norwood.

It had hardly died away when an amazing thing happened. A door suddenly flew open out of what appeared to be solid wall at the end of the corridor, and a little, wizened man darted out of it, like a rabbit out of its burrow.

'Capital!' said Holmes, calmly. 'Watson, a bucket of water over the straw. That will do! Lestrade, allow me to present you with your principal missing witness, Mr Jonas Oldacre.'

The detective stared at the new-comer with blank amazement. The latter was blinking in the bright light of the corridor, and peering at us and at the smouldering fire. It was an odious face – crafty, vicious, malignant, with shifty, light-grey eyes and white eyelashes.

'What's this, then?' said Lestrade at last. 'What have you been doing all this time, eh?'

Oldacre gave an uneasy laugh, shrinking back from the furious red face of the angry detective.

'I have done no harm.'

'No harm? You have done your best to get an innocent man hanged. If it wasn't for this gentleman here, I am not sure that you would not have succeeded.'

The wretched creature began to whimper.

'I am sure, sir, it was only my practical joke.'

'Oh! a joke, was it? You won't find the laugh on your side, I promise you. Take him down and keep him in the sitting-room until I come. Mr Holmes,' he continued, when they had gone, 'I could not speak before the constables, but I don't mind saying, in the presence of Dr Watson, that this is the brightest thing that you have done yet, though it is a mystery to me how you did it. You have saved an innocent man's life, and you have prevented a very grave scandal, which would have ruined my reputation in the Force.'

Holmes smiled and clapped Lestrade upon the shoulder.

'Instead of being ruined, my good sir, you will find that your reputation has been enormously enhanced. Just make a few alterations in that report which you were writing, and they will understand how hard it is to throw dust in the eyes of Inspector Lestrade.'

'And you don't want your name to appear?'

'Not at all. The work is its own reward. Perhaps I shall get the credit also at some distant day when I permit my zealous historian to lay out his foolscap once more – eh, Watson? Well, now, let us see where this rat has been lurking.'

A lath-and-plaster partition had been run across the passage six feet from the end, with a door cunningly concealed in it. It was lit within by slits under the eaves. A few articles of furniture and a supply of food and water were within, together with a number of books and papers.

'There's the advantage of being a builder,' said Holmes, as we came out. 'He was able to fix up his own little hiding-place without any confederate – save, of course, that precious housekeeper of his, whom I should lose no time in adding to your bag, Lestrade.'

'I'll take your advice. But how did you know of this place, Mr Holmes?'

'I made up my mind that the fellow was in hiding in the house. When I paced one corridor and found it six feet shorter than the corresponding one below, it was pretty clear where he was. I thought he had not the nerve to lie quiet before an alarm of fire. We could, of course, have gone in and taken him, but it amused me to make him reveal himself; besides, I owed you a little mystification, Lestrade, for your chaff in the morning.'

'Well, sir, you certainly got equal with me on that. But how in the world did you know that he was in the house at all?'

'The thumb-mark, Lestrade. You said it was final; and so it was, in a very different sense. I knew it had not been there the day before. I pay a good deal of attention to matters of detail, as you may have observed, and I had examined the hall and was sure that the wall was clear. Therefore, it had been put on during the night.'

'But how?'

'Very simply. When those packets were sealed up, Jonas Oldacre got McFarlane to secure one of the seals by putting his thumb upon the soft wax. It would be done so quickly and so naturally that I dare say the young man himself has no recollection of it. Very likely it just so happened, and Oldacre had himself no notion of the use he would put it to. Brooding over the case in that den of his, it suddenly struck him what absolutely damning evidence he could make against McFarlane by using that thumb-mark. It was the simplest thing in the world for him to take a wax impression from the seal, to moisten it in as much blood as he could get from a pinprick, and to put the mark upon the wall during the night, either with his own hand or with that of his housekeeper. If you examine among those documents which he took with him into his retreat I will lay you a wager that you find the seal with the thumb-mark upon it.'

'Wonderful!' said Lestrade. 'Wonderful! It's all as clear as crystal, as you put it. But what is the object of this deep deception, Mr Holmes?'

It was amusing to me to see how the detective's overbearing manner had changed suddenly to that of a child asking questions of its teacher.

'Well, I don't think that is very hard to explain. A very deep, malicious, vindictive person is the gentleman who is now awaiting us downstairs. You know that he was once refused by McFarlane's mother? You don't! I told you that you should go to Blackheath first and Norwood afterwards. Well, this injury, as he would consider it, has rankled in his wicked, scheming brain, and all his life he has longed for vengeance, but never seen his chance. During the last year or two things have gone against him – secret speculation, I think – and he finds himself in a bad way. He determines to swindle his creditors, and for this purpose he pays large cheques to a certain Mr Cornelius, who is, I imagine, himself under another name. I have not traced these cheques yet, but I have no doubt that they were banked under that name at some provincial town where Oldacre from time to time led a double existence. He intended to change his name altogether, draw this money, and vanish, starting life again elsewhere.'

'Well, that's likely enough.'

'It would strike him that in disappearing he might throw all pursuit off his track, and at the same time have an ample and crushing revenge upon his old sweetheart, if he could give the impression that he had been murdered by her only child. It was a masterpiece of villainy, and he carried it out like a master. The idea of the will, which would give an obvious motive for the crime, the secret visit unknown to his own parents, the retention of the stick, the blood, and the animal remains and buttons in the wood-pile, all were admirable. It was a net from which it seemed to me a few hours ago that there was no possible escape. But he had not that supreme gift of the artist, the knowledge of when to stop. He wished to improve that which was already perfect – to draw the rope tighter yet round the neck of his unfortunate victim – and so he ruined all. Let us descend, Lestrade. There are just one or two questions that I would ask him.'

The malignant creature was seated in his own parlour with a policeman upon each side of him.

'It was a joke, my good sir, a practical joke, nothing more,' he whined incessantly. 'I assure you, sir, that I simply concealed myself in order to see the effect of my disappearance, and I am sure that you would not be so unjust as to imagine that I would have allowed any harm to befall poor young Mr McFarlane.'

'That's for a jury to decide,' said Lestrade. 'Anyhow, we shall have you on a charge of conspiracy, if not for attempted murder.'

'And you'll probably find that your creditors will impound the banking account of Mr Cornelius,' said Holmes.

The little man started and turned his malignant eyes upon my friend.

'I have to thank you for a good deal,' said he. 'Perhaps I'll pay my debt some day.'

Holmes smiled indulgently.

'I fancy that for some few years you will find your time very fully occupied,' said he. 'By the way, what was it you put into the wood-pile besides your old trousers? A dead dog, or rabbits, or what? You won't tell? Dear me, how very unkind of you! Well, well, I dare say that a couple of rabbits would account both for the blood and for the charred ashes. If ever you write an account, Watson, you can make rabbits serve your turn.'

3

The Dancing Men

Holmes had been seated for some hours in silence with his long, thin back curved over a chemical vessel in which he was brewing a particularly malodorous product. His head was sunk upon his breast, and he looked from my point of view like a strange, lank bird, with dull grey plumage and a black topknot.

'So, Watson,' said he, suddenly, 'you do not propose to invest in South African securities?'

I gave a start of astonishment. Accustomed as I was to Holmes's curious faculties, this sudden intrusion into my most intimate thoughts was utterly inexplicable.

'How on earth do you know that?' I asked.

He wheeled round upon his stool, with a steaming test-tube in his hand and a gleam of amusement in his deep-set eyes.

'Now, Watson, confess yourself utterly taken aback,' said he.

'I am.'

'I ought to make you sign a paper to that effect.'

'Why?'

'Because in five minutes you will say that it is all so absurdly simple.'

'I am sure that I shall say nothing of the kind.'

'You see, my dear Watson' – he propped his test-tube in the rack and began to lecture with the air of a professor addressing his class – 'it is not really difficult to construct a series of inferences, each dependent upon its predecessor and each simple in itself. If, after doing so, one simply knocks out all the central inferences and presents one's audience with the starting-point and the conclusion, one may produce a startling, though possibly a meretricious, effect. Now, it was not really difficult, by an inspection of the groove between your left forefinger and thumb, to feel sure that you did NOT propose to invest your small capital in the goldfields.'

'I see no connection.'

'Very likely not; but I can quickly show you a close connection. Here are the missing links of the very simple chain: 1. You had chalk between your left finger and thumb when you returned from the club last night. 2. You put chalk there when you play billiards to steady the cue. 3. You never play billiards except with Thurston. 4. You told me four weeks ago that Thurston had an option on some South African property which would expire in a month, and which he desired you to share with him. 5. Your chequebook is locked in my drawer, and you have not asked for the key. 6. You do not propose to invest your money in this manner.'

'How absurdly simple!' I cried.

'Quite so!' said he, a little nettled. 'Every problem becomes very childish when once it is explained to you. Here is an unexplained one. See what you can make of that, friend Watson.' He tossed a sheet of paper upon the table and turned once more to his chemical analysis.

I looked with amazement at the absurd hieroglyphics upon the paper.

'Why, Holmes, it is a child's drawing,' I cried.

'Oh, that's your idea!'

'What else should it be?'

'That is what Mr Hilton Cubitt, of Ridling Thorpe Manor, Norfolk, is very anxious to know. This little conundrum came by the first post, and he was to follow by the next train. There's a ring at the bell, Watson. I should not be very much surprised if this were he.'

A heavy step was heard upon the stairs, and an instant later there entered a tall, ruddy, clean-shaven gentleman, whose clear eyes and florid cheeks told of a life led far from the fogs of Baker Street. He seemed to bring a whiff of his strong, fresh, bracing, east-coast air with him as he entered. Having shaken hands with each of us, he was about to sit down when his eye rested upon the paper with the curious markings, which I had just examined and left upon the table.

'Well, Mr Holmes, what do you make of these?' he cried. 'They told me that you were fond of queer mysteries, and I don't think you can find a queerer one than that. I sent the paper on ahead so that you might have time to study it before I came.'

'It is certainly rather a curious production,' said Holmes. 'At first sight it would appear to be some childish prank. It consists of a number of absurd little figures dancing across the paper upon which they are drawn. Why should you attribute any importance to so grotesque an object?'

'I never should, Mr Holmes. But my wife does. It is frightening her to death. She says nothing, but I can see terror in her eyes. That's why I want to sift the matter to the bottom.'

Holmes held up the paper so that the sunlight shone full upon it. It was a page torn from a notebook. The markings were done in pencil, and ran in this way:

Holmes examined it for some time, and then, folding it carefully up, he placed it in his pocketbook.

'This promises to be a most interesting and unusual case,' said he. 'You gave me a few particulars in your letter, Mr Hilton Cubitt, but I should be very much obliged if you would kindly go over it all again for the benefit of my friend, Dr Watson.'

'I'm not much of a storyteller,' said our visitor, nervously clasping and unclasping his great, strong hands. 'You'll just ask me anything that I don't make clear. I'll begin at the time of my marriage last year; but I want to say first of all that, though I'm not a rich man, my people have been at Ridling Thorpe for a matter of five centuries, and there is no better-known family in the county of Norfolk. Last year I came up to London for the Jubilee, and I stopped at a boarding-house in Russell Square, because Parker, the vicar of our parish, was staying in it. There was an American young lady there – Patrick was the name – Elsie Patrick. In some way we became friends, until before my month was up I was as much in love as a man could be. We were quietly married at a registry office, and we returned to Norfolk a wedded couple. You'll think it very mad, Mr Holmes, that a man of a good old family should marry a wife in this fashion, knowing nothing of her past or of her people; but if you saw her and knew her it would help you to understand.

'She was very straight about it, was Elsie. I can't say that she did not give me every chance of getting out of it if I wished to do so. "I have had some very disagreeable associations in my life," said she; "I wish to forget all about them. I would rather never allude to the past, for it is very painful to me. If you take me, Hilton, you will take a woman who has nothing that she need be personally ashamed of; but you will have to be content with my word for it, and to allow me to be silent as to all that passed up to the time when I became yours. If these conditions are too hard, then go back to Norfolk and leave me to the lonely life in which you found me." It was only the day before our wedding that she said those very words to me. I told her that I was content to take her on her own terms, and I have been as good as my word.

'Well, we have been married now for a year, and very happy we have been. But about a month ago, at the end of June, I saw for the first time signs of trouble. One day my wife received a letter from America. I saw the American stamp. She turned deadly white, read the letter, and threw it into the fire. She made no allusion to it afterwards, and I made none, for a promise is a promise; but she has never known an easy hour from that moment. There is always a look of fear upon her face – a look as if she were waiting and expecting. She would do better to trust me. She would find that I was her best friend. But until she speaks I can say nothing. Mind you, she is a truthful woman, Mr Holmes, and whatever trouble there may have been in her past life it has been no fault of hers. I am only a simple Norfolk squire, but there is not a man in England who ranks his family honour more highly than I do. She knows it well, and she knew it well before she married me. She would never bring any stain upon it – of that I am sure.

'Well, now I come to the queer part of my story. About a week ago – it was the Tuesday of last week – I found on one of the window-sills a number of absurd little dancing figures, like these upon the paper. They were scrawled with chalk. I thought that it was the stable-boy who had drawn them, but the lad swore he knew nothing about it. Anyhow, they had come there during the night. I had them washed out, and I only mentioned the matter to my wife afterwards. To my surprise she took it very seriously, and begged me if any more came to let her see them. None did come for a week, and then yesterday morning I found this paper lying on the sundial in the garden. I showed it to Elsie, and down she dropped in a dead faint. Since then she has looked like a woman in a dream, half dazed, and with terror always lurking in her eyes. It was then that I wrote and sent the paper to you, Mr Holmes. It was not a thing that I could take to the police, for they would have laughed at me, but you will tell me what to do. I am not a rich man; but if there is any danger threatening my little woman I would spend my last copper to shield her.'

He was a fine creature, this man of the old English soil, simple, straight, and gentle, with his great, earnest blue eyes and broad, comely face. His love for his wife and his trust in her shone in his features. Holmes had listened to his story with the utmost attention, and now he sat for some time in silent thought.

'Don't you think, Mr Cubitt,' said he, at last, 'that your best plan would be to make a direct appeal to your wife, and to ask her to share her secret with you?'

Hilton Cubitt shook his massive head.

'A promise is a promise, Mr Holmes. If Elsie wished to tell me she would. If not, it is not for me to force her confidence. But I am justified in taking my own line – and I will.'

'Then I will help you with all my heart. In the first place, have you heard of any strangers being seen in your neighbourhood?'

'No.'

'I presume that it is a very quiet place. Any fresh face would cause comment?'

'In the immediate neighbourhood, yes. But we have several small watering-places not very far away. And the farmers take in lodgers.'

'These hieroglyphics have evidently a meaning. If it is a purely arbitrary one it may be impossible for us to solve it. If, on the other hand, it is systematic, I have no doubt that we shall get to the bottom of it. But this particular sample is so short that I can do nothing, and the facts which you have brought me are so indefinite that we have no basis for an investigation. I would suggest that you return to Norfolk, that you keep a keen lookout, and that you take an exact copy of any fresh dancing men which may appear. It is a thousand pities that we have not a reproduction of those which were done in chalk upon the window-sill. Make a discreet enquiry also as to any strangers in the neighbourhood. When you have collected some fresh evidence come to me again. That is the best advice which I can give you, Mr Hilton Cubitt. If there are any pressing fresh developments I shall be always ready to run down and see you in your Norfolk home.'

The interview left Sherlock Holmes very thoughtful, and several times in the next few days I saw him take his slip of paper from his notebook and look long and earnestly at the curious figures inscribed upon it. He made no allusion to the affair, however, until one afternoon a fortnight or so later. I was going out when he called me back.

'You had better stay here, Watson.'

'Why?'

'Because I had a wire from Hilton Cubitt this morning – you remember Hilton Cubitt, of the dancing men? He was to reach Liverpool Street at one-twenty. He may be here at any moment. I gather from his wire that there have been some new incidents of importance.'

We had not long to wait, for our Norfolk squire came straight from the station as fast as a hansom could bring him. He was looking worried and depressed, with tired eyes and a lined forehead.

'It's getting on my nerves, this business, Mr Holmes,' said he, as he sank, like a wearied man, into an arm-chair. 'It's bad enough to feel that you are surrounded by unseen, unknown folk, who have some kind of design upon you; but when, in addition to that, you know that it is just killing your wife by inches, then it becomes as much as flesh and blood can endure. She's wearing away under it – just wearing away before my eyes.'

'Has she said anything yet?'

'No, Mr Holmes, she has not. And yet there have been times when the poor girl has wanted to speak, and yet could not quite bring herself to take the plunge. I have tried to help her; but I dare say I did it clumsily, and scared her off from it. She has spoken about my old family, and our reputation in the county, and our pride in our unsullied honour, and I always felt it was leading to the point; but somehow it turned off before we got there.'

'But you have found out something for yourself?'

'A good deal, Mr Holmes. I have several fresh dancing men pictures for you to examine, and, what is more important, I have seen the fellow.'

'What, the man who draws them?'

'Yes, I saw him at his work. But I will tell you everything in order. When I got back after my visit to you, the very first thing I saw next morning was a fresh crop of dancing men. They had been drawn in chalk upon the black wooden door of the tool-house, which stands beside the lawn in full view of the front windows. I took an exact copy, and here it is.' He unfolded a paper and laid it upon the table. Here is a copy of the hieroglyphics:

'Excellent!' said Holmes. 'Excellent! Pray continue.'

'When I had taken the copy I rubbed out the marks; but two mornings later a fresh inscription had appeared. I have a copy of it here':

Holmes rubbed his hands and chuckled with delight.

'Our material is rapidly accumulating,' said he.

'Three days later a message was left scrawled upon paper, and placed under a pebble upon the sundial. Here it is. The characters are, as you see, exactly the same as the last one. After that I determined to lie in wait; so I got out my revolver and I sat up in my study, which overlooks the lawn and garden. About two in the morning I was seated by the window, all being dark save for the moonlight outside, when I heard steps behind me, and there was my wife in her dressing-gown. She implored me to come to bed. I told her frankly that I wished to see who it was who played such absurd tricks upon us. She answered that it was some senseless practical joke, and that I should not take any notice of it.

' "If it really annoys you, Hilton, we might go and travel, you and I, and so avoid this nuisance."

' "What, be driven out of our own house by a practical joker?" said I. "Why, we should have the whole county laughing at us."

' "Well, come to bed," said she, "and we can discuss it in the morning."

'Suddenly, as she spoke, I saw her white face grow whiter yet in the moonlight, and her hand tightened upon my shoulder. Something was moving in the shadow of the tool-house. I saw a dark, creeping figure which crawled round the corner and squatted in front of the door. Seizing my pistol I was rushing out, when my wife threw her arms round me and held me with convulsive strength. I tried to throw her off, but she clung to me most desperately. At last I got clear, but by the time I had opened the door and reached the house the creature was gone. He had left a trace of his presence, however, for there on the door was the very same arrangement of dancing men which had already twice appeared, and which I have copied on that paper. There was no other sign of the fellow anywhere, though I ran all over the grounds. And yet the amazing thing is that he must have been there all the time, for when I examined the door again in the morning he had scrawled some more of his pictures under the line which I had already seen.'

'Have you that fresh drawing?'

'Yes; it is very short, but I made a copy of it, and here it is.'

Again he produced a paper. The new dance was in this form:

'Tell me,' said Holmes – and I could see by his eyes that he was much excited – 'was this a mere addition to the first, or did it appear to be entirely separate?'

'It was on a different panel of the door.'

'Excellent! This is far the most important of all for our purpose. It fills me with hopes. Now, Mr Hilton Cubitt, please continue your most interesting statement.'

'I have nothing more to say, Mr Holmes, except that I was angry with my wife that night for having held me back when I might have caught the skulking rascal. She said that she feared that I might come to harm. For an instant it had crossed my mind that perhaps what she really feared was that *he* might come to harm, for I could not doubt that she knew who this man was and what he meant by these strange signals. But there is a tone in my wife's voice, Mr Holmes, and a look in her eyes which forbid doubt, and I am sure that it was indeed my own safety that was in her mind. There's the whole case, and now I want your advice as to what I ought to do. My own inclination is to put half a dozen of my farm lads in the shrubbery, and when this fellow comes again to give him such a hiding that he will leave us in peace for the future.'

'I fear it is too deep a case for such simple remedies,' said Holmes. 'How long can you stay in London?'

'I must go back today. I would not leave my wife

alone all night for anything. She is very nervous and begged me to come back.'

'I dare say you are right. But if you could have stopped I might possibly have been able to return with you in a day or two. Meanwhile you will leave me these papers, and I think that it is very likely that I shall be able to pay you a visit shortly and to throw some light upon your case.'

Sherlock Holmes preserved his calm professional manner until our visitor had left us, although it was easy for me, who knew him so well, to see that he was profoundly excited. The moment that Hilton Cubitt's broad back had disappeared through the door my comrade rushed to the table, laid out all the slips of paper containing dancing men in front of him, and threw himself into an intricate and elaborate calculation. For two hours I watched him as he covered sheet after sheet of paper with figures and letters, so completely absorbed in his task that he had evidently forgotten my presence. Sometimes he was making progress and whistled and sang at his work; sometimes he was puzzled, and would sit for long spells with a furrowed brow and a vacant eye. Finally he sprang from his chair with a cry of satisfaction, and walked up and down the room rubbing his hands together. Then he wrote a long telegram upon a cable form. 'If my answer to this is as I hope, you will have a very pretty case to add to your collection, Watson,' said he. 'I expect that we shall be able to go down to Norfolk tomorrow, and to take our friend some very definite news as to the secret of his annoyance.'

I confess that I was filled with curiosity, but I was aware that Holmes liked to make his disclosures at his own time and in his own way; so I waited until it should suit him to take me into his confidence.

But there was a delay in that answering telegram, and two days of impatience followed, during which Holmes pricked up his ears at every ring of the bell. On the evening of the second there came a letter from Hilton Cubitt. All was quiet with him, save that a long inscription had appeared that morning upon the pedestal of the sundial. He enclosed a copy of it, which is here reproduced:

Holmes bent over this grotesque frieze for some minutes, and then suddenly sprang to his feet with an exclamation of surprise and dismay. His face was haggard with anxiety.

'We have let this affair go far enough,' said he. 'Is there a train to North Walsham tonight?'

I turned up the timetable. The last had just gone.

'Then we shall breakfast early and take the very first in the morning,' said Holmes. 'Our presence is most urgently needed. Ah! here is our expected cablegram. One moment, Mrs Hudson; there may be an answer. No, that is quite as I expected. This message makes it even more essential that we should not lose an hour in letting Hilton Cubitt know how matters stand, for it is a singular and a dangerous web in which our simple Norfolk squire is entangled.'

So, indeed, it proved, and as I come to the dark conclusion of a story which had seemed to me to be only childish and bizarre I experience once again the dismay and horror with which I was filled. Would that I had some brighter ending to communicate to my readers, but these are the chronicles of fact, and I must follow to their dark crisis the strange chain of events which for some days made Ridling Thorpe Manor a household word through the length and breadth of England.

We had hardly alighted at North Walsham, and mentioned the name of our destination, when the station-master hurried towards us. 'I suppose that you are the detectives from London?' said he.

A look of annoyance passed over Holmes's face.

'What makes you think such a thing?'

'Because Inspector Martin from Norwich has just passed through. But maybe you are the surgeons. She's not dead – or wasn't by last accounts. You may be in time to save her yet – though it be for the gallows.'

Holmes's brow was dark with anxiety.

'We are going to Ridling Thorpe Manor,' said he, 'but we have heard nothing of what has passed there.'

'It's a terrible business,' said the station-master. 'They are shot, both Mr Hilton Cubitt and his wife. She shot him and then herself – so the servants say. He's dead and her life is despaired of. Dear, dear, one of the oldest families in the county of Norfolk, and one of the most honoured.'

Without a word Holmes hurried to a carriage, and during the long seven miles' drive he never opened his mouth. Seldom have I seen him so utterly despondent. He had been uneasy during all our journey from town, and I had observed that he had turned over the morning papers with anxious attention; but now this sudden realisation of his worst fears left him in a blank melancholy. He leaned back in his seat, lost in gloomy speculation. Yet there was much around to interest us, for we were passing through as singular a countryside as any in England, where a few scattered cottages represented the population of today, while on every hand enormous square-towered churches bristled up from the flat, green landscape and told of the glory and prosperity of old East Anglia. At last the violet rim of the German Ocean appeared over the green edge of the Norfolk coast, and the driver pointed with his whip to two old brick and timber gables which projected from a grove of trees. 'That's Ridling Thorpe Manor,' said he.

As we drove up to the porticoed front door I observed in front of it, beside the tennis lawn, the black tool-house and the pedestalled sundial with which we had such strange associations. A dapper little man, with a quick, alert manner and a waxed moustache, had just descended from a high dog-cart. He introduced himself as Inspector Martin, of the Norfolk Constabulary, and he was considerably astonished when he heard the name of my companion.

'Why, Mr Holmes, the crime was only committed at three this morning. How could you hear of it in London and get to the spot as soon as I?'

'I anticipated it. I came in the hope of preventing it.'

'Then you must have important evidence of which we are ignorant, for they were said to be a most united couple.'

'I have only the evidence of the dancing men,' said Holmes. 'I will explain the matter to you later. Meanwhile, since it is too late to prevent this tragedy, I am very anxious that I should use the knowledge which I possess in order to ensure that justice be done.

Will you associate me in your investigation, or will you prefer that I should act independently?'

'I should be proud to feel that we were acting together, Mr Holmes,' said the inspector, earnestly.

'In that case I should be glad to hear the evidence and to examine the premises without an instant of unnecessary delay.'

Inspector Martin had the good sense to allow my friend to do things in his own fashion, and contented himself with carefully noting the results. The local surgeon, an old, white-haired man, had just come down from Mrs Hilton Cubitt's room, and he reported that her injuries were serious, but not necessarily fatal. The bullet had passed through the front of her brain, and it would probably be some time before she could regain consciousness. On the question of whether she had been shot or had shot herself he would not venture to express any decided opinion. Certainly the bullet had been discharged at very close quarters. There was only the one pistol found in the room, two barrels of which had been emptied. Mr Hilton Cubitt had been shot through the heart. It was equally conceivable that he had shot her and then himself, or that she had been the criminal, for the revolver lay upon the floor midway between them.

'Has he been moved?' asked Holmes.

'We have moved nothing except the lady. We could not leave her lying wounded upon the floor.'

'How long have you been here, doctor?'

'Since four o'clock.'

'Anyone else?'

'Yes, the constable here.'

'And you have touched nothing?'

'Nothing.'

'You have acted with great discretion. Who sent for you?'

'The housemaid, Saunders.'

'Was it she who gave the alarm?'

'She and Mrs King, the cook.'

'Where are they now?'

'In the kitchen, I believe.'

'Then I think we had better hear their story at once.'

The old hall, oak-panelled and high-windowed, had been turned into a court of investigation. Holmes sat in a great, old-fashioned chair, his inexorable eyes gleaming out of his haggard face. I could read in them a set purpose to devote his life to this quest until the client whom he had failed to save should at last be avenged. The trim Inspector Martin, the old, grey-headed country doctor, myself, and a stolid village policeman made up the rest of that strange company.

The two women told their story clearly enough. They had been aroused from their sleep by the sound of an explosion, which had been followed a minute later by a second one. They slept in adjoining rooms, and Mrs King had rushed in to Saunders. Together they had descended the stairs. The door of the study was open and a candle was burning upon the table. Their master lay upon his face in the centre of the room. He was quite dead. Near the window his wife was crouching, her head leaning against the wall. She was horribly wounded, and the side of her face was red with blood. She breathed heavily, but was incapable of saying anything. The passage, as well as the room, was full of smoke and the smell of powder. The window was certainly shut and fastened upon the inside. Both women were positive upon the point. They had at once sent for the doctor and for the constable. Then, with the aid of the groom and the stable-boy, they had conveyed their injured mistress to her room. Both she and her husband had occupied the bed. She was clad in her dress – he in his dressing-gown, over his night clothes. Nothing had been moved in the study. So far as they knew there had never been any quarrel between husband and wife. They had always looked upon them as a very united couple.

These were the main points of the servants' evidence. In answer to Inspector Martin they were clear that every door was fastened upon the inside, and that no one could have escaped from the house. In answer to Holmes they both remembered that they were conscious of the smell of powder from the moment that they ran out of their rooms upon the top floor. 'I commend that fact very carefully to your attention,' said Holmes to his professional colleague. 'And now I think that we are in a position to undertake a thorough examination of the room.'

The study proved to be a small chamber, lined on three sides with books, and with a writing-table facing an ordinary window, which looked out upon the garden. Our first attention was given to the body of the unfortunate squire, whose huge frame lay stretched across the room. His disordered dress showed that he had been hastily aroused from sleep. The bullet had been fired at him from the front, and had remained in his body after penetrating the heart. His death had certainly been instantaneous and painless. There was no powder-marking either upon his dressing-gown or on his hands. According to the country surgeon the lady had stains upon her face, but none upon her hand.

'The absence of the latter means nothing, though its

presence may mean everything,' said Holmes. 'Unless the powder from a badly-fitting cartridge happens to spurt backwards, one may fire many shots without leaving a sign. I would suggest that Mr Cubitt's body may now be removed. I suppose, doctor, you have not recovered the bullet which wounded the lady?'

'A serious operation will be necessary before that can be done. But there are still four cartridges in the revolver. Two have been fired and two wounds inflicted, so that each bullet can be accounted for.'

'So it would seem,' said Holmes. 'Perhaps you can account also for the bullet which has so obviously struck the edge of the window?'

He had turned suddenly, and his long, thin finger was pointing to a hole which had been drilled right through the lower window-sash about an inch above the bottom.

'By George!' cried the inspector. 'How ever did you see that?'

'Because I looked for it.'

'Wonderful!' said the country doctor. 'You are certainly right, sir. Then a third shot has been fired, and therefore a third person must have been present. But who could that have been and how could he have got away?'

'That is the problem which we are now about to solve,' said Sherlock Holmes. 'You remember, Inspector Martin, when the servants said that on leaving their room they were at once conscious of a smell of powder I remarked that the point was an extremely important one?'

'Yes, sir; but I confess I did not quite follow you.'

'It suggested that at the time of the firing the window as well as the door of the room had been open.

Otherwise the fumes of powder could not have been blown so rapidly through the house. A draught in the room was necessary for that. Both door and window were only open for a very short time, however.'

'How do you prove that?'

'Because the candle has not guttered.'

'Capital!' cried the inspector. 'Capital!'

'Feeling sure that the window had been open at the time of the tragedy I conceived that there might have been a third person in the affair, who stood outside this opening and fired through it. Any shot directed at this person might hit the sash. I looked, and there, sure enough, was the bullet mark!'

'But how came the window to be shut and fastened?'

'The woman's first instinct would be to shut and fasten the window. But, halloa! what is this?'

It was a lady's handbag which stood upon the study table – a trim little handbag of crocodile-skin and silver. Holmes opened it and turned the contents out. There were twenty fifty-pound notes of the Bank of England, held together by an india rubber band – nothing else.

'This must be preserved, for it will figure in the trial,' said Holmes, as he handed the bag with its contents to the inspector. 'It is now necessary that we should try to throw some light upon this third bullet, which has clearly, from the splintering of the wood, been fired from inside the room. I should like to see Mrs King, the cook, again . . . You said, Mrs King, that you were awakened by a *loud* explosion. When you said that, did you mean that it seemed to you to be louder than the second one?'

'Well, sir, it wakened me from my sleep, and so it is hard to judge. But it did seem very loud.'

'You don't think that it might have been two shots fired almost at the same instant?'

'I am sure I couldn't say, sir.'

'I believe that it was undoubtedly so. I rather think, Inspector Martin, that we have now exhausted all that this room can teach us. If you will kindly step round with me, we shall see what fresh evidence the garden has to offer.'

A flower-bed extended up to the study window, and we all broke into an exclamation as we approached it. The flowers were trampled down, and the soft soil was imprinted all over with footmarks. Large, masculine feet they were, with peculiarly long, sharp toes. Holmes hunted about among the grass and leaves like a retriever after a wounded bird. Then, with a cry of satisfaction, he bent forward and picked up a little brazen cylinder.

'I thought so,' said he; 'the revolver had an ejector, and here is the third cartridge. I really think, Inspector Martin, that our case is almost complete.'

The country inspector's face had shown his intense amazement at the rapid and masterful progress of Holmes's investigation. At first he had shown some disposition to assert his own position; but now he was overcome with admiration and ready to follow without question wherever Holmes led.

'Whom do you suspect?' he asked.

'I'll go into that later. There are several points in this problem which I have not been able to explain to you yet. Now that I have got so far I had best proceed on my own lines, and then clear the whole matter up once and for all.'

'Just as you wish, Mr Holmes, so long as we get our man.'

'I have no desire to make mysteries, but it is

impossible at the moment of action to enter into long and complex explanations. I have the threads of this affair all in my hand. Even if this lady should never recover consciousness we can still reconstruct the events of last night and ensure that justice be done. First of all I wish to know whether there is any inn in this neighbourhood known as "Elrige's"?'

The servants were cross-questioned, but none of them had heard of such a place. The stable-boy threw a light upon the matter by remembering that a farmer of that name lived some miles off in the direction of East Ruston.

'Is it a lonely farm?'

'Very lonely, sir.'

'Perhaps they have not heard yet of all that happened here during the night?'

'Maybe not, sir.'

Holmes thought for a little and then a curious smile played over his face.

'Saddle a horse, my lad,' said he. 'I shall wish you to take a note to Elrige's Farm.'

He took from his pocket the various slips of the dancing men. With these in front of him he worked for some time at the study table. Finally he handed a note to the boy, with directions to put it into the hands of the person to whom it was addressed, and especially to answer no questions of any sort which might be put to him. I saw the outside of the note, addressed in straggling, irregular characters, very unlike Holmes's usual precise hand. It was consigned to Mr Abe Slaney, Elrige's Farm, East Ruston, Norfolk.

'I think, inspector,' Holmes remarked, 'that you would do well to telegraph for an escort, as, if my calculations prove to be correct, you may have a particularly dangerous prisoner to convey to the county gaol. The boy who takes this note could no doubt forward your telegram. If there is an afternoon train to town, Watson, I think we should do well to take it, as I have a chemical analysis of some interest to finish, and this investigation draws rapidly to a close.'

When the youth had been dispatched with the note, Sherlock Holmes gave his instructions to the servants. If any visitor were to call asking for Mrs Hilton Cubitt no information should be given as to her condition, but he was to be shown at once into the drawing-room. He impressed these points upon them with the utmost earnestness. Finally he led the way into the drawing-room with the remark that the business was now out of our hands, and that we must while away the time as best we might until we could see what was in store for us. The doctor had departed to his patients, and only the inspector and myself remained.

'I think that I can help you to pass an hour in an interesting and profitable manner,' said Holmes, drawing his chair up to the table and spreading out in front of him the various papers upon which were recorded the antics of the dancing men. 'As to you, friend Watson, I owe you every atonement for having allowed your natural curiosity to remain so long unsatisfied. To you, inspector, the whole incident may appeal as a remarkable professional study. I must tell you first of all the interesting circumstances connected with the previous consultations which Mr Hilton Cubitt has had with me in Baker Street.' He then shortly recapitulated the facts which have already been recorded. 'I have here in front of me these singular productions, at which one might smile had they not proved themselves to be the forerunners of so terrible a tragedy. I am fairly familiar with all forms of secret writings, and am myself the author of a trifling monograph upon the subject, in which I analyse one hundred and sixty separate ciphers; but I confess that this is entirely new to me. The object of those who invented the system has apparently been to conceal that these characters convey a message, and to give the idea that they are the mere random sketches of children.

'Having once recognised, however, that the symbols stood for letters, and having applied the rules which guide us in all forms of secret writings, the solution was easy enough. The first message submitted to me was so short that it was impossible for me to do more than to say with some confidence that the symbol stood for E. As you are aware, E is the most common letter in the English alphabet, and it predominates to so marked an extent that even in a short sentence one would expect to find it most often. Out of fifteen symbols in the first message four were the same, so it was reasonable to set this down as E. It is true that in some cases the figure was bearing a flag and in some cases not, but it was probable from the way in which the flags were distributed that they were used to break the sentence up into words. I accepted this as a hypothesis, and noted that E was represented by

'But now came the real difficulty of the enquiry. The order of the English letters after E is by no means well marked, and any preponderance which may be shown in an average of a printed sheet may be reversed in a single short sentence. Speaking roughly, T, A, O, I, N, S, H, R, D, and L are the numerical order in which letters occur; but T, A, O, and I are very nearly abreast of each other, and it would be an endless task to try each combination until a meaning was arrived at. I, therefore, waited for fresh material. In my second interview with Mr Hilton Cubitt he was able to give me two other short sentences and one message, which appeared – since there was no flag – to be a single word. Here are the symbols. Now, in the single word I have already got the two E's coming second and fourth in a word of five letters. It might be "sever", or "lever'" or "never".' There can be no question that the latter as a reply to an appeal is far the most probable, and the circumstances pointed to its being a reply written by the lady. Accepting it as correct, we are now able to say that the symbols ⚡ ⤴ ⚡ stand respectively for N, V, and R.

'Even now I was in considerable difficulty, but a happy thought put me in possession of several other letters. It occurred to me that if these appeals came, as I expected, from someone who had been intimate with the lady in her early life, a combination which contained two E's with three letters between might very well stand for the name "ELSIE". On examination I found that such a combination formed the termination of the message which was three times repeated. It was certainly some appeal to "Elsie". In this way I had got my L, S, and I. But what appeal could it be? There were only four letters in the word which preceded "Elsie", and it ended in E. Surely the word must be "COME". I tried all other four letters ending in E, but could find none to fit the case. So now I was in possession of C, O, and M, and I was in a position to attack the first message once more, dividing it into words and putting dots for each symbol which was still unknown. So treated it worked out in this fashion:

-M -ERE --E SL-NE-

'Now the first letter *can* only be A, which is a most useful discovery, since it occurs no fewer than three times in this short sentence, and the H is also apparent in the second word. Now it becomes:

AM HERE A-E SLANE-

Or, filling in the obvious vacancies in the name:

AM HERE ABE SLANEY

I had so many letters now that I could proceed with considerable confidence to the second message, which worked out in this fashion:

A- ELRI-ES

Here I could only make sense by putting T and G for the missing letters, and supposing that the name was that of some house or inn at which the writer was staying.'

Inspector Martin and I had listened with the utmost interest to the full and clear account of how my friend had produced results which had led to so complete a command over our difficulties.

'What did you do then, sir?' asked the inspector.

'I had every reason to suppose that this Abe Slaney was an American, since Abe is an American contraction, and since a letter from America had been the starting-point of all the trouble. I had also every cause to think that there was some criminal secret in the matter. The lady's allusions to her past and her refusal to take her husband into her confidence both pointed in that direction. I therefore cabled to my friend, Wilson Hargreave, of the New York Police Bureau, who has more than once made use of my knowledge of London crime. I asked him whether the name of Abe Slaney was known to him. Here is his reply: "The most dangerous crook in Chicago". On the very evening upon which I had his answer Hilton Cubitt sent me the last message from Slaney. Working with known letters it took this form:

ELSIE –RE–ARE TO MEET THY GO–

The addition of two Ps and a D completed a message which showed me that the rascal was proceeding from persuasion to threats, and my knowledge of the crooks of Chicago prepared me to find that he might very rapidly put his words into action. I at once came to Norfolk with my friend and colleague, Dr Watson, but, unhappily, only in time to find that the worst had already occurred.'

'It is a privilege to be associated with you in the handling of a case,' said the inspector, warmly. 'You will excuse me, however, if I speak frankly to you. You are only answerable to yourself, but I have to answer to my superiors. If this Abe Slaney, living at Elrige's, is indeed the murderer, and if he has made his escape while I am seated here, I should certainly get into serious trouble.'

'You need not be uneasy. He will not try to escape.'

'How do you know?'

'To fly would be a confession of guilt.'

'Then let us go to arrest him.'

'I expect him here every instant.'

'But why should he come?'

'Because I have written and asked him.'

'But this is incredible, Mr Holmes! Why should he come because you have asked him? Would not such a request rather rouse his suspicions and cause him to fly?'

'I think I have known how to frame the letter,' said Sherlock Holmes. 'In fact, if I am not very much mistaken, here is the gentleman himself coming up the drive.'

A man was striding up the path which led to the door. He was a tall, handsome, swarthy fellow, clad in a suit of grey flannel, with a Panama hat, a bristling black beard, and a great, aggressive hooked nose, and flourishing a cane as he walked. He swaggered up the path as if the place belonged to him, and we heard his loud, confident peal at the bell.

'I think, gentlemen,' said Holmes, quietly, 'that we had best take up our position behind the door. Every precaution is necessary when dealing with such a fellow. You will need your handcuffs, inspector. You can leave the talking to me.'

We waited in silence for a minute – one of those minutes which one can never forget. Then the door opened and the man stepped in. In an instant Holmes clapped a pistol to his head and Martin slipped the handcuffs over his wrists. It was all done so swiftly and deftly that the fellow was helpless before he knew that he was attacked. He glared from one to the other of us with a pair of blazing black eyes. Then he burst into a bitter laugh.

'Well, gentlemen, you have the drop on me this time. I seem to have knocked up against something hard. But I came here in answer to a letter from Mrs Hilton Cubitt. Don't tell me that she is in this? Don't tell me that she helped to set a trap for me?'

'Mrs Hilton Cubitt was seriously injured and is at death's door.'

The man gave a hoarse cry of grief which rang through the house.

'You're crazy!' he cried, fiercely. 'It was he that was hurt, not she. Who would have hurt little Elsie? I may have threatened her, God forgive me, but I would not have touched a hair of her pretty head. Take it back – you! Say that she is not hurt!'

'She was found badly wounded by the side of her dead husband.'

He sank with a deep groan on to the settee and buried his face in his manacled hands. For five minutes he was silent. Then he raised his face once more, and spoke with the cold composure of despair.

'I have nothing to hide from you, gentlemen,' said he. 'If I shot the man he had his shot at me, and there's no murder in that. But if you think I could have hurt that woman, then you don't know either me or her. I tell you there was never a man in this world loved a woman more than I loved her. I had a right to her. She was pledged to me years ago. Who was this Englishman that he should come between us? I tell you that I had the first right to her, and that I was only claiming my own.'

'She broke away from your influence when she found the man that you are,' said Holmes, sternly. 'She fled from America to avoid you, and she married an honourable gentleman in England. You dogged her and followed her and made her life a misery to her in order to induce her to abandon the husband whom she loved and respected in order to fly with you, whom she feared and hated. You have ended by bringing about the death of a noble man and driving his wife to suicide. That is your record in this business, Mr Abe Slaney, and you will answer for it to the law.'

'If Elsie dies I care nothing what becomes of me,' said the American. He opened one of his hands and looked at a note crumpled up in his palm. 'See here, mister,' he cried, with a gleam of suspicion in his eyes, 'you're not trying to scare me over this, are you? If the lady is hurt as bad as you say, who was it that wrote this note?' He tossed it forward on to the table.

'I wrote it to bring you here.'

'You wrote it? There was no one on earth outside the Joint who knew the secret of the dancing men. How came you to write it?'

'What one man can invent another can discover,' said Holmes. 'There is a cab coming to convey you to Norwich, Mr Slaney. But, meanwhile, you have time to make some small reparation for the injury you have wrought. Are you aware that Mrs Hilton Cubitt has herself lain under grave suspicion of the murder of her husband, and that it was only my presence here and the knowledge which I happened to possess which has saved her from the accusation? The least that you owe her is to make it clear to the whole world that she was in no way, directly or indirectly, responsible for his tragic end.'

'I ask nothing better,' said the American. 'I guess the very best case I can make for myself is the absolute naked truth.'

'It is my duty to warn you that it will be used against you,' cried the inspector, with the magnificent fair-play of the British criminal law.

Slaney shrugged his shoulders.

'I'll chance that,' said he. 'First of all, I want you gentlemen to understand that I have known this lady since she was a child. There were seven of us in a gang in Chicago, and Elsie's father was the boss of the Joint.

He was a clever man, was old Patrick. It was he who invented that writing, which would pass as a child's scrawl unless you just happened to have the key to it. Well, Elsie learned some of our ways; but she couldn't stand the business, and she had a bit of honest money of her own, so she gave us all the slip and got away to London. She had been engaged to me, and she would have married me, I believe, if I had taken over another profession; but she would have nothing to do with anything on the cross. It was only after her marriage to this Englishman that I was able to find out where she was. I wrote to her, but got no answer. After that I came over, and, as letters were no use, I put my messages where she could read them.

'Well, I have been here a month now. I lived in that farm, where I had a room down below, and could get in and out every night, and no one the wiser. I tried all I could to coax Elsie away. I knew that she read the messages, for once she wrote an answer under one of them. Then my temper got the better of me, and I began to threaten her. She sent me a letter then, imploring me to go away and saying that it would break her heart if any scandal should come upon her husband. She said that she would come down when her husband was asleep at three in the morning, and speak with me through the end window, if I would go away afterwards and leave her in peace. She came down and brought money with her, trying to bribe me to go. This made me mad, and I caught her arm and tried to pull her through the window. At that moment in rushed the husband with his revolver in his hand. Elsie had sunk down upon the floor, and we were face to face. I was heeled also, and I held up my gun to scare him off and let me get away. He fired and missed me.

I pulled off almost at the same instant, and down he dropped. I made away across the garden, and as I went I heard the window shut behind me. That's God's truth, gentlemen, every word of it, and I heard no more about it until that lad came riding up with a note which made me walk in here, like a jay, and give myself into your hands.'

A cab had driven up whilst the American had been talking. Two uniformed policemen sat inside. Inspector Martin rose and touched his prisoner on the shoulder.

'It is time for us to go.'

'Can I see her first?'

'No, she is not conscious. Mr Sherlock Holmes, I only hope that if ever again I have an important case I shall have the good fortune to have you by my side.'

We stood at the window and watched the cab drive away. As I turned back my eye caught the pellet of paper which the prisoner had tossed upon the table. It was the note with which Holmes had decoyed him.

'See if you can read it, Watson,' said he, with a smile.

It contained no word, but this little line of dancing men:

'If you use the code which I have explained,' said Holmes, 'you will find that it simply means "Come here at once." I was convinced that it was an invitation which he would not refuse, since he could never imagine that it could come from anyone but the lady. And so, my dear Watson, we have ended by turning the dancing men to good when they have so often been the agents of evil, and I think that I have fulfilled my promise of giving you something unusual for your notebook. Three-forty is our train, and I fancy we should be back in Baker Street for dinner.'

Only one word of epilogue. The American, Abe Slaney, was condemned to death at the winter assizes at Norwich; but his penalty was changed to penal servitude in consideration of mitigating circumstances, and the certainty that Hilton Cubitt had fired the first shot. Of Mrs Hilton Cubitt I only know that I have heard she recovered entirely, and that she still remains a widow, devoting her whole life to the care of the poor and to the administration of her husband's estate.

4

The Solitary Cyclist

From the years 1894 to 1901 inclusive Mr Sherlock Holmes was a very busy man. It is safe to say that there was no public case of any difficulty in which he was not consulted during those eight years, and there were hundreds of private cases, some of them of the most intricate and extraordinary character, in which he played a prominent part. Many startling successes and a few unavoidable failures were the outcome of this long period of continuous work. As I have preserved very full notes of all these cases, and was myself personally engaged in many of them, it may be imagined that it is no easy task to know which I should select to lay before the public. I shall, however, preserve my former rule, and give the preference to those cases which derive their interest not so much from the brutality of the crime as from the ingenuity and dramatic quality of the solution. For this reason I will now lay before the reader the facts connected with Miss Violet Smith, the solitary cyclist of Charlington, and the curious sequel of our investigation, which culminated in unexpected tragedy. It is true that the circumstances did not admit of any striking illustration of those powers for which my friend was famous, but there were some points about the case which made it stand out in those long records of crime from which I gather the material for these little narratives.

On referring to my notebook for the year 1895 I find that it was upon Saturday, the 23rd of April, that we first heard of Miss Violet Smith. Her visit was, I remember, extremely unwelcome to Holmes, for he was immersed at the moment in a very abstruse and complicated problem concerning the peculiar persecution to which John Vincent Harden, the well-known tobacco millionaire, had been subjected. My friend, who loved above all things precision and concentration of thought, resented anything which distracted his attention from the matter in hand. And yet without a harshness which was foreign to his nature it was impossible to refuse to listen to the story of the young and beautiful woman, tall, graceful, and queenly, who presented herself at Baker Street late in the evening and implored his assistance and advice. It was vain to urge that his time was already fully occupied, for the young lady had come with the determination to tell her story, and it was evident that nothing short of force could get her out of the room until she had done so. With a resigned air and a somewhat weary smile, Holmes begged the beautiful intruder to take a seat and to inform us what it was that was troubling her.

'At least it cannot be your health,' said he, as his keen eyes darted over her; 'so ardent a bicyclist must be full of energy.'

She glanced down in surprise at her own feet, and I observed the slight roughening of the side of the sole caused by the friction of the edge of the pedal.

'Yes, I bicycle a good deal, Mr Holmes, and that has something to do with my visit to you today.'

My friend took the lady's ungloved hand and examined it with as close an attention and as little sentiment as a scientist would show to a specimen.

'You will excuse me, I am sure. It is my business,' said he, as he dropped it. 'I nearly fell into the error of supposing that you were typewriting. Of course, it is obvious that it is music. You observe the spatulate finger-end, Watson, which is common to both professions? There is a spirituality about the face, however' – he gently turned it towards the light – 'which the typewriter does not generate. This lady is a musician.'

'Yes, Mr Holmes, I teach music.'

'In the country, I presume, from your complexion.'

'Yes, sir; near Farnham, on the borders of Surrey.'

'A beautiful neighbourhood and full of the most interesting associations. You remember, Watson, that it was near there that we took Archie Stamford, the forger. Now, Miss Violet, what has happened to you near Farnham, on the borders of Surrey?'

The young lady, with great clearness and composure, made the following curious statement.

'My father is dead, Mr Holmes. He was James Smith, who conducted the orchestra at the old Imperial Theatre. My mother and I were left without a relation in the world except one uncle, Ralph Smith, who went to Africa twenty-five years ago, and we have never had a word from him since. When father died we were left very poor, but one day we were told that there was an advertisement in *The Times* enquiring for our whereabouts. You can imagine how excited we were, for we thought that someone had left us a fortune. We went at once to the lawyer whose name was given in the paper. There we met two gentlemen, Mr Carruthers and Mr Woodley, who were home on a visit from South Africa. They said that my uncle was a friend of theirs, that he died some months before in great poverty in Johannesburg, and that he had asked them with his last breath to hunt up his relations and see that they were in no want. It seemed strange to us that Uncle Ralph, who took no notice of us when he was alive, should be so careful to look after us when he was dead; but Mr Carruthers explained that the reason was that my uncle had just heard of the death of his brother, and so felt responsible for our fate.'

'Excuse me,' said Holmes; 'when was this interview?'

'Last December – four months ago.'

'Pray proceed.'

'Mr Woodley seemed to me to be a most odious person. He was for ever making eyes at me – a coarse, puffy-faced, red-moustached young man, with his hair plastered down on each side of his forehead. I thought that he was perfectly hateful – and I was sure that Cyril would not wish me to know such a person.'

'Oh, Cyril is his name!' said Holmes, smiling.

The young lady blushed and laughed.

'Yes, Mr Holmes; Cyril Morton, an electrical engineer, and we hope to be married at the end of the summer. Dear me, how *did* I get talking about him? What I wished to say was that Mr Woodley was perfectly odious, but that Mr Carruthers, who was a much older man, was more agreeable. He was a dark, sallow, clean-shaven, silent person; but he had polite manners and a pleasant smile. He enquired how we were left, and on finding that we were very poor he suggested that I should come and teach music to his only daughter, aged ten. I said that I did not like to leave my mother, on which he suggested that I should go home to her every weekend, and he offered me a hundred a year, which was certainly splendid pay.

So it ended by my accepting, and I went down to Chiltern Grange, about six miles from Farnham. Mr Carruthers was a widower, but he had engaged a lady-housekeeper, a very respectable, elderly person, called Mrs Dixon, to look after his establishment. The child was a dear, and everything promised well. Mr Carruthers was very kind and very musical, and we had most pleasant evenings together. Every weekend I went home to my mother in town.

'The first flaw in my happiness was the arrival of the red-moustached Mr Woodley. He came for a visit of a week, and oh, it seemed three months to me! He was a dreadful person, a bully to everyone else, but to me something infinitely worse. He made odious love to me, boasted of his wealth, said that if I married him I would have the finest diamonds in London, and finally, when I would have nothing to do with him, he seized me in his arms one day after dinner – he was hideously strong – and he swore that he would not let me go until I had kissed him. Mr Carruthers came in and tore him off from me, on which he turned upon his own host, knocking him down and cutting his face open. That was the end of his visit, as you can imagine. Mr Carruthers apologised to me next day, and assured me that I should never be exposed to such an insult again. I have not seen Mr Woodley since.

'And now, Mr Holmes, I come at last to the special thing which has caused me to ask your advice today. You must know that every Saturday forenoon I ride on my bicycle to Farnham Station in order to get the 12.22 to town. The road from Chiltern Grange is a lonely one, and at one spot it is particularly so, for it lies for over a mile between Charlington Heath upon one side and the woods which lie round Charlington Hall upon the other. You could not find a more lonely tract of road anywhere, and it is quite rare to meet so much as a cart, or a peasant, until you reach the high road near Crooksbury Hill. Two weeks ago I was passing this place when I chanced to look back over my shoulder, and about two hundred yards behind me I saw a man, also on a bicycle. He seemed to be a middle-aged man, with a short, dark beard. I looked back before I reached Farnham, but the man was gone, so I thought no more about it. But you can imagine how surprised I was, Mr Holmes, when on my return on the Monday I saw the same man on the same stretch of road. My astonishment was increased when the incident occurred again, exactly as before, on the following Saturday and Monday. He always kept his distance and did not molest me in any way, but still it certainly was very odd. I mentioned it to Mr Carruthers, who seemed interested in what I said, and told me that he had ordered a horse and trap, so that in future I should not pass over these lonely roads without some companion.

'The horse and trap were to have come this week, but for some reason they were not delivered, and again I had to cycle to the station. That was this morning. You can think that I looked out when I came to Charlington Heath, and there, sure enough, was the man, exactly as he had been the two weeks before. He always kept so far from me that I could not clearly see his face, but it was certainly someone whom I did not know. He was dressed in a dark suit with a cloth cap. The only thing about his face that I could clearly see was his dark beard. Today I was not alarmed, but I was filled with curiosity, and I determined to find out who he was and what he wanted. I slowed down my machine, but he slowed down his. Then I stopped altogether, but he stopped also. Then I laid a trap for him. There is a sharp turning of the road, and I pedalled very quickly round this, and then I stopped and waited. I expected him to shoot round and pass me before he could stop. But he never appeared. Then I went back and looked round the corner. I could see a mile of road, but he was not on it. To make it the more extraordinary, there was no side road at this point down which he could have gone.'

Holmes chuckled and rubbed his hands. 'This case certainly presents some features of its own,' said he. 'How much time elapsed between your turning the corner and your discovery that the road was clear?'

'Two or three minutes.'

'Then he could not have retreated down the road, and you say that there are no side roads?'

'None.'

'Then he certainly took a footpath on one side or the other.'

'It could not have been on the side of the heath or I should have seen him.'

'So by the process of exclusion we arrive at the fact that he made his way towards Charlington Hall, which, as I understand, is situated in its own grounds on one side of the road. Anything else?'

'Nothing, Mr Holmes, save that I was so perplexed that I felt I should not be happy until I had seen you and had your advice.'

Holmes sat in silence for some little time.

'Where is the gentleman to whom you are engaged?' he asked, at last.

'He is in the Midland Electrical Company, at Coventry.'

'He would not pay you a surprise visit?'

'Oh, Mr Holmes! As if I should not know him!'

'Have you had any other admirers?'

'Several before I knew Cyril.'

'And since?'

'There was this dreadful man, Woodley, if you can call him an admirer.'

'No one else?'

Our fair client seemed a little confused.

'Who was he?' asked Holmes.

'Oh, it may be a mere fancy of mine; but it has seemed to me sometimes that my employer, Mr Carruthers, takes a great deal of interest in me. We are thrown rather together. I play his accompaniments in the evening. He has never said anything. He is a perfect gentleman. But a girl always knows.'

'Ha!' Holmes looked grave. 'What does he do for a living?'

'He is a rich man.'

'No carriages or horses?'

'Well, at least he is fairly well-to-do. But he goes into the City two or three times a week. He is deeply interested in South African gold shares.'

'You will let me know any fresh development, Miss Smith. I am very busy just now, but I will find time to make some enquiries into your case. In the meantime take no step without letting me know. Goodbye, and I trust that we shall have nothing but good news from you.'

'It is part of the settled order of Nature that such a girl should have followers,' said Holmes, as he pulled at his meditative pipe, 'but for choice not on bicycles in lonely country roads. Some secretive lover, beyond all doubt. But there are curious and suggestive details about the case, Watson.'

'That he should appear only at that point?'

'Exactly. Our first effort must be to find who are the tenants of Charlington Hall. Then, again, how about the connection between Carruthers and Woodley, since they appear to be men of such a different type? How came they *both* to be so keen upon looking up Ralph Smith's relations? One more point. What sort of a *ménage* is it which pays double the market price for a governess, but does not keep a horse although six miles from the station? Odd, Watson – very odd!'

'You will go down?'

'No, my dear fellow, *you* will go down. This may be some trifling intrigue, and I cannot break my other important research for the sake of it. On Monday you will arrive early at Farnham; you will conceal yourself near Charlington Heath; you will observe these facts for yourself, and act as your own judgment advises. Then, having enquired as to the occupants of the Hall, you will come back to me and report. And now, Watson, not another word of the matter until we have a few solid stepping-stones on which we may hope to get across to our solution.'

We had ascertained from the lady that she went down upon the Monday by the train which leaves Waterloo at 9.50, so I started early and caught the 9.13. At Farnham Station I had no difficulty in being directed to Charlington Heath. It was impossible to mistake the scene of the young lady's adventure, for the road runs between the open heath on one side and an old yew hedge upon the other, surrounding a park which is studded with magnificent trees. There was a main gateway of lichen-studded stone, each side pillar surmounted by mouldering heraldic emblems; but besides this central carriage drive I observed several points where there were gaps in the hedge and paths leading through them. The house was invisible from the road, but the surroundings all spoke of gloom and decay.

The heath was covered with golden patches of flowering gorse, gleaming magnificently in the light of the bright spring sunshine. Behind one of these clumps I took up my position, so as to command both the gateway of the Hall and a long stretch of the road upon either side. It had been deserted when I left it, but now I saw a cyclist riding down it from the opposite direction to that in which I had come. He was clad in a dark suit, and I saw that he had a black beard. On reaching the end of the Charlington grounds he sprang from his machine and led it through a gap in the hedge, disappearing from my view.

A quarter of an hour passed and then a second cyclist appeared. This time it was the young lady coming from the station. I saw her look about her as she came to the Charlington hedge. An instant later the man emerged from his hiding-place, sprang upon his cycle, and followed her. In all the broad landscape those were the only moving figures, the graceful girl sitting very straight upon her machine, and the man behind her bending low over his handle-bar, with a curiously furtive suggestion in every movement. She looked back at him and slowed her pace. He slowed also. She stopped. He at once stopped too, keeping two hundred yards behind her. Her next movement was as unexpected as it was spirited. She suddenly whisked her wheels round and dashed straight at him! He was as quick as she, however, and darted off in desperate flight. Presently she came back up the road again, her head haughtily in the air, not deigning to take any further notice of her silent attendant. He had turned also, and still kept his distance until the curve of the road hid them from my sight.

I remained in my hiding-place, and it was well that I did so, for presently the man reappeared cycling slowly back. He turned in at the Hall gates and dismounted from his machine. For some few minutes I could see him standing among the trees. His hands were raised and he seemed to be settling his necktie. Then he mounted his cycle and rode away from me down the drive towards the Hall. I ran across the heath and peered through the trees. Far away I could catch glimpses of the old grey building with its bristling Tudor chimneys, but the drive ran through a dense shrubbery, and I saw no more of my man.

However, it seemed to me that I had done a fairly good morning's work, and I walked back in high spirits to Farnham. The local house-agent could tell me nothing about Charlington Hall, and referred me to a well-known firm in Pall Mall. There I halted on my way home, and met with courtesy from the representative. No, I could not have Charlington Hall for the summer. I was just too late. It had been let about a month ago. Mr Williamson was the name of the tenant. He was a respectable elderly gentleman. The polite agent was afraid he could say no more, as the affairs of his clients were not matters which he could discuss.

Mr Sherlock Holmes listened with attention to the long report which I was able to present to him that evening, but it did not elicit that word of curt praise which I had hoped for and should have valued. On the contrary, his austere face was even more severe than usual as he commented upon the things that I had done and the things that I had not.

'Your hiding-place, my dear Watson, was very faulty. You should have been behind the hedge; then you would have had a close view of this interesting person. As it is you were some hundreds of yards away, and can tell me even less than Miss Smith. She thinks she does not know the man; I am convinced she does. Why, otherwise, should he be so desperately anxious that she should not get so near him as to see his features? You describe him as bending over the handle-bar. Concealment again, you see. You really have done remarkably badly. He returns to the house and you want to find out who he is. You come to a London house-agent!'

'What should I have done?' I cried, with some heat.

'Gone to the nearest public-house. That is the centre of country gossip. They would have told you every name, from the master to the scullery-maid. Williamson! It conveys nothing to my mind. If he is an elderly man he is not this active cyclist who sprints away from that athletic young lady's pursuit. What have we gained by your expedition? The knowledge that the girl's story is true. I never doubted it. That there is a connection between the cyclist and the Hall. I never doubted that either. That the Hall is tenanted by Williamson. Who's the better for that? Well, well, my dear sir, don't look so depressed. We can do little more until next Saturday, and in the meantime I may make one or two enquiries myself.'

Next morning we had a note from Miss Smith, recounting shortly and accurately the very incidents which I had seen, but the pith of the letter lay in the postscript:

I am sure that you will respect my confidence, Mr

Holmes, when I tell you that my place here has become difficult owing to the fact that my employer has proposed marriage to me. I am convinced that his feelings are most deep and most honourable. At the same time my promise is, of course, given. He took my refusal very seriously, but also very gently. You can understand, however, that the situation is a little strained.

'Our young friend seems to be getting into deep waters,' said Holmes, thoughtfully, as he finished the letter. 'The case certainly presents more features of interest and more possibility of development than I had originally thought. I should be none the worse for a quiet, peaceful day in the country, and I am inclined to run down this afternoon and test one or two theories which I have formed.'

Holmes's quiet day in the country had a singular termination, for he arrived at Baker Street late in the evening with a cut lip and a discoloured lump upon his forehead, besides a general air of dissipation which would have made his own person the fitting object of a Scotland Yard investigation. He was immensely tickled by his own adventures, and laughed heartily as he recounted them.

'I get so little active exercise that it is always a treat,' said he. 'You are aware that I have some proficiency in the good old British sport of boxing. Occasionally it is of service. Today, for example, I should have come to very ignominious grief without it.'

I begged him to tell me what had occurred.

'I found that country pub which I had already recommended to your notice, and there I made my discreet enquiries. I was in the bar, and a garrulous landlord was giving me all that I wanted. Williamson is a white-bearded man, and he lives alone with a small staff of servants at the Hall. There is some rumour that he is or has been a clergyman; but one or two incidents of his short residence at the Hall struck me as peculiarly unecclesiastical. I have already made some enquiries at a clerical agency, and they tell me that there *was* a man of that name in orders whose career has been a singularly dark one. The landlord further informed me that there are usually weekend visitors – "a warm lot, sir" – at the Hall, and especially one gentleman with a red moustache, Mr Woodley by name, who was always there. We had got as far as this when who should walk in but the gentleman himself, who had been drinking his beer in the taproom and had heard the whole conversation. Who was I? What did I want? What did I mean by asking questions? He had a fine flow of language, and his adjectives were very vigorous. He ended a string of abuse by a vicious backhander which I failed to entirely avoid. The next few minutes were delicious. It was a straight left against a slogging ruffian. I emerged as you see me. Mr Woodley went home in a cart. So ended my country trip, and it must be confessed that, however enjoyable, my day on the Surrey border has not been much more profitable than your own.'

The Thursday brought us another letter from our client.

You will not be surprised, Mr Holmes, to hear that I am leaving Mr Carruthers's employment. Even the high pay cannot reconcile me to the discomforts of my situation. On Saturday I come up to town and I do not intend to return. Mr Carruthers has got a trap, and so the dangers of the lonely road, if there ever were any dangers, are now over.

As to the special cause of my leaving, it is not merely the strained situation with Mr Carruthers, but it is the reappearance of that odious man, Mr Woodley. He was always hideous, but he looks more awful than ever now, for he appears to have had an accident and he is much disfigured. I saw him out of the window, but I am glad to say I did not meet him. He had a long talk with Mr Carruthers, who seemed much excited afterwards. Woodley must be staying in the neighbourhood, for he did not sleep here, and yet I caught a glimpse of him again this morning slinking about in the shrubbery. I would sooner have a savage wild animal loose about the place. I loathe and fear him more than I can say. How *can* Mr Carruthers endure such a creature for a moment? However, all my troubles will be over on Saturday.

'So I trust, Watson, so I trust,' said Holmes, gravely. 'There is some deep intrigue going on round that little woman, and it is our duty to see that no one molests her upon that last journey. I think, Watson, that we must spare time to run down together on Saturday morning, and make sure that this curious and inconclusive investigation has no untoward ending.'

I confess that I had not up to now taken a very serious view of the case, which had seemed to me rather grotesque and bizarre than dangerous. That a man should lie in wait for and follow a very handsome woman is no unheard-of thing, and if he had so little audacity that he not only dared not address her, but even fled from her approach, he was not a very formidable assailant. The ruffian Woodley was a very different person, but, except on one occasion, he had not molested our client, and now he visited the house of Carruthers without intruding upon her presence. The man on the bicycle was doubtless a member of those weekend parties at the Hall of which the publican had spoken; but who he was or what he wanted was as obscure as ever. It was the severity of Holmes's manner and the fact that he slipped a revolver into his pocket before leaving our rooms which impressed me with the feeling that tragedy might prove to lurk behind this curious train of events.

A rainy night had been followed by a glorious morning, and the heath-covered countryside with the glowing clumps of flowering gorse seemed all the more beautiful to eyes which were weary of the duns and drabs and slate-greys of London. Holmes and I walked along the broad, sandy road inhaling the fresh morning air, and rejoicing in the music of the birds and the fresh breath of the spring. From a rise of the road on the shoulder of Crooksbury Hill we could see the grim Hall bristling out from amidst the ancient oaks, which, old as they were, were still younger than the building which they surrounded. Holmes pointed down the long tract of road which wound, a reddish yellow band, between the brown of the heath and the budding green of the woods. Far away, a black dot, we could see a vehicle moving in our direction. Holmes gave an exclamation of impatience.

'I had given a margin of half an hour,' said he. 'If that is her trap she must be making for the earlier train. I fear, Watson, that she will be past Charlington before we can possibly meet her.'

From the instant that we passed the rise we could no

longer see the vehicle, but we hastened onwards at such a pace that my sedentary life began to tell upon me, and I was compelled to fall behind. Holmes, however, was always in training, for he had inexhaustible stores of nervous energy upon which to draw. His springy step never slowed until suddenly, when he was a hundred yards in front of me, he halted, and I saw him throw up his hand with a gesture of grief and despair. At the same instant an empty dog-cart, the horse cantering, the reins trailing, appeared round the curve of the road and rattled swiftly towards us.

'Too late, Watson; too late!' cried Holmes, as I ran panting to his side. 'Fool that I was not to allow for that earlier train! It's abduction, Watson – abduction! Murder! Heaven knows what! Block the road! Stop the horse! That's right. Now, jump in, and let us see if I can repair the consequences of my own blunder.'

We had sprung into the dog-cart, and Holmes, after turning the horse, gave it a sharp cut with the whip, and we flew back along the road. As we turned the curve the whole stretch of road between the Hall and the heath was opened up. I grasped Holmes's arm.

'That's the man!' I gasped.

A solitary cyclist was coming towards us. His head was down and his shoulders rounded as he put every ounce of energy that he possessed on to the pedals. He was flying like a racer. Suddenly he raised his bearded face, saw us close to him, and pulled up, springing from his machine. That coal-black beard was in singular contrast to the pallor of his face, and his eyes were as bright as if he had a fever. He stared at us and at the dog-cart. Then a look of amazement came over his face.

'Halloa! Stop there!' he shouted, holding his bicycle

to block our road. 'Where did you get that dog-cart? Pull up, man!' he yelled, drawing a pistol from his side pocket. 'Pull up, I say, or, by George, I'll put a bullet into your horse.'

Holmes threw the reins into my lap and sprang down from the cart.

'You're the man we want to see. Where is Miss Violet Smith?' he said, in his quick, clear way.

'That's what I am asking you. You're in her dog-cart. You ought to know where she is.'

'We met the dog-cart on the road. There was no one in it. We drove back to help the young lady.'

'Good Lord! Good Lord! what shall I do?' cried the stranger, in an ecstasy of despair. 'They've got her, that hellhound Woodley and the blackguard parson. Come, man, come, if you really are her friend. Stand by me and we'll save her, if I have to leave my carcass in Charlington Wood.'

He ran distractedly, his pistol in his hand, towards a gap in the hedge. Holmes followed him, and I, leaving the horse grazing beside the road, followed Holmes.

'This is where they came through,' said he, pointing to the marks of several feet upon the muddy path. 'Halloa! Stop a minute! Who's this in the bush?'

It was a young fellow about seventeen, dressed like an ostler, with leather cords and gaiters. He lay upon his back, his knees drawn up, a terrible cut upon his head. He was insensible, but alive. A glance at his wound told me that it had not penetrated the bone.

'That's Peter, the groom,' cried the stranger. 'He drove her. The beasts have pulled him off and clubbed him. Let him lie; we can't do him any good, but we may save her from the worst fate that can befall a woman.'

We ran frantically down the path, which wound among the trees. We had reached the shrubbery which surrounded the house when Holmes pulled up.

'They didn't go to the house. Here are their marks on the left – here, beside the laurel bushes! Ah, I said so!'

As he spoke a woman's shrill scream – a scream which vibrated with a frenzy of horror – burst from the thick green clump of bushes in front of us. It ended suddenly on its highest note with a choke and a gurgle.

'This way! This way! They are in the bowling alley,' cried the stranger, darting through the bushes. 'Ah, the cowardly dogs! Follow me, gentlemen! Too late! too late! by the living Jingo!'

We had broken suddenly into a lovely glade of greensward surrounded by ancient trees. On the farther side of it, under the shadow of a mighty oak, there stood a singular group of three people. One was a woman, our client, drooping and faint, a handkerchief round her mouth. Opposite her stood a brutal, heavy-faced, red-moustached young man, his gaitered legs parted wide, one arm akimbo, the other waving a riding-crop, his whole attitude suggestive of triumphant bravado. Between them an elderly, grey-bearded man, wearing a short surplice over a light tweed suit, had evidently just completed the wedding service, for he pocketed his prayer-book as we appeared and slapped the sinister bridegroom upon the back in jovial congratulation.

'They're married!' I gasped.

'Come on!' cried our guide; 'come on!' He rushed across the glade, Holmes and I at his heels. As we approached, the lady staggered against the trunk of the tree for support. Williamson, the ex-clergyman, bowed to us with mock politeness, and the bully Woodley advanced with a shout of brutal and exultant laughter.

'You can take your beard off, Bob,' said he. 'I know you right enough. Well, you and your pals have just come in time for me to be able to introduce you to Mrs Woodley.'

Our guide's answer was a singular one. He snatched off the dark beard which had disguised him and threw it on the ground, disclosing a long, sallow, clean-shaven face below it. Then he raised his revolver and covered the young ruffian, who was advancing upon him with his dangerous riding-crop swinging in his hand.

'Yes,' said our ally, 'I *am* Bob Carruthers, and I'll see this woman righted if I have to swing for it. I told you what I'd do if you molested her, and, by the Lord, I'll be as good as my word!'

'You're too late. She's my wife!'

'No, she's your widow.'

His revolver cracked, and I saw the blood spurt from the front of Woodley's waistcoat. He spun round with a scream and fell upon his back, his hideous red face turning suddenly to a dreadful mottled pallor. The old man, still clad in his surplice, burst into such a string of foul oaths as I have never heard, and pulled out a revolver of his own, but before he could raise it he was looking down the barrel of Holmes's weapon.

'Enough of this,' said my friend, coldly. 'Drop that pistol! Watson, pick it up! Hold it to his head! Thank you. You, Carruthers, give me that revolver. We'll have no more violence. Come, hand it over!'

'Who are you, then?'

'My name is Sherlock Holmes.'

'Good Lord!'

'You have heard of me, I see. I will represent the official police until their arrival. Here, you!' he shouted to a frightened groom who had appeared at the edge of the glade. 'Come here. Take this note as hard as you can ride to Farnham.' He scribbled a few words upon a leaf from his notebook. 'Give it to the superintendent at the police-station. Until he comes I must detain you all under my personal custody.'

The strong, masterful personality of Holmes dominated the tragic scene, and all were equally puppets in his hands. Williamson and Carruthers found themselves carrying the wounded Woodley into the house, and I gave my arm to the frightened girl. The injured man was laid on his bed, and at Holmes's request I examined him. I carried my report to where he sat in the old tapestry-hung dining-room with his two prisoners before him.

'He will live,' said I.

'What!' cried Carruthers, springing out of his chair. 'I'll go upstairs and finish him first. Do you tell me that that girl, that angel, is to be tied to Roaring Jack Woodley for life?'

'You need not concern yourself about that,' said Holmes. 'There are two very good reasons why she should under no circumstances be his wife. In the first place, we are very safe in questioning Mr Williamson's right to solemnise a marriage.'

'I have been ordained,' cried the old rascal.

'And also unfrocked.'

'Once a clergyman, always a clergyman.'

'I think not. How about the licence?'

'We had a licence for the marriage. I have it here in my pocket.'

'Then you got it by a trick. But in any case a forced marriage is no marriage, but it is a very serious felony, as you will discover before you have finished. You'll have time to think the point out during the next ten years or so, unless I am mistaken. As to you, Carruthers, you would have done better to keep your pistol in your pocket.'

'I begin to think so, Mr Holmes; but when I thought of all the precaution I had taken to shield this girl – for I loved her, Mr Holmes, and it is the only time that ever I knew what love was – it fairly drove me mad to think that she was in the power of the greatest brute and bully in South Africa, a man whose name is a holy terror from Kimberley to Johannesburg. Why, Mr Holmes, you'll hardly believe it, but ever since that girl has been in my employment I never once let her go past this house, where I knew these rascals were lurking, without following her on my bicycle just to see that she came to no harm. I kept my distance from her, and I wore a beard so that she should not recognise me, for she is a good and high-spirited girl, and she wouldn't have stayed in my employment long if she had thought that I was following her about the country roads.'

'Why didn't you tell her of her danger?'

'Because then, again, she would have left me, and I couldn't bear to face that. Even if she couldn't love me it was a great deal to me just to see her dainty form about the house, and to hear the sound of her voice.'

'Well,' said I, 'you call that love, Mr Carruthers, but I should call it selfishness.'

'Maybe the two things go together. Anyhow, I couldn't let her go. Besides, with this crowd about, it was well that she should have someone near to look after her. Then when the cable came I knew they were bound to make a move.'

'What cable?'

Carruthers took a telegram from his pocket.

'That's it,' said he.

It was short and concise: 'The old man is dead.'

'Hum!' said Holmes. 'I think I see how things worked, and I can understand how this message would, as you say, bring them to a head. But while we wait you might tell me what you can.'

The old reprobate with the surplice burst into a volley of bad language.

'By Heaven,' said he, 'if you squeal on us, Bob Carruthers, I'll serve you as you served Jack Woodley. You can bleat about the girl to your heart's content, for that's your own affair, but if you round on your pals to this plain-clothes copper it will be the worst day's work that ever you did.'

'Your reverence need not be excited,' said Holmes, lighting a cigarette. 'The case is clear enough against you, and all I ask is a few details for my private curiosity. However, if there's any difficulty in your telling me I'll do the talking, and then you will see how far you have a chance of holding back your secrets. In the first place, three of you came from South Africa on this game – you, Williamson, you, Carruthers, and Woodley.'

'Lie number one,' said the old man; 'I never saw either of them until two months ago, and I have never been in Africa in my life, so you can put that in your pipe and smoke it, Mr Busybody Holmes!'

'What he says is true,' said Carruthers.

'Well, well, two of you came over. His reverence is our own home-made article. You had known Ralph

Smith in South Africa. You had reason to believe he would not live long. You found out that his niece would inherit his fortune. How's that – eh?'

Carruthers nodded and Williamson swore.

'She was next-of-kin, no doubt, and you were aware that the old fellow would make no will.'

'Couldn't read or write,' said Carruthers.

'So you came over, the two of you, and hunted up the girl. The idea was that one of you was to marry her and the other have a share of the plunder. For some reason Woodley was chosen as the husband. Why was that?'

'We played cards for her on the voyage. He won.'

'I see. You got the young lady into your service, and there Woodley was to do the courting. She recognised the drunken brute that he was, and would have nothing to do with him. Meanwhile, your arrangement was rather upset by the fact that you had yourself fallen in love with the lady. You could no longer bear the idea of this ruffian owning her.'

'No, by George, I couldn't!'

'There was a quarrel between you. He left you in a rage, and began to make his own plans independently of you.'

'It strikes me, Williamson, there isn't very much that we can tell this gentleman,' cried Carruthers, with a bitter laugh. 'Yes, we quarrelled, and he knocked me down. I am level with him on that, anyhow. Then I lost sight of him. That was when he picked up with this cast padre here. I found that they had set up house-keeping together at this place on the line that she had to pass for the station. I kept my eye on her after that, for I knew there was some devilry in the wind. I saw them from time to time, for I was anxious to know what they were after. Two days ago Woodley came up to my house with this cable, which showed that Ralph Smith was dead. He asked me if I would stand by the bargain. I said I would not. He asked me if I would marry the girl myself and give him a share. I said I would willingly do so, but that she would not have me. He said, "Let us get her married first, and after a week or two she may see things a bit different." I said I would have nothing to do with violence. So he went off cursing, like the foul-mouthed blackguard that he was, and swearing that he would have her yet. She was leaving me this weekend, and I had got a trap to take her to the station, but I was so uneasy in my mind that I followed her on my bicycle. She had got a start, however, and before I could catch her the mischief was done. The first thing I knew about it was when I saw you two gentlemen driving back in her dog-cart.'

Holmes rose and tossed the end of his cigarette into the grate. 'I have been very obtuse, Watson,' said he. 'When in your report you said that you had seen the cyclist as you thought arrange his necktie in the shrubbery, that alone should have told me all. However, we may congratulate ourselves upon a curious and in some respects a unique case. I perceive three of the county constabulary in the drive, and I am glad to see that the little ostler is able to keep pace with them; so it is likely that neither he nor the interesting bridegroom will be permanently damaged by their morning's adventures. I think, Watson, that in your medical capacity you might wait upon Miss Smith and tell her that if she is sufficiently recovered we shall be happy to escort her to her mother's home. If she is not quite convalescent you will find that a hint that we were about to telegraph to a young electrician in the

Midlands would probably complete the cure. As to you, Mr Carruthers, I think that you have done what you could to make amends for your share in an evil plot. There is my card, sir, and if my evidence can be of help to you in your trial it shall be at your disposal.'

In the whirl of our incessant activity it has often been difficult for me, as the reader has probably observed, to round off my narratives, and to give those final details which the curious might expect. Each case has been the prelude to another, and the crisis once over the actors have passed for ever out of our busy lives. I find, however, a short note at the end of my manuscripts dealing with this case, in which I have put it upon record that Miss Violet Smith did indeed inherit a large fortune, and that she is now the wife of Cyril Morton, the senior partner of Morton & Kennedy, the famous Westminster electricians. Williamson and Woodley were both tried for abduction and assault, the former getting seven years and the latter ten. Of the fate of Carruthers I have no record, but I am sure that his assault was not viewed very gravely by the Court, since Woodley had the reputation of being a most dangerous ruffian, and I think that a few months were sufficient to satisfy the demands of justice.

5

The Priory School

We have had some dramatic entrances and exits upon our small stage at Baker Street, but I cannot recollect anything more sudden and startling than the first appearance of Thorneycroft Huxtable, M.A., Ph.D., etc. His card, which seemed too small to carry the weight of his academic distinctions, preceded him by a few seconds, and then he entered himself – so large, so pompous, and so dignified that he was the very embodiment of self-possession and solidity. And yet his first action when the door had closed behind him was to stagger against the table, whence he slipped down upon the floor, and there was that majestic figure prostrate and insensible upon our bearskin hearthrug.

We had sprung to our feet, and for a few moments we stared in silent amazement at this ponderous piece of wreckage, which told of some sudden and fatal storm far out on the ocean of life. Then Holmes hurried with a cushion for his head and I with brandy for his lips. The heavy white face was seamed with lines of trouble, the hanging pouches under the closed eyes were leaden in colour, the loose mouth drooped dolorously at the corners, the rolling chins were unshaven. Collar and shirt bore the grime of a long journey, and the hair bristled unkempt from the well-shaped head. It was a sorely stricken man who lay before us.

'What is it, Watson?' asked Holmes.

'Absolute exhaustion – possibly mere hunger and fatigue,' said I, with my finger on the thready pulse, where the stream of life trickled thin and small.

'Return ticket from Mackleton, in the north of England,' said Holmes, drawing it from the watch-pocket. 'It is not twelve o'clock yet. He has certainly been an early starter.'

The puckered eyelids had begun to quiver, and now a pair of vacant, grey eyes looked up at us. An instant later the man had scrambled on to his feet, his face crimson with shame.

'Forgive this weakness, Mr Holmes; I have been a little overwrought. Thank you, if I might have a glass of milk and a biscuit I have no doubt that I should be better. I came personally, Mr Holmes, in order to ensure that you would return with me. I feared that no telegram would convince you of the absolute urgency of the case.'

'When you are quite restored – '

'I am quite well again. I cannot imagine how I came to be so weak. I wish you, Mr Holmes, to come to Mackleton with me by the next train.'

My friend shook his head.

'My colleague, Dr Watson, could tell you that we are very busy at present. I am retained in this case of the Ferrers Documents, and the Abergavenny murder is coming up for trial. Only a very important issue could call me from London at present.'

'Important!' Our visitor threw up his hands. 'Have you heard nothing of the abduction of the only son of the Duke of Holdernesse?'

'What! the late Cabinet Minister?'

'Exactly. We had tried to keep it out of the papers,

but there was some rumour in the *Globe* last night. I thought it might have reached your ears.'

Holmes shot out his long, thin arm and picked out Volume 'H' in his encyclopaedia of reference.

' "Holdernesse, 6th Duke, K.G., P.C." – half the alphabet! "Baron Beverley, Earl of Carston" – dear me, what a list! "Lord Lieutenant of Hallamshire since 1900. Married Edith, daughter of Sir Charles Appledore, 1888. Heir and only child, Lord Saltire. Owns about two hundred and fifty thousand acres. Minerals in Lancashire and Wales. Address: Carlton House Terrace; Holdernesse Hall, Hallamshire; Carston Castle, Bangor, Wales. Lord of the Admiralty, 1872; Chief Secretary of State for – " Well, well, this man is certainly one of the greatest subjects of the Crown!'

'The greatest and perhaps the wealthiest. I am aware, Mr Holmes, that you take a very high line in professional matters, and that you are prepared to work for the work's sake. I may tell you, however, that his Grace has already intimated that a cheque for five thousand pounds will be handed over to the person who can tell him where his son is, and another thousand to him who can name the man, or men, who have taken him.'

'It is a princely offer,' said Holmes. 'Watson, I think that we shall accompany Dr Huxtable back to the north of England. And now, Dr Huxtable, when you have consumed that milk you will kindly tell me what has happened, when it happened, how it happened, and, finally, what Dr Thorneycroft Huxtable, of the Priory School, near Mackleton, has to do with the matter, and why he comes three days after an event – the state of your chin gives the date – to ask for my humble services.'

Our visitor had consumed his milk and biscuits. The light had come back to his eyes and the colour to his cheeks as he set himself with great vigour and lucidity to explain the situation.

'I must inform you, gentlemen, that the Priory is a preparatory school, of which I am the founder and principal. Huxtable's *Sidelights on Horace* may possibly recall my name to your memories. The Priory is, without exception, the best and most select preparatory school in England. Lord Leverstoke, the Earl of Blackwater, Sir Cathcart Soames – they all have entrusted their sons to me. But I felt that my school had reached its zenith when, three weeks ago, the Duke of Holdernesse sent Mr James Wilder, his secretary, with the intimation that young Lord Saltire, ten years old, his only son and heir, was about to be committed to my charge. Little did I think that this would be the prelude to the most crushing misfortune of my life.

'On May 1st the boy arrived, that being the beginning of the summer term. He was a charming youth, and he soon fell into our ways. I may tell you – I trust that I am not indiscreet, but half-confidences are absurd in such a case – that he was not entirely happy at home. It is an open secret that the Duke's married life had not been a peaceful one, and the matter had ended in a separation by mutual consent, the Duchess taking up her residence in the south of France. This had occurred very shortly before, and the boy's sympathies are known to have been strongly with his mother. He moped after her departure from Holdernesse Hall, and it was for this reason that the Duke desired to send him to my establishment. In a fortnight the boy was quite at home with us, and was apparently absolutely happy.

'He was last seen on the night of May 13th – that is, the night of last Monday. His room was on the second floor, and was approached through another larger room in which two boys were sleeping. These boys saw and heard nothing, so that it is certain that young Saltire did not pass out that way. His window was open, and there is a stout ivy plant leading to the ground. We could trace no footmarks below, but it is sure that this is the only possible exit.

'His absence was discovered at seven o'clock on Tuesday morning. His bed had been slept in. He had dressed himself fully before going off in his usual school suit of black Eton jacket and dark grey trousers. There were no signs that anyone had entered the room, and it is quite certain that anything in the nature of cries, or a struggle, would have been heard, since Caunter, the elder boy in the inner room, is a very light sleeper.

'When Lord Saltire's disappearance was discovered I at once called a roll of the whole establishment, boys, masters, and servants. It was then that we ascertained that Lord Saltire had not been alone in his flight. Heidegger, the German master, was missing. His room was on the second floor, at the farther end of the building, facing the same way as Lord Saltire's. His bed had also been slept in; but he had apparently gone away partly dressed, since his shirt and socks were lying on the floor. He had undoubtedly let himself down by the ivy, for we could see the marks of his feet where he had landed on the lawn. His bicycle was kept in a small shed beside this lawn, and it also was gone.

'He had been with me for two years, and came with the best references; but he was a silent, morose man, not very popular either with masters or boys. No trace could be found of the fugitives, and now on Thursday morning we are as ignorant as we were on Tuesday. Enquiry was, of course, made at once at Holdernesse Hall. It is only a few miles away, and we imagined that in some sudden attack of homesickness he had gone back to his father; but nothing had been heard of him. The Duke is greatly agitated – and as to me, you have seen yourselves the state of nervous prostration to which the suspense and the responsibility have reduced me. Mr Holmes, if ever you put forward your full powers, I implore you to do so now, for never in your life could you have a case which is more worthy of them.'

Sherlock Holmes had listened with the utmost intentness to the statement of the unhappy schoolmaster. His drawn brows and the deep furrow between them showed that he needed no exhortation to concentrate all his attention upon a problem which, apart from the tremendous interests involved, must appeal so directly to his love of the complex and the unusual. He now drew out his notebook and jotted down one or two memoranda.

'You have been very remiss in not coming to me sooner,' said he, severely. 'You start me on my investigation with a very serious handicap. It is inconceivable, for example, that this ivy and this lawn would have yielded nothing to an expert observer.'

'I am not to blame, Mr Holmes. His Grace was extremely desirous to avoid all public scandal. He was afraid of his family unhappiness being dragged before the world. He has a deep horror of anything of the kind.'

'But there has been some official investigation?'

'Yes, sir, and it has proved most disappointing. An

apparent clue was at once obtained, since a boy and a young man were reported to have been seen leaving a neighbouring station by an early train. Only last night we had news that the couple had been hunted down in Liverpool, and they prove to have no connection whatever with the matter in hand. Then it was that in my despair and disappointment, after a sleepless night, I came straight to you by the early train.'

'I suppose the local investigation was relaxed while this false clue was being followed up?'

'It was entirely dropped.'

'So that three days have been wasted. The affair has been most deplorably handled.'

'I feel it, and admit it.'

'And yet the problem should be capable of ultimate solution. I shall be very happy to look into it. Have you been able to trace any connection between the missing boy and this German master?'

'None at all.'

'Was he in the master's class?'

'No; he never exchanged a word with him so far as I know.'

'That is certainly very singular. Had the boy a bicycle?'

'No.'

'Was any other bicycle missing?'

'No.'

'Is that certain?'

'Quite.'

'Well, now, you do not mean to seriously suggest that this German rode off upon a bicycle in the dead of the night bearing the boy in his arms?'

'Certainly not.'

'Then what is the theory in your mind?'

'The bicycle may have been a blind. It may have been hidden somewhere and the pair gone off on foot.'

'Quite so; but it seems rather an absurd blind, does it not? Were there other bicycles in this shed?'

'Several.'

'Would he not have hidden a *couple* had he desired to give the idea that they had gone off upon them?'

'I suppose he would.'

'Of course he would. The blind theory won't do. But the incident is an admirable starting-point for an investigation. After all, a bicycle is not an easy thing to conceal or to destroy. One other question. Did anyone call to see the boy on the day before he disappeared?'

'No.'

'Did he get any letters?'

'Yes; one letter.'

'From whom?'

'From his father.'

'Do you open the boys' letters?'

'No.'

'How do you know it was from the father?'

'The coat of arms was on the envelope, and it was addressed in the Duke's peculiar stiff hand. Besides, the Duke remembers having written.'

'When had he a letter before that?'

'Not for several days.'

'Had he ever one from France?'

'No; never.'

'You see the point of my questions, of course. Either the boy was carried off by force or he went of his own free will. In the latter case you would expect that some prompting from outside would be needed to make so young a lad do such a thing. If he has had no visitors, that prompting must have come in letters. Hence I try to find out who were his correspondents.'

'I fear I cannot help you much. His only correspondent, so far as I know, was his own father.'

'Who wrote to him on the very day of his disappearance. Were the relations between father and son very friendly?'

'His Grace is never very friendly with anyone. He is completely immersed in large public questions, and is rather inaccessible to all ordinary emotions. But he was always kind to the boy in his own way.'

'But the sympathies of the latter were with the mother?'

'Yes.'

'Did he say so?'

'No.'

'The Duke, then?'

'Good heavens, no!'

'Then how could you know?'

'I have had some confidential talks with Mr James Wilder, his Grace's secretary. It was he who gave me the information about Lord Saltire's feelings.'

'I see. By the way, that last letter of the Duke's – was it found in the boy's room after he was gone?'

'No; he had taken it with him. I think, Mr Holmes, it is time that we were leaving for Euston.'

'I will order a four-wheeler. In a quarter of an hour we shall be at your service. If you are telegraphing home, Mr Huxtable, it would be well to allow the people in your neighbourhood to imagine that the enquiry is still going on in Liverpool, or wherever else that red herring led your pack. In the meantime I will do a little quiet work at your own doors, and perhaps the scent is not so cold but that two old hounds like Watson and myself may get a sniff of it.'

That evening found us in the cold, bracing atmosphere of the Peak country, in which Dr Huxtable's famous school is situated. It was already dark when we reached it. A card was lying on the hall table, and the butler whispered something to his master, who turned to us with agitation in every heavy feature.

'The Duke is here,' said he. 'The Duke and Mr Wilder are in the study. Come, gentlemen, and I will introduce you.'

I was, of course, familiar with the pictures of the famous statesman, but the man himself was very different from his representation. He was a tall and stately person, scrupulously dressed, with a drawn, thin face, and a nose which was grotesquely curved and long. His complexion was of a dead pallor, which was more startling by contrast with a long, dwindling beard of vivid red, which flowed down over his white waistcoat, with his watch-chain gleaming through its fringe. Such was the stately presence who looked stonily at us from the centre of Dr Huxtable's hearthrug. Beside him stood a very young man, whom I understood to be Wilder, the private secretary. He was small, nervous, alert, with intelligent, light-blue eyes and mobile features. It was he who at once, in an incisive and positive tone, opened the conversation.

'I called this morning, Dr Huxtable, too late to prevent you from starting for London. I learned that your object was to invite Mr Sherlock Holmes to undertake the conduct of this case. His Grace is surprised, Dr Huxtable, that you should have taken such a step without consulting him.'

'When I learned that the police had failed – '

'His Grace is by no means convinced that the police have failed.'

'But surely, Mr Wilder – '

'You are well aware, Dr Huxtable, that his Grace is particularly anxious to avoid all public scandal. He prefers to take as few people as possible into his confidence.'

'The matter can be easily remedied,' said the brow-beaten doctor; 'Mr Sherlock Holmes can return to London by the morning train.'

'Hardly that, Doctor, hardly that,' said Holmes, in his blandest voice. 'This northern air is invigorating and pleasant, so I propose to spend a few days upon your moors, and to occupy my mind as best I may. Whether I have the shelter of your roof or of the village inn is, of course, for you to decide.'

I could see that the unfortunate doctor was in the last stage of indecision, from which he was rescued by the deep, sonorous voice of the red-bearded Duke, which boomed out like a dinner-gong.

'I agree with Mr Wilder, Dr Huxtable, that you would have done wisely to consult me. But since Mr Holmes has already been taken into your confidence, it would indeed be absurd that we should not avail ourselves of his services. Far from going to the inn, Mr Holmes, I should be pleased if you would come and stay with me at Holdernesse Hall.'

'I thank your Grace. For the purposes of my investigation I think that it would be wiser for me to remain at the scene of the mystery.'

'Just as you like, Mr Holmes. Any information which Mr Wilder or I can give you is, of course, at your disposal.'

'It will probably be necessary for me to see you at the Hall,' said Holmes. 'I would only ask you now, sir, whether you have formed any explanation in your own mind as to the mysterious disappearance of your son?'

'No, sir, I have not.'

'Excuse me if I allude to that which is painful to you, but I have no alternative. Do you think that the Duchess had anything to do with the matter?'

The great Minister showed perceptible hesitation.

'I do not think so,' he said, at last.

'The other most obvious explanation is that the child has been kidnapped for the purpose of levying ransom. You have not had any demand of the sort?'

'No, sir.'

'One more question, your Grace. I understand that you wrote to your son upon the day when this incident occurred.'

'No; I wrote upon the day before.'

'Exactly. But he received it on that day?'

'Yes.'

'Was there anything in your letter which might have unbalanced him or induced him to take such a step?'

'No, sir, certainly not.'

'Did you post that letter yourself?'

The nobleman's reply was interrupted by his secretary, who broke in with some heat.

'His Grace is not in the habit of posting letters himself,' said he. 'This letter was laid with others upon the study table, and I myself put them in the postbag.'

'You are sure this one was among them?'

'Yes; I observed it.'

'How many letters did your Grace write that day?'

'Twenty or thirty. I have a large correspondence. But surely this is somewhat irrelevant?'

'Not entirely,' said Holmes.

'For my own part,' the Duke continued, 'I have advised the police to turn their attention to the south of France. I have already said that I do not believe that the Duchess would encourage so monstrous an action, but the lad had the most wrong-headed opinions, and it is possible that he may have fled to her, aided and abetted by this German. I think, Dr Huxtable, that we will now return to the Hall.'

I could see that there were other questions which Holmes would have wished to put; but the nobleman's abrupt manner showed that the interview was at an end. It was evident that to his intensely aristocratic nature this discussion of his intimate family affairs with a stranger was most abhorrent, and that he feared lest every fresh question would throw a fiercer light into the discreetly shadowed corners of his ducal history.

When the nobleman and his secretary had left, my friend flung himself at once with characteristic eagerness into the investigation.

The boy's chamber was carefully examined, and yielded nothing save the absolute conviction that it was only through the window that he could have escaped. The German master's room and effects gave no further clue. In his case a trailer of ivy had given way under his weight, and we saw by the light of a lantern the mark on the lawn where his heels had come down. That one dint in the short green grass was the only material witness left of this inexplicable nocturnal flight.

Sherlock Holmes left the house alone, and only returned after eleven. He had obtained a large ordnance map of the neighbourhood, and this he brought into my room, where he laid it out on the bed, and, having balanced the lamp in the middle of it, he began to smoke over it, and occasionally to point out objects of interest with the reeking amber of his pipe.

'This case grows upon me, Watson,' said he. 'There are decidedly some points of interest in connection with it. In this early stage I want you to realise those geographical features which may have a good deal to do with our investigation.

'Look at this map. This dark square is the Priory School. I'll put a pin in it. Now, this line is the main road. You see that it runs east and west past the school, and you see also that there is no side road for a mile either way. If these two folk passed away by road it was *this* road.'

'Exactly.'

'By a singular and happy chance we are able to some

extent to check what passed along this road during the night in question. At this point, where my pipe is now resting, a country constable was on duty from twelve to six. It is, as you perceive, the first cross road on the east side. This man declares that he was not absent from his post for an instant, and he is positive that neither boy nor man could have gone that way unseen. I have spoken with this policeman tonight, and he appears to me to be a perfectly reliable person. That blocks this end. We have now to deal with the other. There is an inn here, the Red Bull, the landlady of which was ill. She had sent to Mackleton for a doctor, but he did not arrive until morning, being absent at another case. The people at the inn were alert all night, awaiting his coming, and one or other of them seems to have continually had an eye upon the road. They declare that no one passed. If their evidence is good, then we are fortunate enough to be able to block the west, and also to be able to say that the fugitives did *not* use the road at all.'

'But the bicycle?' I objected.

'Quite so. We will come to the bicycle presently. To continue our reasoning: if these people did not go by the road, they must have traversed the country to the north of the house or to the south of the house. That is certain. Let us weigh the one against the other. On the south of the house is, as you perceive, a large district of arable land, cut up into small fields, with stone walls between them. There, I admit that a bicycle is impossible. We can dismiss the idea. We turn to the country on the north. Here there lies a grove of trees, marked as the "Ragged Shaw", and on the farther side stretches a great rolling moor, Lower Gill Moor, extending for ten miles and sloping gradually upwards. Here, at one side of this wilderness, is Holdernesse Hall, ten miles by road, but only six across the moor. It is a peculiarly desolate plain. A few moor farmers have small holdings, where they rear sheep and cattle. Except these, the plover and the curlew are the only inhabitants until you come to the Chesterfield high road. There is a church there, you see, a few cottages, and an inn. Beyond that the hills become precipitous. Surely it is here to the north that our quest must lie.'

'But the bicycle?' I persisted.

'Well, well!' said Holmes, impatiently. 'A good cyclist does not need a high road. The moor is intersected with paths and the moon was at the full. Halloa! what is this?'

There was an agitated knock at the door, and an instant afterwards Dr Huxtable was in the room. In his hand he held a blue cricket-cap, with a white chevron on the peak.

'At last we have a clue!' he cried. 'Thank Heaven! at last we are on the dear boy's track! It is his cap.'

'Where was it found?'

'In the van of the gypsies who camped on the moor. They left on Tuesday. Today the police traced them down and examined their caravan. This was found.'

'How do they account for it?'

'They shuffled and lied – said that they found it on the moor on Tuesday morning. They know where he is, the rascals! Thank goodness, they are all safe under lock and key. Either the fear of the law or the Duke's purse will certainly get out of them all that they know.'

'So far, so good,' said Holmes, when the doctor had at last left the room. 'It at least bears out the theory that it is on the side of the Lower Gill Moor that we must hope for results. The police have really done nothing locally, save the arrest of these gypsies. Look here, Watson! There is a watercourse across the moor. You see it marked here in the map. In some parts it widens into a morass. This is particularly so in the region between Holdernesse Hall and the school. It is vain to look elsewhere for tracks in this dry weather; but at *that* point there is certainly a chance of some record being left. I will call you early tomorrow morning, and you and I will try if we can throw some little light upon the mystery.'

The day was just breaking when I woke to find the long, thin form of Holmes by my bedside. He was fully dressed, and had apparently already been out.

'I have done the lawn and the bicycle shed,' said he. 'I have also had a ramble through the Ragged Shaw. Now, Watson, there is cocoa ready in the next room. I must beg you to hurry, for we have a great day before us.'

His eyes shone, and his cheek was flushed with the exhilaration of the master workman who sees his work lie ready before him. A very different Holmes, this active, alert man, from the introspective and pallid dreamer of Baker Street. I felt, as I looked upon that supple figure, alive with nervous energy, that it was indeed a strenuous day that awaited us.

And yet it opened in the blackest disappointment. With high hopes we struck across the peaty, russet moor, intersected with a thousand sheep paths, until we came to the broad, light-green belt which marked the morass between us and Holdernesse. Certainly, if the lad had gone homewards, he must have passed this, and he could not pass it without leaving his traces. But no sign of him or the German could be seen. With a darkening face my friend strode along the margin, eagerly observant of every muddy stain upon the mossy surface. Sheep-marks there were in profusion, and at one place, some miles down, cows had left their tracks. Nothing more.

'Check number one,' said Holmes, looking gloomily over the rolling expanse of the moor. 'There is another morass down yonder and a narrow neck between. Halloa! halloa! halloa! what have we here?'

We had come on a small black ribbon of pathway. In the middle of it, clearly marked on the sodden soil, was the track of a bicycle.

'Hurrah!' I cried. 'We have it.'

But Holmes was shaking his head, and his face was puzzled and expectant rather than joyous.

'A bicycle, certainly, but not *the* bicycle,' said he. 'I am familiar with forty-two different impressions left by tyres. This, as you perceive, is a Dunlop, with a patch upon the outer cover. Heidegger's tyres were Palmer's, leaving longitudinal stripes. Aveling, the mathematical master, was sure upon the point. Therefore, it is not Heidegger's track.'

'The boy's, then?'

'Possibly, if we could prove a bicycle to have been in his possession. But this we have utterly failed to do. This track, as you perceive, was made by a rider who was going from the direction of the school.'

'Or towards it?'

'No, no, my dear Watson. The more deeply sunk impression is, of course, the hind wheel, upon which the weight rests. You perceive several places where it has passed across and obliterated the more shallow mark of the front one. It was undoubtedly heading away from the school. It may or may not be connected with our enquiry, but we will follow it backwards before we go any farther.'

We did so, and at the end of a few hundred yards lost the tracks as we emerged from the boggy portion of the moor. Following the path backwards, we picked out another spot, where a spring trickled across it. Here, once again, was the mark of the bicycle, though nearly obliterated by the hoofs of cows. After that there was no sign, but the path ran right on into Ragged Shaw, the wood which backed on to the school. From this wood the cycle must have emerged. Holmes sat down on a boulder and rested his chin in his hands. I had smoked two cigarettes before he moved.

'Well, well,' said he, at last. 'It is, of course, possible that a cunning man might change the tyre of his bicycle in order to leave unfamiliar tracks. A criminal who was capable of such a thought is a man whom I should be proud to do business with. We will leave this question undecided and hark back to our morass again, for we have left a good deal unexplored.'

We continued our systematic survey of the edge of the sodden portion of the moor, and soon our perseverance was gloriously rewarded. Right across the lower part of the bog lay a miry path. Holmes gave a cry of delight as he approached it. An impression like a fine bundle of telegraph wires ran down the centre of it. It was the Palmer tyre.

'Here is Herr Heidegger, sure enough!' cried Holmes, exultantly. 'My reasoning seems to have been pretty sound, Watson.'

'I congratulate you.'

'But we have a long way still to go. Kindly walk clear of the path. Now let us follow the trail. I fear that it will not lead very far.'

We found, however, as we advanced, that this portion of the moor is intersected with soft patches, and, though we frequently lost sight of the track, we always succeeded in picking it up once more.

'Do you observe,' said Holmes, 'that the rider is now undoubtedly forcing the pace? There can be no doubt of it. Look at this impression, where you get both tyres clear. The one is as deep as the other. That can only mean that the rider is throwing his weight on to the handlebar, as a man does when he is sprinting. By Jove! he has had a fall.'

There was a broad, irregular smudge covering some yards of the track. Then there were a few footmarks, and the tyre reappeared once more.

'A sideslip,' I suggested.

Holmes held up a crumpled branch of flowering gorse. To my horror I perceived that the yellow blossoms were all dabbled with crimson. On the path, too, and among the heather were dark stains of clotted blood.

'Bad!' said Holmes. 'Bad! Stand clear, Watson! Not an unnecessary footstep! What do I read here? He fell wounded, he stood up, he remounted, he proceeded. But there is no other track. Cattle on this side path. He was surely not gored by a bull? Impossible! But I see no traces of anyone else. We must push on, Watson. Surely with stains as well as the track to guide us he cannot escape us now.'

Our search was not a very long one. The tracks of the tyre began to curve fantastically upon the wet and shining path. Suddenly, as I looked ahead, the gleam of metal caught my eye from amid the thick gorse bushes. Out of them we dragged a bicycle, Palmer-tyred, one pedal bent, and the whole front of it horribly smeared and slobbered with blood. On the other side of the bushes a shoe was projecting. We ran round, and there lay the unfortunate rider. He was a tall man, full bearded, with spectacles, one glass of which had been knocked out. The cause of his death was a frightful blow upon the head, which had crushed in part of his skull. That he could have gone on after receiving such an injury said much for the vitality and courage of the man. He wore shoes, but no socks, and his open coat disclosed a nightshirt beneath it. It was undoubtedly the German master.

Holmes turned the body over reverently, and examined it with great attention. He then sat in deep thought for a time, and I could see by his ruffled brow that this grim discovery had not, in his opinion, advanced us much in our enquiry.

'It is a little difficult to know what to do, Watson,' said he, at last. 'My own inclinations are to push this enquiry on, for we have already lost so much time that we cannot afford to waste another hour. On the other hand, we are bound to inform the police of the discovery, and to see that this poor fellow's body is looked after.'

'I could take a note back.'

'But I need your company and assistance. Wait a bit! There is a fellow cutting peat up yonder. Bring him over here, and he will guide the police.'

I brought the peasant across, and Holmes dispatched the frightened man with a note to Dr Huxtable.

'Now, Watson,' said he, 'we have picked up two clues this morning. One is the bicycle with the Palmer tyre, and we see what that has led to. The other is the bicycle with the patched Dunlop. Before we start to investigate that, let us try to realise what we *do* know, so as to make the most of it, and to separate the essential from the accidental.

'First of all I wish to impress upon you that the boy certainly left of his own free will. He got down from his window and he went off, either alone or with someone. That is sure.'

I assented.

'Well, now, let us turn to this unfortunate German master. The boy was fully dressed when he fled. Therefore, he foresaw what he would do. But the German went without his socks. He certainly acted on very short notice.'

'Undoubtedly.'

'Why did he go? Because, from his bedroom window, he saw the flight of the boy. Because he wished to overtake him and bring him back. He seized his bicycle, pursued the lad, and in pursuing him met his death.'

'So it would seem.'

'Now I come to the critical part of my argument. The natural action of a man in pursuing a little boy would be to run after him. He would know that he could overtake him. But the German does not do so. He turns to his bicycle. I am told that he was an excellent cyclist. He would not do this if he did not see that the boy had some swift means of escape.'

'The other bicycle.'

'Let us continue our reconstruction. He meets his death five miles from the school – not by a bullet, mark you, which even a lad might conceivably discharge, but by a savage blow dealt by a vigorous arm. The lad, then, *had* a companion in his flight. And the flight was a swift one, since it took five miles before an expert cyclist could overtake them. Yet we survey the ground round the scene of the tragedy. What do we find? A few cattle tracks, nothing more. I took a wide sweep round, and there is no path within fifty yards. Another cyclist could have had nothing to do with the actual murder. Nor were there any human footmarks.'

'Holmes,' I cried, 'this is impossible.'

'Admirable!' he said. 'A most illuminating remark. It *is* impossible as I state it, and therefore I must in some respect have stated it wrong. Yet you saw for yourself. Can you suggest any fallacy?'

'He could not have fractured his skull in a fall?'

'In a morass, Watson?'

'I am at my wit's end.'

'Tut, tut; we have solved some worse problems. At least we have plenty of material, if we can only use it. Come, then, and, having exhausted the Palmer, let us see what the Dunlop with the patched cover has to offer us.'

We picked up the track and followed it onwards for some distance; but soon the moor rose into a long, heather-tufted curve, and we left the watercourse behind us. No further help from tracks could be hoped for. At the spot where we saw the last of the Dunlop tyre it might equally have led to Holdernesse Hall, the stately towers of which rose some miles to our left, or to a low, grey village which lay in front of us, and marked the position of the Chesterfield high road.

As we approached the forbidding and squalid inn, with the sign of a gamecock above the door, Holmes gave a sudden groan and clutched me by the shoulder to save himself from falling. He had had one of those violent strains of the ankle which leave a man helpless. With difficulty he limped up to the door, where a squat, dark, elderly man was smoking a black clay pipe.

'How are you, Mr Reuben Hayes?' said Holmes.

'Who are you, and how do you get my name so pat?' the countryman answered, with a suspicious flash of a pair of cunning eyes.

'Well, it's printed on the board above your head. It's easy to see a man who is master of his own house. I suppose you haven't such a thing as a carriage in your stables?'

'No; I have not.'

'I can hardly put my foot to the ground.'

'Don't put it to the ground.'

'But I can't walk.'

'Well, then, hop.'

Mr Reuben Hayes's manner was far from gracious, but Holmes took it with admirable good-humour.

'Look here, my man,' said he. 'This is really rather an awkward fix for me. I don't mind how I get on.'

'Neither do I,' said the morose landlord.

'The matter is very important. I would offer you a sovereign for the use of a bicycle.'

The landlord pricked up his ears.

'Where do you want to go?'

'To Holdernesse Hall.'

'Pals of the Dook, I suppose?' said the landlord, surveying our mud-stained garments with ironical eyes.

Holmes laughed good-naturedly.

'He'll be glad to see us, anyhow.'

'Why?'

'Because we bring him news of his lost son.'

The landlord gave a very visible start.

'What, you're on his track?'

'He has been heard of in Liverpool. They expect to get him every hour.'

Again a swift change passed over the heavy, unshaven face. His manner was suddenly genial.

'I've less reason to wish the Dook well than most men,' said he, 'for I was his head coachman once, and cruel bad he treated me. It was him that sacked me without a character on the word of a lying cornchandler. But I'm glad to hear that the young lord was heard of in Liverpool, and I'll help you to take the news to the Hall.'

'Thank you,' said Holmes. 'We'll have some food first. Then you can bring round the bicycle.'

'I haven't got a bicycle.'

Holmes held up a sovereign.

'I tell you, man, that I haven't got one. I'll let you have two horses as far as the Hall.'

'Well, well,' said Holmes, 'we'll talk about it when we've had something to eat.'

When we were left alone in the stone-flagged kitchen it was astonishing how rapidly that sprained ankle recovered. It was nearly nightfall, and we had eaten nothing since early morning, so that we spent some time over our meal. Holmes was lost in thought, and once or twice he walked over to the window and stared earnestly out. It opened on to a squalid courtyard. In the far corner was a smithy, where a grimy lad was at work. On the other side were the stables. Holmes had sat down again after one of these excursions, when he suddenly sprang out of his chair with a loud exclamation.

'By Heaven, Watson, I believe that I've got it!' he cried. 'Yes, yes, it must be so. Watson, do you remember seeing any cow-tracks today?'

'Yes, several.'

'Where?'

'Well, everywhere. They were at the morass, and again on the path, and again near where poor Heidegger met his death.'

'Exactly. Well, now, Watson, how many cows did you see on the moor?'

'I don't remember seeing any.'

'Strange, Watson, that we should see tracks all along our line, but never a cow on the whole moor; very strange, Watson, eh?'

'Yes, it is strange.'

'Now, Watson, make an effort; throw your mind back! Can you see those tracks upon the path?'

'Yes, I can.'

'Can you recall that the tracks were sometimes like that, Watson' – he arranged a number of bread-crumbs in this fashion – : : : : : – 'and sometimes like this' – : · : · : · : · – 'and occasionally like this' – . · . · . .

'Can you remember that?'

'No, I cannot.'

'But I can. I could swear to it. However, we will go back at our leisure and verify it. What a blind beetle I have been not to draw my conclusion!'

'And what is your conclusion?'

'Only that it is a remarkable cow which walks, canters, and gallops. By George, Watson, it was no brain of a country publican that thought out such a blind as that! The coast seems to be clear, save for that lad in the smithy. Let us slip out and see what we can see.'

There were two rough-haired, unkempt horses in the tumble-down stable. Holmes raised the hind leg of one of them and laughed aloud.

'Old shoes, but newly shod – old shoes, but new

nails. This case deserves to be a classic. Let us go across to the smithy.'

The lad continued his work without regarding us. I saw Holmes's eye darting to right and left among the litter of iron and wood which was scattered about the floor. Suddenly, however, we heard a step behind us, and there was the landlord, his heavy eyebrows drawn over his savage eyes, his swarthy features convulsed with passion. He held a short, metal-headed stick in his hand, and he advanced in so menacing a fashion that I was right glad to feel the revolver in my pocket.

'You infernal spies!' the man cried. 'What are you doing there?'

'Why, Mr Reuben Hayes,' said Holmes, coolly, 'one might think that you were afraid of our finding something out.'

The man mastered himself with a violent effort, and his grim mouth loosened into a false laugh, which was more menacing than his frown.

'You're welcome to all you can find out in my smithy,' said he. 'But look here, mister, I don't care for folk poking about my place without my leave, so the sooner you pay your score and get out of this the better I shall be pleased.'

'All right, Mr Hayes – no harm meant,' said Holmes. 'We have been having a look at your horses, but I think I'll walk after all. It's not far, I believe.'

'Not more than two miles to the Hall gates. That's the road to the left.' He watched us with sullen eyes until we had left his premises.

We did not go very far along the road, for Holmes stopped the instant that the curve hid us from the landlord's view.

'We were warm, as the children say, at that inn,' said

he. 'I seem to grow colder every step that I take away from it. No, no; I can't possibly leave it.'

'I am convinced,' said I, 'that this Reuben Hayes knows all about it. A more self-evident villain I never saw.'

'Oh! he impressed you in that way, did he? There are the horses, there is the smithy. Yes, it is an interesting place, this Fighting Cock. I think we shall have another look at it in an unobtrusive way.'

A long, sloping hillside, dotted with grey limestone boulders, stretched behind us. We had turned off the road, and were making our way up the hill, when, looking in the direction of Holdernesse Hall, I saw a cyclist coming swiftly along.

'Get down, Watson!' cried Holmes, with a heavy hand upon my shoulder. We had hardly sunk from view when the man flew past us on the road. Amid a rolling cloud of dust I caught a glimpse of a pale, agitated face – a face with horror in every lineament, the mouth open, the eyes staring wildly in front. It was like some strange caricature of the dapper James Wilder whom we had seen the night before.

'The Duke's secretary!' cried Holmes. 'Come, Watson, let us see what he does.'

We scrambled from rock to rock until in a few moments we had made our way to a point from which we could see the front door of the inn. Wilder's bicycle was leaning against the wall beside it. No one was moving about the house, nor could we catch a glimpse of any faces at the windows. Slowly the twilight crept down as the sun sank behind the high towers of Holdernesse Hall. Then in the gloom we saw the two side-lamps of a trap light up in the stable-yard of the inn, and shortly afterwards heard the rattle of hoofs, as it wheeled out into the road and tore off at a furious pace in the direction of Chesterfield.

'What do you make of that, Watson?' Holmes whispered.

'It looks like a flight.'

'A single man in a dog cart, so far as I could see. Well, it certainly was not Mr James Wilder, for there he is at the door.'

A red square of light had sprung out of the darkness. In the middle of it was the black figure of the secretary, his head advanced, peering out into the night. It was evident that he was expecting someone. Then at last there were steps in the road, a second figure was visible for an instant against the light, the door shut, and all was black once more. Five minutes later a lamp was lit in a room upon the first floor.

'It seems to be a curious class of custom that is done by the Fighting Cock,' said Holmes.

'The bar is on the other side.'

'Quite so. These are what one may call the private guests. Now, what in the world is Mr James Wilder doing in that den at this hour of night, and who is the companion who comes to meet him there? Come, Watson, we must really take a risk and try to investigate this a little more closely.'

Together we stole down to the road and crept across to the door of the inn. The bicycle still leaned against the wall. Holmes struck a match and held it to the back wheel, and I heard him chuckle as the light fell upon a patched Dunlop tyre. Up above us was the lighted window.

'I must have a peep through that, Watson. If you bend your back and support yourself upon the wall, I think that I can manage.'

An instant later his feet were on my shoulders. But he was hardly up before he was down again.

'Come, my friend,' said he, 'our day's work has been quite long enough. I think that we have gathered all that we can. It's a long walk to the school, and the sooner we get started the better.'

He hardly opened his lips during that weary trudge across the moor, nor would he enter the school when he reached it, but went on to Mackleton Station, whence he could send some telegrams. Late at night I heard him consoling Dr Huxtable, prostrated by the tragedy of his master's death, and later still he entered my room as alert and vigorous as he had been when he started in the morning. 'All goes well, my friend,' said he. 'I promise that before tomorrow evening we shall have reached the solution of the mystery.'

At eleven o'clock next morning my friend and I were walking up the famous yew avenue of Holdernesse Hall. We were ushered through the magnificent Elizabethan doorway and into his Grace's study. There we found Mr James Wilder, demure and courtly, but with some trace of that wild terror of the night before still lurking in his furtive eyes and in his twitching features.

'You have come to see his Grace? I am sorry; but the fact is that the Duke is far from well. He has been very much upset by the tragic news. We received a telegram from Dr Huxtable yesterday afternoon, which told us of your discovery.'

'I must see the Duke, Mr Wilder.'

'But he is in his room.'

'Then I must go to his room.'

'I believe he is in his bed.'

'I will see him there.'

Holmes's cold and inexorable manner showed the secretary that it was useless to argue with him.

'Very good, Mr Holmes; I will tell him that you are here.'

After half an hour's delay the great nobleman appeared. His face was more cadaverous than ever, his shoulders had rounded, and he seemed to me to be an altogether older man than he had been the morning before. He greeted us with a stately courtesy and seated himself at his desk, his red beard streaming down on to the table.

'Well, Mr Holmes?' said he.

But my friend's eyes were fixed upon the secretary, who stood by his master's chair.

'I think, your Grace, that I could speak more freely in Mr Wilder's absence.'

The man turned a shade paler and cast a malignant glance at Holmes.

'If your Grace wishes – '

'Yes, yes; you had better go. Now, Mr Holmes, what have you to say?'

My friend waited until the door had closed behind the retreating secretary.

'The fact is, your Grace,' said he, 'that my colleague, Dr Watson, and myself had an assurance from Dr Huxtable that a reward had been offered in this case. I should like to have this confirmed from your own lips.'

'Certainly, Mr Holmes.'

'It amounted, if I am correctly informed, to five thousand pounds to anyone who will tell you where your son is?'

'Exactly.'

'And another thousand to the man who will name the person or persons who keep him in custody?'

'Exactly.'

'Under the latter heading is included, no doubt, not only those who may have taken him away, but also those who conspire to keep him in his present position?'

'Yes, yes,' cried the Duke, impatiently. 'If you do your work well, Mr Sherlock Holmes, you will have no reason to complain of niggardly treatment.'

My friend rubbed his thin hands together with an appearance of avidity which was a surprise to me, who knew his frugal tastes.

'I fancy that I see your Grace's chequebook upon the table,' said he. 'I should be glad if you would make me out a cheque for six thousand pounds. It would be as well, perhaps, for you to cross it. The Capital and Counties Bank, Oxford Street branch, are my agents.'

His Grace sat very stern and upright in his chair, and looked stonily at my friend.

'Is this a joke, Mr Holmes? It is hardly a subject for pleasantry.'

'Not at all, your Grace. I was never more earnest in my life.'

'What do you mean, then?'

'I mean that I have earned the reward. I know where your son is, and I know some, at least, of those who are holding him.'

The Duke's beard had turned more aggressively red than ever against his ghastly white face.

'Where is he?' he gasped.

'He is, or was last night, at the Fighting Cock Inn, about two miles from your park gate.'

The Duke fell back in his chair.

'And whom do you accuse?'

Sherlock Holmes's answer was an astounding one.

He stepped swiftly forward and touched the Duke upon the shoulder.

'I accuse *you*,' said he. 'And now, your Grace, I'll trouble you for that cheque.'

Never shall I forget the Duke's appearance as he sprang up and clawed with his hands like one who is sinking into an abyss. Then, with an extraordinary effort of aristocratic self-command, he sat down and sank his face in his hands. It was some minutes before he spoke.

'How much do you know?' he asked at last, without raising his head.

'I saw you together last night.'

'Does anyone else besides your friend know?'

'I have spoken to no one.'

The Duke took a pen in his quivering fingers and opened his chequebook.

'I shall be as good as my word, Mr Holmes. I am about to write your cheque, however unwelcome the information which you have gained may be to me. When the offer was first made I little thought the turn which events might take. But you and your friend are men of discretion, Mr Holmes?'

'I hardly understand your Grace.'

'I must put it plainly, Mr Holmes. If only you two know of this incident, there is no reason why it should go any farther. I think twelve thousand pounds is the sum that I owe you, is it not?'

But Holmes smiled and shook his head.

'I fear, your Grace, that matters can hardly be arranged so easily. There is the death of this schoolmaster to be accounted for.'

'But James knew nothing of that. You cannot hold him responsible for that. It was the work of this brutal ruffian whom he had the misfortune to employ.'

'I must take the view, your Grace, that when a man embarks upon a crime he is morally guilty of any other crime which may spring from it.'

'Morally, Mr Holmes. No doubt you are right. But surely not in the eyes of the law. A man cannot be condemned for a murder at which he was not present, and which he loathes and abhors as much as you do. The instant that he heard of it he made a complete confession to me, so filled was he with horror and remorse. He lost not an hour in breaking entirely with the murderer. Oh, Mr Holmes, you must save him – you must save him! I tell you that you must save him!' The Duke had dropped the last attempt at self-command, and was pacing the room with a convulsed face and with his clenched hands raving in the air. At last he mastered himself and sat down once more at his desk. 'I appreciate your conduct in coming here before you spoke to anyone else,' said he. 'At least, we may take counsel how far we can minimise this hideous scandal.'

'Exactly,' said Holmes. 'I think, your Grace, that this can only be done by absolute and complete frankness between us. I am disposed to help your Grace to the best of my ability; but in order to do so I must understand to the last detail how the matter stands. I realise that your words applied to Mr James Wilder, and that he is not the murderer.'

'No; the murderer has escaped.'

Sherlock Holmes smiled demurely.

'Your Grace can hardly have heard of any small reputation which I possess, or you would not imagine that it is so easy to escape me. Mr Reuben Hayes was arrested at Chesterfield on my information at eleven o'clock last night. I had a telegram from the head of the local police before I left the school this morning.'

The Duke leaned back in his chair and stared with amazement at my friend.

'You seem to have powers that are hardly human,' said he. 'So Reuben Hayes is taken? I am right glad to hear it, if it will not react upon the fate of James.'

'Your secretary?'

'No, sir; my son.'

It was Holmes's turn to look astonished.

'I confess that this is entirely new to me, your Grace. I must beg you to be more explicit.'

'I will conceal nothing from you. I agree with you that complete frankness, however painful it may be to me, is the best policy in this desperate situation to which James's folly and jealousy have reduced us. When I was a very young man, Mr Holmes, I loved with such a love as comes only once in a lifetime. I offered the lady marriage, but she refused it on the grounds that such a match might mar my career. Had she lived I would certainly never have married anyone else. She died, and left this one child, whom for her sake I have cherished and cared for. I could not acknowledge the paternity to the world; but I gave him the best of educations, and since he came to manhood I have kept him near my person. He surprised my secret, and has presumed ever since upon the claim which he has upon me and upon his power of provoking a scandal, which would be abhorrent to me. His presence had something to do with the unhappy issue of my marriage. Above all, he hated my young legitimate heir from the first with a persistent hatred. You may well ask me why, under these circumstances, I still kept James under my roof. I answer that it was because I could see his mother's face in his, and that for her dear sake there was no end to my long-suffering. All her pretty ways, too – there was not one of them which he could not suggest and bring back to my memory. I *could* not send him away. But I feared so much lest he should do Arthur – that is, Lord Saltire – a mischief that I dispatched him for safety to Dr Huxtable's school.

'James came into contact with this fellow Hayes because the man was a tenant of mine, and James acted as agent. The fellow was a rascal from the beginning; but in some extraordinary way James became intimate with him. He had always a taste for low company. When James determined to kidnap Lord Saltire it was of this man's service that he availed himself. You remember that I wrote to Arthur upon that last day. Well, James opened the letter and inserted a note asking Arthur to meet him in a little wood called the Ragged Shaw, which is near to the school. He used the Duchess's name, and in that way got the boy to come. That evening James bicycled over – I am telling you what he has himself confessed to me – and he told Arthur, whom he met in the wood, that his mother longed to see him, that she was awaiting him on the moor, and that if he would come back into the wood at midnight he would find a man with a horse, who would take him to her. Poor Arthur fell into the trap. He came to the appointment and found this fellow Hayes with a led pony. Arthur mounted, and they set off together. It appears – though this James only heard yesterday – that they were pursued, that Hayes struck the pursuer with his stick, and that the man died of his injuries. Hayes brought Arthur to his public-house, the Fighting Cock, where he was confined in an upper room, under the care of Mrs Hayes, who is a kindly woman, but entirely under the control of her brutal husband.

'Well, Mr Holmes, that was the state of affairs when I first saw you two days ago. I had no more idea of the truth than you. You will ask me what was James's motive in doing such a deed. I answer that there was a great deal which was unreasoning and fanatical in the hatred which he bore my heir. In his view he should himself have been heir of all my estates, and he deeply resented those social laws which made it impossible. At the same time he had a definite motive also. He was eager that I should break the entail, and he was of opinion that it lay in my power to do so. He intended to make a bargain with me – to restore Arthur if I would break the entail, and so make it possible for the estate to be left to him by will. He knew well that I should never willingly invoke the aid of the police against him. I say that he would have proposed such a bargain to me, but he did not actually do so, for events moved too quickly for him, and he had not time to put his plans into practice.

'What brought all his wicked scheme to wreck was your discovery of this man Heidegger's dead body. James was seized with horror at the news. It came to us yesterday as we sat together in this study. Dr Huxtable had sent a telegram. James was so overwhelmed with grief and agitation that my suspicions, which had never been entirely absent, rose instantly to a certainty, and I taxed him with the deed. He made a complete voluntary confession. Then he implored me to keep his secret for three days longer, so as to give his wretched accomplice a chance of saving his guilty life. I yielded – as I have always yielded – to his prayers, and instantly James hurried off to the Fighting Cock to warn Hayes and give him the means of flight. I could not go there by daylight without provoking comment, but as soon as night fell I hurried off to see my dear Arthur. I found him safe and well, but horrified beyond expression by the dreadful deed he had witnessed. In deference to my promise, and much against my will, I consented to leave him there for three days under the charge of Mrs Hayes, since it was evident that it was impossible to inform the police where he was without telling them also who was the murderer, and I could not see how that murderer could be punished without ruin to my unfortunate James. You asked for frankness, Mr Holmes, and I have taken you at your word, for I have now told you everything without an attempt at circumlocution or concealment. Do you in turn be as frank with me.'

'I will,' said Holmes. 'In the first place, your Grace, I am bound to tell you that you have placed yourself in a most serious position in the eyes of the law. You have condoned a felony and you have aided the escape of a murderer; for I cannot doubt that any money which was taken by James Wilder to aid his accomplice in his flight came from your Grace's purse.'

The Duke bowed his assent.

'This is indeed a most serious matter. Even more culpable in my opinion, your Grace, is your attitude towards your younger son. You leave him in this den for three days.'

'Under solemn promises – '

'What are promises to such people as these? You have no guarantee that he will not be spirited away again. To humour your guilty elder son you have exposed your innocent younger son to imminent and unnecessary danger. It was a most unjustifiable action.'

The proud lord of Holdernesse was not accustomed to be so rated in his own ducal hall. The blood flushed

into his high forehead, but his conscience held him dumb.

'I will help you, but on one condition only. It is that you ring for the footman and let me give such orders as I like.'

Without a word the Duke pressed the electric bell. A servant entered.

'You will be glad to hear,' said Holmes, 'that your young master is found. It is the Duke's desire that the carriage shall go at once to the Fighting Cock Inn to bring Lord Saltire home.

'Now,' said Holmes, when the rejoicing lackey had disappeared, 'having secured the future, we can afford to be more lenient with the past. I am not in an official position, and there is no reason, so long as the ends of justice are served, why I should disclose all that I know. As to Hayes I say nothing. The gallows awaits him, and I would do nothing to save him from it. What he will divulge I cannot tell, but I have no doubt that your Grace could make him understand that it is to his interest to be silent. From the police point of view he will have kidnapped the boy for the purpose of ransom. If they do not themselves find it out I see no reason why I should prompt them to take a broader point of view. I would warn your Grace, however, that the continued presence of Mr James Wilder in your household can only lead to misfortune.'

'I understand that, Mr Holmes, and it is already settled that he shall leave me for ever and go to seek his fortune in Australia.'

'In that case, your Grace, since you have yourself stated that any unhappiness in your married life was caused by his presence, I would suggest that you make such amends as you can to the Duchess, and that you

THE RETURN OF SHERLOCK HOLMES

try to resume those relations which have been so unhappily interrupted.'

'That also I have arranged, Mr Holmes. I wrote to the Duchess this morning.'

'In that case,' said Holmes, rising, 'I think that my friend and I can congratulate ourselves upon several most happy results from our little visit to the north. There is one other small point upon which I desire some light. This fellow Hayes had shod his horses with shoes which counterfeited the tracks of cows. Was it from Mr Wilder that he learned so extraordinary a device?'

The Duke stood in thought for a moment, with a look of intense surprise on his face. Then he opened a door and showed us into a large room furnished as a museum. He led the way to a glass case in a corner, and pointed to the inscription.

'These shoes,' it ran, 'were dug up in the moat of Holdernesse Hall. They are for the use of horses; but they are shaped below with a cloven foot of iron, so as to throw pursuers off the track. They are supposed to have belonged to some of the marauding Barons of Holdernesse in the Middle Ages.'

Holmes opened the case, and moistening his finger, he passed it along the shoe. A thin film of recent mud was left upon his skin.

'Thank you,' said he, as he replaced the glass. 'It is the second most interesting object that I have seen in the north.'

'And the first?'

Holmes folded up his cheque and placed it carefully in his notebook. 'I am a poor man,' said he, as he patted it affectionately and thrust it into the depths of his inner pocket.

6

Black Peter

I have never known my friend to be in better form, both mental and physical, than in the year 1895. His increasing fame had brought with it an immense practice, and I should be guilty of an indiscretion if I were even to hint at the identity of some of the illustrious clients who crossed our humble threshold in Baker Street. Holmes, however, like all great artists, lived for his art's sake, and, save in the case of the Duke of Holdernesse, I have seldom known him claim any large reward for his inestimable services. So unworldly was he – or so capricious – that he frequently refused his help to the powerful and wealthy where the problem made no appeal to his sympathies, while he would devote weeks of most intense application to the affairs of some humble client whose case presented those strange and dramatic qualities which appealed to his imagination and challenged his ingenuity.

In this memorable year 1895 a curious and incongruous succession of cases had engaged his attention, ranging from his famous investigation of the sudden death of Cardinal Tosca – an enquiry which was carried out by him at the express desire of His Holiness the Pope – down to his arrest of Wilson, the notorious canary-trainer, which removed a plague-spot from the East End of London. Close on the heels of these two famous cases came the tragedy of Woodman's Lee, and the very obscure circumstances which surrounded the death of Captain Peter Carey. No record of the doings of Mr Sherlock Holmes would be complete which did not include some account of this very unusual affair.

During the first week of July my friend had been absent so often and so long from our lodgings that I knew he had something on hand. The fact that several rough-looking men called during that time and enquired for Captain Basil made me understand that Holmes was working somewhere under one of the numerous disguises and names with which he concealed his own formidable identity. He had at least five small refuges in different parts of London in which he was able to change his personality. He said nothing of his business to me, and it was not my habit to force a confidence. The first positive sign which he gave me of the direction which his investigation was taking was an extraordinary one. He had gone out before breakfast, and I had sat down to mine, when he strode into the room, his hat upon his head and a huge barbed-headed spear tucked like an umbrella under his arm.

'Good gracious, Holmes!' I cried. 'You don't mean to say that you have been walking about London with that thing?'

'I drove to the butcher's and back.'

'The butcher's?'

'And I return with an excellent appetite. There can be no question, my dear Watson, of the value of exercise before breakfast. But I am prepared to bet that you will not guess the form that my exercise has taken.'

'I will not attempt it.'

He chuckled as he poured out the coffee.

'If you could have looked into Allardyce's back shop you would have seen a dead pig swung from a hook in the ceiling, and a gentleman in his shirtsleeves furiously stabbing at it with this weapon. I was that energetic person, and I have satisfied myself that by no exertion of my strength can I transfix the pig with a single blow. Perhaps you would care to try?'

'Not for worlds. But why were you doing this?'

'Because it seemed to me to have an indirect bearing upon the mystery of Woodman's Lee. Ah, Hopkins, I got your wire last night, and I have been expecting you. Come and join us.'

Our visitor was an exceedingly alert man, thirty years of age, dressed in a quiet tweed suit, but retaining the erect bearing of one who was accustomed to official uniform. I recognised him at once as Stanley Hopkins, a young police inspector for whose future Holmes had high hopes, while he in turn professed the admiration and respect of a pupil for the scientific methods of the famous amateur. Hopkins's brow was clouded, and he sat down with an air of deep dejection.

'No, thank you, sir. I breakfasted before I came round. I spent the night in town, for I came up yesterday to report.'

'And what had you to report?'

'Failure, sir; absolute failure.'

'You have made no progress?'

'None.'

'Dear me! I must have a look at the matter.'

'I wish to heavens that you would, Mr Holmes. It's my first big chance, and I am at my wit's end. For goodness' sake come down and lend me a hand.'

'Well, well, it just happens that I have already read

all the available evidence, including the report of the inquest, with some care. By the way, what do you make of that tobacco-pouch found on the scene of the crime? Is there no clue there?'

Hopkins looked surprised.

'It was the man's own pouch, sir. His initials were inside it. And it was of sealskin – and he an old sealer.'

'But he had no pipe.'

'No, sir, we could find no pipe; indeed, he smoked very little. And yet he might have kept some tobacco for his friends.'

'No doubt. I only mention it because if I had been handling the case I should have been inclined to make that the starting-point of my investigation. However, my friend Dr Watson knows nothing of this matter, and I should be none the worse for hearing the sequence of events once more. Just give us some short sketch of the essentials.'

Stanley Hopkins drew a slip of paper from his pocket.

'I have a few dates here which will give you the career of the dead man, Captain Peter Carey. He was born in 1845 – fifty years of age. He was a most daring and successful seal and whale fisher. In 1883 he commanded the steam sealer *Sea Unicorn*, of Dundee. He had then had several successful voyages in succession, and in the following year, 1884, he retired. After that he travelled for some years, and finally he bought a small place called Woodman's Lee, near Forest Row, in Sussex. There he has lived for six years, and there he died just a week ago today.

'There were some most singular points about the man. In ordinary life he was a strict Puritan – a silent, gloomy fellow. His household consisted of his wife, his daughter, aged twenty, and two female servants. These last were continually changing, for it was never a very cheery situation, and sometimes it became past all bearing. The man was an intermittent drunkard, and when he had the fit on him he was a perfect fiend. He has been known to drive his wife and his daughter out of doors in the middle of the night, and flog them through the park until the whole village outside the gates was aroused by their screams.

'He was summoned once for a savage assault upon the old vicar, who had called upon him to remonstrate with him upon his conduct. In short, Mr Holmes, you would go far before you found a more dangerous man than Peter Carey, and I have heard that he bore the same character when he commanded his ship. He was known in the trade as Black Peter, and the name was given him, not only on account of his swarthy features and the colour of his huge beard, but for the humours which were the terror of all around him. I need not say that he was loathed and avoided by every one of his neighbours, and that I have not heard one single word of sorrow about his terrible end.

'You must have read in the account of the inquest about the man's cabin, Mr Holmes; but perhaps your friend here has not heard of it. He had built himself a wooden outhouse – he always called it "the cabin" – a few hundred yards from his house, and it was here that he slept every night. It was a little, single-roomed hut, sixteen feet by ten. He kept the key in his pocket, made his own bed, cleaned it himself, and allowed no other foot to cross the threshold. There are small windows on each side, which were covered by curtains and never opened. One of these windows was turned towards the high road, and when the light burned in it at night the folk used to point it out to each other and wonder what Black Peter was doing in there. That's the window, Mr Holmes, which gave us one of the few bits of positive evidence that came out at the inquest.

'You remember that a stonemason, named Slater, walking from Forest Row about one o'clock in the morning – two days before the murder – stopped as he passed the grounds and looked at the square of light still shining among the trees. He swears that the shadow of a man's head turned sideways was clearly visible on the blind, and that this shadow was certainly not that of Peter Carey, whom he knew well. It was that of a bearded man, but the beard was short and bristled forwards in a way very different from that of the captain. So he says, but he had been two hours in the public-house, and it is some distance from the road to the window. Besides, this refers to the Monday, and the crime was done upon the Wednesday.

'On the Tuesday Peter Carey was in one of his blackest moods, flushed with drink and as savage as a dangerous wild beast. He roamed about the house, and the women ran for it when they heard him coming. Late in the evening he went down to his own hut. About two o'clock the following morning his daughter, who slept with her window open, heard a most fearful yell from that direction, but it was no unusual thing for him to bawl and shout when he was in drink, so no notice was taken. On rising at seven one of the maids noticed that the door of the hut was open, but so great was the terror which the man caused that it was midday before anyone would venture down to see what had become of him. Peeping into the open door they saw a sight which sent them flying with white faces into the village.

Within an hour I was on the spot and had taken over the case.

'Well, I have fairly steady nerves, as you know, Mr Holmes, but I give you my word that I got a shake when I put my head into that little house. It was droning like a harmonium with the flies and bluebottles, and the floor and walls were like a slaughterhouse. He had called it a cabin, and a cabin it was sure enough, for you would have thought that you were in a ship. There was a bunk at one end, a sea-chest, maps and charts, a picture of the *Sea Unicorn*, a line of logbooks on a shelf, all exactly as one would expect to find it in a captain's room. And there in the middle of it was the man himself, his face twisted like a lost soul in torment, and his great brindled beard stuck upwards in his agony. Right through his broad breast a steel harpoon had been driven, and it had sunk deep into the wood of the wall behind him. He was pinned like a beetle on a card. Of course, he was quite dead, and had been so from the instant that he had uttered that last yell of agony.

'I know your methods, sir, and I applied them. Before I permitted anything to be moved I examined most carefully the ground outside, and also the floor of the room. There were no footmarks.'

'Meaning that you saw none?'

'I assure you, sir, that there were none.'

'My good Hopkins, I have investigated many crimes, but I have never yet seen one which was committed by a flying creature. As long as the criminal remains upon two legs so long must there be some indentation, some abrasion, some trifling displacement which can be detected by the scientific searcher. It is incredible that this blood-bespattered room contained no trace which could have aided us. I understand, however, from the inquest that there were some objects which you failed to overlook?'

The young inspector winced at my companion's ironical comments.

'I was a fool not to call you in at the time, Mr Holmes. However, that's past praying for now. Yes, there were several objects in the room which called for special attention. One was the harpoon with which the deed was committed. It had been snatched down from a rack on the wall. Two others remained there, and there was a vacant place for the third. On the stock was engraved "S.S. *Sea Unicorn*, Dundee". This seemed to establish that the crime had been done in a moment of fury, and that the murderer had seized the first weapon which came in his way. The fact that the crime was committed at two in the morning, and yet Peter Carey was fully dressed, suggested that he had an appointment with the murderer, which is borne out by the fact that a bottle of rum and two dirty glasses stood upon the table.'

'Yes,' said Holmes; 'I think that both inferences are permissible. Was there any other spirit but rum in the room?'

'Yes; there was a tantalus containing brandy and whisky on the sea-chest. It is of no importance to us, however, since the decanters were full, and it had therefore not been used.'

'For all that its presence has some significance,' said Holmes. 'However, let us hear some more about the objects which do seem to you to bear upon the case.'

'There was this tobacco-pouch upon the table.'

'What part of the table?'

'It lay in the middle. It was of coarse sealskin – the straight-haired skin, with a leather thong to bind it.

Inside was "P.C." on the flap. There was half an ounce of strong ship's tobacco in it.'

'Excellent! What more?'

Stanley Hopkins drew from his pocket a drab-covered notebook. The outside was rough and worn, the leaves discoloured. On the first page were written the initials 'J.H.N.' and the date '1883'. Holmes laid it on the table and examined it in his minute way, while Hopkins and I gazed over each shoulder. On the second page were the printed letters 'C.P.R.', and then came several sheets of numbers. Another heading was Argentine, another Costa Rica, and another San Paulo, each with pages of signs and figures after it.

'What do you make of these?' asked Holmes.

'They appear to be lists of Stock Exchange securities. I thought that "J.H.N." were the initials of a broker, and that "C.P.R." may have been his client.'

'Try Canadian Pacific Railway,' said Holmes.

Stanley Hopkins swore between his teeth and struck his thigh with his clenched hand.

'What a fool I have been!' he cried. 'Of course, it is as you say. Then "J.H.N." are the only initials we have to solve. I have already examined the old Stock Exchange lists, and I can find no one in 1883 either in the House or among the outside brokers whose initials correspond with these. Yet I feel that the clue is the most important one that I hold. You will admit, Mr Holmes, that there is a possibility that these initials are those of the second person who was present – in other words, of the murderer. I would also urge that the introduction into the case of a document relating to large masses of valuable securities gives us for the first time some indication of a motive for the crime.'

Sherlock Holmes's face showed that he was

thoroughly taken aback by this new development.

'I must admit both your points,' said he. 'I confess that this notebook, which did not appear at the inquest, modifies any views which I may have formed. I had come to a theory of the crime in which I can find no place for this. Have you endeavoured to trace any of the securities here mentioned?'

'Enquiries are now being made at the offices, but I fear that the complete register of the stockholders of these South American concerns is in South America, and that some weeks must elapse before we can trace the shares.'

Holmes had been examining the cover of the note-book with his magnifying lens.

'Surely there is some discoloration here,' said he.

'Yes, sir, it is a bloodstain. I told you that I picked the book off the floor.'

'Was the bloodstain above or below?'

'On the side next the boards.'

'Which proves, of course, that the book was dropped after the crime was committed.'

'Exactly, Mr Holmes. I appreciated that point, and I conjectured that it was dropped by the murderer in his hurried flight. It lay near the door.'

'I suppose that none of these securities have been found among the property of the dead man?'

'No, sir.'

'Have you any reason to suspect robbery?'

'No, sir. Nothing seemed to have been touched.'

'Dear me, it is certainly a very interesting case. Then there was a knife, was there not?'

'A sheath-knife, still in its sheath. It lay at the feet of the dead man. Mrs Carey has identified it as being her husband's property.'

Holmes was lost in thought for some time.

'Well,' said he, at last, 'I suppose I shall have to come out and have a look at it.'

Stanley Hopkins gave a cry of joy.

'Thank you, sir. That will indeed be a weight off my mind.'

Holmes shook his finger at the inspector.

'It would have been an easier task a week ago,' said he. 'But even now my visit may not be entirely fruitless. Watson, if you can spare the time I should be very glad of your company. If you will call a four-wheeler, Hopkins, we shall be ready to start for Forest Row in a quarter of an hour.'

Alighting at the small wayside station, we drove for some miles through the remains of widespread woods, which were once part of that great forest which for so long held the Saxon invaders at bay – the impenetrable 'weald', for sixty years the bulwark of Britain. Vast sections of it have been cleared, for this is the seat of the first ironworks of the country, and the trees have been felled to smelt the ore. Now the richer fields of the north have absorbed the trade, and nothing save these ravaged groves and great scars in the earth show the work of the past. Here in a clearing upon the green slope of a hill stood a long, low stone house, approached by a curving drive running through the fields. Nearer the road, and surrounded on three sides by bushes, was a small outhouse, one window and the door facing in our direction. It was the scene of the murder!

Stanley Hopkins led us first to the house, where he introduced us to a haggard, grey-haired woman, the widow of the murdered man, whose gaunt and deep-lined face, with the furtive look of terror in the depths of her red-rimmed eyes, told of the years of hardship and ill-usage which she had endured. With her was her daughter, a pale, fair-haired girl, whose eyes blazed defiantly at us as she told us that she was glad that her father was dead, and that she blessed the hand which had struck him down. It was a terrible household that Black Peter Carey had made for himself, and it was with a sense of relief that we found ourselves in the sunlight again and making our way along a path which had been worn across the fields by the feet of the dead man.

The outhouse was the simplest of dwellings, wooden-walled, shingle-roofed, one window beside the door and one on the farther side. Stanley Hopkins drew the key from his pocket, and had stooped to the lock, when he paused with a look of attention and surprise upon his face.

'Someone has been tampering with it,' he said.

There could be no doubt of the fact. The woodwork was cut and the scratches showed white through the paint, as if they had been that instant done. Holmes had been examining the window.

'Someone has tried to force this also. Whoever it was has failed to make his way in. He must have been a very poor burglar.'

'This is a most extraordinary thing,' said the inspector; 'I could swear that these marks were not here yesterday evening.'

'Some curious person from the village, perhaps,' I suggested.

'Very unlikely. Few of them would dare to set foot in the grounds, far less try to force their way into the cabin. What do you think of it, Mr Holmes?'

'I think that fortune is very kind to us.'

'You mean that the person will come again?'

'It is very probable. He came expecting to find the door open. He tried to get in with the blade of a very small penknife. He could not manage it. What would he do?'

'Come again next night with a more useful tool.'

'So I should say. It will be our fault if we are not there to receive him. Meanwhile, let me see the inside of the cabin.'

The traces of the tragedy had been removed, but the furniture within the little room still stood as it had been on the night of the crime. For two hours, with most intense concentration, Holmes examined every object in turn, but his face showed that his quest was not a successful one. Once only he paused in his patient investigation.

'Have you taken anything off this shelf, Hopkins?'

'No; I have moved nothing.'

'Something has been taken. There is less dust in this corner of the shelf than elsewhere. It may have been a book lying on its side. It may have been a box. Well, well, I can do nothing more. Let us walk in these beautiful woods, Watson, and give a few hours to the birds and the flowers. We shall meet you here later, Hopkins, and see if we can come to closer quarters with the gentleman who has paid this visit in the night.'

It was past eleven o'clock when we formed our little ambuscade. Hopkins was for leaving the door of the hut open, but Holmes was of the opinion that this would rouse the suspicions of the stranger. The lock was a perfectly simple one, and only a strong blade was needed to push it back. Holmes also suggested that we should wait, not inside the hut, but outside it among the bushes which grew round the farther window. In this way we should be able to watch our man if he struck a light, and see what his object was in this stealthy nocturnal visit.

It was a long and melancholy vigil, and yet brought with it something of the thrill which the hunter feels when he lies beside the water pool and waits for the coming of the thirsty beast of prey. What savage creature was it which might steal upon us out of the darkness? Was it a fierce tiger of crime, which could only be taken fighting hard with flashing fang and claw, or would it prove to be some skulking jackal, dangerous only to the weak and unguarded?

In absolute silence we crouched amongst the bushes, waiting for whatever might come. At first the steps of a few belated villagers, or the sound of voices from the village, lightened our vigil; but one by one these interruptions died away and an absolute stillness fell upon us, save for the chimes of the distant church, which told us of the progress of the night, and for the rustle and whisper of a fine rain falling amid the foliage which roofed us in.

Half-past two had chimed, and it was the darkest hour which precedes the dawn, when we all started as a low but sharp click came from the direction of the gate. Someone had entered the drive. Again there was a long silence, and I had begun to fear that it was a false alarm, when a stealthy step was heard upon the other side of the hut, and a moment later a metallic scraping and clinking. The man was trying to force the lock! This time his skill was greater or his tool was better, for there was a sudden snap and the creak of the hinges. Then a match was struck, and next instant the steady light from a candle filled the interior of the hut.

Through the gauze curtain our eyes were all riveted upon the scene within.

The nocturnal visitor was a young man, frail and thin, with a black moustache which intensified the deadly pallor of his face. He could not have been much above twenty years of age. I have never seen any human being who appeared to be in such a pitiable fright, for his teeth were visibly chattering and he was shaking in every limb. He was dressed like a gentleman, in Norfolk jacket and knickerbockers, with a cloth cap upon his head. We watched him staring round with frightened eyes. Then he laid the candle-end upon the table and disappeared from our view into one of the corners. He returned with a large book, one of the logbooks which formed a line upon the shelves. Leaning on the table he rapidly turned over the leaves of this volume until he came to the entry which he sought. Then, with an angry gesture of his clenched hand, he closed the book, replaced it in the corner, and put out the light. He had hardly turned to leave the hut when Hopkins's hand was on the fellow's collar, and I heard his loud gasp of terror as he understood that he was taken. The candle was re-lit, and there was our wretched captive shivering and cowering in the grasp of the detective. He sank down upon the sea-chest, and looked helplessly from one of us to the other.

'Now, my fine fellow,' said Stanley Hopkins, 'who are you, and what do you want here?'

The man pulled himself together and faced us with an effort at self-composure.

'You are detectives, I suppose?' said he. 'You imagine I am connected with the death of Captain Peter Carey. I assure you that I am innocent.'

'We'll see about that,' said Hopkins. 'First of all, what is your name?'

'It is John Hopley Neligan.'

I saw Holmes and Hopkins exchange a quick glance.

'What are you doing here?'

'Can I speak confidentially?'

'No, certainly not.'

'Why should I tell you?'

'If you have no answer it may go badly with you at the trial.'

The young man winced.

'Well, I will tell you,' he said. 'Why should I not? And yet I hate to think of this old scandal gaining a new lease of life. Did you ever hear of Dawson and Neligan?'

I could see from Hopkins's face that he never had; but Holmes was keenly interested.

'You mean the West Country bankers,' said he. 'They failed for a million, ruined half the county families of Cornwall, and Neligan disappeared.'

'Exactly. Neligan was my father.'

At last we were getting something positive, and yet it seemed a long gap between an absconding banker and Captain Peter Carey pinned against the wall with one of his own harpoons. We all listened intently to the young man's words.

'It was my father who was really concerned. Dawson had retired. I was only ten years of age at the time, but I was old enough to feel the shame and horror of it all. It has always been said that my father stole all the securities and fled. It is not true. It was his belief that if he were given time in which to realise them all would be well and every creditor paid in full. He started in his little yacht for Norway just before the warrant was issued for his arrest. I can remember that last night when he bade farewell to my mother. He left us a list of the securities he was taking, and he swore that he would come back with his honour cleared, and that none who had trusted him would suffer. Well, no word was ever heard from him again. Both the yacht and he vanished utterly. We believed, my mother and I, that he and it, with the securities that he had taken with him, were at the bottom of the sea. We had a faithful friend, however, who is a business man, and it was he who discovered some time ago that some of the securities which my father had with him have reappeared on the London market. You can imagine our amazement. I spent months in trying to trace them, and at last, after many doublings and difficulties, I discovered that the original seller had been Captain Peter Carey, the owner of this hut.

'Naturally, I made some enquiries about the man. I found that he had been in command of a whaler which was due to return from the Arctic seas at the very time when my father was crossing to Norway. The autumn of that year was a stormy one, and there was a long succession of southerly gales. My father's yacht may well have been blown to the north, and there met by Captain Peter Carey's ship. If that were so, what had become of my father? In any case, if I could prove from Peter Carey's evidence how these securities came on the market it would be a proof that my father had not sold them, and that he had no view to personal profit when he took them.

'I came down to Sussex with the intention of seeing the captain, but it was at this moment that his terrible death occurred. I read at the inquest a description of his cabin, in which it stated that the old logbooks of his vessel were preserved in it. It struck me that if I could see what occurred in the month of August, 1883, on board the *Sea Unicorn*, I might settle the mystery of my father's fate. I tried last night to get at these logbooks, but was unable to open the door. Tonight I tried again, and succeeded; but I find that the pages which deal with that month have been torn from the book. It was at that moment I found myself a prisoner in your hands.'

'Is that all?' asked Hopkins.

'Yes, that is all.' His eyes shifted as he said it.

'You have nothing else to tell us?'

He hesitated.

'No; there is nothing.'

'You have not been here before last night?'

'No.'

'Then how do you account for *that*?' cried Hopkins, as he held up the damning notebook, with the initials of our prisoner on the first leaf and the bloodstain on the cover.

The wretched man collapsed. He sank his face in his hands and trembled all over.

'Where did you get it?' he groaned. 'I did not know. I thought I had lost it at the hotel.'

'That is enough,' said Hopkins, sternly. 'Whatever else you have to say you must say in court. You will walk down with me now to the police-station. Well, Mr Holmes, I am very much obliged to you and to your friend for coming down to help me. As it turns out your presence was unnecessary, and I would have brought the case to this successful issue without you; but none the less I am very grateful. Rooms have been reserved for you at the Brambletye Hotel, so we can all walk down to the village together.'

'Well, Watson, what do you think of it?' asked Holmes, as we travelled back next morning.

'I can see that you are not satisfied.'

'Oh, yes, my dear Watson, I am perfectly satisfied. At the same time Stanley Hopkins's methods do not commend themselves to me. I am disappointed in Stanley Hopkins. I had hoped for better things from him. One should always look for a possible alternative and provide against it. It is the first rule of criminal investigation.'

'What, then, is the alternative?'

'The line of investigation which I have myself been pursuing. It may give us nothing. I cannot tell. But at least I shall follow it to the end.'

Several letters were waiting for Holmes at Baker Street. He snatched one of them up, opened it, and burst out into a triumphant chuckle of laughter.

'Excellent, Watson. The alternative develops. Have you telegraph forms? Just write a couple of messages for me: "Sumner, Shipping Agent, Ratcliff Highway. Send three men on, to arrive ten tomorrow morning. – Basil." That's my name in those parts. The other is: "Inspector Stanley Hopkins, 46 Lord Street, Brixton. Come breakfast tomorrow at nine-thirty. Important. Wire if unable to come. – Sherlock Holmes." There, Watson, this infernal case has haunted me for ten days. I hereby banish it completely from my presence. Tomorrow I trust that we shall hear the last of it for ever.'

Sharp at the hour named Inspector Stanley Hopkins appeared, and we sat down together to the excellent breakfast which Mrs Hudson had prepared. The young detective was in high spirits at his success.

'You really think that your solution must be correct?' asked Holmes.

'I could not imagine a more complete case.'

'It did not seem to me conclusive.'

'You astonish me, Mr Holmes. What more could one ask for?'

'Does your explanation cover every point?'

'Undoubtedly. I find that young Neligan arrived at the Brambletye Hotel on the very day of the crime. He came on the pretence of playing golf. His room was on the ground floor, and he could get out when he liked. That very night he went down to Woodman's Lee, saw Peter Carey at the hut, quarrelled with him, and killed him with the harpoon. Then, horrified by what he had done, he fled out of the hut, dropping the notebook which he had brought with him in order to question Peter Carey about these different securities. You may have observed that some of them were marked with ticks, and the others – the great majority – were not. Those which are ticked have been traced on the London market; but the others presumably were still in the possession of Carey, and young Neligan, according to his own account, was anxious to recover them in order to do the right thing by his father's creditors. After his flight he did not dare to approach the hut again for some time; but at last he forced himself to do so in order to obtain the information which he needed. Surely that is all simple and obvious?'

Holmes smiled and shook his head.

'It seems to me to have only one drawback, Hopkins, and that is that it is intrinsically impossible. Have you tried to drive a harpoon through a body? No? Tut, tut, my dear sir, you must really pay attention to these details. My friend Watson could tell you that I spent a whole morning in that exercise. It is no easy matter, and requires a strong and practised arm. But this blow was delivered with such violence that the head of the weapon sank deep into the wall. Do you imagine that this anaemic youth was capable of so frightful an assault? Is he the man who hobnobbed in rum and water with Black Peter in the dead of the night? Was it his profile that was seen on the blind two nights before? No, no, Hopkins; it is another and a more formidable person for whom we must seek.'

The detective's face had grown longer and longer during Holmes's speech. His hopes and his ambitions were all crumbling about him. But he would not abandon his position without a struggle.

'You can't deny that Neligan was present that night, Mr Holmes. The book will prove that. I fancy that I have evidence enough to satisfy a jury, even if you are able to pick a hole in it. Besides, Mr Holmes, I have laid my hand upon *my* man. As to this terrible person of yours, where is he?'

'I rather fancy that he is on the stair,' said Holmes, serenely. 'I think, Watson, that you would do well to put that revolver where you can reach it.' He rose, and laid a written paper upon a side-table. 'Now we are ready,' said he.

There had been some talking in gruff voices outside, and now Mrs Hudson opened the door to say that there were three men enquiring for Captain Basil.

'Show them in one by one,' said Holmes.

The first who entered was a little ribston-pippin of a man, with ruddy cheeks and fluffy white side-whiskers. Holmes had drawn a letter from his pocket.

'What name?' he asked.

'James Lancaster.'

'I am sorry, Lancaster, but the berth is full. Here is

half a sovereign for your trouble. Just step into this room and wait there for a few minutes.'

The second man was a long, dried-up creature, with lank hair and sallow cheeks. His name was Hugh Pattins. He also received his dismissal, his half-sovereign, and the order to wait.

The third applicant was a man of remarkable appearance. A fierce bulldog face was framed in a tangle of hair and beard, and two bold dark eyes gleamed behind the cover of thick, tufted, overhung eyebrows. He saluted and stood sailor-fashion, turning his cap round in his hands.

'Your name?' asked Holmes.

'Patrick Cairns.'

'Harpooner?'

'Yes, sir. Twenty-six voyages.'

'Dundee, I suppose?'

'Yes, sir.'

'And ready to start with an exploring ship?'

'Yes, sir.'

'What wages?'

'Eight pounds a month.'

'Could you start at once?'

'As soon as I get my kit.'

'Have you your papers?'

'Yes, sir.' He took a sheaf of worn and greasy forms from his pocket. Holmes glanced over them and returned them.

'You are just the man I want,' said he. 'Here's the agreement on the side-table. If you sign it the whole matter will be settled.'

The seaman lurched across the room and took up the pen.

'Shall I sign here?' he asked, stooping over the table.

Holmes leaned over his shoulder and passed both hands over his neck.

'This will do,' said he.

I heard a click of steel and a bellow like an enraged bull. The next instant Holmes and the seaman were rolling on the ground together. He was a man of such gigantic strength that, even with the handcuffs which Holmes had so deftly fastened upon his wrists, he would have very quickly overpowered my friend had Hopkins and I not rushed to his rescue. Only when I pressed the cold muzzle of the revolver to his temple did he at last understand that resistance was vain. We lashed his ankles with cord and rose breathless from the struggle.

'I must really apologise, Hopkins,' said Sherlock Holmes; 'I fear that the scrambled eggs are cold. However, you will enjoy the rest of your breakfast all the better, will you not, for the thought that you have brought your case to a triumphant conclusion.'

Stanley Hopkins was speechless with amazement.

'I don't know what to say, Mr Holmes,' he blurted out at last, with a very red face. 'It seems to me that I have been making a fool of myself from the beginning. I understand now, what I should never have forgotten, that I am the pupil and you are the master. Even now I see what you have done, but I don't know how you did it, or what it signifies.'

'Well, well,' said Holmes, good-humouredly. 'We all learn by experience, and your lesson this time is that you should never lose sight of the alternative. You were so absorbed in young Neligan that you could not spare a thought to Patrick Cairns, the true murderer of Peter Carey.'

The hoarse voice of the seaman broke in on our conversation.

'See here, mister,' said he, 'I make no complaint of being manhandled in this fashion, but I would have you call things by their right names. You say I murdered Peter Carey; I say I *killed* Peter Carey, and there's all the difference. Maybe you don't believe what I say. Maybe you think I am just slinging you a yarn.'

'Not at all,' said Holmes. 'Let us hear what you have to say.'

'It's soon told, and, by the Lord, every word of it is truth. I knew Black Peter, and when he pulled out his knife I whipped a harpoon through him sharp, for I knew that it was him or me. That's how he died. You can call it murder. Anyhow, I'd as soon die with a rope round my neck as with Black Peter's knife in my heart.'

'How came you there?' asked Holmes.

'I'll tell it you from the beginning. Just sit me up a little so as I can speak easy. It was in 1883 that it happened – August of that year. Peter Carey was master of the *Sea Unicorn*, and I was spare harpooner. We were coming out of the ice-pack on our way home, with head winds and a week's southerly gale, when we picked up a little craft that had been blown north. There was one man on her – a landsman. The crew had thought she would founder, and had made for the Norwegian coast in the dinghy. I guess they were all drowned. Well, we took him on board, this man, and he and the skipper had some long talks in the cabin. All the baggage we took off with him was one tin box. So far as I know, the man's name was never mentioned, and on the second night he disappeared as if he had never been. It was given out that he had either thrown himself overboard or fallen overboard in the heavy weather that we were having. Only one man knew what had happened to him, and that was me, for with my own eyes I saw the skipper tip up his heels and put him over the rail in the middle watch of a dark night, two days before we sighted the Shetland lights.

'Well, I kept my knowledge to myself and waited to see what would come of it. When we got back to Scotland it was easily hushed up, and nobody asked any questions. A stranger died by an accident, and it was nobody's business to enquire. Shortly after Peter Carey gave up the sea, and it was long years before I could find where he was. I guessed that he had done the deed for the sake of what was in that tin box, and that he could afford now to pay me well for keeping my mouth shut.

'I found out where he was through a sailor man that had met him in London, and down I went to squeeze him. The first night he was reasonable enough, and was ready to give me what would make me free of the sea for life. We were to fix it all two nights later. When I came I found him three parts drunk and in a vile temper. We sat down and we drank and we yarned about old times, but the more he drank the less I liked the look on his face. I spotted that harpoon upon the wall, and I thought I might need it before I was through. Then at last he broke out at me, spitting and cursing, with murder in his eyes and a great clasp-knife in his hand. He had not time to get it from the sheath before I had the harpoon through him. Heavens! what a yell he gave; and his face gets between me and my sleep! I stood there, with his blood splashing round me, and I waited for a bit; but all was quiet, so I took heart once more. I looked round, and there was the tin box on a shelf. I had as much right to it as Peter Carey,

193

anyhow, so I took it with me and left the hut. Like a
fool I left my baccy-pouch upon the table.

'Now I'll tell you the queerest part of the whole
story. I had hardly got outside the hut when I heard
someone coming, and I hid among the bushes. A man
came slinking along, went into the hut, gave a cry as if
he had seen a ghost, and legged it as hard as he could
run until he was out of sight. Who he was or what he
wanted is more than I can tell. For my part I walked
ten miles, got a train at Tunbridge Wells, and so
reached London, and no one the wiser.

'Well, when I came to examine the box I found there
was no money in it, and nothing but papers that I would
not dare to sell. I had lost my hold on Black Peter, and
was stranded in London without a shilling. There was
only my trade left. I saw these advertisements about
harpooners and high wages, so I went to the shipping
agents, and they sent me here. That's all I know, and I
say again that if I killed Black Peter the law should give
me thanks, for I saved them the price of a hempen rope.'

'A very clear statement,' said Holmes, rising and
lighting his pipe. 'I think, Hopkins, that you should lose
no time in conveying your prisoner to a place of safety.
This room is not well adapted for a cell, and Mr Patrick
Cairns occupies too large a proportion of our carpet.'

'Mr Holmes,' said Hopkins, 'I do not know how to
express my gratitude. Even now I do not understand
how you attained this result.'

'Simply by having the good fortune to get the right
clue from the beginning. It is very possible if I had
known about this notebook it might have led away my
thoughts, as it did yours. But all I heard pointed in the
one direction. The amazing strength, the skill in the
use of the harpoon, the rum and water, the sealskin

tobacco-pouch, with the coarse tobacco – all these pointed to a seaman, and one who had been a whaler. I was convinced that the initials "P.C." upon the pouch were a coincidence, and not those of Peter Carey, since he seldom smoked, and no pipe was found in his cabin. You remember that I asked whether whisky and brandy were in the cabin. You said they were. How many landsmen are there who would drink rum when they could get these other spirits? Yes, I was certain it was a seaman.'

'And how did you find him?'

'My dear sir, the problem had become a very simple one. If it were a seaman, it could only be a seaman who had been with him on the *Sea Unicorn*. So far as I could learn he had sailed in no other ship. I spent three days in wiring to Dundee, and at the end of that time I had ascertained the names of the crew of the *Sea Unicorn* in 1883. When I found Patrick Cairns among the harpooners my research was nearing its end. I argued that the man was probably in London, and that he would desire to leave the country for a time. I therefore spent some days in the East End, devised an Arctic expedition, put forth tempting terms for harpooners who would serve under Captain Basil – and behold the result!'

'Wonderful!' cried Hopkins. 'Wonderful!'

'You must obtain the release of young Neligan as soon as possible,' said Holmes. 'I confess that I think you owe him some apology. The tin box must be returned to him, but, of course, the securities which Peter Carey has sold are lost for ever. There's the cab, Hopkins, and you can remove your man. If you want me for the trial, my address and that of Watson will be somewhere in Norway – I'll send particulars later.'

7

Charles Augustus Milverton

It is years since the incidents of which I speak took place, and yet it is with diffidence that I allude to them. For a long time, even with the utmost discretion and reticence, it would have been impossible to make the facts public; but now the principal person concerned is beyond the reach of human law, and with due suppression the story may be told in such fashion as to injure no one. It records an absolutely unique experience in the career both of Mr Sherlock Holmes and of myself. The reader will excuse me if I conceal the date or any other fact by which he might trace the actual occurrence.

We had been out for one of our evening rambles, Holmes and I, and had returned about six o'clock on a cold, frosty winter's evening. As Holmes turned up the lamp the light fell upon a card on the table. He glanced at it, and then, with an ejaculation of disgust, threw it on the floor. I picked it up and read:

CHARLES AUGUSTUS MILVERTON
Appledore Towers
Agent   *Hampstead*

'Who is he?' I asked.

'The worst man in London,' Holmes answered, as he sat down and stretched his legs before the fire. 'Is anything on the back of the card?'

I turned it over.

'Will call at 6.30 – C.A.M.,' I read.

'Hum! He's about due. Do you feel a creeping, shrinking sensation, Watson, when you stand before the serpents in the Zoo and see the slithery, gliding, venomous creatures, with their deadly eyes and wicked, flattened faces? Well, that's how Milverton impresses me. I've had to do with fifty murderers in my career, but the worst of them never gave me the repulsion which I have for this fellow. And yet I can't get out of doing business with him – indeed, he is here at my invitation.'

'But who is he?'

'I'll tell you, Watson. He is the king of all the blackmailers. Heaven help the man, and still more the woman, whose secret and reputation come into the power of Milverton. With a smiling face and a heart of marble he will squeeze and squeeze until he has drained them dry. The fellow is a genius in his way, and would have made his mark in some more savoury trade. His method is as follows: He allows it to be known that he is prepared to pay very high sums for letters which compromise people of wealth or position. He receives these wares not only from treacherous valets or maids, but frequently from genteel ruffians who have gained the confidence and affection of trusting women. He deals with no niggard hand. I happen to know that he paid seven hundred pounds to a footman for a note two lines in length, and that the ruin of a noble family was the result. Everything which is in the market goes to Milverton, and there are hundreds in this great city who turn white at his name. No one knows where his grip may fall, for he is far too rich and far too cunning to work from hand to mouth. He will hold a card back for years in order to play it at the moment when the stake is best worth winning. I have said that he is the worst man in London, and I would ask you how could one compare the ruffian who in hot blood bludgeons his mate with this man, who methodically and at his leisure tortures the soul and wrings the nerves in order to add to his already swollen money-bags?'

I had seldom heard my friend speak with such intensity of feeling.

'But surely,' said I, 'the fellow must be within the grasp of the law?'

'Technically, no doubt, but practically not. What would it profit a woman, for example, to get him a few months' imprisonment if her own ruin must immediately follow? His victims dare not hit back. If ever he blackmailed an innocent person, then, indeed, we should have him; but he is as cunning as the Evil One. No, no; we must find other ways to fight him.'

'And why is he here?'

'Because an illustrious client has placed her piteous case in my hands. It is the Lady Eva Brackwell, the most beautiful débutante of last season. She is to be married in a fortnight to the Earl of Dovercourt. This fiend has several imprudent letters – imprudent, Watson, nothing worse – which were written to an impecunious young squire in the country. They would suffice to break off the match. Milverton will send the letters to the Earl unless a large sum of money is paid him. I have been commissioned to meet him, and – to make the best terms I can.'

At that instant there was a clatter and a rattle in the street below. Looking down I saw a stately carriage and pair, the brilliant lamps gleaming on the glossy haunches of the noble chestnuts. A footman opened the door, and a small, stout man in a shaggy astrakhan overcoat descended. A minute later he was in the room.

Charles Augustus Milverton was a man of fifty, with a large, intellectual head, a round, plump, hairless face, a perpetual frozen smile, and two keen grey eyes, which gleamed brightly from behind broad, golden-rimmed glasses. There was something of Mr Pickwick's benevolence in his appearance, marred only by the insincerity of the fixed smile and by the hard glitter of those restless and penetrating eyes. His voice was as smooth and suave as his countenance, as he advanced with a plump little hand extended, murmuring his regret for having missed us at his first visit. Holmes disregarded the outstretched hand and looked at him with a face of granite. Milverton's smile broadened; he shrugged his shoulders, removed his overcoat, folded it with great deliberation over the back of a chair, and then took a seat.

'This gentleman?' said he, with a wave in my direction. 'Is it discreet? Is it right?'

'Dr Watson is my friend and partner.'

'Very good, Mr Holmes. It is only in your client's interests that I protested. The matter is so very delicate – '

'Dr Watson has already heard of it.'

'Then we can proceed to business. You say that you are acting for Lady Eva. Has she empowered you to accept my terms?'

'What are your terms?'

'Seven thousand pounds.'

'And the alternative?'

'My dear sir, it is painful for me to discuss it; but if the money is not paid on the 14th there certainly will be no marriage on the 18th.' His insufferable smile was more complacent than ever.

Holmes thought for a little.

'You appear to me,' he said, at last, 'to be taking matters too much for granted. I am, of course, familiar with the contents of these letters. My client will certainly do what I may advise. I shall counsel her to tell her future husband the whole story and to trust to his generosity.'

Milverton chuckled.

'You evidently do not know the Earl,' said he.

From the baffled look upon Holmes's face I could see clearly that he did.

'What harm is there in the letters?' he asked.

'They are sprightly – very sprightly,' Milverton answered. 'The lady was a charming correspondent. But I can assure you that the Earl of Dovercourt would fail to appreciate them. However, since you think otherwise, we will let it rest at that. It is purely a matter of business. If you think that it is in the best interests of your client that these letters should be placed in the hands of the Earl, then you would indeed be foolish to pay so large a sum of money to regain them.' He rose and seized his astrakhan coat.

Holmes was grey with anger and mortification.

'Wait a little,' he said. 'You go too fast. We would certainly make every effort to avoid scandal in so delicate a matter.'

Milverton relapsed into his chair.

'I was sure that you would see it in that light,' he purred.

'At the same time,' Holmes continued, 'Lady Eva is not a wealthy woman. I assure you that two thousand pounds would be a drain upon her resources, and that the sum you name is utterly beyond her power. I beg, therefore, that you will moderate your demands, and that you will return the letters at the price I indicate, which is, I assure you, the highest that you can get.'

Milverton's smile broadened and his eyes twinkled humorously.

'I am aware that what you say is true about the lady's resources,' said he. 'At the same time, you must admit that the occasion of a lady's marriage is a very suitable time for her friends and relatives to make some little effort upon her behalf. They may hesitate as to an acceptable wedding present. Let me assure them that this little bundle of letters would give more joy than all the candelabra and butter-dishes in London.'

'It is impossible,' said Holmes.

'Dear me, dear me, how unfortunate!' cried Milverton, taking out a bulky pocketbook. 'I cannot help thinking that ladies are ill-advised in not making an effort. Look at this!' He held up a little note with a coat-of-arms upon the envelope. 'That belongs to – well, perhaps it is hardly fair to tell the name until tomorrow morning. But at that time it will be in the hands of the lady's husband. And all because she will not find a beggarly sum which she could get by turning her diamonds into paste. It *is* such a pity. Now, you remember the sudden end of the engagement between the Honourable Miss Miles and Colonel Dorking? Only two days before the wedding there was a paragraph in the *Morning Post* to say that it was all off. And why? It is almost incredible, but the absurd sum of twelve hundred pounds would have settled the whole question. Is it not pitiful? And here I find you, a man of sense, boggling about terms when your client's future and honour are at stake. You surprise me, Mr Holmes.'

'What I say is true,' Holmes answered. 'The money cannot be found. Surely it is better for you to take the substantial sum which I offer than to ruin this woman's career, which can profit you in no way?'

'There you make a mistake, Mr Holmes. An exposure would profit me indirectly to a considerable extent. I have eight or ten similar cases maturing. If it was circulated among them that I had made a severe example of the Lady Eva I should find all of them much more open to reason. You see my point?'

Holmes sprang from his chair.

'Get behind him, Watson! Don't let him out! Now, sir, let us see the contents of that notebook.'

Milverton had glided as quick as a rat to the side of the room, and stood with his back against the wall.

'Mr Holmes, Mr Holmes,' he said, turning the front of his coat and exhibiting the butt of a large revolver, which projected from the inside pocket. 'I have been expecting you to do something original. This has been done so often, and what good has ever come from it? I assure you that I am armed to the teeth, and I am perfectly prepared to use my weapons, knowing that the law will support me. Besides, your supposition that I would bring the letters here in a notebook is entirely mistaken. I would do nothing so foolish. And now, gentlemen, I have one or two little interviews this evening, and it is a long drive to Hampstead.' He stepped forward, took up his coat, laid his hand on his revolver, and turned to the door. I picked up a chair, but Holmes shook his head and I laid it down again. With a bow, a smile, and a twinkle Milverton was out of the room, and a few moments after we heard the slam of the carriage door and the rattle of the wheels as he drove away.

Holmes sat motionless by the fire, his hands buried deep in his trouser pockets, his chin sunk upon his breast, his eyes fixed upon the glowing embers. For half an hour he was silent and still. Then, with the gesture of a man who has taken his decision, he sprang to his feet and passed into his bedroom. A little later a rakish young workman with a goatee beard and a swagger lit his clay pipe at the lamp before descending into the street. 'I'll be back some time, Watson,' said he, and vanished into the night. I understood that he had opened his campaign against Charles Augustus Milverton; but I little dreamed the strange shape which that campaign was destined to take.

For some days Holmes came and went at all hours in this attire, but beyond a remark that his time was spent at Hampstead, and that it was not wasted, I knew nothing of what he was doing. At last, however, on a wild, tempestuous evening, when the wind screamed and rattled against the windows, he returned from his last expedition, and having removed his disguise he sat before the fire and laughed heartily in his silent inward fashion.

'You would not call me a marrying man, Watson?'

'No, indeed!'

'You'll be interested to hear that I am engaged.'

'My dear fellow! I congrat – '

'To Milverton's housemaid.'

'Good heavens, Holmes!'

'I wanted information, Watson.'

'Surely you have gone too far?'

'It was a most necessary step. I am a plumber with a rising business, Escott by name. I have walked out with her each evening, and I have talked with her. Good heavens, those talks! However, I have got all I wanted. I know Milverton's house as I know the palm of my hand.'

'But the girl, Holmes?'

He shrugged his shoulders.

'You can't help it, my dear Watson. You must play your cards as best you can when such a stake is on the table. However, I rejoice to say that I have a hated rival who will certainly cut me out the instant that my back is turned. What a splendid night it is!'

'You like this weather?'

'It suits my purpose. Watson, I mean to burgle Milverton's house tonight.'

I had a catching of the breath, and my skin went cold at the words, which were slowly uttered in a tone of concentrated resolution. As a flash of lightning in the night shows up in an instant every detail of a wide landscape, so at one glance I seemed to see every possible result of such an action – the detection, the capture, the honoured career ending in irreparable failure and disgrace, my friend himself lying at the mercy of the odious Milverton.

'For Heaven's sake, Holmes, think what you are doing,' I cried.

'My dear fellow, I have given it every consideration. I am never precipitate in my actions, nor would I adopt so energetic and indeed so dangerous a course if any other were possible. Let us look at the matter clearly and fairly. I suppose that you will admit that the action is morally justifiable, though technically criminal. To burgle his house is no more than to forcibly take his pocketbook – an action in which you were prepared to aid me.'

I turned it over in my mind.

'Yes,' I said; 'it is morally justifiable so long as our object is to take no articles save those which are used for an illegal purpose.'

'Exactly. Since it is morally justifiable I have only to consider the question of personal risk. Surely a gentleman should not lay much stress upon this when a lady is in most desperate need of his help?'

'You will be in such a false position.'

'Well, that is part of the risk. There is no other possible way of regaining these letters. The unfortunate lady has not the money, and there are none of her people in whom she could confide. Tomorrow is the last day of grace, and unless we can get the letters tonight this villain will be as good as his word and will bring about her ruin. I must, therefore, abandon my client to her fate or I must play this last card. Between ourselves, Watson, it's a sporting duel between this fellow Milverton and me. He had, as you saw, the best of the first exchanges; but my self-respect and my reputation are concerned to fight it to a finish.'

'Well, I don't like it; but I suppose it must be,' said I. 'When do we start?'

'You are not coming.'

'Then you are not going,' said I. 'I give you my word of honour – and I never broke it in my life – that I will take a cab straight to the police-station and give you away unless you let me share this adventure with you.'

'You can't help me.'

'How do you know that? You can't tell what may happen. Anyway, my resolution is taken. Other people besides you have self-respect and even reputations.'

Holmes had looked annoyed, but his brow cleared, and he clapped me on the shoulder.

'Well, well, my dear fellow, be it so. We have shared the same room for some years, and it would be amusing if we ended by sharing the same cell. You know, Watson, I don't mind confessing to you that I have always had an idea that I would have made a highly efficient criminal. This is the chance of my lifetime in that direction. See here!' He took a neat little leather case out of a drawer, and opening it he exhibited a number of shining instruments. 'This is a first-class, up-to-date burgling kit, with nickel-plated jemmy, diamond-tipped glass-cutter, adaptable keys, and every modern improvement which the march of civilisation demands. Here, too, is my dark lantern. Everything is in order. Have you a pair of silent shoes?'

'I have rubber-soled tennis shoes.'

'Excellent. And a mask?'

'I can make a couple out of black silk.'

'I can see that you have a strong natural turn for this sort of thing. Very good; do you make the masks. We shall have some cold supper before we start. It is now nine-thirty. At eleven we shall drive as far as Church Row. It is a quarter of an hour's walk from there to Appledore Towers. We shall be at work before midnight. Milverton is a heavy sleeper and retires punctually at ten-thirty. With any luck we should be back here by two, with the Lady Eva's letters in my pocket.'

Holmes and I put on our dress-clothes, so that we might appear to be two theatre-goers homeward bound. In Oxford Street we picked up a hansom and drove to an address in Hampstead. Here we paid off our cab, and with our greatcoats buttoned up, for it was bitterly cold and the wind seemed to blow through us, we walked along the edge of the Heath.

'It's a business that needs delicate treatment,' said Holmes. 'These documents are contained in a safe in the fellow's study, and the study is the anteroom of his bedchamber. On the other hand, like all these stout, little men who do themselves well, he is a plethoric sleeper. Agatha – that's my fiancée – says it is a joke in the servants' hall that it's impossible to wake the master. He has a secretary who is devoted to his interests and never budges from the study all day. That's why we are going at night. Then he has a beast of a dog which roams the garden. I met Agatha late the last two evenings, and she locks the brute up so as to give me a clear run. This is the house, this big one in its own grounds. Through the gate – now to the right among the laurels. We might put on our masks here, I think. You see, there is not a glimmer of light in any of the windows, and everything is working splendidly.'

With our black silk face-coverings, which turned us into two of the most truculent figures in London, we stole up to the silent, gloomy house. A sort of tiled veranda extended along one side of it, lined by several windows and two doors.

'That's his bedroom,' Holmes whispered. 'This door opens straight into the study. It would suit us best, but it is bolted as well as locked, and we should make too much noise getting in. Come round here. There's a greenhouse which opens into the drawing-room.'

The place was locked, but Holmes removed a circle of glass and turned the key from the inside. An instant afterwards he had closed the door behind us, and we had become felons in the eyes of the law. The thick, warm air of the conservatory and the rich, choking fragrance of exotic plants took us by the throat. He seized my hand in the darkness and led me swiftly past banks of shrubs which brushed against our faces. Holmes had remarkable powers, carefully cultivated, of seeing in the dark. Still holding my hand in one of his, he opened a door, and I was vaguely conscious that we had entered a large room in which a cigar had been smoked not long before. He felt his way among the furniture, opened another door, and closed it behind us. Putting out my hand I felt several coats hanging from the wall, and I understood that I was in a passage. We passed along it, and Holmes very gently opened a door upon the right-hand side. Something rushed out at us and my heart sprang into my mouth, but I could have laughed when I realised that it was the cat. A fire was burning in this new room, and again the air was heavy with tobacco smoke. Holmes entered on tiptoe, waited for me to follow, and then very gently closed the door. We were in Milverton's study, and a *portière* at the farther side showed the entrance to his bedroom.

It was a good fire, and the room was illuminated by it. Near the door I saw the gleam of an electric switch, but it was unnecessary, even if it had been safe, to turn it on. At one side of the fireplace was a heavy curtain, which covered the bay window we had seen from outside. On the other side was the door which communicated with the veranda. A desk stood in the centre, with a turning chair of shining red leather. Opposite was a large bookcase, with a marble bust of Athene on the top. In the corner between the bookcase and the wall there stood a tall green safe, the firelight flashing back from the polished brass knobs upon its face. Holmes stole across and looked at it. Then he crept to the door of the bedroom, and stood with slanting head listening intently. No sound came from within. Meanwhile it had struck me that it would be wise to secure our retreat through the outer door, so I examined it. To my amazement it was neither locked nor bolted! I touched

Holmes on the arm, and he turned his masked face in that direction. I saw him start, and he was evidently as surprised as I.

'I don't like it,' he whispered, putting his lips to my very ear. 'I can't quite make it out. Anyhow, we have no time to lose.'

'Can I do anything?'

'Yes; stand by the door. If you hear anyone come, bolt it on the inside, and we can get away as we came. If they come the other way, we can get through the door if our job is done, or hide behind these window curtains if it is not. Do you understand?'

I nodded and stood by the door. My first feeling of fear had passed away, and I thrilled now with a keener zest than I had ever enjoyed when we were the defenders of the law instead of its defiers. The high object of our mission, the consciousness that it was unselfish and chivalrous, the villainous character of our opponent, all added to the sporting interest of the adventure. Far from feeling guilty, I rejoiced and exulted in our dangers. With a glow of admiration I watched Holmes unrolling his case of instruments and choosing his tool with the calm, scientific accuracy of a surgeon who performs a delicate operation. I knew that the opening of safes was a particular hobby with him, and I understood the joy which it gave him to be confronted with this green and gold monster, the dragon which held in its maw the reputations of many fair ladies. Turning up the cuffs of his dress-coat – he had placed his overcoat on a chair – Holmes laid out two drills, a jemmy, and several skeleton keys. I stood at the centre door with my eyes glancing at each of the others, ready for any emergency; though, indeed, my plans were somewhat vague as to what I should do if we were interrupted. For half an hour Holmes worked with concentrated energy, laying down one tool, picking up another, handling each with the strength and delicacy of the trained mechanic. Finally I heard a click, the broad green door swung open, and inside I had a glimpse of a number of paper packets, each tied, sealed, and inscribed. Holmes picked one out, but it was hard to read by the flickering fire, and he drew out his little dark lantern, for it was too dangerous, with Milverton in the next room, to switch on the electric light. Suddenly I saw him halt, listen intently, and then in an instant he had swung the door of the safe to, picked up his coat, stuffed his tools into the pockets, and darted behind the window curtain, motioning me to do the same.

It was only when I had joined him there that I heard what had alarmed his quicker senses. There was a noise somewhere within the house. A door slammed in the distance. Then a confused, dull murmur broke itself into the measured thud of heavy footsteps rapidly approaching. They were in the passage outside the room. They paused at the door. The door opened. There was a sharp snick as the electric light was turned on. The door closed once more, and the pungent reek of a strong cigar was borne to our nostrils. Then the footsteps continued backwards and forwards, backwards and forwards, within a few yards of us. Finally, there was a creak from a chair, and the footsteps ceased. Then a key clicked in a lock and I heard the rustle of papers.

So far I had not dared to look out, but now I gently parted the division of the curtains in front of me and peeped through. From the pressure of Holmes's shoulder against mine I knew that he was sharing my observations. Right in front of us, and almost within our reach, was the broad, rounded back of Milverton. It was evident that we had entirely miscalculated his movements, that he had never been to his bedroom, but that he had been sitting up in some smoking or billiard room in the farther wing of the house, the windows of which we had not seen. His broad, grizzled head, with its shining patch of baldness, was in the immediate foreground of our vision. He was leaning far back in the red leather chair, his legs outstretched, a long black cigar projecting at an angle from his mouth. He wore a semi-military smoking-jacket, claret-coloured, with a black velvet collar. In his hand he held a long legal document, which he was reading in an indolent fashion, blowing rings of tobacco smoke from his lips as he did so. There was no promise of a speedy departure in his composed bearing and his comfortable attitude.

I felt Holmes's hand steal into mine and give me a reassuring shake, as if to say that the situation was within his powers and that he was easy in his mind. I was not sure whether he had seen what was only too obvious from my position, that the door of the safe was imperfectly closed, and that Milverton might at any moment observe it. In my own mind I had determined that if I were sure, from the rigidity of his gaze, that it had caught his eye, I would at once spring out, throw my greatcoat over his head, pinion him, and leave the rest to Holmes. But Milverton never looked up. He was languidly interested by the papers in his hand, and page after page was turned as he followed the argument of the lawyer. At least, I thought, when he has finished the document and the cigar he will go to his room; but before he had reached the end of either there came a remarkable development which turned our thoughts into quite another channel.

Several times I had observed that Milverton looked at his watch, and once he had risen and sat down again, with a gesture of impatience. The idea, however, that he might have an appointment at so strange an hour never occurred to me until a faint sound reached my ears from the veranda outside. Milverton dropped his papers and sat rigid in his chair. The sound was repeated, and then there came a gentle tap at the door. Milverton rose and opened it.

'Well,' said he, curtly, 'you are nearly half an hour late.'

So this was the explanation of the unlocked door and of the nocturnal vigil of Milverton. There was the gentle rustle of a woman's dress. I had closed the slit between the curtains as Milverton's face had turned in our direction, but now I ventured very carefully to open it once more. He had resumed his seat, the cigar still projecting at an insolent angle from the corner of his mouth. In front of him, in the full glare of the electric light, there stood a tall, slim, dark woman, a veil over her face, a mantle drawn round her chin. Her breath came quick and fast, and every inch of the lithe figure was quivering with strong emotion.

'Well,' said Milverton, 'you've made me lose a good night's rest, my dear. I hope you'll prove worth it. You couldn't come any other time – eh?'

The woman shook her head.

'Well, if you couldn't you couldn't. If the Countess is a hard mistress you have your chance to get level with her now. Bless the girl, what are you shivering about? That's right! Pull yourself together! Now, let us get down to business.' He took a note from the drawer of his desk. 'You say that you have five letters which compromise the Countess d'Albert. You want to sell them. I want to buy them. So far so good. It only remains to fix a price. I should want to inspect the letters, of course. If they are really good specimens – Great heavens, is it you?'

The woman without a word had raised her veil and dropped the mantle from her chin. It was a dark, handsome, clear-cut face which confronted Milverton, a face with a curved nose, strong, dark eyebrows shading hard, glittering eyes, and a straight, thin-lipped mouth set in a dangerous smile.

'It is I,' she said – 'the woman whose life you have ruined.'

Milverton laughed, but fear vibrated in his voice. 'You were so very obstinate,' said he. 'Why did you drive me to such extremities? I assure you I wouldn't hurt a fly of my own accord, but every man has his business, and what was I to do? I put the price well within your means. You would not pay.'

'So you sent the letters to my husband, and he – the noblest gentleman that ever lived, a man whose boots I was never worthy to lace – he broke his gallant heart and died. You remember that last night when I came through that door I begged and prayed you for mercy, and you laughed in my face as you are trying to laugh now, only your coward heart cannot keep your lips from twitching? Yes, you never thought to see me here again, but it was that night which taught me how I could meet you face to face, and alone. Well, Charles Milverton, what have you to say?'

'Don't imagine that you can bully me,' said he, rising to his feet. 'I have only to raise my voice, and I could call my servants and have you arrested. But I will make allowance for your natural anger. Leave the room at once as you came, and I will say no more.'

The woman stood with her hand buried in her bosom, and the same deadly smile on her thin lips.

'You will ruin no more lives as you ruined mine. You will wring no more hearts as you wrung mine. I will free the world of a poisonous thing. Take that, you hound, and that! – and that! – and that!'

She had drawn a little, gleaming revolver, and emptied barrel after barrel into Milverton's body, the muzzle within two feet of his shirt front. He shrank away and then fell forward upon the table, coughing furiously and clawing among the papers. Then he staggered to his feet, received another shot, and rolled upon the floor. 'You've done me,' he cried, and lay still. The woman looked at him intently and ground her heel into his upturned face. She looked again, but there was no sound or movement. I heard a sharp rustle, the night air blew into the heated room, and the avenger was gone.

No interference upon our part could have saved the man from his fate; but as the woman poured bullet after bullet into Milverton's shrinking body I was about to spring out, when I felt Holmes's cold, strong grasp upon my wrist. I understood the whole argument of that firm, restraining grip – that it was no affair of ours; that justice had overtaken a villain; that we had our own duties and our own objects which were not to be lost sight of. But hardly had the woman rushed from the room when Holmes, with swift, silent steps, was over at the other door. He turned the key in the lock. At the same instant we heard voices in the house and the sound of hurrying feet. The revolver shots had roused the household. With perfect coolness Holmes slipped across to the safe, filled his two arms with bundles of letters, and poured them all into the fire. Again and again he did it, until the safe was empty. Someone turned the handle and beat upon the outside of the door. Holmes looked swiftly round. The letter which had been the messenger of death for Milverton lay, all mottled with his blood, upon the table. Holmes tossed it in among the blazing papers. Then he drew the key from the outer door, passed through after me, and locked it on the outside. 'This way, Watson,' said he; 'we can scale the garden wall in this direction.'

I could not have believed that an alarm could have spread so swiftly. Looking back, the huge house was one blaze of light. The front door was open, and figures were rushing down the drive. The whole garden was alive with people, and one fellow raised a view-halloa as we emerged from the veranda and followed hard at our heels. Holmes seemed to know the ground perfectly, and he threaded his way swiftly among a plantation of small trees, I close at his heels, and our foremost pursuer panting behind us. It was a six-foot wall which barred our path, but he sprang to the top and over. As I did the same I felt the hand of the man behind me grab at my ankle; but I kicked myself free and scrambled over a glass-strewn coping. I fell upon my face among some bushes; but Holmes had me on my feet in an instant, and together we dashed away across the huge expanse of Hampstead Heath. We had run two miles, I suppose, before Holmes at last halted and listened intently. All was absolute silence behind us. We had shaken off our pursuers and were safe.

We had breakfasted and were smoking our morning pipe on the day after the remarkable experience which

I have recorded when Mr Lestrade, of Scotland Yard, very solemn and impressive, was ushered into our modest sitting-room.

'Good morning, Mr Holmes,' said he; 'good morning. May I ask if you are very busy just now?'

'Not too busy to listen to you.'

'I thought that, perhaps, if you had nothing particular on hand, you might care to assist us in a most remarkable case which occurred only last night at Hampstead.'

'Dear me!' said Holmes. 'What was that?'

'A murder – a most dramatic and remarkable murder. I know how keen you are upon these things, and I would take it as a great favour if you would step down to Appledore Towers and give us the benefit of your advice. It is no ordinary crime. We have had our eyes upon this Mr Milverton for some time, and, between ourselves, he was a bit of a villain. He is known to have held papers which he used for blackmailing purposes. These papers have all been burned by the murderers. No article of value was taken, as it is probable that the criminals were men of good position, whose sole object was to prevent social exposure.'

'Criminals!' said Holmes. 'Plural!'

'Yes, there were two of them. They were, as nearly as possible, captured red-handed. We have their footmarks, we have their description; it's ten to one that we trace them. The first fellow was a bit too active, but the second was caught by the under-gardener and only got away after a struggle. He was a middle-sized, strongly-built man – square jaw, thick neck, moustache, a mask over his eyes.'

'That's rather vague,' said Sherlock Holmes. 'Why, it might be a description of Watson!'

CHARLES AUGUSTUS MILVERTON

'It's true,' said the inspector, with much amusement. 'It might be a description of Watson.'

'Well, I am afraid I can't help you, Lestrade,' said Holmes. 'The fact is that I knew this fellow Milverton, that I considered him one of the most dangerous men in London, and that I think there are certain crimes which the law cannot touch, and which therefore, to some extent, justify private revenge. No, it's no use arguing. I have made up my mind. My sympathies are with the criminals rather than with the victim, and I will not handle this case.'

Holmes had not said one word to me about the tragedy which we had witnessed, but I observed all the morning that he was in his most thoughtful mood, and he gave me the impression, from his vacant eyes and his abstracted manner, of a man who is striving to recall something to his memory. We were in the middle of our lunch when he suddenly sprang to his feet. 'By Jove, Watson; I've got it!' he cried. 'Take your hat! Come with me!' He hurried at his top speed down Baker Street and along Oxford Street, until we had almost reached Regent Circus. Here on the left hand there stands a shop window filled with photographs of the celebrities and beauties of the day. Holmes's eyes fixed themselves upon one of them, and following his gaze I saw the picture of a regal and stately lady in Court dress, with a high diamond tiara upon her noble head. I looked at that delicately-curved nose, at the marked eyebrows, at the straight mouth, and the strong little chin beneath it. Then I caught my breath as I read the time-honoured title of the great nobleman and statesman whose wife she had been. My eyes met those of Holmes, and he put his finger to his lips as we turned away from the window.

8

The Six Napoleons

It was no very unusual thing for Mr Lestrade, of Scotland Yard, to look in upon us of an evening, and his visits were welcome to Sherlock Holmes, for they enabled him to keep in touch with all that was going on at the police headquarters. In return for the news which Lestrade would bring, Holmes was always ready to listen with attention to the details of any case upon which the detective was engaged, and was able occasionally, without any active interference, to give some hint or suggestion drawn from his own vast knowledge and experience.

On this particular evening Lestrade had spoken of the weather and the newspapers. Then he had fallen silent, puffing thoughtfully at his cigar. Holmes looked keenly at him.

'Anything remarkable on hand?' he asked.

'Oh, no, Mr Holmes, nothing very particular.'

'Then tell me about it.'

Lestrade laughed.

'Well, Mr Holmes, there is no use denying that there *is* something on my mind. And yet it is such an absurd business that I hesitated to bother you about it. On the other hand, although it is trivial, it is undoubtedly queer, and I know that you have a taste for all that is out of the common. But in my opinion it comes more in Dr Watson's line than ours.'

'Disease?' said I.

'Madness, anyhow. And a queer madness too! You wouldn't think there was anyone living at this time of day who had such a hatred of Napoleon the First that he would break any image of him that he could see.'

Holmes sank back in his chair.

'That's no business of mine,' said he.

'Exactly. That's what I said. But then, when the man commits burglary in order to break images which are not his own, that brings it away from the doctor and on to the policeman.'

Holmes sat up again.

'Burglary! This is more interesting. Let me hear the details.'

Lestrade took out his official notebook and refreshed his memory from its pages.

'The first case reported was four days ago,' said he. 'It was at the shop of Morse Hudson, who has a place for the sale of pictures and statues in the Kennington Road. The assistant had left the front shop for an instant when he heard a crash, and hurrying in he found a plaster bust of Napoleon, which stood with several other works of art upon the counter, lying shivered into fragments. He rushed out into the road, but, although several passers-by declared that they had noticed a man run out of the shop, he could neither see anyone nor could he find any means of identifying the rascal. It seemed to be one of those senseless acts of hooliganism which occur from time to time, and it was reported to the constable on the beat as such. The plaster cast was not worth more than a few shillings, and the whole affair appeared to be too childish for any particular investigation.

'The second case, however, was more serious and also more singular. It occurred only last night.

'In Kennington Road, and within a few hundred yards of Morse Hudson's shop, there lives a well-known medical practitioner, named Dr Barnicot, who has one of the largest practices upon the south side of the Thames. His residence and principal consulting-room is at Kennington Road, but he has a branch surgery and dispensary at Lower Brixton Road, two miles away. This Dr Barnicot is an enthusiastic admirer of Napoleon, and his house is full of books, pictures, and relics of the French Emperor. Some little time ago he purchased from Morse Hudson two duplicate plaster casts of the famous head of Napoleon by the French sculptor, Devine. One of these he placed in his hall in the house at Kennington Road, and the other on the mantel-piece of the surgery at Lower Brixton. Well, when Dr Barnicot came down this morning he was astonished to find that his house had been burgled during the night, but that nothing had been taken save the plaster head from the hall. It had been carried out and had been dashed savagely against the garden wall, under which its splintered fragments were discovered.'

Holmes rubbed his hands.

'This is certainly very novel,' said he.

'I thought it would please you. But I have not got to the end yet. Dr Barnicot was due at his surgery at twelve o'clock, and you can imagine his amazement when, on arriving there, he found that the window had been opened in the night, and that the broken pieces of his second bust were strewn all over the room. It had been smashed to atoms where it stood. In neither case were there any signs which could give us a clue as to the criminal or lunatic who had done the mischief. Now, Mr Holmes, you have got the facts.'

'They are singular, not to say grotesque,' said Holmes. 'May I ask whether the two busts smashed in Dr Barnicot's rooms were the exact duplicates of the one which was destroyed in Morse Hudson's shop?'

'They were taken from the same mould.'

'Such a fact must tell against the theory that the man who breaks them is influenced by any general hatred of Napoleon. Considering how many hundreds of statues of the great Emperor must exist in London, it is too much to suppose such a coincidence as that a promiscuous iconoclast should chance to begin upon three specimens of the same bust.'

'Well, I thought as you do,' said Lestrade. 'On the other hand, this Morse Hudson is the purveyor of busts in that part of London, and these three were the only ones which had been in his shop for years. So, although, as you say, there are many hundreds of statues in London, it is very probable that these three were the only ones in that district. Therefore, a local fanatic would begin with them. What do you think, Dr Watson?'

'There are no limits to the possibilities of monomania,' I answered. 'There is the condition which the modern French psychologists have called the *idée fixe*, which may be trifling in character, and accompanied by complete sanity in every other way. A man who had read deeply about Napoleon, or who had possibly received some hereditary family injury through the great war, might conceivably form such an *idée fixe* and under its influence be capable of any fantastic outrage.'

'That won't do, my dear Watson,' said Holmes, shaking his head; 'for no amount of *idée fixe* would enable your interesting monomaniac to find out where these busts were situated.'

'Well, how do *you* explain it?'

'I don't attempt to do so. I would only observe that there is a certain method in the gentleman's eccentric proceedings. For example, in Dr Barnicot's hall, where a sound might arouse the family, the bust was taken outside before being broken, whereas in the surgery, where there was less danger of an alarm, it was smashed where it stood. The affair seems absurdly trifling, and yet I dare call nothing trivial when I reflect that some of my most classic cases have had the least promising commencement. You will remember, Watson, how the dreadful business of the Abernetty family was first brought to my notice by the depth which the parsley had sunk into the butter upon a hot day. I can't afford, therefore, to smile at your three broken busts, Lestrade, and I shall be very much obliged to you if you will let me hear of any fresh developments of so singular a chain of events.'

The development for which my friend had asked came in a quicker and an infinitely more tragic form than he could have imagined. I was still dressing in my bedroom next morning when there was a tap at the door and Holmes entered, a telegram in his hand. He read it aloud:

'Come instantly, 131 Pitt Street, Kensington.

LESTRADE.'

'What is it, then?' I asked.

'Don't know – may be anything. But I suspect it is the sequel of the story of the statues. In that case our friend, the image-breaker, has begun operations in another quarter of London. There's coffee on the table, Watson, and I have a cab at the door.'

In half an hour we had reached Pitt Street, a quiet little backwater just beside one of the briskest currents of London life. Number 131 was one of a row, all flat-chested, respectable, and most unromantic dwellings. As we drove up we found the railings in front of the house lined by a curious crowd. Holmes whistled.

'By George! it's attempted murder at the least. Nothing less will hold the London message-boy. There's a deed of violence indicated in that fellow's round shoulders and outstretched neck. What's this, Watson? The top steps swilled down and the other ones dry. Footsteps enough, anyhow! Well, well, there's Lestrade at the front window, and we shall soon know all about it.'

The official received us with a very grave face and showed us into a sitting-room, where an exceedingly unkempt and agitated elderly man, clad in a flannel dressing-gown, was pacing up and down. He was introduced to us as the owner of the house – Mr Horace Harker, of the Central Press Syndicate.

'It's the Napoleon bust business again,' said Lestrade. 'You seemed interested last night, Mr Holmes, so I thought perhaps you would be glad to be present now that the affair has taken a very much graver turn.'

'What has it turned to, then?'

'To murder. Mr Harker, will you tell these gentlemen exactly what has occurred?'

The man in the dressing-gown turned upon us with a most melancholy face.

'It's an extraordinary thing,' said he, 'that all my life I have been collecting other people's news, and now that a real piece of news has come my own way I am so confused and bothered that I can't put two words together. If I had come in here as a journalist I should have interviewed myself and had two columns in every evening paper. As it is I am giving away valuable copy by telling my story over and over to a string of different people, and I can make no use of it myself. However, I've heard your name, Mr Sherlock Holmes, and if you'll only explain this queer business I shall be paid for my trouble in telling you the story.'

Holmes sat down and listened.

'It all seems to centre round that bust of Napoleon which I bought for this very room about four months ago. I picked it up cheap from Harding Brothers, two doors from the High Street Station. A great deal of my journalistic work is done at night, and I often write until the early morning. So it was today. I was sitting in my den, which is at the back of the top of the house, about three o'clock, when I was convinced that I heard some sounds downstairs. I listened, but they were not repeated, and I concluded that they came from outside. Then suddenly, about five minutes later, there came a most horrible yell – the most dreadful sound, Mr Holmes, that ever I heard. It will ring in my ears as long as I live. I sat frozen with horror for a minute or two. Then I seized the poker and went downstairs. When I entered this room I found the window wide open, and I at once observed that the bust was gone from the mantelpiece. Why any burglar should take such a thing passes my understanding, for it was only a plaster cast and of no real value whatever.

'You can see for yourself that anyone going out through that open window could reach the front doorstep by taking a long stride. This was clearly what the burglar had done, so I went round and opened the door. Stepping out into the dark I nearly fell over a dead man who was lying there. I ran back for a light, and there was the poor fellow, a great gash in his throat and the whole place swimming in blood. He lay on his back, his knees drawn up, and his mouth horribly open. I shall see him in my dreams. I had just time to blow on my police-whistle, and then I must have fainted, for I knew nothing more until I found the policeman standing over me in the hall.'

'Well, who was the murdered man?' asked Holmes.

'There's nothing to show who he was,' said Lestrade. 'You shall see the body at the mortuary, but we have made nothing of it up to now. He is a tall man, sunburned, very powerful, not more than thirty. He is poorly dressed, and yet does not appear to be a labourer. A horn-handled clasp-knife was lying in a pool of blood beside him. Whether it was the weapon which did the deed, or whether it belonged to the dead man, I do not know. There was no name on his clothing, and nothing in his pockets save an apple, some string, a shilling map of London, and a photograph. Here it is.'

It was evidently taken by a snapshot from a small camera. It represented an alert, sharp-featured simian man with thick eyebrows, and a very peculiar projection of the lower part of the face like the muzzle of a baboon.

'And what became of the bust?' asked Holmes, after a careful study of this picture.

'We had news of it just before you came. It has been found in the front garden of an empty house in Campden House Road. It was broken into fragments. I am going round now to see it. Will you come?'

'Certainly. I must just take one look round.' He examined the carpet and the window. 'The fellow had either very long legs or was a most active man,' said he. 'With an area beneath, it was no mean feat to reach that window-ledge and open that window. Getting back was comparatively simple. Are you coming with us to see the remains of your bust, Mr Harker?'

The disconsolate journalist had seated himself at a writing-table.

'I must try and make something of it,' said he, 'though I have no doubt that the first editions of the evening papers are out already with full details. It's like my luck! You remember when the stand fell at Doncaster? Well, I was the only journalist in the stand, and my journal the only one that had no account of it, for I was too shaken to write it. And now I'll be too late with a murder done on my own doorstep.'

As we left the room we heard his pen travelling shrilly over the foolscap.

The spot where the fragments of the bust had been found was only a few hundred yards away. For the first time our eyes rested upon this presentment of the great Emperor, which seemed to raise such frantic and destructive hatred in the mind of the unknown. It lay scattered in splintered shards upon the grass. Holmes picked up several of them and examined them carefully. I was convinced from his intent face and his purposeful manner that at last he was upon a clue.

'Well?' asked Lestrade.

Holmes shrugged his shoulders.

'We have a long way to go yet,' said he. 'And yet – and yet – well, we have some suggestive facts to act upon. The possession of this trifling bust was worth more in the eyes of this strange criminal than a human life. That is one point. Then there is the singular fact that he did not break it in the house, or immediately outside the house, if to break it was his sole object.'

'He was rattled and bustled by meeting this other fellow. He hardly knew what he was doing.'

'Well, that's likely enough. But I wish to call your attention very particularly to the position of this house in the garden of which the bust was destroyed.'

Lestrade looked about him.

'It was an empty house, and so he knew that he would not be disturbed in the garden.'

'Yes, but there is another empty house farther up the street which he must have passed before he came to this one. Why did he not break it there, since it is evident that every yard that he carried it increased the risk of someone meeting him?'

'I give it up,' said Lestrade.

Holmes pointed to the street lamp above our heads.

'He could see what he was doing here and he could not there. That was his reason.'

'By Jove! that's true,' said the detective. 'Now that I come to think of it, Dr Barnicot's bust was broken not far from his red lamp. Well, Mr Holmes, what are we to do with that fact?'

'To remember it – to docket it. We may come on something later which will bear upon it. What steps do you propose to take now, Lestrade?'

'The most practical way of getting at it, in my opinion, is to identify the dead man. There should be no difficulty about that. When we have found who he is and who his associates are, we should have a good start in learning what he was doing in Pitt Street last night, and who it was who met him and killed him on the doorstep of Mr Horace Harker. Don't you think so?'

'No doubt; and yet it is not quite the way in which I should approach the case.'

'What would you do, then?'

'Oh, you must not let me influence you in any way! I suggest that you go on your line and I on mine. We can compare notes afterwards, and each will supplement the other.'

'Very good,' said Lestrade.

'If you are going back to Pitt Street you might see Mr Horace Harker. Tell him from me that I have quite made up my mind, and that it is certain that a dangerous homicidal lunatic with Napoleonic delusions was in his house last night. It will be useful for his article.'

Lestrade stared.

'You don't seriously believe that?'

Holmes smiled.

'Don't I? Well, perhaps I don't. But I am sure that it will interest Mr Horace Harker and the subscribers of the Central Press Syndicate. Now, Watson, I think that we shall find that we have a long and rather complex day's work before us. I should be glad, Lestrade, if you could make it convenient to meet us at Baker Street at six o'clock this evening. Until then I should like to keep this photograph found in the dead man's pocket. It is possible that I may have to ask your company and assistance upon a small expedition which will have to be undertaken tonight, if my chain of reasoning should prove to be correct. Until then, goodbye and good luck!'

Sherlock Holmes and I walked together to the High Street, where he stopped at the shop of Harding Brothers, whence the bust had been purchased. A young assistant informed us that Mr Harding would be absent until after noon, and that he was himself a newcomer who could give us no information. Holmes's face showed his disappointment and annoyance.

'Well, well, we can't expect to have it all our own way, Watson,' he said, at last. 'We must come back in the afternoon if Mr Harding will not be here until then. I am, as you have no doubt surmised, endeavouring to trace these busts to their source, in order to find if there is not something peculiar which may account for their remarkable fate. Let us make for Mr Morse Hudson, of the Kennington Road, and see if he can throw any light upon the problem.'

A drive of an hour brought us to the picture-dealer's establishment. He was a small, stout man with a red face and a peppery manner.

'Yes, sir. On my very counter, sir,' said he. 'What we pay rates and taxes for I don't know, when any ruffian can come in and break one's goods. Yes, sir, it was I who sold Dr Barnicot his two statues. Disgraceful, sir! A Nihilist plot, that's what I make it. No one but an Anarchist would go about breaking statues. Red republicans, that's what I call 'em. Who did I get the statues from? I don't see what that has to do with it. Well, if you really want to know, I got them from Gelder and Co., in Church Street, Stepney. They are a well-known house in the trade, and have been this twenty years. How many had I? Three – two and one are three – two of Dr Barnicot's and one smashed in broad daylight on my own counter. Do I know that photograph? No, I don't. Yes, I do, though. Why, it's Beppo. He was a kind of Italian piece-work man, who made himself useful in the shop. He could carve a bit and gild and frame, and do odd jobs. The fellow left me last week, and I've heard nothing of him since. No,

I don't know where he came from nor where he went to. I have nothing against him while he was here. He was gone two days before the bust was smashed.'

'Well, that's all we could reasonably expect to get from Morse Hudson,' said Holmes, as we emerged from the shop. 'We have this Beppo as a common factor, both in Kennington and in Kensington, so that is worth a ten-mile drive. Now, Watson, let us make for Gelder and Co., of Stepney, the source and origin of busts. I shall be surprised if we don't get some help down there.'

In rapid succession we passed through the fringe of fashionable London, hotel London, theatrical London, literary London, commercial London, and, finally, maritime London, till we came to a riverside city of a hundred thousand souls, where the tenement houses swelter and reek with the outcasts of Europe. Here, in a broad thoroughfare, once the abode of wealthy City merchants, we found the sculpture works for which we searched. Outside was a considerable yard full of monumental masonry. Inside was a large room in which fifty workers were carving or moulding. The manager, a big blond German, received us civilly, and gave a clear answer to all Holmes's questions. A reference to his books showed that hundreds of casts had been taken from a marble copy of Devine's head of Napoleon, but that the three which had been sent to Morse Hudson a year or so before had been half of a batch of six, the other three being sent to Harding Brothers, of Kensington. There was no reason why those six should be different to any of the other casts. He could suggest no possible cause why anyone should wish to destroy them – in fact, he laughed at the idea. Their wholesale price was six shillings, but the retailer would get twelve or more. The cast was taken in two moulds from each side of the face, and then these two profiles of plaster of Paris were joined together to make the complete bust. The work was usually done by Italians in the room we were in. When finished the busts were put on a table in the passage to dry, and afterwards stored. That was all he could tell us.

But the production of the photograph had a remarkable effect upon the manager. His face flushed with anger, and his brows knotted over his blue Teutonic eyes.

'Ah, the rascal!' he cried. 'Yes, indeed, I know him very well. This has always been a respectable establishment, and the only time that we have ever had the police in it was over this very fellow. It was more than a year ago now. He knifed another Italian in the street, and then he came to the works with the police on his heels, and he was taken here. Beppo was his name – his second name I never knew. Serve me right for engaging a man with such a face. But he was a good workman, one of the best.'

'What did he get?'

'The man lived and he got off with a year. I have no doubt he is out now; but he has not dared to show his nose here. We have a cousin of his here, and I dare say he could tell you where he is.'

'No, no,' cried Holmes, 'not a word to the cousin – not a word, I beg you. The matter is very important, and the farther I go with it the more important it seems to grow. When you referred in your ledger to the sale of those casts I observed that the date was June 3rd of last year. Could you give me the date when Beppo was arrested?'

'I could tell you roughly by the pay-list,' the manager

answered. 'Yes,' he continued, after some turning over of pages, 'he was paid last on May 20th.'

'Thank you,' said Holmes. 'I don't think that I need intrude upon your time and patience any more.' With a last word of caution that he should say nothing as to our researches we turned our faces westward once more.

The afternoon was far advanced before we were able to snatch a hasty luncheon at a restaurant. A news-bill at the entrance announced 'Kensington Outrage. Murder by a Madman', and the contents of the paper showed that Mr Horace Harker had got his account into print after all. Two columns were occupied with a highly sensational and flowery rendering of the whole incident. Holmes propped it against the cruet-stand and read it while he ate. Once or twice he chuckled.

'This is all right, Watson,' said he. 'Listen to this: "It is satisfactory to know that there can be no difference of opinion upon this case, since Mr Lestrade, one of the most experienced members of the official force, and Mr Sherlock Holmes, the well-known consulting expert, have each come to the conclusion that the grotesque series of incidents, which have ended in so tragic a fashion, arise from lunacy rather than from deliberate crime. No explanation save mental aberration can cover the facts." The Press, Watson, is a most valuable institution if you only know how to use it. And now, if you have quite finished, we will hark back to Kensington and see what the manager of Harding Brothers has to say to the matter.'

The founder of that great emporium proved to be a brisk, crisp little person, very dapper and quick, with a clear head and a ready tongue.

'Yes, sir, I have already read the account in the

evening papers. Mr Horace Harker is a customer of ours. We supplied him with the bust some months ago. We ordered three busts of that sort from Gelder and Co., of Stepney. They are all sold now. To whom? Oh, I dare say by consulting our sales book we could very easily tell you. Yes, we have the entries here. One to Mr Harker, you see, and one to Mr Josiah Brown, of Laburnum Lodge, Laburnum Vale, Chiswick, and one to Mr Sandeford, of Lower Grove Road, Reading. No, I have never seen this face which you show me in the photograph. You would hardly forget it, would you, sir, for I've seldom seen an uglier. Have we any Italians on the staff? Yes, sir, we have several among our work people and cleaners. I dare say they might get a peep at that sales book if they wanted to. There is no particular reason for keeping a watch upon that book. Well, well, it's a very strange business, and I hope that you'll let me know if anything comes of your enquiries.'

Holmes had taken several notes during Mr Harding's evidence, and I could see that he was thoroughly satisfied by the turn which affairs were taking. He made no remark, however, save that, unless we hurried, we should be late for our appointment with Lestrade. Sure enough, when we reached Baker Street the detective was already there, and we found him pacing up and down in a fever of impatience. His look of importance showed that his day's work had not been in vain.

'Well?' he asked. 'What luck, Mr Holmes?'

'We have had a very busy day, and not entirely a wasted one,' my friend explained. 'We have seen both the retailers and also the wholesale manufacturers. I can trace each of the busts now from the beginning.'

'The busts!' cried Lestrade. 'Well, well, you have your own methods, Mr Sherlock Holmes, and it is not for me to say a word against them, but I think I have done a better day's work than you. I have identified the dead man.'

'You don't say so?'

'And found a cause for the crime.'

'Splendid!'

'We have an inspector who makes a speciality of Saffron Hill and the Italian quarter. Well, this dead man had some Catholic emblem round his neck, and that, along with his colour, made me think he was from the south. Inspector Hill knew him the moment he caught sight of him. His name is Pietro Venucci, from Naples, and he is one of the greatest cut-throats in London. He is connected with the Mafia, which, as you know, is a secret political society, enforcing its decrees by murder. Now you see how the affair begins to clear up. The other fellow is probably an Italian also, and a member of the Mafia. He has broken the rules in some fashion. Pietro is set upon his track. Probably the photograph we found in his pocket is the man himself, so that he may not knife the wrong person. He dogs the fellow, he sees him enter a house, he waits outside for him, and in the scuffle he receives his own death-wound. How is that, Mr Sherlock Holmes?'

Holmes clapped his hands approvingly.

'Excellent, Lestrade, excellent!' he cried. 'But I didn't quite follow your explanation of the destruction of the busts.'

'The busts! You never can get those busts out of your head. After all, that is nothing; petty larceny, six months at the most. It is the murder that we are really investigating, and I tell you that I am gathering all the threads into my hands.'

'And the next stage?'

'Is a very simple one. I shall go down with Hill to the Italian quarter, find the man whose photograph we have got, and arrest him on the charge of murder. Will you come with us?'

'I think not. I fancy we can attain our end in a simpler way. I can't say for certain, because it all depends – well, it all depends upon a factor which is completely outside our control. But I have great hopes – in fact, the betting is exactly two to one – that if you will come with us tonight I shall be able to help you to lay him by the heels.'

'In the Italian quarter?'

'No; I fancy Chiswick is an address which is more likely to find him. If you will come with me to Chiswick tonight, Lestrade, I'll promise to go to the Italian quarter with you tomorrow, and no harm will be done by the delay. And now I think that a few hours' sleep would do us all good, for I do not propose to leave before eleven o'clock, and it is unlikely that we shall be back before morning. You'll dine with us, Lestrade, and then you are welcome to the sofa until it is time for us to start. In the meantime, Watson, I should be glad if you would ring for an express messenger, for I have a letter to send, and it is important that it should go at once.'

Holmes spent the evening in rummaging among the files of the old daily papers with which one of our lumber-rooms was packed. When at last he descended it was with triumph in his eyes, but he said nothing to either of us as to the result of his researches. For my own part, I had followed step by step the methods by which he had traced the various windings of this complex case, and, though I could not yet perceive the goal which we would reach, I understood clearly that Holmes expected this grotesque criminal to make an attempt upon the two remaining busts, one of which, I remembered, was at Chiswick. No doubt the object of our journey was to catch him in the very act, and I could not but admire the cunning with which my friend had inserted a wrong clue in the evening paper, so as to give the fellow the idea that he could continue his scheme with impunity. I was not surprised when Holmes suggested that I should take my revolver with me. He had himself picked up the loaded hunting-crop which was his favourite weapon.

A four-wheeler was at the door at eleven, and in it we drove to a spot at the other side of Hammersmith Bridge. Here the cabman was directed to wait. A short walk brought us to a secluded road fringed with pleasant houses, each standing in its own grounds. In the light of a street lamp we read 'Laburnum Villa' upon the gatepost of one of them. The occupants had evidently retired to rest, for all was dark save for a fanlight over the hall door, which shed a single blurred circle on to the garden path. The wooden fence which separated the grounds from the road threw a dense black shadow upon the inner side, and here it was that we crouched.

'I fear that you'll have a long wait,' Holmes whispered. 'We may thank our stars that it is not raining. I don't think we can even venture to smoke to pass the time. However, it's a two to one chance that we get something to pay us for our trouble.'

It proved, however, that our vigil was not to be so long as Holmes had led us to fear, and it ended in a very sudden and singular fashion. In an instant, without the least sound to warn us of his coming, the garden gate swung open, and a lithe, dark figure, as swift and active as an ape, rushed up the garden path. We saw it whisk past the light thrown from over the door and disappear against the black shadow of the house. There was a long pause, during which we held our breath, and then a very gentle creaking sound came to our ears. The window was being opened. The noise ceased, and again there was a long silence. The fellow was making his way into the house. We saw the sudden flash of a dark lantern inside the room. What he sought was evidently not there, for again we saw the flash through another blind, and then through another.

'Let us get to the open window. We will nab him as he climbs out,' Lestrade whispered.

But before we could move the man had emerged again. As he came out into the glimmering patch of light we saw that he carried something white under his arm. He looked stealthily all round him. The silence of the deserted street reassured him. Turning his back upon us he laid down his burden, and the next instant there was the sound of a sharp tap, followed by a clatter and rattle. The man was so intent upon what he was doing that he never heard our steps as we stole across the grass plot. With the bound of a tiger Holmes was on his back, and an instant later Lestrade and I had him by either wrist and the handcuffs had been fastened. As we turned him over I saw a hideous, sallow face, with writhing, furious features, glaring up at us, and I knew that it was indeed the man of the photograph whom we had secured.

But it was not our prisoner to whom Holmes was giving his attention. Squatted on the doorstep, he was engaged in most carefully examining that which the man had brought from the house. It was a bust of Napoleon like the one which we had seen that morning, and it had been broken into similar fragments. Carefully Holmes held each separate shard to the light, but in no way did it differ from any other shattered piece of plaster. He had just completed his examination when the hall lights flew up, the door opened, and the owner of the house, a jovial, rotund figure in shirt and trousers, presented himself.

'Mr Josiah Brown, I suppose?' said Holmes.

'Yes, sir; and you, no doubt, are Mr Sherlock Holmes? I had the note which you sent by the express messenger, and I did exactly what you told me. We locked every door on the inside and awaited developments. Well, I'm very glad to see that you have got the rascal. I hope, gentlemen, that you will come in and have some refreshment.'

However, Lestrade was anxious to get his man into safe quarters, so within a few minutes our cab had been summoned and we were all four upon our way to London. Not a word would our captive say; but he glared at us from the shadow of his matted hair, and once, when my hand seemed within his reach, he snapped at it like a hungry wolf. We stayed long enough at the police-station to learn that a search of his clothing revealed nothing save a few shillings and a long sheath knife, the handle of which bore copious traces of recent blood.

'That's all right,' said Lestrade, as we parted. 'Hill knows all these gentry, and he will give a name to him. You'll find that my theory of the Mafia will work out all right. But I'm sure I am exceedingly obliged to you, Mr Holmes, for the workmanlike way in which you laid hands upon him. I don't quite understand it all yet.'

'I fear it is rather too late an hour for explanations,' said Holmes. 'Besides, there are one or two details which are not finished off, and it is one of those cases which are worth working out to the very end. If you will come round once more to my rooms at six o'clock tomorrow I think I shall be able to show you that even now you have not grasped the entire meaning of this business, which presents some features which make it absolutely original in the history of crime. If ever I permit you to chronicle any more of my little problems, Watson, I foresee that you will enliven your pages by an account of the singular adventure of the Napoleonic busts.'

When we met again next evening Lestrade was furnished with much information concerning our prisoner. His name, it appeared, was Beppo, second name unknown. He was a well-known ne'er-do-well among the Italian colony. He had once been a skilful sculptor and had earned an honest living, but he had taken to evil courses and had twice already been in gaol – once for a petty theft and once, as we had already heard, for stabbing a fellow-countryman. He could talk English perfectly well. His reasons for destroying the busts were still unknown, and he refused to answer any questions upon the subject; but the police had discovered that these same busts might very well have been made by his own hands, since he was engaged in this class of work at the establishment of Gelder and Co. To all this information, much of which we already knew, Holmes listened with polite attention; but I, who knew him so well, could clearly see that his thoughts were elsewhere, and I detected a mixture of mingled uneasiness and expectation beneath that mask which he was wont to assume. At last he started in his chair and his eyes brightened. There had been a ring at the bell. A minute later we heard steps upon the stairs, and an elderly, red-faced man with grizzled side-whiskers was ushered in. In his right hand he carried an old-fashioned carpetbag, which he placed upon the table.

'Is Mr Sherlock Holmes here?'

My friend bowed and smiled. 'Mr Sandeford, of Reading, I suppose?' said he.

'Yes, sir, I fear that I am a little late; but the trains were awkward. You wrote to me about a bust that is in my possession.'

'Exactly.'

'I have your letter here. You said, "I desire to possess a copy of Devine's Napoleon, and am prepared to pay you ten pounds for the one which is in your possession." Is that right?'

'Certainly.'

'I was very much surprised at your letter, for I could not imagine how you knew that I owned such a thing.'

'Of course you must have been surprised, but the explanation is very simple. Mr Harding, of Harding Brothers, said that they had sold you their last copy, and he gave me your address.'

'Oh, that was it, was it? Did he tell you what I paid for it?'

'No, he did not.'

'Well, I am an honest man, though not a very rich one. I only gave fifteen shillings for the bust, and I think you ought to know that before I take ten pounds from you.'

'I am sure the scruple does you honour, Mr Sandeford. But I have named that price, so I intend to stick to it.'

'Well, it is very handsome of you, Mr Holmes. I brought the bust up with me, as you asked me to do. Here it is!' He opened his bag, and at last we saw placed upon our table a complete specimen of that bust which we had already seen more than once in fragments.

Holmes took a paper from his pocket and laid a ten-pound note upon the table.

'You will kindly sign that paper, Mr Sandeford, in the presence of these witnesses. It is simply to say that you transfer every possible right that you ever had in the bust to me. I am a methodical man, you see, and you never know what turn events might take afterwards. Thank you, Mr Sandeford; here is your money, and I wish you a very good evening.'

When our visitor had disappeared Sherlock Holmes's movements were such as to rivet our attention. He began by taking a clean white cloth from a drawer and laying it over the table. Then he placed his newly-acquired bust in the centre of the cloth. Finally, he picked up his hunting-crop and struck Napoleon a sharp blow on the top of the head. The figure broke into fragments, and Holmes bent eagerly over the shattered remains. Next instant, with a loud shout of triumph, he held up one splinter, in which a round, dark object was fixed like a plum in a pudding.

'Gentlemen,' he cried, 'let me introduce you to the famous black pearl of the Borgias.'

Lestrade and I sat silent for a moment, and then, with a spontaneous impulse, we both broke out clapping as at the well-wrought crisis of a play. A flush of colour sprang to Holmes's pale cheeks, and he bowed to us like the master dramatist who receives the homage of his audience. It was at such moments that for an instant he ceased to be a reasoning machine, and betrayed his human love for admiration and applause. The same singularly proud and reserved nature which turned away with disdain from popular notoriety was capable of being moved to its depths by spontaneous wonder and praise from a friend.

'Yes, gentlemen,' said he, 'it is the most famous pearl now existing in the world, and it has been my good fortune, by a connected chain of inductive reasoning, to trace it from the Prince of Colonna's bedroom at the Dacre Hotel, where it was lost, to the interior of this, the last of the six busts of Napoleon which were manufactured by Gelder and Co., of Stepney. You will remember, Lestrade, the sensation caused by the disappearance of this valuable jewel, and the vain efforts of the London police to recover it. I was myself consulted upon the case; but I was unable to throw any light upon it. Suspicion fell upon the maid of the Princess, who was an Italian, and it was proved that she had a brother in London, but we failed to trace any connection between them. The maid's name was Lucretia Venucci, and there is no doubt in my mind that this Pietro who was murdered two nights ago was the brother. I have been looking up the dates in the old files of the paper, and I find that the disappearance of the pearl was exactly two days before the arrest of Beppo for some crime of violence, an event which took place in the factory of Gelder and Co., at the very moment when these busts were being made. Now you clearly see the sequence of events, though you see them, of course, in the inverse order to the way in which they presented themselves to me. Beppo had the pearl in his possession. He may have stolen it from Pietro, he may have been Pietro's confederate, he may have been the go-between of Pietro and his sister. It is of no consequence to us which is the correct solution.

'The main fact is that he *had* the pearl, and at that moment, when it was on his person, he was pursued by the police. He made for the factory in which he worked, and he knew that he had only a few minutes in which to conceal this enormously valuable prize, which would otherwise be found on him when he was searched. Six plaster casts of Napoleon were drying in the passage. One of them was still soft. In an instant Beppo, a skilful workman, made a small hole in the wet plaster, dropped in the pearl, and with a few touches covered over the aperture once more. It was an admirable hiding-place. No one could possibly find it. But Beppo was condemned to a year's imprisonment, and in the meanwhile his six busts were scattered over London. He could not tell which contained his treasure. Only by breaking them could he see. Even shaking would tell him nothing, for as the plaster was wet it was probable that the pearl would adhere to it – as, in fact, it has done. Beppo did not despair, and he conducted his search with considerable ingenuity and perseverance. Through a cousin who works with Gelder he found out the retail firms who had bought the busts. He managed to find employment with Morse Hudson, and in that way tracked down three of them. The pearl was not there. Then, with the help of some Italian employee, he succeeded in finding out where the other three busts had gone. The first was at Harker's. There he was dogged by his confederate, who held Beppo responsible for the loss of the pearl, and he stabbed him in the scuffle which followed.'

'If he was his confederate why should he carry his photograph?' I asked.

'As a means of tracing him if he wished to enquire about him from any third person. That was the obvious reason. Well, after the murder I calculated that Beppo would probably hurry rather than delay his movements. He would fear that the police would read his secret, and so he hastened on before they should get ahead of him. Of course, I could not say that he had not found the pearl in Harker's bust. I had not even concluded for certain that it was the pearl; but it was evident to me that he was looking for something, since he carried the bust past the other houses in order to break it in the garden which had a lamp overlooking it. Since Harker's bust was one in three the chances were exactly as I told you, two to one against the pearl being inside it. There remained two busts, and it was obvious that he would go for the London one first. I warned the inmates of the house, so as to avoid a second tragedy, and we went down with the happiest results. By that time, of course, I knew for certain that it was the Borgia pearl that we were after. The name of the murdered man linked the one event with the other. There only remained a single bust – the Reading one – and the pearl must be there. I bought it in your presence from the owner – and there it lies.'

We sat in silence for a moment.

'Well,' said Lestrade, 'I've seen you handle a good many cases, Mr Holmes, but I don't know that I ever knew a more workmanlike one than that. We're not jealous of you at Scotland Yard. No, sir, we are very proud of you, and if you come down tomorrow there's not a man, from the oldest inspector to the youngest constable, who wouldn't be glad to shake you by the hand.'

'Thank you!' said Holmes. 'Thank you!' and as he turned away it seemed to me that he was more nearly moved by the softer human emotions than I had ever seen him. A moment later he was the cold and practical thinker once more. 'Put the pearl in the safe, Watson,' said he, 'and get out the papers of the Conk-Singleton forgery case. Goodbye, Lestrade. If any little problem comes your way I shall be happy, if I can, to give you a hint or two as to its solution.'

9

The Three Students

It was in the year 1895 that a combination of events, into which I need not enter, caused Mr Sherlock Holmes and myself to spend some weeks in one of our great University towns, and it was during this time that the small but instructive adventure which I am about to relate befell us. It will be obvious that any details which would help the reader to exactly identify the college or the criminal would be injudicious and offensive. So painful a scandal may well be allowed to die out. With due discretion the incident itself may, however, be described, since it serves to illustrate some of those qualities for which my friend was remarkable. I will endeavour in my statement to avoid such terms as would serve to limit the events to any particular place, or give a clue as to the people concerned.

We were residing at the time in furnished lodgings close to a library where Sherlock Holmes was pursuing some laborious researches in early English charters – researches which led to results so striking that they may be the subject of one of my future narratives. Here it was that one evening we received a visit from an acquaintance, Mr Hilton Soames, tutor and lecturer at the College of St Luke's. Mr Soames was a tall, spare man, of a nervous and excitable temperament. I had always known him to be restless in his manner, but on this particular occasion he was in such a state of uncontrollable agitation that it was clear something very unusual had occurred.

'I trust, Mr Holmes, that you can spare me a few hours of your valuable time. We have had a very painful incident at St Luke's, and really, but for the happy chance of your being in the town, I should have been at a loss what to do.'

'I am very busy just now, and I desire no distractions,' my friend answered. 'I should much prefer that you called in the aid of the police.'

'No, no, my dear sir; such a course is utterly impossible. When once the law is evoked it cannot be stayed again, and this is just one of those cases where, for the credit of the college, it is most essential to avoid scandal. Your discretion is as well known as your powers, and you are the one man in the world who can help me. I beg you, Mr Holmes, to do what you can.'

My friend's temper had not improved since he had been deprived of the congenial surroundings of Baker Street. Without his scrapbook, his chemicals, and his homely untidiness, he was an uncomfortable man. He shrugged his shoulders in ungracious acquiescence, while our visitor in hurried words and with much excitable gesticulation poured forth his story.

'I must explain to you, Mr Holmes, that tomorrow is the first day of the examination for the Fortescue Scholarship. I am one of the examiners. My subject is Greek, and the first of the papers consists of a large passage of Greek translation which the candidate has not seen. This passage is printed on the examination paper, and it would naturally be an immense advantage if the candidate could prepare it in advance. For this reason great care is taken to keep the paper secret.

'Today about three o'clock the proofs of this paper

arrived from the printers. The exercise consists of half a chapter of Thucydides. I had to read it over carefully, as the text must be absolutely correct. At four-thirty my task was not yet completed. I had, however, promised to take tea in a friend's rooms, so I left the proof upon my desk. I was absent rather more than an hour.

'You are aware, Mr Holmes, that our college doors are double – a green baize one within and a heavy oak one without. As I approached my outer door I was amazed to see a key in it. For an instant I imagined that I had left my own there, but on feeling in my pocket I found that it was all right. The only duplicate which existed, so far as I knew, was that which belonged to my servant, Bannister, a man who has looked after my room for ten years, and whose honesty is absolutely above suspicion. I found that the key was indeed his, that he had entered my room to know if I wanted tea, and that he had very carelessly left the key in the door when he came out. His visit to my room must have been within a very few minutes of my leaving it. His forgetfulness about the key would have mattered little upon any other occasion, but on this one day it has produced the most deplorable consequences.

'The moment I looked at my table I was aware that someone had rummaged among my papers. The proof was in three long slips. I had left them all together. Now, I found that one of them was lying on the floor, one was on the side table near the window, and the third was where I had left it.'

Holmes stirred for the first time.

'The first page on the floor, the second in the window, the third where you left it,' said he.

'Exactly, Mr Holmes. You amaze me. How could you possibly know that?'

'Pray continue your very interesting statement.'

'For an instant I imagined that Bannister had taken the unpardonable liberty of examining my papers. He denied it, however, with the utmost earnestness, and I am convinced that he was speaking the truth. The alternative was that someone passing had observed the key in the door, had known that I was out, and had entered to look at the papers. A large sum of money is at stake, for the scholarship is a very valuable one, and an unscrupulous man might very well run a risk in order to gain an advantage over his fellows.

'Bannister was very much upset by the incident. He had nearly fainted when we found that the papers had undoubtedly been tampered with. I gave him a little brandy and left him collapsed in a chair while I made a most careful examination of the room. I soon saw that the intruder had left other traces of his presence besides the rumpled papers. On the table in the window were several shreds from a pencil which had been sharpened. A broken tip of lead was lying there also. Evidently the rascal had copied the paper in a great hurry, had broken his pencil, and had been compelled to put a fresh point to it.'

'Excellent!' said Holmes, who was recovering his good-humour as his attention became more engrossed by the case. 'Fortune has been your friend.'

'This was not all. I have a new writing-table with a fine surface of red leather. I am prepared to swear, and so is Bannister, that it was smooth and unstained. Now I found a clean cut in it about three inches long – not a mere scratch, but a positive cut. Not only this, but on the table I found a small ball of black dough, or clay, with specks of something which looks like sawdust in it. I am convinced that these marks were left by the man who rifled the papers. There were no footmarks and no other evidence as to his identity. I was at my wits' ends, when suddenly the happy thought occurred to me that you were in the town, and I came straight round to put the matter into your hands. Do help me, Mr Holmes! You see my dilemma. Either I must find the man or else the examination must be postponed until fresh papers are prepared, and since this cannot be done without explanation there will ensue a hideous scandal, which will throw a cloud not only on the college, but on the University. Above all things I desire to settle the matter quietly and discreetly.'

'I shall be happy to look into it and to give you such advice as I can,' said Holmes, rising and putting on his overcoat. 'The case is not entirely devoid of interest. Had anyone visited you in your room after the papers came to you?'

'Yes; young Daulat Ras, an Indian student who lives on the same stair, came in to ask me some particulars about the examination.'

'For which he was entered?'

'Yes.'

'And the papers were on your table?'

'To the best of my belief they were rolled up.'

'But might be recognised as proofs?'

'Possibly.'

'No one else in your room?'

'No.'

'Did anyone know that these proofs would be there?'

'No one save the printer.'

'Did this man Bannister know?'

'No, certainly not. No one knew.'

'Where is Bannister now?'

'He was very ill, poor fellow. I left him collapsed in the chair. I was in such a hurry to come to you.'

'You left your door open?'

'I locked up the papers first.'

'Then it amounts to this, Mr Soames, that unless the Indian student recognised the roll as being proofs, the man who tampered with them came upon them accidentally without knowing that they were there.'

'So it seems to me.'

Holmes gave an enigmatic smile.

'Well,' said he, 'let us go round. Not one of your cases, Watson – mental, not physical. All right; come if you want to. Now, Mr Soames – at your disposal!'

The sitting-room of our client opened by a long, low, latticed window on to the ancient lichen-tinted court of the old college. A Gothic arched door led to a worn stone staircase. On the ground floor was the tutor's room. Above were three students, one on each storey. It was already twilight when we reached the scene of our problem. Holmes halted and looked earnestly at the window. Then he approached it, and, standing on tiptoe with his neck craned, he looked into the room.

'He must have entered through the door. There is no opening except the one pane,' said our learned guide.

'Dear me!' said Holmes, and he smiled in a singular way as he glanced at our companion. 'Well, if there is nothing to be learned here we had best go inside.'

The lecturer unlocked the outer door and ushered us into his room. We stood at the entrance while Holmes made an examination of the carpet.

'I am afraid there are no signs here,' said he. 'One could hardly hope for any upon so dry a day. Your servant seems to have quite recovered. You left him in a chair, you say; which chair?'

'By the window there.'

'I see. Near this little table. You can come in now. I have finished with the carpet. Let us take the little table first. Of course, what has happened is very clear. The man entered and took the papers, sheet by sheet, from the central table. He carried them over to the window table, because from there he could see if you came across the courtyard, and so could effect an escape.'

'As a matter of fact he could not,' said Soames, 'for I entered by the side door.'

'Ah, that's good! Well, anyhow, that was in his mind. Let me see the three strips. No finger impressions – no! Well, he carried over this one first and he copied it. How long would it take him to do that, using every possible contraction? A quarter of an hour, not less. Then he tossed it down and seized the next. He was in the midst of that when your return caused him to make a very hurried retreat – *very* hurried, since he had not time to replace the papers which would tell you that he had been there. You were not aware of any hurrying feet on the stair as you entered the outer door?'

'No, I can't say I was.'

'Well, he wrote so furiously that he broke his pencil, and had, as you observe, to sharpen it again. This is of interest, Watson. The pencil was not an ordinary one. It was above the usual size, with a soft lead; the outer colour was dark blue, the maker's name was printed in silver lettering, and the piece remaining is only about an inch and a half long. Look for such a pencil, Mr Soames, and you have got your man. When I add that he possesses a large and very blunt knife, you have an additional aid.'

Mr Soames was somewhat overwhelmed by this flood of information. 'I can follow the other points,' said he, 'but really, in this matter of the length – '

Holmes held out a small chip with the letters NN and a space of clear wood after them.

'You see?'

'No, I fear that even now – '

'Watson, I have always done you an injustice. There are others. What could this NN be? It is at the end of a word. You are aware that Johann Faber is the most common maker's name. Is it not clear that there is just as much of the pencil left as usually follows the Johann?' He held the small table sideways to the electric light. 'I was hoping that if the paper on which he wrote was thin some trace of it might come through upon this polished surface. No, I see nothing. I don't think there is anything more to be learned here. Now for the central table. This small pellet is, I presume, the black, doughy mass you spoke of. Roughly pyramidal in shape and hollowed out, I perceive. As you say, there appear to be grains of sawdust in it. Dear me, this is very interesting. And the cut – a positive tear, I see. It began with a thin scratch and ended in a jagged hole. I am much indebted to you for directing my attention to this case, Mr Soames. Where does that door lead to?'

'To my bedroom.'

'Have you been in it since your adventure?'

'No; I came straight away for you.'

'I should like to have a glance round. What a charming, old-fashioned room! Perhaps you will kindly wait a minute until I have examined the floor. No, I see nothing. What about this curtain? You hang your clothes behind it. If anyone were forced to conceal himself in this room he must do it there, since the bed

253

is too low and the wardrobe too shallow. No one there, I suppose?'

As Holmes drew the curtain I was aware, from some little rigidity and alertness of his attitude, that he was prepared for an emergency. As a matter of fact the drawn curtain disclosed nothing but three or four suits of clothes hanging from a line of pegs. Holmes turned away and stooped suddenly to the floor.

'Halloa! What's this?' said he.

It was a small pyramid of black, putty-like stuff, exactly like the one upon the table of the study. Holmes held it out on his open palm in the glare of the electric light.

'Your visitor seems to have left traces in your bedroom as well as in your sitting-room, Mr Soames.'

'What could he have wanted there?'

'I think it is clear enough. You came back by an unexpected way, and so he had no warning until you were at the very door. What could he do? He caught up everything which would betray him and he rushed into your bedroom to conceal himself.'

'Good gracious, Mr Holmes, do you mean to tell me that all the time I was talking to Bannister in this room we had the man prisoner if we had only known it?'

'So I read it.'

'Surely there is another alternative, Mr Holmes. I don't know whether you observed my bedroom window?'

'Lattice-paned, lead framework, three separate windows, one swinging on hinge and large enough to admit a man.'

'Exactly. And it looks out on an angle of the courtyard so as to be partly invisible. The man might have effected his entrance there, left traces as he passed through the bedroom, and, finally, finding the door open, have escaped that way.'

Holmes shook his head impatiently.

'Let us be practical,' said he. 'I understand you to say that there are three students who use this stair and are in the habit of passing your door?'

'Yes, there are.'

'And they are all in for this examination?'

'Yes.'

'Have you any reason to suspect any one of them more than the others?'

Soames hesitated.

'It is a very delicate question,' said he. 'One hardly likes to throw suspicion where there are no proofs.'

'Let us hear the suspicions. I will look after the proofs.'

'I will tell you, then, in a few words the character of the three men who inhabit these rooms. The lower of the three is Gilchrist, a fine scholar and athlete; plays in the Rugby team and the cricket team for the college, and got his Blue for the hurdles and the long jump. He is a fine, manly fellow. His father was the notorious Sir Jabez Gilchrist, who ruined himself on the turf. My scholar has been left very poor, but he is hard-working and industrious. He will do well.

'The second floor is inhabited by Daulat Ras, the Indian. He is a quiet, inscrutable fellow, as most of those Indians are. He is well up in his work, though his Greek is his weak subject. He is steady and methodical.

'The top floor belongs to Miles McLaren. He is a brilliant fellow when he chooses to work – one of the brightest intellects of the University, but he is wayward, dissipated, and unprincipled. He was nearly expelled over a card scandal in his first year. He has been idling all this term, and he must look forward with dread to the examination.'

'Then it is he whom you suspect?'

'I dare not go so far as that. But of the three he is perhaps the least unlikely.'

'Exactly. Now, Mr Soames, let us have a look at your servant, Bannister.'

He was a little, white-faced, clean-shaven, grizzly-haired fellow of fifty. He was still suffering from this sudden disturbance of the quiet routine of his life. His plump face was twitching with his nervousness, and his fingers could not keep still.

'We are investigating this unhappy business, Bannister,' said his master.

'Yes, sir.'

'I understand,' said Holmes, 'that you left your key in the door?'

'Yes, sir.'

'Was it not very extraordinary that you should do this on the very day when there were these papers inside?'

'It was most unfortunate, sir. But I have occasionally done the same thing at other times.'

'When did you enter the room?'

'It was about half-past four. That is Mr Soames's tea time.'

'How long did you stay?'

'When I saw that he was absent I withdrew at once.'

'Did you look at these papers on the table?'

'No, sir; certainly not.'

'How came you to leave the key in the door?'

'I had the tea-tray in my hand. I thought I would come back for the key. Then I forgot.'

'Has the outer door a spring lock?'

'No, sir.'

'Then it was open all the time?'

'Yes, sir.'

'Anyone in the room could get out?'

'Yes, sir.'

'When Mr Soames returned and called for you, you were very much disturbed?'

'Yes, sir. Such a thing has never happened during the many years that I have been here. I nearly fainted, sir.'

'So I understand. Where were you when you began to feel bad?'

'Where was I, sir? Why, here, near the door.'

'That is singular, because you sat down in that chair over yonder near the corner. Why did you pass these other chairs?'

'I don't know, sir. It didn't matter to me where I sat.'

'I really don't think he knew much about it, Mr Holmes. He was looking very bad – quite ghastly.'

'You stayed here when your master left?'

'Only for a minute or so. Then I locked the door and went to my room.'

'Whom do you suspect?'

'Oh, I would not venture to say, sir. I don't believe there is any gentleman in this University who is capable of profiting by such an action. No, sir, I'll not believe it.'

'Thank you; that will do,' said Holmes. 'Oh, one more word. You have not mentioned to any of the three gentlemen whom you attend that anything is amiss?'

'No, sir; not a word.'

'You haven't seen any of them?'

'No, sir.'

THE RETURN OF SHERLOCK HOLMES

'Very good. Now, Mr Soames, we will take a walk in the quadrangle, if you please.'

Three yellow squares of light shone above us in the gathering gloom.

'Your three birds are all in their nests,' said Holmes, looking up. 'Halloa! What's that? One of them seems restless enough.'

It was the Indian, whose dark silhouette appeared suddenly upon his blind. He was pacing swiftly up and down his room.

'I should like to have a peep at each of them,' said Holmes. 'Is it possible?'

'No difficulty in the world,' Soames answered. 'This set of rooms is quite the oldest in the college, and it is not unusual for visitors to go over them. Come along, and I will personally conduct you.'

'No names, please!' said Holmes, as we knocked at Gilchrist's door. A tall, flaxen-haired, slim young fellow opened it, and made us welcome when he understood our errand. There were some really curious pieces of mediaeval domestic architecture within. Holmes was so charmed with one of them that he insisted on drawing it on his notebook, broke his pencil, had to borrow one from our host, and finally borrowed a knife to sharpen his own. The same curious accident happened to him in the rooms of the Indian – a silent, little, hook-nosed fellow, who eyed us askance and was obviously glad when Holmes's architectural studies had come to an end. I could not see that in either case Holmes had come upon the clue for which he was searching. Only at the third did our visit prove abortive. The outer door would not open to our knock, and nothing more substantial than a torrent of bad language came from behind it. 'I don't care who you are. You can go to blazes!' roared the angry voice. 'Tomorrow's the exam, and I won't be drawn by anyone.'

'A rude fellow,' said our guide, flushing with anger as we withdrew down the stair. 'Of course, he did not realise that it was I who was knocking, but none the less his conduct was very uncourteous, and, indeed, under the circumstances rather suspicious.'

Holmes's response was a curious one.

'Can you tell me his exact height?' he asked.

'Really, Mr Holmes, I cannot undertake to say. He is taller than the Indian, not so tall as Gilchrist. I suppose five foot six would be about it.'

'That is very important,' said Holmes. 'And now, Mr Soames, I wish you good-night.'

Our guide cried aloud in his astonishment and dismay. 'Good gracious, Mr Holmes, you are surely not going to leave me in this abrupt fashion! You don't seem to realise the position. Tomorrow is the examination. I must take some definite action tonight. I cannot allow the examination to be held if one of the papers has been tampered with. The situation must be faced.'

'You must leave it as it is. I shall drop round early tomorrow morning and chat the matter over. It is possible that I may be in a position then to indicate some course of action. Meanwhile you change nothing – nothing at all.'

'Very good, Mr Holmes.'

'You can be perfectly easy in your mind. We shall certainly find some way out of your difficulties. I will take the black clay with me, also the pencil cuttings. Goodbye.'

When we were out in the darkness of the quadrangle

we again looked up at the windows. The Indian still paced his room. The others were invisible.

'Well, Watson, what do you think of it?' Holmes asked, as we came out into the main street. 'Quite a little parlour game – sort of three-card trick, is it not? There are your three men. It must be one of them. You take your choice. Which is yours?'

'The foul-mouthed fellow at the top. He is the one with the worst record. And yet that Indian was a sly fellow also. Why should he be pacing his room all the time?'

'There is nothing in that. Many men do it when they are trying to learn anything by heart.'

'He looked at us in a queer way.'

'So would you if a flock of strangers came in on you when you were preparing for an examination next day, and every moment was of value. No, I see nothing in that. Pencils, too, and knives – all was satisfactory. But that fellow *does* puzzle me.'

'Who?'

'Why, Bannister, the servant. What's his game in the matter?'

'He impressed me as being a perfectly honest man.'

'So he did me. That's the puzzling part. Why should a perfectly honest man – well, well, here's a large stationer's. We shall begin our researches here.'

There were only four stationers of any consequence in the town, and at each Holmes produced his pencil chips and bid high for a duplicate. All were agreed that one could be ordered, but that it was not a usual size of pencil and that it was seldom kept in stock. My friend did not appear to be depressed by his failure, but shrugged his shoulders in half-humorous resignation.

'No good, my dear Watson. This, the best and only final clue, has run to nothing. But, indeed, I have little doubt that we can build up a sufficient case without it. By Jove! my dear fellow, it is nearly nine, and the landlady babbled of green peas at seven-thirty. What with your eternal tobacco, Watson, and your irregularity at meals, I expect that you will get notice to quit and that I shall share your downfall – not, however, before we have solved the problem of the nervous tutor, the careless servant, and the three enterprising students.'

Holmes made no further allusion to the matter that day, though he sat lost in thought for a long time after our belated dinner. At eight in the morning he came into my room just as I finished my toilet.

'Well, Watson,' said he, 'it is time we went down to St Luke's. Can you do without breakfast?'

'Certainly.'

'Soames will be in a dreadful fidget until we are able to tell him something positive.'

'Have you anything positive to tell him?'

'I think so.'

'You have formed a conclusion?'

'Yes, my dear Watson; I have solved the mystery.'

'But what fresh evidence could you have got?'

'Aha! It is not for nothing that I have turned myself out of bed at the untimely hour of six. I have put in two hours' hard work and covered at least five miles, with something to show for it. Look at that!'

He held out his hand. On the palm were three little pyramids of black, doughy clay.

'Why, Holmes, you had only two yesterday!'

'And one more this morning. It is a fair argument

that wherever number three came from is also the source of numbers one and two. Eh, Watson? Well, come along and put friend Soames out of his pain.'

The unfortunate tutor was certainly in a state of pitiable agitation when we found him in his chambers. In a few hours the examination would commence, and he was still in the dilemma between making the facts public and allowing the culprit to compete for the valuable scholarship. He could hardly stand still, so great was his mental agitation, and he ran towards Holmes with two eager hands outstretched.

'Thank Heaven that you have come! I feared that you had given it up in despair. What am I to do? Shall the examination proceed?'

'Yes; let it proceed by all means.'

'But this rascal – ?'

'He shall not compete.'

'You know him?'

'I think so. If this matter is not to become public we must give ourselves certain powers, and resolve ourselves into a small private court-martial. You there, if you please, Soames! Watson, you here! I'll take the armchair in the middle. I think that we are now sufficiently imposing to strike terror into a guilty breast. Kindly ring the bell!'

Bannister entered, and shrunk back in evident surprise and fear at our judicial appearance.

'You will kindly close the door,' said Holmes. 'Now, Bannister, will you please tell us the truth about yesterday's incident?'

The man turned white to the roots of his hair.

'I have told you everything, sir.'

'Nothing to add?'

'Nothing at all, sir.'

'Well, then, I must make some suggestions to you. When you sat down on that chair yesterday, did you do so in order to conceal some object which would have shown who had been in the room?'

Bannister's face was ghastly.

'No, sir; certainly not.'

'It is only a suggestion,' said Holmes, suavely. 'I frankly admit that I am unable to prove it. But it seems probable enough, since the moment that Mr Soames's back was turned you released the man who was hiding in that bedroom.'

Bannister licked his dry lips.

'There was no man, sir.'

'Ah, that's a pity, Bannister. Up to now you may have spoken the truth, but now I know that you have lied.'

The man's face set in sullen defiance.

'There was no man, sir.'

'Come, come, Bannister!'

'No, sir; there was no one.'

'In that case you can give us no further information. Would you please remain in the room? Stand over there near the bedroom door. Now, Soames, I am going to ask you to have the great kindness to go up to the room of young Gilchrist, and to ask him to step down into yours.'

An instant later the tutor returned, bringing with him the student. He was a fine figure of a man, tall, lithe, and agile, with a springy step and a pleasant, open face. His troubled blue eyes glanced at each of us, and finally rested with an expression of blank dismay upon Bannister in the farther corner.

'Just close the door,' said Holmes. 'Now, Mr

Gilchrist, we are all quite alone here, and no one need ever know one word of what passes between us. We can be perfectly frank with each other. We want to know, Mr Gilchrist, how you, an honourable man, ever came to commit such an action as that of yesterday?'

The unfortunate young man staggered back and cast a look full of horror and reproach at Bannister.

'No, no, Mr Gilchrist, sir; I never said a word – never one word!' cried the servant.

'No, but you have now,' said Holmes. 'Now, sir, you must see that after Bannister's words your position is hopeless, and that your only chance lies in a frank confession.'

For a moment Gilchrist, with upraised hand, tried to control his writhing features. The next he had thrown himself on his knees beside the table and, burying his face in his hands, he had burst into a storm of passionate sobbing.

'Come, come,' said Holmes, kindly; 'it is human to err, and at least no one can accuse you of being a callous criminal. Perhaps it would be easier for you if I were to tell Mr Soames what occurred, and you can check me where I am wrong. Shall I do so? Well, well, don't trouble to answer. Listen, and see that I do you no injustice.

'From the moment, Mr Soames, that you said to me that no one, not even Bannister, could have told that the papers were in your room, the case began to take a definite shape in my mind. The printer one could, of course, dismiss. He could examine the papers in his own office. The Indian I also thought nothing of. If the proofs were in a roll he could not possibly know what they were. On the other hand, it seemed an unthinkable coincidence that a man should dare to enter the room, and that by chance on that very day the papers were on the table. I dismissed that. The man who entered knew that the papers were there. How did he know?

'When I approached your room I examined the window. You amused me by supposing that I was contemplating the possibility of someone having in broad daylight, under the eyes of all these opposite rooms, forced himself through it. Such an idea was absurd. I was measuring how tall a man would need to be in order to see as he passed what papers were on the central table. I am six feet high, and I could do it with an effort. No one less than that would have a chance. Already you see I had reason to think that if one of your three students was a man of unusual height he was the most worth watching of the three.

'I entered and I took you into my confidence as to the suggestions of the side table. Of the centre table I could make nothing, until in your description of Gilchrist you mentioned that he was a long-distance jumper. Then the whole thing came to me in an instant, and I only needed certain corroborative proofs, which I speedily obtained.

'What happened was this. This young fellow had employed his afternoon at the athletic grounds, where he had been practising the jump. He returned carrying his jumping shoes, which are provided, as you are aware, with several sharp spikes. As he passed your window he saw, by means of his great height, these proofs upon your table, and conjectured what they were. No harm would have been done had it not been that as he passed your door he perceived the key which had been left by the carelessness of your servant. A sudden impulse came over him to enter and see if they were indeed the proofs. It was not a dangerous exploit, for he could always pretend that he had simply looked in to ask a question.

'Well, when he saw that they were indeed the proofs, it was then that he yielded to temptation. He put his shoes on the table. What was it you put on that chair near the window?'

'Gloves,' said the young man.

Holmes looked triumphantly at Bannister. 'He put his gloves on the chair, and he took the proofs, sheet by sheet, to copy them. He thought the tutor must return by the main gate, and that he would see him. As we know, he came back by the side gate. Suddenly he heard him at the very door. There was no possible escape. He forgot his gloves, but he caught up his shoes and darted into the bedroom. You observe that the scratch on that table is slight at one side, but deepens in the direction of the bedroom door. That in itself is enough to show us that the shoe had been drawn in that direction and that the culprit had taken refuge there. The earth round the spike had been left on the table, and a second sample was loosened and fell in the bedroom. I may add that I walked out to the athletic grounds this morning, saw that tenacious black clay is used in the jumping-pit, and carried away a specimen of it, together with some of the fine tan or sawdust which is strewn over it to prevent the athlete from slipping. Have I told the truth, Mr Gilchrist?'

The student had drawn himself erect.

'Yes, sir, it is true,' said he.

'Good heavens, have you nothing to add?' cried Soames.

'Yes, sir, I have, but the shock of this disgraceful

exposure has bewildered me. I have a letter here, Mr Soames, which I wrote to you early this morning in the middle of a restless night. It was before I knew that my sin had found me out. Here it is, sir. You will see that I have said, "I have determined not to go in for the examination. I have been offered a commission in the Rhodesian Police, and I am going out to South Africa at once." '

'I am indeed pleased to hear that you did not intend to profit by your unfair advantage,' said Soames. 'But why did you change your purpose?'

Gilchrist pointed to Bannister.

'There is the man who set me in the right path,' said he.

'Come now, Bannister,' said Holmes. 'It will be clear to you from what I have said that only you could have let this young man out, since you were left in the room, and must have locked the door when you went out. As to his escaping by that window, it was incredible. Can you not clear up the last point in this mystery, and tell us the reasons for your action?'

'It was simple enough, sir, if you only had known; but with all your cleverness it was impossible that you could know. Time was, sir, when I was butler to old Sir Jabez Gilchrist, this young gentleman's father. When he was ruined I came to the college as servant, but I never forgot my old employer because he was down in the world. I watched his son all I could for the sake of the old days. Well, sir, when I came into this room yesterday when the alarm was given, the very first thing I saw was Mr Gilchrist's tan gloves a-lying in that chair. I knew those gloves well, and I understood their message. If Mr Soames saw them the game was up. I flopped down into that chair, and nothing would budge me until Mr Soames he went for you. Then out came my poor young master, whom I had dandled on my knee, and confessed it all to me. Wasn't it natural, sir, that I should save him, and wasn't it natural also that I should try to speak to him as his dead father would have done, and make him understand that he could not profit by such a deed? Could you blame me, sir?'

'No, indeed,' said Holmes, heartily, springing to his feet. 'Well, Soames, I think we have cleared your little problem up, and our breakfast awaits us at home. Come, Watson! As to you, sir, I trust that a bright future awaits you in Rhodesia. For once you have fallen low. Let us see in the future how high you can rise.'

10

The Golden Pince-Nez

When I look at the three massive manuscript volumes which contain our work for the year 1894 I confess that it is very difficult for me, out of such a wealth of material, to select the cases which are most interesting in themselves and at the same time most conducive to a display of those peculiar powers for which my friend was famous. As I turn over the pages I see my notes upon the repulsive story of the red leech and the terrible death of Crosby the banker. Here also I find an account of the Addleton tragedy and the singular contents of the ancient British barrow. The famous Smith-Mortimer succession case comes also within this period, and so does the tracking and arrest of Huret, the Boulevard assassin – an exploit which won for Holmes an autograph letter of thanks from the French President and the Order of the Legion of Honour. Each of these would furnish a narrative, but on the whole I am of opinion that none of them unite so many singular points of interest as the episode of Yoxley Old Place, which includes not only the lamentable death of young Willoughby Smith, but also those subsequent developments which threw so curious a light upon the causes of the crime.

It was a wild, tempestuous night towards the close of November. Holmes and I sat together in silence all the evening, he engaged with a powerful lens deciphering the remains of the original inscription upon a palimpsest, I deep in a recent treatise upon surgery. Outside the wind howled down Baker Street, while the rain beat fiercely against the windows. It was strange there in the very depths of the town, with ten miles of man's handiwork on every side of us, to feel the iron grip of Nature, and to be conscious that to the huge elemental forces all London was no more than the molehills that dot the fields. I walked to the window and looked out on the deserted street. The occasional lamps gleamed on the expanse of muddy road and shining pavement. A single cab was splashing its way from the Oxford Street end.

'Well, Watson, it's as well we have not to turn out tonight,' said Holmes, laying aside his lens and rolling up the palimpsest. 'I've done enough for one sitting. It is trying work for the eyes. So far as I can make out it is nothing more exciting than an Abbey's accounts dating from the second half of the fifteenth century. Halloa! halloa! halloa! What's this?'

Amid the droning of the wind there had come the stamping of a horse's hoofs and the long grind of a wheel as it rasped against the kerb. The cab which I had seen had pulled up at our door.

'What can he want?' I ejaculated, as a man stepped out of it.

'Want! He wants us. And we, my poor Watson, want overcoats and cravats and goloshes, and every aid that man ever invented to fight the weather. Wait a bit, though! There's the cab off again! There's hope yet. He'd have kept it if he had wanted us to come. Run down, my dear fellow, and open the door, for all virtuous folk have been long in bed.'

When the light of the hall lamp fell upon our midnight visitor I had no difficulty in recognising him.

It was young Stanley Hopkins, a promising detective, in whose career Holmes had several times shown a very practical interest.

'Is he in?' he asked, eagerly.

'Come up, my dear sir,' said Holmes's voice from above. 'I hope you have no designs upon us on such a night as this.'

The detective mounted the stairs, and our lamp gleamed upon his shining waterproof. I helped him out of it while Holmes knocked a blaze out of the logs in the grate.

'Now, my dear Hopkins, draw up and warm your toes,' said he. 'Here's a cigar, and the doctor has a prescription containing hot water and a lemon which is good medicine on a night like this. It must be something important which has brought you out in such a gale.'

'It is indeed, Mr Holmes. I've had a bustling afternoon, I promise you. Did you see anything of the Yoxley case in the latest editions?'

'I've seen nothing later than the fifteenth century today.'

'Well, it was only a paragraph, and all wrong at that, so you have not missed anything. I haven't let the grass grow under my feet. It's down in Kent, seven miles from Chatham and three from the railway line. I was wired for at three-fifteen, reached Yoxley Old Place at five, conducted my investigation, was back at Charing Cross by the last train, and straight to you by cab.'

'Which means, I suppose, that you are not quite clear about your case?'

'It means that I can make neither head nor tail of it. So far as I can see it is just as tangled a business as ever I handled, and yet at first it seemed so simple that one couldn't go wrong. There's no motive, Mr Holmes. That's what bothers me – I can't put my hand on a motive. Here's a man dead – there's no denying that – but, so far as I can see, no reason on earth why anyone should wish him harm.'

Holmes lit his cigar and leaned back in his chair.

'Let us hear about it,' said he.

'I've got my facts pretty clear,' said Stanley Hopkins. 'All I want now is to know what they all mean. The story, so far as I can make it out, is like this. Some years ago this country house, Yoxley Old Place, was taken by an elderly man, who gave the name of Professor Coram. He was an invalid, keeping his bed half the time, and the other half hobbling round the house with a stick or being pushed about the grounds by the gardener in a bath-chair. He was well liked by the few neighbours who called upon him, and he has the reputation down there of being a very learned man. His household used to consist of an elderly housekeeper, Mrs Marker, and of a maid, Susan Tarlton. These have both been with him since his arrival, and they seem to be women of excellent character. The Professor is writing a learned book, and he found it necessary about a year ago to engage a secretary. The first two that he tried were not successes; but the third, Mr Willoughby Smith, a very young man straight from the University, seems to have been just what his employer wanted. His work consisted in writing all the morning to the Professor's dictation, and he usually spent the evening in hunting up references and passages which bore upon the next day's work. This Willoughby Smith has nothing against him either as a boy at Uppingham or as a young man at Cambridge. I have seen his testimonials, and from the first he was a decent, quiet, hard-working fellow, with no weak spot in him at all. And yet this is the lad who has met his death this morning in the Professor's study under circumstances which can point only to murder.'

The wind howled and screamed at the windows. Holmes and I drew closer to the fire while the young inspector slowly and point by point developed his singular narrative.

'If you were to search all England,' said he, 'I don't suppose you could find a household more self-contained or free from outside influences. Whole weeks would pass and not one of them go past the garden gate. The Professor was buried in his work and existed for nothing else. Young Smith knew nobody in the neighbourhood, and lived very much as his employer did. The two women had nothing to take them from the house. Mortimer the gardener, who wheels the bath-chair, is an Army pensioner – an old Crimean man of excellent character. He does not live in the house, but in a three-roomed cottage at the other end of the garden. Those are the only people that you would find within the grounds of Yoxley Old Place. At the same time, the gate of the garden is a hundred yards from the main London to Chatham road. It opens with a latch, and there is nothing to prevent anyone from walking in.

'Now I will give you the evidence of Susan Tarlton, who is the only person who can say anything positive about the matter. It was in the forenoon, between eleven and twelve. She was engaged at the moment in hanging some curtains in the upstairs front bedroom. Professor Coram was still in bed, for when the weather is bad he seldom rises before midday. The housekeeper was busied with some work in the back of the house. Willoughby Smith had been in his bedroom, which he uses as a sitting-room; but the maid heard him at that moment pass along the passage and descend to the study immediately below her. She did not see him, but she says that she could not be mistaken in his quick, firm tread. She did not hear the study door close, but a minute or so later there was a dreadful cry in the room below. It was a wild, hoarse scream, so strange and unnatural that it might have come either from a man or a woman. At the same instant there was a heavy thud, which shook the old house, and then all was silence. The maid stood petrified for a moment, and then, recovering her courage, she ran downstairs. The study door was shut, and she opened it. Inside young Mr Willoughby Smith was stretched upon the floor. At first she could see no injury, but as she tried to raise him she saw that blood was pouring from the underside of his neck. It was pierced by a very small but very deep wound, which had divided the carotid artery. The instrument with which the injury had been inflicted lay upon the carpet beside him. It was one of those small sealing-wax knives to be found on old-fashioned writing-tables, with an ivory handle and a stiff blade. It was part of the fittings of the Professor's own desk.

'At first the maid thought that young Smith was already dead, but on pouring some water from the carafe over his forehead he opened his eyes for an instant. "The Professor," he murmured – "it was she." The maid is prepared to swear that those were the exact words. He tried desperately to say something else, and he held his right hand up in the air. Then he fell back dead.

'In the meantime the housekeeper had also arrived upon the scene, but she was just too late to catch the young man's dying words. Leaving Susan with the body, she hurried to the Professor's room. He was sitting up in bed horribly agitated, for he had heard enough to convince him that something terrible had occurred. Mrs Marker is prepared to swear that the Professor was still in his night-clothes, and, indeed, it was impossible for him to dress without the help of Mortimer, whose orders were to come at twelve o'clock. The Professor declares that he heard the distant cry, but that he knows nothing more. He can give no explanation of the young man's last words, "The Professor – it was she," but imagines that they were the outcome of delirium. He believes that Willoughby Smith had not an enemy in the world, and can give no reason for the crime. His first action was to send Mortimer the gardener for the local police. A little later the chief constable sent for me. Nothing was moved before I got there, and strict orders were given that no one should walk upon the paths leading to the house. It was a splendid chance of putting your theories into practice, Mr Sherlock Holmes. There was really nothing wanting.'

'Except Mr Sherlock Holmes,' said my companion, with a somewhat bitter smile. 'Well, let us hear about it. What sort of job did you make of it?'

'I must ask you first, Mr Holmes, to glance at this rough plan, which will give you a general idea of the position of the Professor's study and the various points of the case. It will help you in following my investigation.'

He unfolded the rough chart, which I here reproduce, and he laid it across Holmes's knee. I rose, and, standing behind Holmes, I studied it over his shoulder.

'It is very rough, of course, and it only deals with the points which seem to me to be essential. All the rest you will see later for yourself. Now, first of all, presuming that the assassin entered the house, how did he or she come in? Undoubtedly by the garden path and the back door, from which there is direct access to the study. Any other way would have been exceedingly complicated. The escape must have also been made along that line, for of the two other exits from the room one was blocked by Susan as she ran downstairs and the other leads straight to the Professor's bedroom. I therefore directed my attention at once to the garden path, which was saturated with recent rain and would certainly show any footmarks.

'My examination showed me that I was dealing with a cautious and expert criminal. No footmarks were to be found on the path. There could be no question, however, that someone had passed along the grass border which lines the path, and that he had done so in order to avoid leaving a track. I could not find anything in the nature of a distinct impression, but the grass was trodden down and someone had undoubtedly passed.

It could only have been the murderer, since neither the gardener nor anyone else had been there that morning and the rain had only begun during the night.'

'One moment,' said Holmes. 'Where does this path lead to?'

'To the road.'

'How long is it?'

'A hundred yards or so.'

'At the point where the path passes through the gate you could surely pick up the tracks?'

'Unfortunately, the path was tiled at that point.'

'Well, on the road itself?'

'No; it was all trodden into mire.'

'Tut-tut! Well, then, these tracks upon the grass, were they coming or going?'

'It was impossible to say. There was never any outline.'

'A large foot or a small?'

'You could not distinguish.'

Holmes gave an ejaculation of impatience.

'It has been pouring rain and blowing a hurricane ever since,' said he. 'It will be harder to read now than that palimpsest. Well, well, it can't be helped. What did you do, Hopkins, after you had made certain that you had made certain of nothing?'

'I think I made certain of a good deal, Mr Holmes. I knew that someone had entered the house cautiously from without. I next examined the corridor. It is lined with cocoanut matting and had taken no impression of any kind. This brought me into the study itself. It is a scantily-furnished room. The main article is a large writing-table with a fixed bureau. This bureau consists of a double column of drawers with a central small cupboard between them. The drawers were open, the cupboard locked. The drawers, it seems, were always open, and nothing of value was kept in them. There were some papers of importance in the cupboard, but there were no signs that this had been tampered with, and the Professor assures me that nothing was missing. It is certain that no robbery has been committed.

'I come now to the body of the young man. It was found near the bureau, and just to the left of it, as marked upon that chart. The stab was on the right side of the neck and from behind forwards, so that it is almost impossible that it could have been self-inflicted.'

'Unless he fell upon the knife,' said Holmes.

'Exactly. The idea crossed my mind. But we found the knife some feet away from the body, so that seems impossible. Then, of course, there are the man's own dying words. And, finally, there was this very important piece of evidence which was found clasped in the dead man's right hand.'

From his pocket Stanley Hopkins drew a small paper packet. He unfolded it and disclosed a golden pince-nez, with two broken ends of black silk cord dangling from the end of it. 'Willoughby Smith had excellent sight,' he added. 'There can be no question that this was snatched from the face or the person of the assassin.'

Sherlock Holmes took the glasses into his hand and examined them with the utmost attention and interest. He held them on his nose, endeavoured to read through them, went to the window and stared up the street with them, looked at them most minutely in the full light of the lamp, and finally, with a chuckle, seated himself at the table and wrote a few lines upon a sheet of paper, which he tossed across to Stanley Hopkins.

'That's the best I can do for you,' said he. 'It may prove to be of some use.'

The astonished detective read the note aloud. It ran as follows:

'Wanted, a woman of good address, attired like a lady. She has a remarkably thick nose, with eyes which are set close upon either side of it. She has a puckered forehead, a peering expression, and probably rounded shoulders. There are indications that she has had recourse to an optician at least twice during the last few months. As her glasses are of remarkable strength and as opticians are not very numerous, there should be no difficulty in tracing her.'

Holmes smiled at the astonishment of Hopkins, which must have been reflected upon my features.

'Surely my deductions are simplicity itself,' said he. 'It would be difficult to name any articles which afford a finer field for inference than a pair of glasses, especially so remarkable a pair as these. That they belong to a woman I infer from their delicacy, and also, of course, from the last words of the dying man. As to her being a person of refinement and well dressed, they are, as you perceive, handsomely mounted in solid gold, and it is inconceivable that anyone who wore such glasses could be slatternly in other respects. You will find that the clips are too wide for your nose, showing that the lady's nose was very broad at the base. This sort of nose is usually a short and coarse one, but there are a sufficient number of exceptions to prevent me from being dogmatic or from insisting upon this point in my description. My own face is a narrow one, and yet I find that I cannot get my eyes into the centre, or near the centre, of these glasses. Therefore the lady's eyes are set very near to the sides of the nose. You will perceive, Watson, that the glasses are concave and of unusual strength. A lady whose vision has been so extremely contracted all her life is sure to have the physical characteristics of such vision, which are seen in the forehead, the eyelids, and the shoulders.'

'Yes,' I said, 'I can follow each of your arguments. I confess, however, that I am unable to understand how you arrive at the double visit to the optician.'

Holmes took the glasses in his hand.

'You will perceive,' he said, 'that the clips are lined with tiny bands of cork to soften the pressure upon the nose. One of these is discoloured and worn to some slight extent, but the other is new. Evidently one has fallen off and been replaced. I should judge that the older of them has not been there more than a few months. They exactly correspond, so I gather that the lady went back to the same establishment for the second.'

'By George, it's marvellous!' cried Hopkins, in an ecstasy of admiration. 'To think that I had all that evidence in my hand and never knew it! I had intended, however, to go the round of the London opticians.'

'Of course you would. Meanwhile, have you anything more to tell us about the case?'

'Nothing, Mr Holmes. I think that you know as much as I do now – probably more. We have had enquiries made as to any stranger seen on the country roads or at the railway station. We have heard of none. What beats me is the utter want of all object in the crime. Not a ghost of a motive can anyone suggest.'

'Ah! there I am not in a position to help you. But I suppose you want us to come out tomorrow?'

'If it is not asking too much, Mr Holmes. There's a train from Charing Cross to Chatham at six in the morning, and we should be at Yoxley Old Place between eight and nine.'

'Then we shall take it. Your case has certainly some features of great interest, and I shall be delighted to look into it. Well, it's nearly one, and we had best get a few hours' sleep. I dare say you can manage all right on the sofa in front of the fire. I'll light my spirit-lamp and give you a cup of coffee before we start.'

The gale had blown itself out next day, but it was a bitter morning when we started upon our journey. We saw the cold winter sun rise over the dreary marshes of the Thames and the long, sullen reaches of the river, which I shall ever associate with our pursuit of the Andaman Islander in the earlier days of our career. After a long and weary journey we alighted at a small station some miles from Chatham. While a horse was being put into a trap at the local inn we snatched a hurried breakfast, and so we were all ready for business when we at last arrived at Yoxley Old Place. A constable met us at the garden gate.

'Well, Wilson, any news?'

'No, sir, nothing.'

'No reports of any stranger seen?'

'No, sir. Down at the station they are certain that no stranger either came or went yesterday.'

'Have you had enquiries made at inns and lodgings?'

'Yes, sir; there is no one that we cannot account for.'

'Well, it's only a reasonable walk to Chatham. Anyone might stay there, or take a train without being observed. This is the garden path of which I spoke, Mr Holmes. I'll pledge my word there was no mark on it yesterday.'

'On which side were the marks on the grass?'

'This side, sir. This narrow margin of grass between the path and the flower-bed. I can't see the traces now, but they were clear to me then.'

'Yes, yes; someone has passed along,' said Holmes, stooping over the grass border. 'Our lady must have picked her steps carefully, must she not, since on the one side she would leave a track on the path, and on the other an even clearer one on the soft bed?'

'Yes, sir, she must have been a cool hand.'

I saw an intent look pass over Holmes's face.

'You say that she must have come back this way?'

'Yes, sir; there is no other.'

'On this strip of grass?'

'Certainly, Mr Holmes.'

'Hum! It was a very remarkable performance – very remarkable. Well, I think we have exhausted the path. Let us go farther. This garden door is usually kept open, I suppose? Then this visitor had nothing to do but to walk in. The idea of murder was not in her mind, or she would have provided herself with some sort of weapon, instead of having to pick this knife off the writing-table. She advanced along this corridor, leaving no traces upon the cocoanut matting. Then she found herself in this study. How long was she there? We have no means of judging.'

'Not more than a few minutes, sir. I forgot to tell you that Mrs Marker, the housekeeper, had been in there tidying not very long before – about a quarter of an hour, she says.'

'Well, that gives us a limit. Our lady enters this room

and what does she do? She goes over to the writing-table. What for? Not for anything in the drawers. If there had been anything worth her taking it would surely have been locked up. No; it was for something in that wooden bureau. Halloa! what is that scratch upon the face of it? Just hold a match, Watson. Why did you not tell me of this, Hopkins?'

The mark which he was examining began upon the brass work on the right-hand side of the keyhole, and extended for about four inches, where it had scratched the varnish from the surface.

'I noticed it, Mr Holmes. But you'll always find scratches round a keyhole.'

'This is recent, quite recent. See how the brass shines where it is cut. An old scratch would be the same colour as the surface. Look at it through my lens. There's the varnish, too, like earth on each side of a furrow. Is Mrs Marker there?'

A sad-faced, elderly woman came into the room.

'Did you dust this bureau yesterday morning?'

'Yes, sir.'

'Did you notice this scratch?'

'No, sir, I did not.'

'I am sure you did not, for a duster would have swept away these shreds of varnish. Who has the key of this bureau?'

'The Professor keeps it on his watch-chain.'

'Is it a simple key?'

'No, sir; it is a Chubb's key.'

'Very good. Mrs Marker, you can go. Now we are making a little progress. Our lady enters the room, advances to the bureau, and either opens it or tries to do so. While she is thus engaged young Willoughby Smith enters the room. In her hurry to withdraw the key she makes this scratch upon the door. He seizes her, and she, snatching up the nearest object, which happens to be this knife, strikes at him in order to make him let go his hold. The blow is a fatal one. He falls and she escapes, either with or without the object for which she has come. Is Susan the maid there? Could anyone have got away through that door after the time that you heard the cry, Susan?'

'No sir; it is impossible. Before I got down the stair I'd have seen anyone in the passage. Besides, the door never opened, for I would have heard it.'

'That settles this exit. Then no doubt the lady went out the way she came. I understand that this other passage leads only to the Professor's room. There is no exit that way?'

'No, sir.'

'We shall go down it and make the acquaintance of the Professor. Halloa, Hopkins! this is very important, very important indeed. The Professor's corridor is also lined with cocoanut matting.'

'Well, sir, what of that?'

'Don't you see any bearing upon the case? Well, well, I don't insist upon it. No doubt I am wrong. And yet it seems to me to be suggestive. Come with me and introduce me.'

We passed down the passage, which was of the same length as that which led to the garden. At the end was a short flight of steps ending in a door. Our guide knocked, and then ushered us into the Professor's bedroom.

It was a very large chamber, lined with innumerable volumes, which had overflowed from the shelves and lay in piles in the corners, or were stacked all round at the base of the cases. The bed was in the centre of the room, and in it, propped up with pillows, was the owner of the house. I have seldom seen a more remarkable-looking person. It was a gaunt, aquiline face which was turned towards us, with piercing dark eyes, which lurked in deep hollows under overhung and tufted brows. His hair and beard were white, save that the latter was curiously stained with yellow around his mouth. A cigarette glowed amid the tangle of white hair, and the air of the room was fetid with stale tobacco-smoke. As he held out his hand to Holmes I perceived that it also was stained yellow with nicotine.

'A smoker, Mr Holmes?' said he, speaking well-chosen English with a curious little mincing accent. 'Pray take a cigarette. And you, sir? I can recommend them, for I have them especially prepared by Ionides of Alexandria. He sends me a thousand at a time, and I grieve to say that I have to arrange for a fresh supply every fortnight. Bad, sir, very bad, but an old man has few pleasures. Tobacco and my work – that is all that is left to me.'

Holmes had lit a cigarette, and was shooting little darting glances all over the room.

'Tobacco and my work, but now only tobacco,' the old man exclaimed. 'Alas! what a fatal interruption! Who could have foreseen such a terrible catastrophe? So estimable a young man! I assure you that after a few months' training he was an admirable assistant. What do you think of the matter, Mr Holmes?'

'I have not yet made up my mind.'

'I shall indeed be indebted to you if you can throw a light where all is so dark to us. To a poor bookworm and invalid like myself such a blow is paralysing. I seem to have lost the faculty of thought. But you are a man of action – you are a man of affairs. It is part of the everyday routine of your life. You can preserve your balance in every emergency. We are fortunate indeed in having you at our side.'

Holmes was pacing up and down one side of the room whilst the old Professor was talking. I observed that he was smoking with extraordinary rapidity. It was evident that he shared our host's liking for the fresh Alexandrian cigarettes.

'Yes, sir, it is a crushing blow,' said the old man. 'That is my *magnum opus* – the pile of papers on the side table yonder. It is my analysis of the documents found in the Coptic monasteries of Syria and Egypt, a work which will cut deep at the very foundations of revealed religion. With my enfeebled health I do not know whether I shall ever be able to complete it now that my assistant has been taken from me. Dear me, Mr Holmes; why, you are even a quicker smoker than I am myself.'

Holmes smiled.

'I am a connoisseur,' said he, taking another cigarette from the box – his fourth – and lighting it from the stub of that which he had finished. 'I will not trouble you with any lengthy cross-examination, Professor Coram, since I gather that you were in bed at the time of the crime and could know nothing about it. I would only ask this. What do you imagine that this poor fellow meant by his last words: "The Professor – it was she"?'

The Professor shook his head.

'Susan is a country girl,' said he, 'and you know the incredible stupidity of that class. I fancy that the poor fellow murmured some incoherent delirious words, and that she twisted them into this meaningless message.'

'I see. You have no explanation yourself of the tragedy?'

'Possibly an accident; possibly – I only breathe it among ourselves – a suicide. Young men have their hidden troubles – some affair of the heart, perhaps, which we have never known. It is a more probable supposition than murder.'

'But the eyeglasses?'

'Ah! I am only a student – a man of dreams. I cannot explain the practical things of life. But still, we are aware, my friend, that love-gages may take strange shapes. By all means take another cigarette. It is a pleasure to see anyone appreciate them so. A fan, a glove, glasses – who knows what article may be carried as a token or treasured when a man puts an end to his life? This gentleman speaks of footsteps in the grass; but, after all, it is easy to be mistaken on such a point. As to the knife, it might well be thrown far from the unfortunate man as he fell. It is possible that I speak as a child, but to me it seems that Willoughby Smith has met his fate by his own hand.'

Holmes seemed struck by the theory thus put forward, and he continued to walk up and down for some time, lost in thought and consuming cigarette after cigarette.

'Tell me, Professor Coram,' he said, at last, 'what is in that cupboard in the bureau?'

'Nothing that would help a thief. Family papers, letters from my poor wife, diplomas of Universities which have done me honour. Here is the key. You can look for yourself.'

Holmes picked up the key and looked at it for an instant; then he handed it back.

'No; I hardly think that it would help me,' said he. 'I

should prefer to go quietly down to your garden and turn the whole matter over in my head. There is something to be said for the theory of suicide which you have put forward. We must apologise for having intruded upon you, Professor Coram, and I promise that we won't disturb you until after lunch. At two o'clock we will come again and report to you anything which may have happened in the interval.'

Holmes was curiously distrait, and we walked up and down the garden path for some time in silence.

'Have you a clue?' I asked, at last.

'It depends upon those cigarettes that I smoked,' said he. 'It is possible that I am utterly mistaken. The cigarettes will show me.'

'My dear Holmes,' I exclaimed, 'how on earth – '

'Well, well, you may see for yourself. If not, there's no harm done. Of course, we always have the optician clue to fall back upon, but I take a short cut when I can get it. Ah, here is the good Mrs Marker! Let us enjoy five minutes of instructive conversation with her.'

I may have remarked before that Holmes had, when he liked, a peculiarly ingratiating way with women, and that he very readily established terms of confidence with them. In half the time which he had named he had captured the housekeeper's goodwill, and was chatting with her as if he had known her for years.

'Yes, Mr Holmes, it is as you say, sir. He does smoke something terrible. All day and sometimes all night, sir. I've seen that room of a morning – well, sir, you'd have thought it was a London fog. Poor young Mr Smith, he was a smoker also, but not as bad as the Professor. His health – well, I don't know that it's better nor worse for the smoking.'

'Ah!' said Holmes, 'but it kills the appetite.'

'Well, I don't know about that, sir.'

'I suppose the Professor eats hardly anything?'

'Well, he is variable. I'll say that for him.'

'I'll wager he took no breakfast this morning, and won't face his lunch after all the cigarettes I saw him consume.'

'Well, you're out there, sir, as it happens, for he ate a remarkable big breakfast this morning. I don't know when I've known him make a better one, and he's ordered a good dish of cutlets for his lunch. I'm surprised myself, for since I came into that room yesterday and saw young Mr Smith lying there on the floor I couldn't bear to look at food. Well, it takes all sorts to make a world, and the Professor hasn't let it take his appetite away.'

We loitered the morning away in the garden. Stanley Hopkins had gone down to the village to look into some rumours of a strange woman who had been seen by some children on the Chatham Road the previous morning. As to my friend, all his usual energy seemed to have deserted him. I had never known him handle a case in such a half-hearted fashion. Even the news brought back by Hopkins that he had found the children and that they had undoubtedly seen a woman exactly corresponding with Holmes's description, and wearing either spectacles or eyeglasses, failed to rouse any sign of keen interest. He was more attentive when Susan, who waited upon us at lunch, volunteered the information that she believed Mr Smith had been out for a walk yesterday morning, and that he had only returned half an hour before the tragedy occurred. I could not myself see the bearing of this incident, but I clearly perceived that Holmes was weaving it into the general scheme which he had formed in his brain. Suddenly he sprang from his chair and glanced at his watch. 'Two o'clock, gentlemen,' said he. 'We must go up and have it out with our friend the Professor.'

The old man had just finished his lunch, and certainly his empty dish bore evidence to the good appetite with which his housekeeper had credited him. He was, indeed, a weird figure as he turned his white mane and his glowing eyes towards us. The eternal cigarette smouldered in his mouth. He had been dressed and was seated in an armchair by the fire.

'Well, Mr Holmes, have you solved this mystery yet?' He shoved the large tin of cigarettes which stood on a table beside him towards my companion. Holmes stretched out his hand at the same moment, and between them they tipped the box over the edge. For a minute or two we were all on our knees retrieving stray cigarettes from impossible places. When we rose again I observed that Holmes's eyes were shining and his cheeks tinged with colour. Only at a crisis have I seen those battle-signals flying.

'Yes,' said he, 'I have solved it.'

Stanley Hopkins and I stared in amazement. Something like a sneer quivered over the gaunt features of the old Professor.

'Indeed! In the garden?'

'No, here.'

'Here! When?'

'This instant.'

'You are surely joking, Mr Sherlock Holmes. You compel me to tell you that this is too serious a matter to be treated in such a fashion.'

'I have forged and tested every link of my chain, Professor Coram, and I am sure that it is sound. What your motives are or what exact part you play in this strange business I am not yet able to say. In a few minutes I shall probably hear it from your own lips. Meanwhile I will reconstruct what is past for your benefit, so that you may know the information which I still require.

'A lady yesterday entered your study. She came with the intention of possessing herself of certain documents which were in your bureau. She had a key of her own. I have had an opportunity of examining yours, and I do not find that slight discoloration which the scratch made upon the varnish would have produced. You were not an accessory, therefore, and she came, so far as I can read the evidence, without your knowledge to rob you.'

The Professor blew a cloud from his lips. 'This is most interesting and instructive,' said he. 'Have you no more to add? Surely, having traced this lady so far, you can also say what has become of her.'

'I will endeavour to do so. In the first place she was seized by your secretary, and stabbed him in order to escape. This catastrophe I am inclined to regard as an unhappy accident, for I am convinced that the lady had no intention of inflicting so grievous an injury. An assassin does not come unarmed. Horrified by what she had done she rushed wildly away from the scene of the tragedy. Unfortunately for her she had lost her glasses in the scuffle, and as she was extremely short-sighted she was really helpless without them. She ran down a corridor, which she imagined to be that by which she had come – both were lined with cocoanut matting – and it was only when it was too late that she understood that she had taken the wrong passage and that her retreat was cut off behind her. What was she to

THE RETURN OF SHERLOCK HOLMES

do? She could not go back. She could not remain where she was. She must go on. She went on. She mounted a stair, pushed open a door, and found herself in your room.'

The old man sat with his mouth open staring wildly at Holmes. Amazement and fear were stamped upon his expressive features. Now, with an effort, he shrugged his shoulders and burst into insincere laughter.

'All very fine, Mr Holmes,' said he. 'But there is one little flaw in your splendid theory. I was myself in my room, and I never left it during the day.'

'I am aware of that, Professor Coram.'

'And you mean to say that I could lie upon that bed and not be aware that a woman had entered my room?'

'I never said so. You *were* aware of it. You spoke with her. You recognised her. You aided her to escape.'

Again the Professor burst into high-keyed laughter. He had risen to his feet and his eyes glowed like embers.

'You are mad!' he cried. 'You are talking insanely. I helped her to escape? Where is she now?'

'She is there,' said Holmes, and he pointed to a high bookcase in the corner of the room.

I saw the old man throw up his arms, a terrible convulsion passed over his grim face, and he fell back in his chair. At the same instant the bookcase at which Holmes pointed swung round upon a hinge, and a woman rushed out into the room. 'You are right!' she cried, in a strange foreign voice. 'You are right! I am here.'

She was brown with the dust and draped with the cobwebs which had come from the walls of her hiding-place. Her face, too, was streaked with grime, and at the best she could never have been handsome, for she had the exact physical characteristics which Holmes had divined, with, in addition, a long and obstinate chin. What with her natural blindness, and what with the change from dark to light, she stood as one dazed, blinking about her to see where and who we were. And yet, in spite of all these disadvantages, there was a certain nobility in the woman's bearing, a gallantry in the defiant chin and in the upraised head, which compelled something of respect and admiration. Stanley Hopkins had laid his hand upon her arm and claimed her as his prisoner, but she waved him aside gently, and yet with an over-mastering dignity which compelled obedience. The old man lay back in his chair, with a twitching face, and stared at her with brooding eyes.

'Yes, sir, I am your prisoner,' she said. 'From where I stood I could hear everything, and I know that you have learned the truth. I confess it all. It was I who killed the young man. But you are right, you who say it was an accident. I did not even know that it was a knife which I held in my hand, for in my despair I snatched anything from the table and struck at him to make him let me go. It is the truth that I tell.'

'Madam,' said Holmes, 'I am sure that it is the truth. I fear that you are far from well.'

She had turned a dreadful colour, the more ghastly under the dark dust-streaks upon her face. She seated herself on the side of the bed; then she resumed.

'I have only a little time here,' she said, 'but I would have you to know the whole truth. I am this man's wife. He is not an Englishman. He is a Russian. His name I will not tell.'

For the first time the old man stirred. 'God bless you, Anna!' he cried. 'God bless you!'

She cast a look of the deepest disdain in his direction. 'Why should you cling so hard to that wretched life of yours, Sergius?' said she. 'It has done harm to many and good to none – not even to yourself. However, it is not for me to cause the frail thread to be snapped before God's time. I have enough already upon my soul since I crossed the threshold of this cursed house. But I must speak or I shall be too late.

'I have said, gentlemen, that I am this man's wife. He was fifty and I a foolish girl of twenty when we married. It was in a city of Russia, a University – I will not name the place.'

'God bless you, Anna!' murmured the old man again.

'We were reformers – revolutionists – Nihilists, you understand. He and I and many more. Then there came a time of trouble, a police officer was killed, many were arrested, evidence was wanted, and in order to save his own life and to earn a great reward my husband betrayed his own wife and his companions. Yes, we were all arrested upon his confession. Some of us found our way to the gallows and some to Siberia. I was among these last, but my term was not for life. My husband came to England with his ill-gotten gains, and has lived in quiet ever since, knowing well that if the Brotherhood knew where he was not a week would pass before justice would be done.'

The old man reached out a trembling hand and helped himself to a cigarette. 'I am in your hands, Anna,' said he. 'You were always good to me.'

'I have not yet told you the height of his villainy,' said she. 'Among our comrades of the Order there was one who was the friend of my heart. He was noble, unselfish, loving – all that my husband was not. He hated violence. We were all guilty – if that is guilt – but he was not. He wrote for ever dissuading us from such a course. These letters would have saved him. So would my diary, in which from day to day I had entered both my feelings towards him and the view which each of us had taken. My husband found and kept both diary and letters. He hid them, and he tried hard to swear away the young man's life. In this he failed, but Alexis was sent a convict to Siberia, where now, at this moment, he works in a salt mine. Think of that, you villain, you villain; now, now, at this very moment, Alexis, a man whose name you are not worthy to speak, works and lives like a slave, and yet I have your life in my hands and I let you go.'

'You were always a noble woman, Anna,' said the old man, puffing at his cigarette.

She had risen, but she fell back again with a little cry of pain.

'I must finish,' she said. 'When my term was over I set myself to get the diary and letters which, if sent to the Russian Government, would procure my friend's release. I knew that my husband had come to England. After months of searching I discovered where he was. I knew that he still had the diary, for when I was in Siberia I had a letter from him once reproaching me and quoting some passages from its pages. Yet I was sure that with his revengeful nature he would never give it to me of his own free will. I must get it for myself. With this object I engaged an agent from a private detective firm, who entered my husband's house as secretary – it was your second secretary, Sergius, the one who left you so hurriedly. He found that papers were kept in the cupboard, and he got an impression of the key. He would not go farther. He furnished me with a plan of the house, and he told me that in the forenoon the study was always empty, as the secretary was employed up here. So at last I took my courage in both hands and I came down to get the papers for myself. I succeeded, but at what a cost!

'I had just taken the papers and was locking the cupboard when the young man seized me. I had seen him already that morning. He had met me in the road and I had asked him to tell me where Professor Coram lived, not knowing that he was in his employ.'

'Exactly! exactly!' said Holmes. 'The secretary came back and told his employer of the woman he had met. Then in his last breath he tried to send a message that it was she – the she whom he had just discussed with him.'

'You must let me speak,' said the woman, in an imperative voice, and her face contracted as if in pain. 'When he had fallen I rushed from the room, chose the wrong door, and found myself in my husband's room. He spoke of giving me up. I showed him that if he did so his life was in my hands. If he gave me to the law I could give him to the Brotherhood. It was not that I wished to live for my own sake, but it was that I desired to accomplish my purpose. He knew that I would do what I said – that his own fate was involved in mine. For that reason and for no other he shielded me. He thrust me into that dark hiding-place, a relic of old days, known only to himself. He took his meals in his own room, and so was able to give me part of his food. It was agreed that when the police left the house I should slip away by night and come back no more. But in some way you have read our plans.' She tore from the bosom of her dress a small packet. 'These are my last words,' said she; 'here is the packet which will save Alexis. I confide it to your honour and to your love of justice. Take it! You will deliver it at the Russian Embassy. Now I have done my duty, and – '

'Stop her!' cried Holmes. He had bounded across the room and had wrenched a small phial from her hand.

'Too late!' she said, sinking back on the bed. 'Too late! I took the poison before I left my hiding-place. My head swims! I am going! I charge you, sir, to remember the packet.'

'A simple case, and yet in some ways an instructive one,' Holmes remarked, as we travelled back to town. 'It hinged from the outset upon the pince-nez. But for the fortunate chance of the dying man having seized these I am not sure that we could ever have reached our solution. It was clear to me from the strength of the glasses that the wearer must have been very blind and helpless when deprived of them. When you asked me to believe that she walked along a narrow strip of grass without once making a false step I remarked, as you may remember, that it was a noteworthy performance. In my mind I set it down as an impossible performance, save in the unlikely case that she had a second pair of glasses. I was forced, therefore, to seriously consider the hypothesis that she had remained within the house. On perceiving the similarity of the two corridors it became clear that she might very easily have made such a mistake, and in that case it was evident that she must have entered the Professor's room. I was keenly on the alert, therefore, for whatever would bear out this supposition, and I examined the room narrowly for anything in the shape of a hiding-place. The carpet seemed continuous and firmly nailed, so I dismissed the idea of a trap-door. There might well be a recess behind the books. As you are aware, such devices are common in old libraries. I observed that books were piled on the floor at all other points, but that one bookcase was left clear. This, then, might be the door. I could see no marks to guide me, but the carpet was of a dun colour, which lends itself very well to examination. I therefore smoked a great number of those excellent cigarettes, and I dropped the ash all over the space in front of the suspected bookcase. It was a simple trick, but exceedingly effective. I then went downstairs and I ascertained, in your presence, Watson, without your perceiving the drift of my remarks, that Professor Coram's consumption of food had increased – as one would expect when he is supplying a second person. We then ascended to the room again, when, by upsetting the cigarette-box, I obtained a very excellent view of the floor, and was able to see quite clearly, from the traces upon the cigarette ash, that the prisoner had, in our absence, come out from her retreat. Well, Hopkins, here we are at Charing Cross, and I congratulate you on having brought your case to a successful conclusion. You are going to headquarters, no doubt. I think, Watson, you and I will drive together to the Russian Embassy.'

11

The Missing Three-Quarter

We were fairly accustomed to receive weird telegrams at Baker Street, but I have a particular recollection of one which reached us on a gloomy February morning some seven or eight years ago and gave Mr Sherlock Holmes a puzzled quarter of an hour. It was addressed to him, and ran thus:

> Please await me. Terrible misfortune. Right wing three-quarter missing; indispensable tomorrow.
>
> OVERTON

'Strand postmark and dispatched ten-thirty-six,' said Holmes, reading it over and over. 'Mr Overton was evidently considerably excited when he sent it, and somewhat incoherent in consequence. Well, well, he will be here, I dare say, by the time I have looked through *The Times*, and then we shall know all about it. Even the most insignificant problem would be welcome in these stagnant days.'

Things had indeed been very slow with us, and I had learned to dread such periods of inaction, for I knew by experience that my companion's brain was so abnormally active that it was dangerous to leave it without material upon which to work. For years I had gradually weaned him from that drug mania which had threatened once to check his remarkable career. Now I knew that under ordinary conditions he no longer craved for this artificial stimulus, but I was well aware that the fiend was not dead, but sleeping; and I have known that the sleep was a light one and the waking near when in periods of idleness I have seen the drawn look upon Holmes's ascetic face, and the brooding of his deep-set and inscrutable eyes. Therefore I blessed this Mr Overton, whoever he might be, since he had come with his enigmatic message to break that dangerous calm which brought more peril to my friend than all the storms of his tempestuous life.

As we had expected, the telegram was soon followed by its sender, and the card of Mr Cyril Overton, of Trinity College, Cambridge, announced the arrival of an enormous young man, sixteen stone of solid bone and muscle, who spanned the doorway with his broad shoulders and looked from one of us to the other with a comely face which was haggard with anxiety.

'Mr Sherlock Holmes?'

My companion bowed.

'I've been down to Scotland Yard, Mr Holmes. I saw Inspector Stanley Hopkins. He advised me to come to you. He said the case, so far as he could see, was more in your line than in that of the regular police.'

'Pray sit down and tell me what is the matter.'

'It's awful, Mr Holmes, simply awful! I wonder my hair isn't grey. Godfrey Staunton – you've heard of him, of course? He's simply the hinge that the whole team turns on. I'd rather spare two from the pack and have Godfrey for my three-quarter line. Whether it's passing, or tackling, or dribbling, there's no one to touch him; and then, he's got the head and can hold us all together. What am I to do? That's what I ask you, Mr Holmes. There's Moorhouse, first reserve, but he is trained as a half, and he always edges right in on to the scrum instead of keeping out on the touchline. He's a fine place-kick, it's true, but, then, he has no judgment, and he can't sprint for nuts. Why, Morton or Johnson, the Oxford fliers, could romp round him. Stevenson is fast enough, but he couldn't drop from the twenty-five line, and a three-quarter who can't either punt or drop isn't worth a place for pace alone. No, Mr Holmes, we are done unless you can help me to find Godfrey Staunton.'

My friend had listened with amused surprise to this long speech, which was poured forth with extraordinary vigour and earnestness, every point being driven home by the slapping of a brawny hand upon the speaker's knee. When our visitor was silent Holmes stretched out his hand and took down letter 'S' of his commonplace book. For once he dug in vain into that mine of varied information.

'There is Arthur H. Staunton, the rising young forger,' said he, 'and there was Henry Staunton, whom I helped to hang, but Godfrey Staunton is a new name to me.'

It was our visitor's turn to look surprised.

'Why, Mr Holmes, I thought you knew things,' said he. 'I suppose, then, if you have never heard of Godfrey Staunton you don't know Cyril Overton either?'

Holmes shook his head good-humouredly.

'Great Scot!' cried the athlete. 'Why, I was first reserve for England against Wales, and I've skippered the 'Varsity all this year. But that's nothing! I didn't think there was a soul in England who didn't know Godfrey Staunton, the crack three-quarter, Cambridge, Blackheath, and five Internationals. Good Lord! Mr Holmes, where *have* you lived?'

Holmes laughed at the young giant's naive astonishment.

'You live in a different world to me, Mr Overton, a sweeter and healthier one. My ramifications stretch out into many sections of society, but never, I am happy to say, into amateur sport, which is the best and soundest thing in England. However, your unexpected visit this morning shows me that even in that world of fresh air and fair play there may be work for me to do; so now, my good sir, I beg you to sit down and to tell me slowly and quietly exactly what it is that has occurred, and how you desire that I should help you.'

Young Overton's face assumed the bothered look of the man who is more accustomed to using his muscles than his wits; but by degrees, with many repetitions and obscurities which I may omit from his narrative, he laid his strange story before us.

'It's this way, Mr Holmes. As I have said, I am the skipper of the rugger team of Cambridge 'Varsity, and Godfrey Staunton is my best man. Tomorrow we play Oxford. Yesterday we all came up and we settled at Bentley's private hotel. At ten o'clock I went round and saw that all the fellows had gone to roost, for I believe in strict training and plenty of sleep to keep a team fit. I had a word or two with Godfrey before he turned in. He seemed to me to be pale and bothered. I asked him what was the matter. He said he was all right – just a touch of headache. I bade him good-night and left him. Half an hour later the porter tells me that a rough-looking man with a beard called with a note for Godfrey. He had not gone to bed and the note was taken to his room. Godfrey read it and fell back in a chair as if he had been poleaxed. The porter was so scared that he was going to fetch me, but Godfrey stopped him, had a drink of water, and pulled himself together. Then he went downstairs, said a few words to the man who was waiting in the hall, and the two of them went off together. The last that the porter saw of them, they were almost running down the street in the direction of the Strand. This morning Godfrey's room was empty, his bed had never been slept in, and his things were all just as I had seen them the night before. He had gone off at a moment's notice with this stranger, and no word has come from him since. I don't believe he will ever come back. He was a sportsman, was Godfrey, down to his marrow, and he wouldn't have stopped his training and let in his skipper if it were not for some cause that was too strong for him. No; I feel as if he were gone for good and we should never see him again.'

Sherlock Holmes listened with the deepest attention to this singular narrative.

'What did you do?' he asked.

'I wired to Cambridge to learn if anything had been heard of him there. I have had an answer. No one has seen him.'

'Could he have got back to Cambridge?'

'Yes, there is a late train – quarter-past eleven.'

'But so far as you can ascertain he did not take it?'

'No, he has not been seen.'

'What did you do next?'

'I wired to Lord Mount-James.'

'Why to Lord Mount-James?'

'Godfrey is an orphan, and Lord Mount-James is his nearest relative – his uncle, I believe.'

'Indeed. This throws new light upon the matter. Lord

Mount-James is one of the richest men in England.'

'So I've heard Godfrey say.'

'And your friend was closely related?'

'Yes, he was his heir, and the old boy is nearly eighty – cram full of gout, too. They say he could chalk his billiard-cue with his knuckles. He never allowed Godfrey a shilling in his life, for he is an absolute miser, but it will all come to him right enough.'

'Have you heard from Lord Mount-James?'

'No.'

'What motive could your friend have in going to Lord Mount-James?'

'Well, something was worrying him the night before, and if it was to do with money it is possible that he would make for his nearest relative who had so much of it, though from all I have heard he would not have much chance of getting it. Godfrey was not fond of the old man. He would not go if he could help it.'

'Well, we can soon determine that. If your friend was going to his relative, Lord Mount-James, you have then to explain the visit of this rough-looking fellow at so late an hour, and the agitation that was caused by his coming.'

Cyril Overton pressed his hands to his head. 'I can make nothing of it,' said he.

'Well, well, I have a clear day, and I shall be happy to look into the matter,' said Holmes. 'I should strongly recommend you to make your preparations for your match without reference to this young gentleman. It must, as you say, have been an overpowering necessity which tore him away in such a fashion, and the same necessity is likely to hold him away. Let us step round together to this hotel, and see if the porter can throw any fresh light upon the matter.'

Sherlock Holmes was a past-master in the art of putting a humble witness at his ease, and very soon, in the privacy of Godfrey Staunton's abandoned room, he had extracted all that the porter had to tell. The visitor of the night before was not a gentleman, neither was he a working man. He was simply what the porter described as a 'medium-looking chap'; a man of fifty, beard grizzled, pale face, quietly dressed. He seemed himself to be agitated. The porter had observed his hand trembling when he had held out the note. Godfrey Staunton had crammed the note into his pocket. Staunton had not shaken hands with the man in the hall. They had exchanged a few sentences, of which the porter had only distinguished the one word 'time'. Then they had hurried off in the manner described. It was just half-past ten by the hall clock.

'Let me see,' said Holmes, seating himself on Staunton's bed. 'You are the day porter, are you not?'

'Yes, sir; I go off duty at eleven.'

'The night porter saw nothing, I suppose?'

'No, sir; one theatre party came in late. No one else.'

'Were you on duty all day yesterday?'

'Yes, sir.'

'Did you take any messages to Mr Staunton?'

'Yes, sir; one telegram.'

'Ah! that's interesting. What o'clock was this?'

'About six.'

'Where was Mr Staunton when he received it?'

'Here in his room.'

'Were you present when he opened it?'

'Yes, sir; I waited to see if there was an answer.'

'Well, was there?'

'Yes, sir. He wrote an answer.'

'Did you take it?'

'No; he took it himself.'

'But he wrote it in your presence?'

'Yes, sir. I was standing by the door, and he with his back turned at that table. When he had written it he said, "All right, porter, I will take this myself." '

'What did he write it with?'

'A pen, sir.'

'Was the telegraphic form one of these on the table?'

'Yes, sir; it was the top one.'

Holmes rose. Taking the forms he carried them over to the window and carefully examined that which was uppermost.

'It is a pity he did not write in pencil,' said he, throwing them down again with a shrug of disappointment. 'As you have no doubt frequently observed, Watson, the impression usually goes through – a fact which has dissolved many a happy marriage. However, I can find no trace here. I rejoice, however, to perceive that he wrote with a broad-pointed quill pen, and I can hardly doubt that we will find some impression upon this blotting-pad. Ah, yes, surely this is the very thing!'

He tore off a strip of the blotting-paper and turned towards us the following hieroglyphic:

Cyril Overton was much excited. 'Hold it to the glass!' he cried.

'That is unnecessary,' said Holmes. 'The paper is thin, and the reverse will give the message. Here it is.' He turned it over and we read:

come Stand by us for God's sake

'So that is the tail end of the telegram which Godfrey Staunton dispatched within a few hours of his disappearance. There are at least six words of the message which have escaped us; but what remains – "Stand by us for God's sake!" – proves that this young man saw a formidable danger which approached him, and from which someone else could protect him. "*Us*", mark you! Another person was involved. Who should it be but the pale-faced, bearded man, who seemed himself in so nervous a state? What, then, is the connection between Godfrey Staunton and the bearded man? And what is the third source from which each of them sought for help against pressing danger? Our enquiry has already narrowed down to that.'

'We have only to find to whom that telegram is addressed,' I suggested.

'Exactly, my dear Watson. Your reflection, though profound, had already crossed my mind. But I dare say it may have come to your notice that if you walk into a post-office and demand to see the counterfoil of another man's message there may be some disinclination on the part of the officials to oblige you. There is so much red tape in these matters! However, I have no doubt that with a little delicacy and finesse the end may be attained. Meanwhile, I should like in your presence, Mr Overton, to go through these papers which have been left upon the table.'

There were a number of letters, bills, and notebooks, which Holmes turned over and examined with quick, nervous fingers and darting, penetrating eyes. 'Nothing here,' he said, at last. 'By the way, I suppose your friend was a healthy young fellow – nothing amiss with him?'

'Sound as a bell.'

'Have you ever known him ill?'

'Not a day. He has been laid up with a hack, and once he slipped his kneecap, but that was nothing.'

'Perhaps he was not so strong as you suppose. I should think he may have had some secret trouble. With your assent I will put one or two of these papers in my pocket, in case they should bear upon our future enquiry.'

'One moment, one moment!' cried a querulous voice, and we looked up to find a queer little old man jerking and twitching in the doorway. He was dressed in rusty black, with a very broad-brimmed top-hat and a loose white necktie – the whole effect being that of a very rustic parson or of an undertaker's mute. Yet, in spite of his shabby and even absurd appearance, his voice had a sharp crackle, and his manner a quick intensity which commanded attention.

'Who are you, sir, and by what right do you touch this gentleman's papers?' he asked.

'I am a private detective, and I am endeavouring to explain his disappearance.'

'Oh, you are, are you? And who instructed you, eh?'

'This gentleman, Mr Staunton's friend, was referred to me by Scotland Yard.'

'Who are you, sir?'

'I am Cyril Overton.'

'Then it is you who sent me a telegram. My name is Lord Mount-James. I came round as quickly as the Bayswater bus would bring me. So you have instructed a detective?'

'Yes, sir.'

'And are you prepared to meet the cost?'

'I have no doubt, sir, that my friend Godfrey, when we find him, will be prepared to do that.'

'But if he is never found, eh? Answer me that!'

'In that case no doubt his family – '

'Nothing of the sort, sir!' screamed the little man. 'Don't look to me for a penny – not a penny! You understand that, Mr Detective! I am all the family that this young man has got, and I tell you that I am not responsible. If he has any expectations it is due to the fact that I have never wasted money, and I do not propose to begin to do so now. As to those papers with which you are making so free, I may tell you that in case there should be anything of any value among them you will be held strictly to account for what you do with them.'

'Very good, sir,' said Sherlock Holmes. 'May I ask in the meanwhile whether you have yourself any theory to account for this young man's disappearance?'

'No, sir, I have not. He is big enough and old enough to look after himself, and if he is so foolish as to lose himself I entirely refuse to accept the responsibility of hunting for him.'

'I quite understand your position,' said Holmes, with a mischievous twinkle in his eyes. 'Perhaps you don't quite understand mine. Godfrey Staunton appears to have been a poor man. If he has been kidnapped it could not have been for anything which he himself possesses. The fame of your wealth has gone abroad, Lord Mount-James, and it is entirely possible that a gang of thieves have secured your nephew in order to gain from him some information as to your house, your habits, and your treasure.'

The face of our unpleasant little visitor turned as white as his neckcloth.

'Heavens, sir, what an idea! I never thought of such villainy! What inhuman rogues there are in the world! But Godfrey is a fine lad – a staunch lad. Nothing would induce him to give his old uncle away. I'll have the plate moved over to the bank this evening. In the meantime spare no pains, Mr Detective! I beg you to leave no stone unturned to bring him safely back. As to money, well, so far as a fiver, or even a tenner, goes, you can always look to me.'

Even in his chastened frame of mind the noble miser could give us no information which could help us, for he knew little of the private life of his nephew. Our only clue lay in the truncated telegram, and with a copy of this in his hand Holmes set forth to find a second link for his chain. We had shaken off Lord Mount-James, and Overton had gone to consult with the other members of his team over the misfortune which had befallen them.

There was a telegraph-office at a short distance from the hotel. We halted outside it.

'It's worth trying, Watson,' said Holmes. 'Of course, with a warrant we could demand to see the counter-foils, but we have not reached that stage yet. I don't suppose they remember faces in so busy a place. Let us venture it.'

'I am sorry to trouble you,' said he, in his blandest manner, to the young woman behind the grating; 'there is some small mistake about a telegram I sent yesterday. I have had no answer, and I very much fear that I must have omitted to put my name at the end. Could you tell me if this was so?'

The young woman turned over a sheaf of counterfoils.

'What o'clock was it?' she asked.

'A little after six.'

'Whom was it to?'

Holmes put his finger to his lips and glanced at me. 'The last words in it were "for God's sake",' he whispered, confidentially; 'I am very anxious at getting no answer.'

The young woman separated one of the forms.

'This is it. There is no name,' said she, smoothing it out upon the counter.

'Then that, of course, accounts for my getting no answer,' said Holmes. 'Dear me, how very stupid of me, to be sure! Good morning, miss, and many thanks for having relieved my mind.' He chuckled and rubbed his hands when we found ourselves in the street once more.

'Well?' I asked.

'We progress, my dear Watson, we progress. I had seven different schemes for getting a glimpse of that telegram, but I could hardly hope to succeed the very first time.'

'And what have you gained?'

'A starting-point for our investigation.' He hailed a cab. 'King's Cross Station,' said he.

'We have a journey, then?'

'Yes; I think we must run down to Cambridge together. All the indications seem to me to point in that direction.'

'Tell me,' I asked, as we rattled up Gray's Inn Road, 'have you any suspicion yet as to the cause of the disappearance? I don't think that among all our cases I have known one where the motives are more obscure. Surely you don't really imagine that he may be kidnapped in order to give information against his wealthy uncle?'

'I confess, my dear Watson, that that does not appeal to me as a very probable explanation. It struck me, however, as being the one which was most likely to interest that exceedingly unpleasant old person.'

'It certainly did that. But what are your alternatives?'

'I could mention several. You must admit that it is curious and suggestive that this incident should occur on the eve of this important match, and should involve the only man whose presence seems essential to the success of the side. It may, of course, be coincidence, but it is interesting. Amateur sport is free from betting, but a good deal of outside betting goes on among the public, and it is possible that it might be worth someone's while to get at a player as the ruffians of the turf get at a racehorse. There is one explanation. A second very obvious one is that this young man really is the heir of a great property, however modest his means may at present be, and it is not impossible that a plot to hold him for ransom might be concocted.'

'These theories take no account of the telegram.'

'Quite true, Watson. The telegram still remains the only solid thing with which we have to deal, and we must not permit our attention to wander away from it. It is to gain light upon the purpose of this telegram that we are now upon our way to Cambridge. The path of our investigation is at present obscure, but I shall be very much surprised if before evening we have not cleared it up or made a considerable advance along it.'

It was already dark when we reached the old University city. Holmes took a cab at the station, and ordered the man to drive to the house of Dr Leslie Armstrong. A few minutes later we had stopped at a large mansion in the busiest thoroughfare. We were shown in, and after a long wait were at last admitted into the consulting-room, where we found the doctor seated behind his table.

It argues the degree in which I had lost touch with my profession that the name of Leslie Armstrong was unknown to me. Now I am aware that he is not only one of the heads of the medical school of the University, but a thinker of European reputation in more than one branch of science. Yet even without knowing his brilliant record one could not fail to be impressed by a mere glance at the man, the square, massive face, the brooding eyes under the thatched brows, and the granite moulding of the inflexible jaw. A man of deep character, a man with an alert mind, grim, ascetic, self-contained, formidable – so I read Dr Leslie Armstrong. He held my friend's card in his hand, and he looked up with no very pleased expression upon his dour features.

'I have heard your name, Mr Sherlock Holmes, and I am aware of your profession, one of which I by no means approve.'

'In that, doctor, you will find yourself in agreement with every criminal in the country,' said my friend, quietly.

'So far as your efforts are directed towards the suppression of crime, sir, they must have the support of every reasonable member of the community, though I cannot doubt that the official machinery is amply sufficient for the purpose. Where your calling is more open to criticism is when you pry into the secrets of private individuals, when you rake up family matters which are better hidden, and when you incidentally waste the time of men who are more busy than yourself. At the present moment, for example, I should be writing a treatise instead of conversing with you.'

'No doubt, doctor; and yet the conversation may prove more important than the treatise. Incidentally I may tell you that we are doing the reverse of what you very justly blame, and that we are endeavouring to prevent anything like public exposure of private matters which must necessarily follow when once the case is fairly in the hands of the official police. You may look upon me simply as an irregular pioneer who goes in front of the regular forces of the country. I have come to ask you about Mr Godfrey Staunton.'

'What about him?'

'You know him, do you not?'

'He is an intimate friend of mine.'

'You are aware that he has disappeared?'

'Ah, indeed!' There was no change of expression in the rugged features of the doctor.

'He left his hotel last night. He has not been heard of.'

'No doubt he will return.'

'Tomorrow is the 'Varsity football match.'

'I have no sympathy with these childish games. The young man's fate interests me deeply, since I know him and like him. The football match does not come within my horizon at all.'

'I claim your sympathy, then, in my investigation of Mr Staunton's fate. Do you know where he is?'

'Certainly not.'

'You have not seen him since yesterday?'

'No, I have not.'

'Was Mr Staunton a healthy man?'

'Absolutely.'

'Did you ever know him ill?'

'Never.'

Holmes popped a sheet of paper before the doctor's eyes. 'Then perhaps you will explain this receipted bill for thirteen guineas, paid by Mr Godfrey Staunton last month to Dr Leslie Armstrong of Cambridge. I picked it out from among the papers upon his desk.'

The doctor flushed with anger.

'I do not feel that there is any reason why I should render an explanation to you, Mr Holmes.'

Holmes replaced the bill in his notebook. 'If you prefer a public explanation it must come sooner or later,' said he. 'I have already told you that I can hush up that which others will be bound to publish, and you would really be wiser to take me into your complete confidence.'

'I know nothing about it.'

'Did you hear from Mr Staunton in London?'

'Certainly not.'

'Dear me, dear me; the post-office again!' Holmes sighed, wearily. 'A most urgent telegram was dispatched to you from London by Godfrey Staunton at six-fifteen yesterday evening – a telegram which is undoubtedly associated with his disappearance – and yet you have not had it. It is most culpable. I shall certainly go down to the office here and register a complaint.'

Dr Leslie Armstrong sprang up from behind his desk, and his dark face was crimson with fury.

'I'll trouble you to walk out of my house, sir,' said he. 'You can tell your employer, Lord Mount-James, that I do not wish to have anything to do either with him or with his agents. No, sir, not another word!' He rang the bell furiously. 'John, show these gentlemen out!' A pompous butler ushered us severely to the door, and we found ourselves in the street. Holmes burst out laughing.

'Dr Leslie Armstrong is certainly a man of energy and character,' said he. 'I have not seen a man who, if he turned his talents that way, was more calculated to fill the gap left by the illustrious Moriarty. And now, my poor Watson, here we are, stranded and friendless in this inhospitable town, which we cannot leave without abandoning our case. This little inn just opposite Armstrong's house is singularly adapted to our needs. If you would engage a front room and purchase the necessaries for the night, I may have time to make a few enquiries.'

These few enquiries proved, however, to be a more lengthy proceeding than Holmes had imagined, for he did not return to the inn until nearly nine o'clock. He was pale and dejected, stained with dust, and exhausted with hunger and fatigue. A cold supper was ready upon the table, and when his needs were satisfied and his pipe alight he was ready to take that half comic and wholly philosophic view which was natural to him when his affairs were going awry. The sound of carriage wheels caused him to rise and glance out of the window. A brougham and pair of greys under the glare of a gas-lamp stood before the doctor's door.

'It's been out three hours,' said Holmes; 'started at half-past six, and here it is back again. That gives a radius of ten or twelve miles, and he does it once, or sometimes twice, a day.'

'No unusual thing for a doctor in practice.'

'But Armstrong is not really a doctor in practice. He is a lecturer and a consultant, but he does not care for general practice, which distracts him from his literary work. Why, then, does he make these long journeys, which must be exceedingly irksome to him, and who is it that he visits?'

'His coachman – '

'My dear Watson, can you doubt that it was to him that I first applied? I do not know whether it came from his own innate depravity or from the promptings of his master, but he was rude enough to set a dog at me. Neither dog nor man liked the look of my stick, however, and the matter fell through. Relations were strained after that, and further enquiries out of the question. All that I have learned I got from a friendly native in the yard of our own inn. It was he who told me of the doctor's habits and of his daily journey. At that instant, to give point to his words, the carriage came round to the door.'

'Could you not follow it?'

'Excellent, Watson! You are scintillating this evening. The idea did cross my mind. There is, as you may have observed, a bicycle shop next to our inn. Into this I rushed, engaged a bicycle, and was able to get started before the carriage was quite out of sight. I rapidly overtook it, and then, keeping at a discreet distance of a hundred yards or so, I followed its lights until we were clear of the town. We had got well out on the country road when a somewhat mortifying incident occurred. The carriage stopped, the doctor alighted, walked swiftly back to where I had also halted, and told me in an excellent sardonic fashion that he feared the road was narrow, and that he hoped his carriage did not impede the passage of my bicycle. Nothing could have been more admirable than his way of putting it. I at once rode past the carriage, and, keeping to the main road, I went on for a few miles, and then halted in a convenient place to see if the carriage passed. There was no sign of it, however, and so it became evident that it had turned down one of several side roads which I had observed. I rode back, but again saw nothing of the carriage, and now, as you perceive, it has returned after me. Of course, I had at the outset no particular reason to connect these journeys with the disappearance of Godfrey Staunton, and was only inclined to investigate them on the general grounds that everything which concerns Dr Armstrong is at present of interest to us; but, now that I find he keeps so keen a lookout upon anyone who may follow him on these excursions, the affair appears more important, and I shall not be satisfied until I have made the matter clear.'

'We can follow him tomorrow.'

'Can we? It is not so easy as you seem to think. You are not familiar with Cambridgeshire scenery, are you? It does not lend itself to concealment. All this country that I passed over tonight is as flat and clean as the palm of your hand, and the man we are following is no fool, as he very clearly showed tonight. I have wired to Overton to let us know any fresh London developments at this address, and in the meantime we can only concentrate our attention upon Dr Armstrong, whose name the obliging young lady at the office allowed me to read upon the counterfoil of Staunton's urgent message. He knows where the young man is – to that I'll swear – and if he knows, then it must be our own fault if we cannot manage to know also. At present it must be admitted that the odd trick is in his possession, and, as you are aware, Watson, it is not my habit to leave the game in that condition.'

And yet the next day brought us no nearer to the

solution of the mystery. A note was handed in after breakfast, which Holmes passed across to me with a smile.

SIR [it ran] – I can assure you that you are wasting your time in dogging my movements. I have, as you discovered last night, a window at the back of my brougham, and if you desire a twenty-mile ride which will lead you to the spot from which you started, you have only to follow me. Meanwhile, I can inform you that no spying upon me can in any way help Mr Godfrey Staunton, and I am convinced that the best service you can do to that gentleman is to return at once to London and to report to your employer that you are unable to trace him. Your time in Cambridge will certainly be wasted.

Yours faithfully,

LESLIE ARMSTRONG

'An outspoken, honest antagonist is the doctor,' said Holmes. 'Well, well, he excites my curiosity, and I must really know more before I leave him.'

'His carriage is at his door now,' said I. 'There he is stepping into it. I saw him glance up at our window as he did so. Suppose I try my luck upon the bicycle?'

'No, no, my dear Watson! With all respect for your natural acumen I do not think that you are quite a match for the worthy doctor. I think that possibly I can attain our end by some independent explorations of my own. I am afraid that I must leave you to your own devices, as the appearance of *two* enquiring strangers upon a sleepy countryside might excite more gossip than I care for. No doubt you will find some sights to amuse you in this venerable city, and I hope to bring back a more favourable report to you before evening.'

Once more, however, my friend was destined to be disappointed. He came back at night weary and unsuccessful.

'I have had a blank day, Watson. Having got the doctor's general direction, I spent the day in visiting all the villages upon that side of Cambridge, and comparing notes with publicans and other local news agencies. I have covered some ground: Chesterton, Histon, Waterbeach, and Oakington have each been explored and have each proved disappointing. The daily appearance of a brougham and pair could hardly have been overlooked in such Sleepy Hollows. The doctor has scored once more. Is there a telegram for me?'

'Yes; I opened it. Here it is: "Ask for Pompey from Jeremy Dixon, Trinity College." I don't understand it.'

'Oh, it is clear enough. It is from our friend Overton, and is in answer to a question from me. I'll just send round a note to Mr Jeremy Dixon, and then I have no doubt that our luck will turn. By the way, is there any news of the match?'

'Yes, the local evening paper has an excellent account in its last edition. Oxford won by a goal and two tries. The last sentences of the description say: "The defeat of the Light Blues may be entirely attributed to the unfortunate absence of the crack International, Godfrey Staunton, whose want was felt at every instant of the game. The lack of combination in the three-quarter line and their weakness both in attack and defence more than neutralised the efforts of a heavy and hard-working pack." '

'Then our friend Overton's forebodings have been justified,' said Holmes. 'Personally I am in agreement with Dr Armstrong, and football does not come within

320

my horizon. Early to bed tonight, Watson, for I foresee that tomorrow may be an eventful day.'

I was horrified by my first glimpse of Holmes next morning, for he sat by the fire holding his tiny hypodermic syringe. I associated that instrument with the single weakness of his nature, and I feared the worst when I saw it glittering in his hand. He laughed at my expression of dismay, and laid it upon the table.

'No, no, my dear fellow, there is no cause for alarm. It is not upon this occasion the instrument of evil, but it will rather prove to be the key which will unlock our mystery. On this syringe I base all my hopes. I have just returned from a small scouting expedition and everything is favourable. Eat a good breakfast, Watson, for I propose to get upon Dr Armstrong's trail today, and once on it I will not stop for rest or food until I run him to his burrow.'

'In that case,' said I, 'we had best carry our breakfast with us, for he is making an early start. His carriage is at the door.'

'Never mind. Let him go. He will be clever if he can drive where I cannot follow him. When you have finished come downstairs with me, and I will introduce you to a detective who is a very eminent specialist in the work that lies before us.'

When we descended I followed Holmes into the stable-yard, where he opened the door of a loose-box and led out a squat, lop-eared, white-and-tan dog, something between a beagle and a foxhound.

'Let me introduce you to Pompey,' said he. 'Pompey is the pride of the local draghounds, no very great flier, as his build will show, but a staunch hound on a scent. Well, Pompey, you may not be fast, but I expect you will be too fast for a couple of middle-aged London gentlemen, so I will take the liberty of fastening this leather leash to your collar. Now, boy, come along, and show what you can do.' He led him across to the doctor's door. The dog sniffed round for an instant, and then with a shrill whine of excitement started off down the street, tugging at his leash in his efforts to go faster. In half an hour, we were clear of the town and hastening down a country road.

'What have you done, Holmes?' I asked.

'A threadbare and venerable device, but useful upon occasion. I walked into the doctor's yard this morning and shot my syringe full of aniseed over the hind wheel. A draghound will follow aniseed from here to John o' Groat's, and our friend Armstrong would have to drive through the Cam before he would shake Pompey off his trail. Oh, the cunning rascal! This is how he gave me the slip the other night.'

The dog had suddenly turned out of the main road into a grass-grown lane. Half a mile farther this opened into another broad road, and the trail turned hard to the right in the direction of the town, which we had just quitted. The road took a sweep to the south of the town and continued in the opposite direction to that in which we started.

'This detour has been entirely for our benefit, then?' said Holmes. 'No wonder that my enquiries among those villages led to nothing. The doctor has certainly played the game for all it is worth, and one would like to know the reason for such elaborate deception. This should be the village of Trumpington to the right of us. And, by Jove! here is the brougham coming round the corner. Quick, Watson, quick, or we are done!'

He sprang through a gate into a field, dragging the

reluctant Pompey after him. We had hardly got under the shelter of the hedge when the carriage rattled past. I caught a glimpse of Dr Armstrong within, his shoulders bowed, his head sunk on his hands, the very image of distress. I could tell by my companion's graver face that he also had seen.

'I fear there is some dark ending to our quest,' said he. 'It cannot be long before we know it. Come, Pompey! Ah, it is the cottage in the field!'

There could be no doubt that we had reached the end of our journey. Pompey ran about and whined eagerly outside the gate where the marks of the brougham's wheels were still to be seen. A footpath led across to the lonely cottage. Holmes tied the dog to the hedge, and we hastened onwards. My friend knocked at the little rustic door, and knocked again without response. And yet the cottage was not deserted, for a low sound came to our ears – a kind of drone of misery and despair, which was indescribably melancholy. Holmes paused irresolute, and then he glanced back at the road which we had just traversed. A brougham was coming down it, and there could be no mistaking those grey horses.

'By Jove, the doctor is coming back!' cried Holmes. 'That settles it. We are bound to see what it means before he comes.'

He opened the door and we stepped into the hall. The droning sound swelled louder upon our ears until it became one long, deep wail of distress. It came from upstairs. Holmes darted up and I followed him. He pushed open a half-closed door and we both stood appalled at the sight before us.

A woman, young and beautiful, was lying dead upon the bed. Her calm, pale face, with dim, wide-opened blue eyes, looked upwards from amid a great tangle of golden hair. At the foot of the bed, half sitting, half kneeling, his face buried in the clothes, was a young man, whose frame was racked by his sobs. So absorbed was he by his bitter grief that he never looked up until Holmes's hand was on his shoulder.

'Are you Mr Godfrey Staunton?'

'Yes, yes; I am – but you are too late. She is dead.'

The man was so dazed that he could not be made to understand that we were anything but doctors who had been sent to his assistance. Holmes was endeavouring to utter a few words of consolation, and to explain the alarm which had been caused to his friends by his sudden disappearance, when there was a step upon the stairs, and there was the heavy, stern, questioning face of Dr Armstrong at the door.

'So, gentlemen,' said he, 'you have attained your end, and have certainly chosen a particularly delicate moment for your intrusion. I would not brawl in the presence of death, but I can assure you that if I were a younger man your monstrous conduct would not pass with impunity.'

'Excuse me, Dr Armstrong, I think we are a little at cross-purposes,' said my friend, with dignity. 'If you could step downstairs with us we may each be able to give some light to the other upon this miserable affair.'

A minute later the grim doctor and ourselves were in the sitting-room below.

'Well, sir?' said he.

'I wish you to understand, in the first place, that I am not employed by Lord Mount-James, and that my sympathies in this matter are entirely against that nobleman. When a man is lost it is my duty to ascertain his fate, but having done so the matter ends so far as I am concerned; and so long as there is nothing criminal, I am much more anxious to hush up private scandals than to give them publicity. If, as I imagine, there is no breach of the law in this matter, you can absolutely depend upon my discretion and my co-operation in keeping the facts out of the papers.'

Dr Armstrong took a quick step forward and wrung Holmes by the hand.

'You are a good fellow,' said he. 'I had misjudged you. I thank Heaven that my compunction at leaving poor Staunton all alone in this plight caused me to turn my carriage back, and so to make your acquaintance. Knowing as much as you do, the situation is very easily explained. A year ago Godfrey Staunton lodged in London for a time, and became passionately attached to his landlady's daughter, whom he married. She was as good as she was beautiful, and as intelligent as she was good. No man need be ashamed of such a wife. But Godfrey was the heir to this crabbed old nobleman, and it was quite certain that the news of his marriage would have been the end of his inheritance. I knew the lad well, and I loved him for his many excellent qualities. I did all I could to help him to keep things straight. We did our very best to keep the thing from everyone, for when once such a whisper gets about it is not long before everyone has heard it. Thanks to this lonely cottage and his own discretion, Godfrey has up to now succeeded. Their secret was known to no one save to me and to one excellent servant who has at present gone for assistance to Trumpington. But at last there came a terrible blow in the shape of dangerous illness to his wife. It was consumption of the most virulent kind. The poor boy was half crazed with grief, and yet he had to go to London to play this match, for he could not get out of it without explanations which would expose his secret. I tried to cheer him up by a wire, and he sent me one in reply imploring me to do all I could. This was the telegram which you appear in some inexplicable way to have seen. I did not tell him how urgent the danger was, for I knew that he could do no good here, but I sent the truth to the girl's father, and he very injudiciously communicated it to Godfrey. The result was that he came straight away in a state bordering on frenzy, and has remained in the same state, kneeling at the end of her bed, until this morning death put an end to her sufferings. That is all, Mr Holmes, and I am sure that I can rely upon your discretion and that of your friend.'

Holmes grasped the doctor's hand.

'Come, Watson,' said he, and we passed from that house of grief into the pale sunlight of the winter day.

12

The Abbey Grange

It was on a bitterly cold and frosty morning during the winter of 1897 that I was awakened by a tugging at my shoulder. It was Holmes. The candle in his hand shone upon his eager, stooping face and told me at a glance that something was amiss.

'Come, Watson, come!' he cried. 'The game is afoot. Not a word! Into your clothes and come!'

Ten minutes later we were both in a cab and rattling through the silent streets on our way to Charing Cross Station. The first faint winter's dawn was beginning to appear, and we could dimly see the occasional figure of an early workman as he passed us, blurred and indistinct in the opalescent London reek. Holmes nestled in silence into his heavy coat, and I was glad to do the same, for the air was most bitter and neither of us had broken our fast. It was not until we had consumed some hot tea at the station, and taken our places in the Kentish train, that we were sufficiently thawed, he to speak and I to listen. Holmes drew a note from his pocket and read it aloud:

'*Abbey Grange, Marsham, Kent, 3.30 a.m.*
'MY DEAR MR HOLMES – I should be very glad of your immediate assistance in what promises to be a most remarkable case. It is something quite in your line. Except for releasing the lady I will see that everything is kept exactly as I have found it, but I

beg you not to lose an instant, as it is difficult to leave Sir Eustace there.

'Yours faithfully,

STANLEY HOPKINS

'Hopkins has called me in seven times, and on each occasion his summons has been entirely justified,' said Holmes. 'I fancy that every one of his cases has found its way into your collection, and I must admit, Watson, that you have some power of selection which atones for much which I deplore in your narratives. Your fatal habit of looking at everything from the point of view of a story instead of as a scientific exercise has ruined what might have been an instructive and even classical series of demonstrations. You slur over work of the utmost finesse and delicacy in order to dwell upon sensational details which may excite, but cannot possibly instruct, the reader.'

'Why do you not write them yourself?' I said, with some bitterness.

'I will, my dear Watson, I will. At present I am, as you know, fairly busy, but I propose to devote my declining years to the composition of a textbook which shall focus the whole art of detection into one volume. Our present research appears to be a case of murder.'

'You think this Sir Eustace is dead, then?'

'I should say so. Hopkins's writing shows considerable agitation, and he is not an emotional man. Yes, I gather there has been violence, and that the body is left for our inspection. A mere suicide would not have caused him to send for me. As to the release of the lady, it would appear that she has been locked in her room during the tragedy. We are moving in high life, Watson – crackling paper, "E.B." monogram, coat-of-arms, picturesque address. I think that friend Hopkins will live up to his reputation and that we shall have an interesting morning. The crime was committed before twelve last night.'

'How can you possibly tell?'

'By an inspection of the trains and by reckoning the time. The local police had to be called in, they had to communicate with Scotland Yard, Hopkins had to go out, and he in turn had to send for me. All that makes a fair night's work. Well, here we are at Chislehurst Station, and we shall soon set our doubts at rest.'

A drive of a couple of miles through narrow country lanes brought us to a park gate, which was opened for us by an old lodge-keeper, whose haggard face bore the reflection of some great disaster. The avenue ran through a noble park, between lines of ancient elms, and ended in a low, widespread house, pillared in front after the fashion of Palladio. The central part was evidently of a great age and shrouded in ivy, but the large windows showed that modern changes had been carried out, and one wing of the house appeared to be entirely new. The youthful figure and alert, eager face of Inspector Stanley Hopkins confronted us in the open doorway.

'I'm very glad you have come, Mr Holmes. And you too, Dr Watson! But, indeed, if I had my time over again I should not have troubled you, for since the lady has come to herself she has given so clear an account of the affair that there is not much left for us to do. You remember that Lewisham gang of burglars?'

'What, the three Randalls?'

'Exactly; the father and two sons. It's their work. I have not a doubt of it. They did a job at Sydenham a fortnight ago, and were seen and described. Rather cool to do another so soon and so near, but it is they, beyond all doubt. It's a hanging matter this time.'

'Sir Eustace is dead, then?'

'Yes; his head was knocked in with his own poker.'

'Sir Eustace Brackenstall, the driver tells me.'

'Exactly – one of the richest men in Kent. Lady Brackenstall is in the morning-room. Poor lady, she has had a most dreadful experience. She seemed half dead when I saw her first. I think you had best see her and hear her account of the facts. Then we will examine the dining-room together.'

Lady Brackenstall was no ordinary person. Seldom have I seen so graceful a figure, so womanly a presence, and so beautiful a face. She was a blonde, golden-haired, blue-eyed, and would, no doubt, have had the perfect complexion which goes with such colouring had not her recent experience left her drawn and haggard. Her sufferings were physical as well as mental, for over one eye rose a hideous, plum-coloured swelling, which her maid, a tall, austere woman, was bathing assiduously with vinegar and water. The lady lay back exhausted upon a couch, but her quick, observant gaze as we entered the room, and the alert expression of her beautiful features, showed that neither her wits nor her courage had been shaken by her terrible experience. She was enveloped in a loose dressing-gown of blue and silver, but a black sequin-covered dinner-dress was hung upon the couch beside her.

'I have told you all that happened, Mr Hopkins,' she said, wearily; 'could you not repeat it for me? Well, if you think it necessary, I will tell these gentlemen what occurred. Have they been in the dining-room yet?'

'I thought they had better hear your ladyship's story first.'

'I shall be glad when you can arrange matters. It is horrible to me to think of him still lying there.' She shuddered and buried her face in her hands. As she did so the loose gown fell back from her forearms. Holmes uttered an exclamation.

'You have other injuries, madam! What is this?' Two vivid red spots stood out on one of the white, round limbs. She hastily covered it.

'It is nothing. It has no connection with the hideous business of last night. If you and your friend will sit down I will tell you all I can.

'I am the wife of Sir Eustace Brackenstall. I have been married about a year. I suppose that it is no use my attempting to conceal that our marriage has not been a happy one. I fear that all our neighbours would tell you that, even if I were to attempt to deny it. Perhaps the fault may be partly mine. I was brought up in the freer, less conventional atmosphere of south Australia, and this English life, with its proprieties and its primness, is not congenial to me. But the main reason lies in the one fact which is notorious to everyone, and that is that Sir Eustace was a confirmed drunkard. To be with such a man for an hour is unpleasant. Can you imagine what it means for a sensitive and high-spirited woman to be tied to him for day and night? It is a sacrilege, a crime, a villainy to hold that such a marriage is binding. I say that these monstrous laws of yours will bring a curse upon the land – Heaven will not let such wickedness endure.' For an instant she sat up, her cheeks flushed, and her eyes blazing from under the terrible mark upon her brow. Then the strong, soothing hand of the austere maid drew her head down on to the cushion, and the wild anger died away into passionate sobbing. At last she continued.

'I will tell you about last night. You are aware, perhaps, that in this house all servants sleep in the modern wing. This central block is made up of the dwelling-rooms, with the kitchen behind and our bedroom above. My maid Theresa sleeps above my room. There is no one else, and no sound could alarm those who are in the farther wing. This must have been well known to the robbers, or they would not have acted as they did.

'Sir Eustace retired about half-past ten. The servants had already gone to their quarters. Only my maid was up, and she had remained in her room at the top of the house until I needed her services. I sat until after eleven in this room, absorbed in a book. Then I walked round to see that all was right before I went upstairs. It was my custom to do this myself, for, as I have explained, Sir Eustace was not always to be trusted. I went into the kitchen, the butler's pantry, the gunroom, the billiard-room, the drawing-room, and finally the dining-room. As I approached the window, which is covered with thick curtains, I suddenly felt the wind blow upon my face and realised that it was open. I flung the curtain aside and found myself face to face with a broad-shouldered, elderly man who had just stepped into the room. The window is a long French one, which really forms a door leading to the lawn. I held my bedroom candle lit in my hand, and, by its light, behind the first man I saw two others, who were in the act of entering. I stepped back, but the fellow was on me in an instant. He caught me first by the wrist and then by the throat. I opened my mouth to scream, but he struck me a savage blow with his fist over the eye, and felled me to the ground. I must have been unconscious for a few minutes, for when I came to myself I found that they had torn down the bell-rope and had secured me tightly to the oaken chair which stands at the head of the dining-room table. I was so firmly bound that I could not move, and a handkerchief round my mouth prevented me from uttering any sound. It was at this instant that my unfortunate husband entered the room. He had evidently heard some suspicious sounds, and he came prepared for such a scene as he found. He was dressed in his shirt and trousers, with his favourite blackthorn cudgel in his hand. He rushed at one of the burglars, but another – it was the elderly man – stooped, picked the poker out of the grate, and struck him a horrible blow as he passed. He fell without a groan, and never moved again. I fainted once more, but again it could only have been a very few minutes during which I was insensible. When I opened my eyes I found that they had collected the silver from the sideboard, and they had drawn a bottle of wine which stood there. Each of them had a glass in his hand. I have already told you, have I not, that one was elderly, with a beard, and the others young, hairless lads. They might have been a father with his two sons. They talked together in whispers. Then they came over and made sure that I was still securely bound. Finally they withdrew, closing the window after them. It was quite a quarter of an hour before I got my mouth free. When I did so my screams brought the maid to my assistance. The other servants were soon alarmed, and we sent for the local police, who instantly communicated with London. That is really all that I can tell you, gentlemen, and I trust that it will not be necessary for me to go over so painful a story again.'

'Any questions, Mr Holmes?' asked Hopkins.

'I will not impose any further tax upon Lady Bracken-stall's patience and time,' said Holmes. 'Before I go into the dining-room I should like to hear your experience.' He looked at the maid.

'I saw the men before ever they came into the house,' said she. 'As I sat by my bedroom window I saw three men in the moonlight down by the lodge gate yonder, but I thought nothing of it at the time. It was more than an hour after that I heard my mistress scream, and down I ran, to find her, poor lamb, just as she says, and him on the floor with his blood and brains over the room. It was enough to drive a woman out of her wits, tied there, and her very dress spotted with him; but she never wanted courage, did Miss Mary Fraser of Adelaide, and Lady Brackenstall of Abbey Grange hasn't learned new ways. You've questioned her long enough, you gentlemen, and now she is coming to her own room, just with her old Theresa, to get the rest that she badly needs.'

With a motherly tenderness the gaunt woman put her arm round her mistress and led her from the room.

'She has been with her all her life,' said Hopkins. 'Nursed her as a baby, and came with her to England when they first left Australia eighteen months ago. Theresa Wright is her name, and the kind of maid you don't pick up nowadays. This way, Mr Holmes, if you please!'

The keen interest had passed out of Holmes's expressive face, and I knew that with the mystery all the charm of the case had departed. There still remained an arrest to be effected, but what were these commonplace rogues that he should soil his hands with them? An abstruse and learned specialist who finds that he has been called in for a case of measles would experience something of the annoyance which I read in my friend's eyes. Yet the scene in the dining-room of the Abbey Grange was sufficiently strange to arrest his attention and to recall his waning interest.

It was a very large and high chamber, with carved oak ceiling, oaken panelling, and a fine array of deer's heads and ancient weapons around the walls. At the farther end from the door was the high French window of which we had heard. Three smaller windows on the right-hand side filled the apartment with cold winter sunshine. On the left was a large, deep fireplace, with a massive, overhanging oak mantelpiece. Beside the fireplace was a heavy oaken chair with arms and crossbars at the bottom. In and out through the open woodwork was woven a crimson cord, which was secured at each side to the crosspiece below. In releasing the lady the cord had been slipped off her, but the knots with which it had been secured still remained. These details only struck our attention afterwards, for our thoughts were entirely absorbed by the terrible object which lay upon the tiger-skin hearthrug in front of the fire.

It was the body of a tall, well-made man, about forty years of age. He lay upon his back, his face upturned, with his white teeth grinning through his short black beard. His two clenched hands were raised above his head, and a heavy blackthorn stick lay across them. His dark, handsome, aquiline features were convulsed into a spasm of vindictive hatred, which had set his dead face in a terribly fiendish expression. He had evidently been in his bed when the alarm had broken out, for he wore a foppish embroidered nightshirt, and his bare feet projected from his trousers. His head was horribly injured, and the whole room bore witness to the savage ferocity of the blow which had struck him down. Beside him lay the heavy poker, bent into a curve by the concussion. Holmes examined both it and the indescribable wreck which it had wrought.

'He must be a powerful man, this elder Randall,' he remarked.

'Yes,' said Hopkins. 'I have some record of the fellow, and he is a rough customer.'

'You should have no difficulty in getting him.'

'Not the slightest. We have been on the lookout for him, and there was some idea that he had got away to America. Now that we know the gang are here I don't see how they can escape. We have the news at every seaport already, and a reward will be offered before evening. What beats me is how they could have done so mad a thing, knowing that the lady could describe them, and that we could not fail to recognise the description.'

'Exactly. One would have expected that they would have silenced Lady Brackenstall as well.'

'They may not have realised,' I suggested, 'that she had recovered from her faint.'

'That is likely enough. If she seemed to be senseless they would not take her life. What about this poor fellow, Hopkins? I seem to have heard some queer stories about him.'

'He was a good-hearted man when he was sober, but a perfect fiend when he was drunk, or rather when he was half drunk, for he seldom really went the whole way. The devil seemed to be in him at such times, and he was capable of anything. From what I hear, in spite of all his wealth and his title, he very nearly came our way once or twice. There was a scandal about his drenching a dog with petroleum and setting it on fire – her ladyship's dog, to make the matter worse – and that was only hushed up with difficulty. Then he threw a decanter at that maid, Theresa Wright; there was trouble about that. On the whole, and between ourselves, it will be a brighter house without him. What are you looking at now?'

Holmes was down on his knees examining with great attention the knots upon the red cord with which the lady had been secured. Then he carefully scrutinised the broken and frayed end where it had snapped off when the burglar had dragged it down.

'When this was pulled down the bell in the kitchen must have rung loudly,' he remarked.

'No one could hear it. The kitchen stands right at the back of the house.'

'How did the burglar know no one would hear it? How dared he pull at a bell-rope in that reckless fashion?'

'Exactly, Mr Holmes, exactly. You put the very question which I have asked myself again and again. There can be no doubt that this fellow must have known the house and its habits. He must have perfectly understood that the servants would all be in bed at that comparatively early hour, and that no one could possibly hear a bell ring in the kitchen. Therefore he must have been in close league with one of the servants. Surely that is evident. But there are eight servants, and all of good character.'

'Other things being equal,' said Holmes, 'one would suspect the one at whose head the master threw a decanter. And yet that would involve treachery towards the mistress to whom this woman seems devoted. Well, well, the point is a minor one, and when you have Randall you will probably find no difficulty in securing his accomplice. The lady's story certainly seems to be corroborated, if it needed corroboration, by every detail which we see before us.' He walked to the French window and threw it open. 'There are no signs here, but the ground is iron hard, and one would not expect them. I see that these candles on the mantelpiece have been lighted.'

'Yes; it was by their light and that of the lady's bedroom candle that the burglars saw their way about.'

'And what did they take?'

'Well, they did not take much – only half a dozen articles of plate off the sideboard. Lady Brackenstall thinks that they were themselves so disturbed by the death of Sir Eustace that they did not ransack the house as they would otherwise have done.'

'No doubt that is true. And yet they drank some wine, I understand.'

'To steady their own nerves.'

'Exactly. These three glasses upon the sideboard have been untouched, I suppose?'

'Yes; and the bottle stands as they left it.'

'Let us look at it. Halloa! halloa! what is this?'

The three glasses were grouped together, all of them tinged with wine, and one of them containing some dregs of bees-wing. The bottle stood near them, two-thirds full, and beside it lay a long, deeply-stained cork. Its appearance and the dust upon the bottle showed that it was no common vintage which the murderers had enjoyed.

A change had come over Holmes's manner. He had

lost his listless expression, and again I saw an alert light of interest in his keen, deep-set eyes. He raised the cork and examined it minutely.

'How did they draw it?' he asked.

Hopkins pointed to a half-opened drawer. In it lay some table linen and a large corkscrew.

'Did Lady Brackenstall say that screw was used?'

'No; you remember that she was senseless at the moment when the bottle was opened.'

'Quite so. As a matter of fact that screw was *not* used. This bottle was opened by a pocket-screw, probably contained in a knife, and not more than an inch and a half long. If you examine the top of the cork you will observe that the screw was driven in three times before the cork was extracted. It has never been transfixed. This long screw would have transfixed it and drawn it with a single pull. When you catch this fellow you will find that he has one of these multiplex knives in his possession.'

'Excellent!' said Hopkins.

'But these glasses do puzzle me, I confess. Lady Brackenstall actually *saw* the three men drinking, did she not?'

'Yes; she was clear about that.'

'Then there is an end of it. What more is to be said? And yet you must admit that the three glasses are very remarkable, Hopkins. What, you see nothing remarkable! Well, well, let it pass. Perhaps when a man has special knowledge and special powers like my own it rather encourages him to seek a complex explanation when a simpler one is at hand. Of course, it must be a mere chance about the glasses. Well, good morning, Hopkins. I don't see that I can be of any use to you, and you appear to have your case very clear.

You will let me know when Randall is arrested, and any further developments which may occur. I trust that I shall soon have to congratulate you upon a successful conclusion. Come, Watson, I fancy that we may employ ourselves more profitably at home.'

During our return journey I could see by Holmes's face that he was much puzzled by something which he had observed. Every now and then, by an effort, he would throw off the impression and talk as if the matter were clear, but then his doubts would settle down upon him again, and his knitted brows and abstracted eyes would show that his thoughts had gone back once more to the great dining-room of the Abbey Grange in which this midnight tragedy had been enacted. At last, by a sudden impulse, just as our train was crawling out of a suburban station, he sprang on to the platform and pulled me out after him.

'Excuse me, my dear fellow,' said he, as we watched the rear carriages of our train disappearing round a curve; 'I am sorry to make you the victim of what may seem a mere whim, but on my life, Watson, I simply *can't* leave that case in this condition. Every instinct that I possess cries out against it. It's wrong – it's all wrong – I'll swear that it's wrong. And yet the lady's story was complete, the maid's corroboration was sufficient, the detail was fairly exact. What have I to put against that? Three wine glasses, that is all. But if I had not taken things for granted, if I had examined everything with care which I would have shown had we approached the case *de novo* and had no cut-and-dried story to warp my mind, would I not then have found something more definite to go upon? Of course I should. Sit down on this bench, Watson, until a train for Chislehurst arrives, and allow me to lay the evidence before you, imploring you in the first instance to dismiss from your mind the idea that anything which the maid or her mistress may have said must necessarily be true. The lady's charming personality must not be permitted to warp our judgment.

'Surely there are details in her story which, if we looked at it in cold blood, would excite our suspicion. These burglars made a considerable haul at Sydenham a fortnight ago. Some account of them and of their appearance was in the papers, and would naturally occur to anyone who wished to invent a story in which imaginary robbers should play a part. As a matter of fact, burglars who have done a good stroke of business are, as a rule, only too glad to enjoy the proceeds in peace and quiet without embarking on another perilous undertaking. Again, it is unusual for burglars to operate at so early an hour; it is unusual for burglars to strike a lady to prevent her screaming, since one would imagine that was the sure way to make her scream; it is unusual for them to commit murder when their numbers are sufficient to overpower one man; it is unusual for them to be content with a limited plunder when there is much more within their reach; and finally I should say that it was very unusual for such men to leave a bottle half empty. How do all these unusuals strike you, Watson?'

'Their cumulative effect is certainly considerable, and yet each of them is quite possible in itself. The most unusual thing of all, as it seems to me, is that the lady should be tied to the chair.'

'Well, I am not so clear about that, Watson; for it is evident that they must either kill her or else secure her in such a way that she could not give immediate notice of their escape. But at any rate I have shown, have I

THE RETURN OF SHERLOCK HOLMES

not, that there is a certain element of improbability about the lady's story? And now on the top of this comes the incident of the wine glasses.'

'What about the wine glasses?'

'Can you see them in your mind's eye?'

'I see them clearly.'

'We are told that three men drank from them. Does that strike you as likely?'

'Why not? There was wine in each glass.'

'Exactly; but there was bees-wing only in one glass. You must have noticed that fact. What does that suggest to your mind?'

'The last glass filled would be most likely to contain bees-wing.'

'Not at all. The bottle was full of it, and it is inconceivable that the first two glasses were clear and the third heavily charged with it. There are two possible explanations, and only two. One is that after the second glass was filled the bottle was violently agitated, and so the third glass received the bees-wing. That does not appear probable. No, no; I am sure that I am right.'

'What, then, do you suppose?'

'That only two glasses were used, and that the dregs of both were poured into a third glass, so as to give the false impression that three people had been here. In that way all the bees-wing would be in the last glass, would it not? Yes, I am convinced that this is so. But if I have hit upon the true explanation of this one small phenomenon, then in an instant the case rises from the commonplace to the exceedingly remarkable, for it can only mean that Lady Brackenstall and her maid have deliberately lied to us, that not one word of their story is to be believed, that they have some very strong reason for covering the real criminal, and that we must construct our case for ourselves without any help from them. That is the mission which now lies before us, and here, Watson, is the Chislehurst train.'

The household of the Abbey Grange were much surprised at our return, but Sherlock Holmes, finding that Stanley Hopkins had gone off to report to head-quarters, took possession of the dining-room, locked the door upon the inside, and devoted himself for two hours to one of those minute and laborious investigations which formed the solid basis on which his brilliant edifices of deduction were reared. Seated in a corner like an interested student who observes the demonstration of his professor, I followed every step of that remarkable research. The window, the curtains, the carpet, the chair, the rope – each in turn was minutely examined and duly pondered. The body of the unfortunate baronet had been removed, but all else remained as we had seen it in the morning. Then, to my astonishment, Holmes climbed up on to the massive mantelpiece. Far above his head hung the few inches of red cord which were still attached to the wire. For a long time he gazed upwards at it, and then in an attempt to get nearer to it he rested his knee upon a wooden bracket on the wall. This brought his hand within a few inches of the broken end of the rope, but it was not this so much as the bracket itself which seemed to engage his attention. Finally he sprang down with an ejaculation of satisfaction.

'It's all right, Watson,' said he. 'We have got our case – one of the most remarkable in our collection. But, dear me, how slow-witted I have been, and how nearly I have committed the blunder of my lifetime! Now, I think that with a few missing links my chain is almost complete.'

'You have got your men?'

'Man, Watson, man. Only one, but a very formidable person. Strong as a lion – witness the blow that bent that poker. Six foot three in height, active as a squirrel, dexterous with his fingers; finally, remarkably quick-witted, for this whole ingenious story is of his concoction. Yes, Watson, we have come upon the handi-work of a very remarkable individual. And yet in that bell-rope he has given us a clue which should not have left us a doubt.'

'Where was the clue?'

'Well, if you were to pull down a bell-rope, Watson, where would you expect it to break? Surely at the spot where it is attached to the wire. Why should it break three inches from the top as this one has done?'

'Because it is frayed there?'

'Exactly. This end, which we can examine, is frayed. He was cunning enough to do that with his knife. But the other end is not frayed. You could not observe that from here, but if you were on the mantelpiece you would see that it is cut clean off without any mark of fraying whatever. You can reconstruct what occurred. The man needed the rope. He would not tear it down for fear of giving the alarm by ringing the bell. What did he do? He sprang up on the mantelpiece, could not quite reach it, put his knee on the bracket – you will see the impression in the dust – and so got his knife to bear upon the cord. I could not reach the place by at least three inches, from which I infer that he is at least three inches a bigger man than I. Look at that mark upon the seat of the oaken chair! What is it?'

'Blood.'

'Undoubtedly it is blood. This alone puts the lady's story out of court. If she were seated on the chair when the crime was done, how comes that mark? No, no; she was placed in the chair *after* the death of her husband. I'll wager that the black dress shows a corresponding mark to this. We have not yet met our Waterloo, Watson, but this is our Marengo, for it begins in defeat and ends in victory. I should like now to have a few words with the nurse Theresa. We must be wary for awhile, if we are to get the information which we want.'

She was an interesting person, this stern Australian nurse. Taciturn, suspicious, ungracious, it took some time before Holmes's pleasant manner and frank acceptance of all that she said thawed her into a corresponding amiability. She did not attempt to conceal her hatred for her late employer.

'Yes, sir, it is true that he threw the decanter at me. I heard him call my mistress a name, and I told him that he would not dare to speak so if her brother had been there. Then it was that he threw it at me. He might have thrown a dozen if he had but left my bonny bird alone. He was for ever ill-treating her, and she too proud to complain. She will not even tell me all that he has done to her. She never told me of those marks on her arm that you saw this morning, but I know very well that they come from a stab with a hat-pin. The sly fiend – Heaven forgive me that I should speak of him so, now that he is dead, but a fiend he was if ever one walked the earth. He was all honey when first we met him, only eighteen months ago, and we both feel as if it were eighteen years. She had only just arrived in London. Yes, it was her first voyage – she had never been from home before. He won her with his title and his money and his false London ways. If she made a mistake she has paid for it, if ever a woman did. What month did we meet him? Well, I tell you it was just after we arrived. We arrived in June, and it was July. They were married in January of last year. Yes, she is down in the morning-room again, and I have no doubt she will see you, but you must not ask too much of her, for she has gone through all that flesh and blood will stand.'

Lady Brackenstall was reclining on the same couch, but looked brighter than before. The maid had entered with us, and began once more to foment the bruise upon her mistress's brow.

'I hope,' said the lady, 'that you have not come to cross-examine me again?'

'No,' Holmes answered, in his gentlest voice, 'I will not cause you any unnecessary trouble, Lady Brackenstall, and my whole desire is to make things easy for you, for I am convinced that you are a much-tried woman. If you will treat me as a friend and trust me you may find that I will justify your trust.'

'What do you want me to do?'

'To tell me the truth.'

'Mr Holmes!'

'No, no, Lady Brackenstall, it is no use. You may have heard of any little reputation which I possess. I will stake it all on the fact that your story is an absolute fabrication.'

Mistress and maid were both staring at Holmes with pale faces and frightened eyes.

'You are an impudent fellow!' cried Theresa. 'Do you mean to say that my mistress has told a lie?'

Holmes rose from his chair.

'Have you nothing to tell me?'

'I have told you everything.'

'Think once more, Lady Brackenstall. Would it not be better to be frank?'

For an instant there was hesitation in her beautiful face. Then some new strong thought caused it to set like a mask.

'I have told you all I know.'

Holmes took his hat and shrugged his shoulders. 'I am sorry,' he said, and without another word we left the room and the house. There was a pond in the park, and to this my friend led the way. It was frozen over, but a single hole was left for the convenience of a solitary swan. Holmes gazed at it and then passed on to the lodge gate. There he scribbled a short note for Stanley Hopkins and left it with the lodge-keeper.

'It may be a hit or it may be a miss, but we are bound to do something for friend Hopkins, just to justify this second visit,' said he. 'I will not quite take him into my confidence yet. I think our next scene of operations must be the shipping office of the Adelaide–Southampton line, which stands at the end of Pall Mall, if I remember right. There is a second line of steamers which connect south Australia with England, but we will draw the larger cover first.'

Holmes's card sent in to the manager ensured instant attention, and he was not long in acquiring all the information which he needed. In June of 1895 only one of their line had reached a home port. It was the *Rock of Gibraltar*, their largest and best boat. A reference to the passenger list showed that Miss Fraser of Adelaide, with her maid, had made the voyage in her. The boat was now on her way to Australia, somewhere to the south of the Suez Canal. Her officers were the same as in 1895, with one exception. The first officer, Mr Jack Croker, had been made a captain and was to take charge of their new ship, the *Bass Rock*, sailing in two days' time from Southampton. He lived at

Sydenham, but he was likely to be in that morning for instructions, if we cared to wait for him.

No; Mr Holmes had no desire to see him, but would be glad to know more about his record and character.

His record was magnificent. There was not an officer in the fleet to touch him. As to his character, he was reliable on duty, but a wild, desperate fellow off the deck of his ship, hot-headed, excitable, but loyal, honest, and kind-hearted. That was the pith of the information with which Holmes left the office of the Adelaide–Southampton company. Thence he drove to Scotland Yard, but instead of entering he sat in his cab with his brows drawn down, lost in profound thought. Finally he drove round to the Charing Cross telegraph-office, sent off a message, and then, at last, we made for Baker Street once more.

'No, I couldn't do it, Watson,' said he, as we re-entered our room. 'Once that warrant was made out nothing on earth would save him. Once or twice in my career I feel that I have done more real harm by my discovery of the criminal than ever he had done by his crime. I have learned caution now, and I had rather play tricks with the law of England than with my own conscience. Let us know a little more before we act.'

Before evening we had a visit from Inspector Stanley Hopkins. Things were not going very well with him.

'I believe that you are a wizard, Mr Holmes. I really do sometimes think that you have powers that are not human. Now, how on earth could you know that the stolen silver was at the bottom of that pond?'

'I didn't know it.'

'But you told me to examine it.'

'You got it, then?'

'Yes, I got it.'

'I am very glad if I have helped you.'

'But you haven't helped me. You have made the affair far more difficult. What sort of burglars are they who steal silver and then throw it into the nearest pond?'

'It was certainly rather eccentric behaviour. I was merely going on the idea that if the silver had been taken by persons who did not want it, who merely took it for a blind as it were, then they would naturally be anxious to get rid of it.'

'But why should such an idea cross your mind?'

'Well, I thought it was possible. When they came out through the French window there was the pond, with one tempting little hole in the ice, right in front of their noses. Could there be a better hiding-place?'

'Ah, a hiding-place – that is better!' cried Stanley Hopkins. 'Yes, yes, I see it all now! It was early, there were folk upon the roads, they were afraid of being seen with the silver, so they sank it in the pond, intending to return for it when the coast was clear. Excellent, Mr Holmes – that is better than your idea of a blind.'

'Quite so; you have got an admirable theory. I have no doubt that my own ideas were quite wild, but you must admit that they have ended in discovering the silver.'

'Yes, sir, yes. It was all your doing. But I have had a bad setback.'

'A setback?'

'Yes, Mr Holmes. The Randall gang were arrested in New York this morning.'

'Dear me, Hopkins! That is certainly rather against your theory that they committed a murder in Kent last night.'

'It is fatal, Mr Holmes, absolutely fatal. Still, there

are other gangs of three besides the Randalls, or it may be some new gang of which the police have never heard.'

'Quite so; it is perfectly possible. What, are you off?'

'Yes, Mr Holmes; there is no rest for me until I have got to the bottom of the business. I suppose you have no hint to give me?'

'I have given you one.'

'Which?'

'Well, I suggested a blind.'

'But why, Mr Holmes, why?'

'Ah, that's the question, of course. But I commend the idea to your mind. You might possibly find that there was something in it. You won't stop for dinner? Well, goodbye, and let us know how you get on.'

Dinner was over and the table cleared before Holmes alluded to the matter again. He had lit his pipe and held his slippered feet to the cheerful blaze of the fire. Suddenly he looked at his watch.

'I expect developments, Watson.'

'When?'

'Now – within a few minutes. I dare say you thought I acted rather badly to Stanley Hopkins just now?'

'I trust your judgment.'

'A very sensible reply, Watson. You must look at it this way: what I know is unofficial; what he knows is official. I have the right to private judgment, but he has none. He must disclose all, or he is a traitor to his service. In a doubtful case I would not put him in so painful a position, and so I reserve my information until my own mind is clear upon the matter.'

'But when will that be?'

'The time has come. You will now be present at the last scene of a remarkable little drama.'

There was a sound upon the stairs, and our door was opened to admit as fine a specimen of manhood as ever passed through it. He was a very tall young man, golden-moustached, blue-eyed, with a skin which had been burned by tropical suns, and a springy step which showed that the huge frame was as active as it was strong. He closed the door behind him, and then he stood with clenched hands and heaving breast, choking down some over-mastering emotion.

'Sit down, Captain Croker. You got my telegram?'

Our visitor sank into an armchair and looked from one to the other of us with questioning eyes.

'I got your telegram, and I came at the hour you said. I heard that you had been down to the office. There was no getting away from you. Let's hear the worst. What are you going to do with me? Arrest me? Speak out, man! You can't sit there and play with me like a cat with a mouse.'

'Give him a cigar,' said Holmes. 'Bite on that, Captain Croker, and don't let your nerves run away with you. I should not sit here smoking with you if I thought that you were a common criminal, you may be sure of that. Be frank with me, and we may do some good. Play tricks with me, and I'll crush you.'

'What do you wish me to do?'

'To give me a true account of all that happened at the Abbey Grange last night – a *true* account, mind you, with nothing added and nothing taken off. I know so much already that if you go one inch off the straight I'll blow this police whistle from my window and the affair goes out of my hands for ever.'

The sailor thought for a little. Then he struck his leg with his great, sunburned hand.

'I'll chance it,' he cried. 'I believe you are a man of

THE RETURN OF SHERLOCK HOLMES

your word, and a white man, and I'll tell you the whole story. But one thing I will say first. So far as I am concerned I regret nothing and I fear nothing, and I would do it all again and be proud of the job. Curse the beast, if he had as many lives as a cat he would owe them all to me! But it's the lady, Mary – Mary Fraser – for never will I call her by that accursed name. When I think of getting her into trouble, I who would give my life just to bring one smile to her dear face, it's that that turns my soul into water. And yet – and yet – what less could I do? I'll tell you my story, gentlemen, and then I'll ask you as man to man what less could I do.

'I must go back a bit. You seem to know everything, so I expect that you know that I met her when she was a passenger and I was first officer of the *Rock of Gibraltar*. From the first day I met her she was the only woman to me. Every day of that voyage I loved her more, and many a time since have I kneeled down in the darkness of the night watch and kissed the deck of that ship because I knew her dear feet had trod it. She was never engaged to me. She treated me as fairly as ever a woman treated a man. I have no complaint to make. It was all love on my side, and all good comradeship and friendship on hers. When we parted she was a free woman, but I could never again be a free man.

'Next time I came back from sea I heard of her marriage. Well, why shouldn't she marry whom she liked? Title and money – who could carry them better than she? She was born for all that is beautiful and dainty. I didn't grieve over her marriage. I was not such a selfish hound as that. I just rejoiced that good luck had come her way, and that she had not thrown herself away on a penniless sailor. That's how I loved Mary Fraser.

'Well, I never thought to see her again; but last voyage I was promoted, and the new boat was not yet launched, so I had to wait for a couple of months with my people at Sydenham. One day out in a country lane I met Theresa Wright, her old maid. She told me about her, about him, about everything. I tell you, gentlemen, it nearly drove me mad. This drunken hound, that he should dare to raise his hand to her whose boots he was not worthy to lick! I met Theresa again. Then I met Mary herself – and met her again. Then she would meet me no more. But the other day I had a notice that I was to start on my voyage within a week, and I determined that I would see her once before I left. Theresa was always my friend, for she loved Mary and hated this villain almost as much as I did. From her I learned the ways of the house. Mary used to sit up reading in her own little room downstairs. I crept round there last night and scratched at the window. At first she would not open to me, but in her heart I know that now she loves me, and she could not leave me in the frosty night. She whispered to me to come round to the big front window, and I found it open before me so as to let me into the dining-room. Again I heard from her own lips things that made my blood boil, and again I cursed this brute who mishandled the woman that I loved. Well, gentlemen, I was standing with her just inside the window, in all innocence, as Heaven is my judge, when he rushed like a madman into the room, called her the vilest name that a man could use to a woman, and welted her across the face with the stick he had in his hand. I had sprung for the poker, and it was a fair fight between us. See here on my arm where his first blow fell. Then it was my turn, and I went through him as if he had been a rotten pumpkin. Do you think I was sorry? Not I! It was his life or mine, but far more than that it was his life or hers, for how could I leave her in the power of this madman? That was how I killed him. Was I wrong? Well, then, what would either of you gentlemen have done if you had been in my position?

'She had screamed when he struck her, and that brought old Theresa down from the room above. There was a bottle of wine on the sideboard, and I opened it and poured a little between Mary's lips, for she was half dead with the shock. Then I took a drop myself. Theresa was as cool as ice, and it was her plot as much as mine. We must make it appear that burglars had done the thing. Theresa kept on repeating our story to her mistress, while I swarmed up and cut the rope of the bell. Then I lashed her in her chair, and frayed out the end of the rope to make it look natural, else they would wonder how in the world a burglar could have got up there to cut it. Then I gathered up a few plates and pots of silver, to carry out the idea of a robbery, and there I left them with orders to give the alarm when I had a quarter of an hour's start. I dropped the silver into the pond and made off for Sydenham, feeling that for once in my life I had done a real good night's work. And that's the truth and the whole truth, Mr Holmes, if it costs me my neck.'

Holmes smoked for some time in silence. Then he crossed the room and shook our visitor by the hand.

'That's what I think,' said he. 'I know that every word is true, for you have hardly said a word which I did not know. No one but an acrobat or a sailor could have got up to that bell-rope from the bracket, and no one but a sailor could have made the knots with which the cord was fastened to the chair. Only once had this lady been brought into contact with sailors, and that was on her voyage, and it was someone of her own class of life, since she was trying hard to shield him and so showing that she loved him. You see how easy it was for me to lay my hands upon you when once I had started upon the right trail.'

'I thought the police never could have seen through our dodge.'

'And the police haven't; nor will they, to the best of my belief. Now, look here, Captain Croker, this is a very serious matter, though I am willing to admit that you acted under the most extreme provocation to which any man could be subjected. I am not sure that in defence of your own life your action will not be pronounced legitimate. However, that is for a British jury to decide. Meanwhile I have so much sympathy for you that if you choose to disappear in the next twenty-four hours I will promise you that no one will hinder you.'

'And then it will all come out?'

'Certainly it will come out.'

The sailor flushed with anger.

'What sort of proposal is that to make a man? I know enough of law to understand that Mary would be had as accomplice. Do you think I would leave her alone to face the music while I slunk away? No, sir; let them do their worst upon me, but for Heaven's sake, Mr Holmes, find some way of keeping my poor Mary out of the courts.'

Holmes for a second time held out his hand to the sailor.

'I was only testing you, and you ring true every time. Well, it is a great responsibility that I take upon myself, but I have given Hopkins an excellent hint, and if he can't avail himself of it I can do no more. See here,

Captain Croker, we'll do this in due form of law. You are the prisoner. Watson, you are a British jury, and I never met a man who was more eminently fitted to represent one. I am the judge. Now, gentleman of the jury, you have heard the evidence. Do you find the prisoner guilty or not guilty?'

'Not guilty, my lord,' said I.

'*Vox populi, vox Dei*. You are acquitted, Captain Croker. So long as the law does not find some other victim you are safe from me. Come back to this lady in a year, and may her future and yours justify us in the judgment which we have pronounced this night.'

13

The Second Stain

I had intended 'The Adventure of the Abbey Grange' to be the last of those exploits of my friend, Mr Sherlock Holmes, which I should ever communicate to the public. This resolution of mine was not due to any lack of material, since I have notes of many hundreds of cases to which I have never alluded, nor was it caused by any waning interest on the part of my readers in the singular personality and unique methods of this remarkable man. The real reason lay in the reluctance which Mr Holmes has shown to the continued publication of his experiences. So long as he was in actual professional practice the records of his successes were of some practical value to him; but since he has definitely retired from London and betaken himself to study and bee-farming on the Sussex Downs, notoriety has become hateful to him, and he has peremptorily requested that his wishes in this matter should be strictly observed. It was only upon my representing to him that I had given a promise that 'The Adventure of the Second Stain' should be published when the times were ripe, and pointing out to him that it is only appropriate that this long series of episodes should culminate in the most important international case which he has ever been called upon to handle, that I at last succeeded in obtaining his consent that a carefully-guarded account of the incident should at last be laid before the public. If in telling the story I seem to be somewhat vague in certain details the public will readily understand that there is an excellent reason for my reticence.

It was, then, in a year, and even in a decade, that shall be nameless, that upon one Tuesday morning in autumn we found two visitors of European fame within the walls of our humble room in Baker Street. The one, austere, high-nosed, eagle-eyed, and dominant, was none other than the illustrious Lord Bellinger, twice Premier of Britain. The other, dark, clear-cut, and elegant, hardly yet of middle age, and endowed with every beauty of body and of mind, was the Right Honourable Trelawney Hope, Secretary for European Affairs, and the most rising statesman in the country. They sat side by side upon our paper-littered settee, and it was easy to see from their worn and anxious faces that it was business of the most pressing importance which had brought them. The Premier's thin, blue-veined hands were clasped tightly over the ivory head of his umbrella, and his gaunt, ascetic face looked gloomily from Holmes to me. The European Secretary pulled nervously at his moustache and fidgeted with the seals of his watch-chain.

'When I discovered my loss, Mr Holmes, which was at eight o'clock this morning, I at once informed the Prime Minister. It was at his suggestion that we have both come to you.'

'Have you informed the police?'

'No, sir,' said the Prime Minister, with the quick, decisive manner for which he was famous. 'We have not done so, nor is it possible that we should do so. To inform the police must, in the long run, mean to inform the public. This is what we particularly desire to avoid.'

'And why, sir?'

'Because the document in question is of such immense importance that its publication might very easily – I might almost say probably – lead to European complications of the utmost moment. It is not too much to say that peace or war may hang upon the issue. Unless its recovery can be attended with the utmost secrecy, then it may as well not be recovered at all, for all that is aimed at by those who have taken it is that its contents should be generally known.'

'I understand. Now, Mr Trelawney Hope, I should be much obliged if you would tell me exactly the circumstances under which this document disappeared.'

'That can be done in a very few words, Mr Holmes. The letter – for it was a letter from a foreign potentate – was received six days ago. It was of such importance that I have never left it in my safe, but I have taken it across each evening to my house in Whitehall Terrace, and kept it in my bedroom in a locked despatch-box. It was there last night. Of that I am certain. I actually opened the box while I was dressing for dinner, and saw the document inside. This morning it was gone. The despatch-box had stood beside the glass upon my dressing-table all night. I am a light sleeper, and so is my wife. We are both prepared to swear that no one could have entered the room during the night. And yet I repeat that the paper is gone.'

'What time did you dine?'

'Half-past seven.'

'How long was it before you went to bed?'

'My wife had gone to the theatre. I waited up for

her. It was half-past eleven before we went to our room.'

'Then for four hours the despatch-box had lain unguarded?'

'No one is ever permitted to enter that room save the housemaid in the morning, and my valet, or my wife's maid, during the rest of the day. They are both trusty servants who have been with us for some time. Besides, neither of them could possibly have known that there was anything more valuable than the ordinary departmental papers in my despatch-box.'

'Who did know of the existence of that letter?'

'No one in the house.'

'Surely your wife knew?'

'No, sir; I had said nothing to my wife until I missed the paper this morning.'

The Premier nodded approvingly.

'I have long known, sir, how high is your sense of public duty,' said he. 'I am convinced that in the case of a secret of this importance it would rise superior to the most intimate domestic ties.'

The European Secretary bowed.

'You do me no more than justice, sir. Until this morning I have never breathed one word to my wife upon this matter.'

'Could she have guessed?'

'No, Mr Holmes, she could not have guessed – nor could anyone have guessed.'

'Have you lost any documents before?'

'No, sir.'

'Who is there in England who did know of the existence of this letter?'

'Each member of the Cabinet was informed of it yesterday; but the pledge of secrecy which attends every Cabinet meeting was increased by the solemn warning which was given by the Prime Minister. Good heavens, to think that within a few hours I should myself have lost it!' His handsome face was distorted with a spasm of despair, and his hands tore at his hair. For a moment we caught a glimpse of the natural man, impulsive, ardent, keenly sensitive. The next the aristocratic mask was replaced, and the gentle voice had returned. 'Besides the members of the Cabinet there are two, or possibly three, departmental officials who know of the letter. No one else in England, Mr Holmes, I assure you.'

'But abroad?'

'I believe that no one abroad has seen it save the man who wrote it. I am well convinced that his Ministers – that the usual official channels have not been employed.'

Holmes considered for some little time.

'Now, sir, I must ask you more particularly what this document is, and why its disappearance should have such momentous consequences?'

The two statesmen exchanged a quick glance and the Premier's shaggy eyebrows gathered in a frown.

'Mr Holmes, the envelope is a long, thin one of pale blue colour. There is a seal of red wax stamped with a crouching lion. It is addressed in large, bold hand-writing to – '

'I fear, sir,' said Holmes, 'that, interesting and indeed essential as these details are, my enquiries must go more to the root of things. What *was* the letter?'

'That is a State secret of the utmost importance, and I fear that I cannot tell you, nor do I see that it is necessary. If by the aid of the powers which you are said to possess you can find such an envelope as I describe with its enclosure, you will have deserved well of your country, and earned any reward which it lies in our power to bestow.'

Sherlock Holmes rose with a smile.

'You are two of the most busy men in the country,' said he, 'and in my own small way I have also a good many calls upon me. I regret exceedingly that I cannot help you in this matter, and any continuation of this interview would be a waste of time.'

The Premier sprang to his feet with that quick, fierce gleam of his deep-set eyes before which a Cabinet has cowered. 'I am not accustomed, sir – ' he began, but mastered his anger and resumed his seat. For a minute or more we all sat in silence. Then the old statesman shrugged his shoulders.

'We must accept your terms, Mr Holmes. No doubt you are right, and it is unreasonable for us to expect you to act unless we give you our entire confidence.'

'I agree with you, sir,' said the younger statesman.

'Then I will tell you, relying entirely upon your honour and that of your colleague, Dr Watson. I may appeal to your patriotism also, for I could not imagine a greater misfortune for the country than that this affair should come out.'

'You may safely trust us.'

'The letter, then, is from a certain foreign potentate who has been ruffled by some recent colonial developments of this country. It has been written hurriedly and upon his own responsibility entirely. Enquiries have shown that his Ministers know nothing of the matter. At the same time it is couched in so unfortunate a manner, and certain phrases in it are of so provocative a character, that its publication would undoubtedly lead to a most dangerous state of feeling in this country. There would be such a ferment, sir, that I do not hesitate to say that within a week of the publication of that letter this country would be involved in a great war.'

Holmes wrote a name upon a slip of paper and handed it to the Premier.

'Exactly. It was he. And it is this letter – this letter which may well mean the expenditure of a thousand millions and the lives of a hundred thousand men – which has become lost in this unaccountable fashion.'

'Have you informed the sender?'

'Yes, sir, a cipher telegram has been despatched.'

'Perhaps he desires the publication of the letter.'

'No, sir, we have strong reason to believe that he already understands that he has acted in an indiscreet and hot-headed manner. It would be a greater blow to him and to his country than to us if this letter were to come out.'

'If this is so, whose interest is it that the letter should come out? Why should anyone desire to steal it or to publish it?'

'There, Mr Holmes, you take me into regions of high international politics. But if you consider the European situation you will have no difficulty in perceiving the motive. The whole of Europe is an armed camp. There is a double league which makes a fair balance of military power. Great Britain holds the scales. If Britain were driven into war with one confederacy, it would assure the supremacy of the other confederacy, whether they joined in the war or not. Do you follow?'

'Very clearly. It is then the interest of the enemies of this potentate to secure and publish this letter, so as to make a breach between his country and ours?'

'Yes, sir.'

'And to whom would this document be sent if it fell into the hands of an enemy?'

'To any of the great Chancelleries of Europe. It is probably speeding on its way thither at the present instant as fast as steam can take it.'

Mr Trelawney Hope dropped his head on his chest and groaned aloud. The Premier placed his hand kindly upon his shoulder.

'It is your misfortune, my dear fellow. No one can blame you. There is no precaution which you have neglected. Now, Mr Holmes, you are in full possession of the facts. What course do you recommend?'

Holmes shook his head mournfully.

'You think, sir, that unless this document is recovered there will be war?'

'I think it is very probable.'

'Then, sir, prepare for war.'

'That is a hard saying, Mr Holmes.'

'Consider the facts, sir. It is inconceivable that it was taken after eleven-thirty at night, since I understand that Mr Hope and his wife were both in the room from that hour until the loss was found out. It was taken, then, yesterday evening between seven-thirty and eleven-thirty, probably near the earlier hour, since whoever took it evidently knew that it was there and would naturally secure it as early as possible. Now, sir, if a document of this importance were taken at that hour, where can it be now? No one has any reason to retain it. It has been passed rapidly on to those who need it. What chance have we now to overtake or even to trace it? It is beyond our reach.'

The Prime Minister rose from the settee.

'What you say is perfectly logical, Mr Holmes. I feel that the matter is indeed out of our hands.'

'Let us presume, for argument's sake, that the document was taken by the maid or by the valet – '

'They are both old and tried servants.'

'I understand you to say that your room is on the second floor, that there is no entrance from without, and that from within no one could go up unobserved. It must, then, be somebody in the house who has taken it. To whom would the thief take it? To one of several international spies and secret agents, whose names are tolerably familiar to me. There are three who may be said to be the heads of their profession. I will begin my research by going round and finding if each of them is at his post. If one is missing – especially if he has disappeared since last night – we will have some indication as to where the document has gone.'

'Why should he be missing?' asked the European Secretary. 'He would take the letter to an Embassy in London, as likely as not.'

'I fancy not. These agents work independently, and their relations with the Embassies are often strained.'

The Prime Minister nodded his acquiescence.

'I believe you are right, Mr Holmes. He would take so valuable a prize to headquarters with his own hands. I think that your course of action is an excellent one. Meanwhile, Hope, we cannot neglect all our other duties on account of this one misfortune. Should there be any fresh developments during the day we shall communicate with you, and you will no doubt let us know the results of your own enquiries.'

The two statesmen bowed and walked gravely from the room.

When our illustrious visitors had departed Holmes lit his pipe in silence, and sat for some time lost in the deepest thought. I had opened the morning paper and was immersed in a sensational crime which had occurred in London the night before, when my friend gave an exclamation, sprang to his feet, and laid his pipe down upon the mantelpiece.

'Yes,' said he, 'there is no better way of approaching it. The situation is desperate, but not hopeless. Even now, if we could be sure which of them has taken it, it is just possible that it has not yet passed out of his hands. After all, it is a question of money with these fellows, and I have the British Treasury behind me. If it's on the market I'll buy it – if it means another penny on the income-tax. It is conceivable that the fellow might hold it back to see what bids come from this side before he tries his luck on the other. There are only those three capable of playing so bold a game; there are Oberstein, La Rothiere, and Eduardo Lucas. I will see each of them.'

I glanced at my morning paper.

'Is that Eduardo Lucas of Godolphin Street?'

'Yes.'

'You will not see him.'

'Why not?'

'He was murdered in his house last night.'

My friend has so often astonished me in the course of our adventures that it was with a sense of exultation that I realised how completely I had astonished him. He stared in amazement, and then snatched the paper from my hands. This was the paragraph which I had been engaged in reading when he rose from his chair:

MURDER IN WESTMINSTER

A crime of mysterious character was committed last night at 16 Godolphin Street, one of the old-fashioned and secluded rows of eighteenth-century houses which lie between the river and the Abbey, almost in the shadow of the great tower of the Houses of Parliament. This small but select mansion has been inhabited for some years by Mr Eduardo Lucas, well known in society circles both on account of his charming personality and because he has the well-deserved reputation of being one of the best amateur tenors in the country. Mr Lucas is an unmarried man, thirty-four years of age, and his establishment consists of Mrs Pringle, an elderly housekeeper, and of Mitton, his valet. The former retires early and sleeps at the top of the house. The valet was out for the evening, visiting a friend at Hammersmith. From ten o'clock onwards Mr Lucas had the house to himself. What occurred during that time has not yet transpired, but at a quarter to twelve Police-constable Barrett, passing along Godolphin Street, observed that the door of Number 16 was ajar. He knocked, but received no answer. Perceiving a light in the front room he advanced into the passage and again knocked, but without reply. He then pushed open the door and entered. The room was in a state of wild disorder, the furniture being all swept to one side, and one chair lying on its back in the centre. Beside this chair, and still grasping one of its legs, lay the unfortunate tenant of the house. He had been stabbed to the heart and must have died instantly. The knife with which the crime had been committed was a curved Indian dagger, plucked down from a trophy of Oriental arms which adorned one of the walls. Robbery does not appear to have been the motive of the crime, for there had been no attempt to remove the valuable contents of the room. Mr Eduardo

Lucas was so well known and popular that his violent and mysterious fate will arouse painful interest and intense sympathy in a widespread circle of friends.

'Well, Watson, what do you make of this?' asked Holmes, after a long pause.

'It is an amazing coincidence.'

'A coincidence! Here is one of the three men whom we had named as possible actors in this drama, and he meets a violent death during the very hours when we know that that drama was being enacted. The odds are enormous against its being coincidence. No figures could express them. No, my dear Watson, the two events are connected – *must* be connected. It is for us to find the connection.'

'But now the official police must know all.'

'Not at all. They know all they see at Godolphin Street. They know – and shall know – nothing of Whitehall Terrace. Only *we* know of both events, and can trace the relation between them. There is one obvious point which would, in any case, have turned my suspicions against Lucas. Godolphin Street, Westminster, is only a few minutes' walk from Whitehall Terrace. The other secret agents whom I have named live in the extreme West End. It was easier, therefore, for Lucas than for the others to establish a connection or receive a message from the European Secretary's household – a small thing, and yet where events are compressed into a few hours it may prove essential. Halloa! what have we here?'

Mrs Hudson had appeared with a lady's card upon her salver. Holmes glanced at it, raised his eyebrows, and handed it over to me.

'Ask Lady Hilda Trelawney Hope if she will be kind enough to step up,' said he.

A moment later our modest apartment, already so distinguished that morning, was further honoured by the entrance of the most lovely woman in London. I had often heard of the beauty of the youngest daughter of the Duke of Belminster, but no description of it, and no contemplation of colourless photographs, had prepared me for the subtle, delicate charm and the beautiful colouring of that exquisite head. And yet as we saw it that autumn morning, it was not its beauty which would be the first thing to impress the observer. The cheek was lovely, but it was paled with emotion; the eyes were bright, but it was the brightness of fever; the sensitive mouth was tight and drawn in an effort after self-command. Terror – not beauty – was what sprang first to the eye as our fair visitor stood framed for an instant in the open door.

'Has my husband been here, Mr Holmes?'

'Yes, madam, he has been here.'

'Mr Holmes, I implore you not to tell him that I came here.' Holmes bowed coldly, and motioned the lady to a chair.

'Your ladyship places me in a very delicate position. I beg that you will sit down and tell me what you desire; but I fear that I cannot make any unconditional promise.'

She swept across the room and seated herself with her back to the window. It was a queenly presence – tall, graceful, and intensely womanly.

'Mr Holmes,' she said, and her white-gloved hands clasped and unclasped as she spoke – 'I will speak frankly to you in the hope that it may induce you to speak frankly in return. There is complete confidence between my husband and me on all matters save one. That one is politics. On this his lips are sealed. He tells me nothing. Now, I am aware that there was a most deplorable occurrence in our house last night. I know that a paper has disappeared. But because the matter is political my husband refuses to take me into his complete confidence. Now it is essential – essential, I say – that I should thoroughly understand it. You are the only other person, save only these politicians, who knows the true facts. I beg you, then, Mr Holmes, to tell me exactly what has happened and what it will lead to. Tell me all, Mr Holmes. Let no regard for your client's interests keep you silent, for I assure you that his interests, if he would only see it, would be best served by taking me into his complete confidence. What was this paper which was stolen?'

'Madam, what you ask me is really impossible.'

She groaned and sank her face in her hands.

'You must see that this is so, madam. If your husband thinks fit to keep you in the dark over this matter, is it for me, who has only learned the true facts under the pledge of professional secrecy, to tell what he has withheld? It is not fair to ask it. It is him whom you must ask.'

'I have asked him. I come to you as a last resource. But without your telling me anything definite, Mr Holmes, you may do a great service if you would enlighten me on one point.'

'What is it, madam?'

'Is my husband's political career likely to suffer through this incident?'

'Well, madam, unless it is set right it may certainly have a very unfortunate effect.'

'Ah!' She drew in her breath sharply as one whose doubts are resolved.

'One more question, Mr Holmes. From an expression which my husband dropped in the first shock of this disaster I understood that terrible public consequences might arise from the loss of this document.'

'If he said so, I certainly cannot deny it.'

'Of what nature are they?'

'Nay, madam, there again you ask me more than I can possibly answer.'

'Then I will take up no more of your time. I cannot blame you, Mr Holmes, for having refused to speak more freely, and you on your side will not, I am sure, think the worse of me because I desire, even against his will, to share my husband's anxieties. Once more I beg that you will say nothing of my visit.' She looked back at us from the door, and I had a last impression of that beautiful haunted face, the startled eyes, and the drawn mouth. Then she was gone.

'Now, Watson, the fair sex is your department,' said Holmes, with a smile, when the dwindling frou-frou of skirts had ended in the slam of the front door. 'What was the fair lady's game? What did she really want?'

'Surely her own statement is clear and her anxiety very natural.'

'Hum! Think of her appearance, Watson – her manner, her suppressed excitement, her restlessness, her tenacity in asking questions. Remember that she comes of a caste who do not lightly show emotion.'

'She was certainly much moved.'

'Remember also the curious earnestness with which she assured us that it was best for her husband that she should know all. What did she mean by that? And you must have observed, Watson, how she manoeuvred to have the light at her back. She did not wish us to read her expression.'

'Yes; she chose the one chair in the room.'

'And yet the motives of women are so inscrutable. You remember the woman at Margate whom I suspected for the same reason. No powder on her nose – that proved to be the correct solution. How can you build on such a quicksand? Their most trivial action may mean volumes, or their most extra-ordinary conduct may depend upon a hairpin or a curling-tongs. Good morning, Watson.'

'You are off?'

'Yes; I will while away the morning at Godolphin Street with our friends of the regular establishment. With Eduardo Lucas lies the solution of our problem, though I must admit that I have not an inkling as to what form it may take. It is a capital mistake to theorise in advance of the facts. Do you stay on guard, my good Watson, and receive any fresh visitors. I'll join you at lunch if I am able.'

All that day and the next and the next Holmes was in a mood which his friends would call taciturn, and others morose. He ran out and ran in, smoked incessantly, played snatches on his violin, sank into reveries, devoured sandwiches at irregular hours, and hardly answered the casual questions which I put to him. It was evident to me that things were not going well with him or his quest. He would say nothing of the case, and it was from the papers that I learned the particulars of the inquest, and the arrest with the subsequent release of John Mitton, the valet of the deceased. The coroner's jury brought in the obvious

'Wilful Murder', but the parties remained as unknown as ever. No motive was suggested. The room was full of articles of value, but none had been taken. The dead man's papers had not been tampered with. They were carefully examined, and showed that he was a keen student of international politics, an indefatigable gossip, a remarkable linguist, and an untiring letter-writer. He had been on intimate terms with the leading politicians of several countries. But nothing sensational was discovered among the documents which filled his drawers. As to his relations with women, they appeared to have been promiscuous but superficial. He had many acquaintances among them, but few friends, and no one whom he loved. His habits were regular, his conduct inoffensive. His death was an absolute mystery, and likely to remain so.

As to the arrest of John Mitton, the valet, it was a counsel of despair as an alternative to absolute inaction. But no case could be sustained against him. He had visited friends in Hammersmith that night. The alibi was complete. It is true that he started home at an hour which should have brought him to Westminster before the time when the crime was discovered, but his own explanation that he had walked part of the way seemed probable enough in view of the fineness of the night. He had actually arrived at twelve o'clock, and appeared to be overwhelmed by the unexpected tragedy. He had always been on good terms with his master. Several of the dead man's possessions – notably a small case of razors – had been found in the valet's boxes, but he explained that they had been presents from the deceased, and the housekeeper was able to corroborate the story. Mitton had been in Lucas's employment for three years. It was noticeable that Lucas did not take

Mitton on the Continent with him. Sometimes he visited Paris for three months on end, but Mitton was left in charge of the Godolphin Street house. As to the housekeeper, she had heard nothing on the night of the crime. If her master had a visitor he had himself admitted him.

So for three mornings the mystery remained, so far as I could follow it in the papers. If Holmes knew more he kept his own counsel, but, as he told me that Inspector Lestrade had taken him into his confidence in the case, I knew that he was in close touch with every development. Upon the fourth day there appeared a long telegram from Paris which seemed to solve the whole question.

A discovery has just been made by the Parisian police [said the *Daily Telegraph*] which raises the veil which hung round the tragic fate of Mr Eduardo Lucas, who met his death by violence last Monday night at Godolphin Street, Westminster. Our readers will remember that the deceased gentleman was found stabbed in his room, and that some suspicion attached to his valet, but that the case broke down on an alibi. Yesterday a lady, who has been known as Mme Henri Fournaye, occupying a small villa in the Rue Austerlitz, was reported to the authorities by her servants as being insane. An examination showed that she had indeed developed mania of a dangerous and permanent form. On enquiry the police have discovered that Mme Henri Fournaye only returned from a journey to London on Tuesday last, and there is evidence to connect her with the crime at Westminster. A comparison of photographs has proved conclusively that M. Henri Fournaye and Eduardo Lucas were really one and the same person, and that the deceased had for some reason lived a double life in London and Paris. Mme Fournaye, who is of Creole origin, is of an extremely excitable nature, and has suffered in the past from attacks of jealousy which have amounted to frenzy. It is conjectured that it was in one of these that she committed the terrible crime which has caused such a sensation in London. Her movements upon the Monday night have not yet been traced, but it is undoubted that a woman answering to her description attracted much attention at Charing Cross Station on Tuesday morning by the wildness of her appearance and the violence of her gestures. It is probable, therefore, that the crime was either committed when insane, or that its immediate effect was to drive the unhappy woman out of her mind. At present she is unable to give any coherent account of the past, and the doctors hold out no hopes of the re-establishment of her reason. There is evidence that a woman, who might have been Mme Fournaye, was seen for some hours on Monday night watching the house in Godolphin Street.

'What do you think of that, Holmes?' I had read the account aloud to him, while he finished his breakfast.

'My dear Watson,' said he, as he rose from the table and paced up and down the room, 'you are most long-suffering, but if I have told you nothing in the last three days it is because there is nothing to tell. Even now this report from Paris does not help us much.'

'Surely it is final as regards the man's death.'

'The man's death is a mere incident – a trivial episode – in comparison with our real task, which is to trace this document and save a European catastrophe. Only one important thing has happened in the last three days, and that is that nothing has happened. I get reports almost hourly from the Government, and it is certain that nowhere in Europe is there any sign of trouble. Now, if this letter were loose – no, it *can't* be loose – but if it isn't loose, where can it be? Who has it? Why is it held back? That's the question that beats in my brain like a hammer. Was it, indeed, a coincidence that Lucas should meet his death on the night when the letter disappeared? Did the letter ever reach him? If so, why is it not among his papers? Did this mad wife of his carry it off with her? If so, is it in her house in Paris? How could I search for it without the French police having their suspicions aroused? It is a case, my dear Watson, where the law is as dangerous to us as the criminals are. Every man's hand is against us, and yet the interests at stake are colossal. Should I bring it to a successful conclusion it will certainly represent the crowning glory of my career. Ah, here is my latest from the front!' He glanced hurriedly at the note which had been handed in. 'Halloa! Lestrade seems to have observed something of interest. Put on your hat, Watson, and we will stroll down together to Westminster.'

It was my first visit to the scene of the crime – a high, dingy, narrow-chested house, prim, formal, and solid, like the century which gave it birth. Lestrade's bulldog features gazed out at us from the front window, and he greeted us warmly when a big constable had opened the door and let us in. The room into which we were shown was that in which the crime had been committed, but no trace of it now remained, save an ugly, irregular stain upon the carpet. This carpet was a small square drugget in the centre of the room, surrounded by a broad expanse of beautiful, old-fashioned wood-flooring in square blocks highly polished. Over the fireplace was a magnificent trophy of weapons, one of which had been used on that tragic night. In the window was a sumptuous writing-desk, and every detail of the apartment, the pictures, the rugs, and the hangings, all pointed to a taste which was luxurious to the verge of effeminacy.

'Seen the Paris news?' asked Lestrade.

Holmes nodded.

'Our French friends seem to have touched the spot this time. No doubt it's just as they say. She knocked at the door – surprise visit, I guess, for he kept his life in watertight compartments. He let her in – couldn't keep her in the street. She told him how she had traced him, reproached him, one thing led to another, and then with that dagger so handy the end soon came. It wasn't all done in an instant, though, for these chairs were all swept over yonder, and he had one in his hand as if he had tried to hold her off with it. We've got it all clear as if we had seen it.'

Holmes raised his eyebrows.

'And yet you have sent for me?'

'Ah, yes, that's another matter – a mere trifle, but the sort of thing you take an interest in – queer, you know, and what you might call freakish. It has nothing to do with the main fact – can't have, on the face of it.'

'What is it, then?'

'Well, you know, after a crime of this sort we are very careful to keep things in their position. Nothing has been moved. Officer in charge here day and night. This morning, as the man was buried and the investigation over – so far as this room is concerned – we thought we could tidy up a bit. This carpet. You see, it is not fastened down; only just laid there. We had occasion to raise it. We found – '

'Yes? You found – '

Holmes's face grew tense with anxiety.

'Well, I'm sure you would never guess in a hundred years what we did find. You see that stain on the carpet? Well, a great deal must have soaked through, must it not?'

'Undoubtedly it must.'

'Well, you will be surprised to hear that there is no stain on the white woodwork to correspond.'

'No stain! But there must – '

'Yes; so you would say. But the fact remains that there isn't.'

He took the corner of the carpet in his hand and, turning it over, he showed that it was indeed as he said.

'But the underside is as stained as the upper. It must have left a mark.'

Lestrade chuckled with delight at having puzzled the famous expert.

'Now I'll show you the explanation. There *is* a second stain, but it does not correspond with the other. See for yourself.' As he spoke he turned over another portion of the carpet, and there, sure enough, was a great crimson spill upon the square white facing of the old-fashioned floor. 'What do you make of that, Mr Holmes?'

'Why, it is simple enough. The two stains did correspond, but the carpet has been turned round. As it was square and unfastened it was easily done.'

'The official police don't need you, Mr Holmes, to tell them that the carpet must have been turned round. That's clear enough, for the stains lie above each other – if you lay it over this way. But what I want to know is, who shifted the carpet, and why?'

I could see from Holmes's rigid face that he was vibrating with inward excitement.

'Look here, Lestrade,' said he, 'has that constable in the passage been in charge of the place all the time?'

'Yes, he has.'

'Well, take my advice. Examine him carefully. Don't do it before us. We'll wait here. You take him into the back room. You'll be more likely to get a confession out of him alone. Ask him how he dared to admit people and leave them alone in this room. Don't ask him if he has done it. Take it for granted. Tell him you *know* someone has been here. Press him. Tell him that a full confession is his only chance of forgiveness. Do exactly what I tell you!'

'By George, if he knows I'll have it out of him!' cried Lestrade. He darted into the hall, and a few moments later his bullying voice sounded from the back room.

'Now, Watson, now!' cried Holmes, with frenzied eagerness. All the demoniacal force of the man masked behind that listless manner burst out in a paroxysm of energy. He tore the drugget from the floor, and in an instant was down on his hands and knees clawing at each of the squares of wood beneath it. One turned sideways as he dug his nails into the edge of it. It hinged back like the lid of a box. A small black cavity opened beneath it. Holmes plunged his eager hand into it, and drew it out with a bitter snarl of anger and disappointment. It was empty.

'Quick, Watson, quick! Get it back again!' The wooden lid was replaced, and the drugget had only just been drawn straight when Lestrade's voice was heard in the passage. He found Holmes leaning languidly against the mantelpiece, resigned and patient, endeavouring to conceal his irrepressible yawns.

'Sorry to keep you waiting, Mr Holmes. I can see that you are bored to death with the whole affair. Well, he has confessed, all right. Come in here, MacPherson. Let these gentlemen hear of your most inexcusable conduct.'

The big constable, very hot and penitent, sidled into the room.

'I meant no harm, sir, I'm sure. The young woman came to the door last evening – mistook the house, she did. And then we got talking. It's lonesome, when you're on duty here all day.'

'Well, what happened then?'

'She wanted to see where the crime was done – had read about it in the papers, she said. She was a very respectable, well-spoken young woman, sir, and I saw no harm in letting her have a peep. When she saw that mark on the carpet, down she dropped on the floor, and lay as if she were dead. I ran to the back and got some water, but I could not bring her to. Then I went round the corner to the Ivy Plant for some brandy, and by the time I had brought it back the young woman had recovered and was off – ashamed of herself, I dare say, and dared not face me.'

'How about moving that drugget?'

'Well, sir, it was a bit rumpled, certainly, when I came back. You see, she fell on it, and it lies on a polished floor with nothing to keep it in place. I straightened it out afterwards.'

'It's a lesson to you that you can't deceive me, Constable MacPherson,' said Lestrade, with dignity. 'No doubt you thought that your breach of duty could never be discovered, and yet a mere glance at that drugget was enough to convince me that someone had been admitted to the room. It's lucky for you, my man, that nothing is missing, or you would find yourself in Queer Street. I'm sorry to have called you down over such a petty business, Mr Holmes, but I thought the point of the second stain not corresponding with the first would interest you.'

'Certainly, it was most interesting. Has this woman only been here once, constable?'

'Yes, sir, only once.'

'Who was she?'

'Don't know the name, sir. Was answering an advertisement about typewriting, and came to the wrong number – very pleasant, genteel young woman, sir.'

'Tall? Handsome?'

'Yes, sir; she was a well-grown young woman. I suppose you might say she was handsome. Perhaps some would say she was very handsome. "Oh, officer, do let me have a peep!" says she. She had pretty, coaxing ways, as you might say, and I thought there was no harm in letting her just put her head through the door.'

'How was she dressed?'

'Quiet, sir – a long mantle down to her feet.'

'What time was it?'

'It was just growing dusk at the time. They were lighting the lamps as I came back with the brandy.'

'Very good,' said Holmes. 'Come, Watson, I think that we have more important work elsewhere.'

As we left the house Lestrade remained in the front room, while the repentant constable opened the door to let us out. Holmes turned on the step and held up something in his hand. The constable stared intently.

'Good Lord, sir!' he cried, with amazement on his face. Holmes put his finger on his lips, replaced his hand in his breast-pocket, and burst out laughing as we turned down the street. 'Excellent!' said he. 'Come, friend Watson, the curtain rings up for the last act. You will be relieved to hear that there will be no war, that the Right Honourable Trelawney Hope will suffer no setback in his brilliant career, that the indiscreet Sovereign will receive no punishment for his indiscretion, that the Prime Minister will have no European complication to deal with, and that with a little tact and management upon our part nobody will be a penny the worse for what might have been a very ugly incident.'

My mind filled with admiration for this extra-ordinary man.

'You have solved it!' I cried.

'Hardly that, Watson. There are some points which are as dark as ever. But we have so much that it will be our own fault if we cannot get the rest. We will go straight to Whitehall Terrace and bring the matter to a head.'

When we arrived at the residence of the European Secretary it was for Lady Hilda Trelawney Hope that Sherlock Holmes enquired. We were shown into the morning-room.

'Mr Holmes!' said the lady, and her face was pink with her indignation, 'this is surely most unfair and ungenerous upon your part. I desired, as I have explained, to keep my visit to you a secret, lest my husband should think that I was intruding into his affairs. And yet you compromise me by coming here and so showing that there are business relations between us.'

'Unfortunately, madam, I had no possible alternative. I have been commissioned to recover this immensely important paper. I must therefore ask you, madam, to be kind enough to place it in my hands.'

The lady sprang to her feet, with the colour all dashed in an instant from her beautiful face. Her eyes glazed – she tottered – I thought that she would faint. Then with a grand effort she rallied from the shock, and a supreme astonishment and indignation chased every other expression from her features.

'You – you insult me, Mr Holmes.'

'Come, come, madam, it is useless. Give up the letter.'

She darted to the bell.

'The butler shall show you out.'

'Do not ring, Lady Hilda. If you do, then all my earnest efforts to avoid a scandal will be frustrated. Give up the letter and all will be set right. If you will work with me I can arrange everything. If you work against me I must expose you.'

She stood grandly defiant, a queenly figure, her eyes fixed upon his as if she would read his very soul. Her hand was on the bell, but she had forborne to ring it.

'You are trying to frighten me. It is not a very manly thing, Mr Holmes, to come here and browbeat a woman. You say that you know something. What is it that you know?'

'Pray sit down, madam. You will hurt yourself there if you fall. I will not speak until you sit down. Thank you.'

'I give you five minutes, Mr Holmes.'

'One is enough, Lady Hilda. I know of your visit to Eduardo Lucas, of your giving him this document, of your ingenious return to the room last night, and of the manner in which you took the letter from the hiding-place under the carpet.'

She stared at him with an ashen face and gulped twice before she could speak.

'You are mad, Mr Holmes – you are mad!' she cried, at last.

He drew a small piece of cardboard from his pocket. It was the face of a woman cut out of a portrait.

'I have carried this because I thought it might be useful,' said he. 'The policeman has recognised it.'

She gave a gasp and her head dropped back in the chair.

'Come, Lady Hilda. You have the letter. The matter may still be adjusted. I have no desire to bring trouble to you. My duty ends when I have returned the lost letter to your husband. Take my advice and be frank with me; it is your only chance.'

Her courage was admirable. Even now she would not own defeat.

'I tell you again, Mr Holmes, that you are under some absurd illusion.'

Holmes rose from his chair.

'I am sorry for you, Lady Hilda. I have done my best for you; I can see that it is all in vain.'

He rang the bell. The butler entered.

'Is Mr Trelawney Hope at home?'

'He will be home, sir, at a quarter to one.'

Holmes glanced at his watch.

'Still a quarter of an hour,' said he. 'Very good, I shall wait.'

The butler had hardly closed the door behind him when Lady Hilda was down on her knees at Holmes's feet, her hands outstretched, her beautiful face up-turned and wet with her tears.

'Oh, spare me, Mr Holmes! Spare me!' she pleaded, in a frenzy of supplication. 'For Heaven's sake, don't tell him! I love him so! I would not bring one shadow on his life, and this I know would break his noble heart.'

Holmes raised the lady. 'I am thankful, madam, that you have come to your senses even at this last moment! There is not an instant to lose. Where is the letter?'

She darted across to a writing-desk, unlocked it, and drew out a long blue envelope.

'Here it is, Mr Holmes. Would to Heaven I had never seen it!'

'How can we return it?' Holmes muttered. 'Quick, quick, we must think of some way! Where is the despatch-box?'

'Still in his bedroom.'

'What a stroke of luck! Quick, madam, bring it here!'

A moment later she had appeared with a red flat box in her hand.

'How did you open it before? You have a duplicate key? Yes, of course you have. Open it!'

From out of her bosom Lady Hilda had drawn a small key. The box flew open. It was stuffed with papers. Holmes thrust the blue envelope deep down into the heart of them, between the leaves of some other document. The box was shut, locked, and returned to the bedroom.

'Now we are ready for him,' said Holmes; 'we have still ten minutes. I am going far to screen you, Lady Hilda. In return you will spend the time in telling me frankly the real meaning of this extraordinary affair.'

'Mr Holmes, I will tell you everything,' cried the lady. 'Oh, Mr Holmes, I would cut off my right hand before I gave him a moment of sorrow! There is no woman in all London who loves her husband as I do, and yet if he knew how I have acted – how I have been compelled to act – he would never forgive me. For his own honour stands so high that he could not forget or pardon a lapse in another. Help me, Mr Holmes! My happiness, his happiness, our very lives are at stake!'

'Quick, madam, the time grows short!'

'It was a letter of mine, Mr Holmes, an indiscreet letter written before my marriage – a foolish letter, a letter of an impulsive, loving girl. I meant no harm, and yet he would have thought it criminal. Had he read that letter his confidence would have been for ever destroyed. It is years since I wrote it. I had thought that the whole matter was forgotten. Then at last I heard from this man, Lucas, that it had passed into his hands, and that he would lay it before my husband. I implored his mercy. He said that he would return my letter if I would bring him a certain document which he described in my husband's despatch-box. He had some spy in the office who had told him of its existence. He assured me that no harm could come to my husband. Put yourself in my position, Mr Holmes! What was I to do?'

'Take your husband into your confidence.'

'I could not, Mr Holmes, I could not! On the one side seemed certain ruin; on the other, terrible as it seemed to take my husband's paper, still in a matter of politics I could not understand the consequences, while in a matter of love and trust they were only too clear to me. I did it, Mr Holmes! I took an impression of his key; this man Lucas furnished a duplicate. I opened his despatch-box, took the paper, and conveyed it to Godolphin Street.'

'What happened there, madam?'

'I tapped at the door as agreed. Lucas opened it. I followed him into his room, leaving the hall door ajar behind me, for I feared to be alone with the man. I remember that there was a woman outside as I entered. Our business was soon done. He had my letter on his desk; I handed him the document. He gave me the letter. At this instant there was a sound at the door. There were steps in the passage. Lucas quickly turned back the drugget, thrust the document into some hiding-place there, and covered it over.

'What happened after that is like some fearful dream. I have a vision of a dark, frantic face, of a woman's voice, which screamed in French, "My waiting is not in vain. At last, at last I have found you with her!" There was a savage struggle. I saw him with a chair in his hand, a knife gleamed in hers. I rushed from the horrible scene, ran from the house, and only next morning in the paper did I learn the dreadful result. That night I was happy, for I had my letter, and I had not seen yet what the future would bring.

'It was the next morning that I realised that I had only exchanged one trouble for another. My husband's anguish at the loss of his paper went to my heart. I could hardly prevent myself from there and then kneeling down at his feet and telling him what I had done. But that again would mean a confession of the past. I came to you that morning in order to understand the full enormity of my offence. From the instant that I grasped it my whole mind was turned to the one thought of getting back my husband's paper. It must still be where Lucas had placed it, for it was concealed before this dreadful woman entered the room. If it had not been for her coming, I should not have known where his hiding-place was. How was I to get into the room? For two days I watched the place, but the door was never left open. Last night I made a last attempt. What I did and how I succeeded, you have already learned. I brought the paper back with me, and thought of destroying it since I could see no way of returning it, without confessing my guilt to my husband. Heavens, I hear his step upon the stair!'

The European Secretary burst excitedly into the room.

'Any news, Mr Holmes, any news?' he cried.

'I have some hopes.'

'Ah, thank Heaven!' His face became radiant. 'The Prime Minister is lunching with me. May he share your hopes? He has nerves of steel, and yet I know that he has hardly slept since this terrible event. Jacobs, will you ask the Prime Minister to come up? As to you, dear, I fear that this is a matter of politics. We will join you in a few minutes in the dining-room.'

The Prime Minister's manner was subdued, but I could see by the gleam of his eyes and the twitchings of his bony hands that he shared the excitement of his young colleague.

'I understand that you have something to report, Mr Holmes?'

'Purely negative as yet,' my friend answered. 'I have enquired at every point where it might be, and I am sure that there is no danger to be apprehended.'

'But that is not enough, Mr Holmes. We cannot live for ever on such a volcano. We must have something definite.'

'I am in hopes of getting it. That is why I am here. The more I think of the matter the more convinced I am that the letter has never left this house.'

'Mr Holmes!'

'If it had it would certainly have been public by now.'

'But why should anyone take it in order to keep it in his house?'

'I am not convinced that anyone did take it.'

'Then how could it leave the despatch-box?'

'I am not convinced that it ever did leave the despatch-box.'

'Mr Holmes, this joking is very ill-timed. You have my assurance that it left the box.'

'Have you examined the box since Tuesday morning?'

'No; it was not necessary.'

'You may conceivably have overlooked it.'

'Impossible, I say.'

'But I am not convinced of it; I have known such things to happen. I presume there are other papers there. Well, it may have got mixed with them.'

'It was on the top.'

'Someone may have shaken the box and displaced it.'

'No, no; I had everything out.'

'Surely it is easily decided, Hope,' said the Premier. 'Let us have the despatch-box brought in.'

The Secretary rang the bell.

'Jacobs, bring down my despatch-box. This is a farcical waste of time, but still, if nothing else will satisfy you, it shall be done. Thank you, Jacobs; put it here. I have always had the key on my watch-chain. Here are the papers, you see. Letter from Lord Merrow, report from Sir Charles Hardy, memorandum from Belgrade, note on the Russo-German grain taxes, letter from Madrid, note from Lord Flowers – good heavens! what is this? Lord Bellinger! Lord Bellinger!'

The Premier snatched the blue envelope from his hand.

'Yes, it is it – and the letter is intact. Hope, I congratulate you.'

'Thank you! Thank you! What a weight from my heart. But this is inconceivable – impossible. Mr Holmes, you are a wizard, a sorcerer! How did you know it was there?'

'Because I knew it was nowhere else.'

'I cannot believe my eyes!' He ran wildly to the door. 'Where is my wife? I must tell her that all is well. Hilda! Hilda!' we heard his voice on the stairs.

The Premier looked at Holmes with twinkling eyes.

'Come, sir,' said he. 'There is more in this than meets the eye. How came the letter back in the box?'

Holmes turned away smiling from the keen scrutiny of those wonderful eyes.

'We also have our diplomatic secrets,' said he, and picking up his hat he turned to the door.

HIS LAST BOW

14

Wisteria Lodge

I

The Singular Experience of Mr John Scott Eccles

I find it recorded in my notebook that it was a bleak and windy day towards the end of March in the year 1892. Holmes had received a telegram while we sat at our lunch, and he had scribbled a reply. He made no remark, but the matter remained in his thoughts, for he stood in front of the fire afterwards with a thoughtful face, smoking his pipe, and casting an occasional glance at the message. Suddenly he turned upon me with a mischievous twinkle in his eyes.

'I suppose, Watson, we must look upon you as a man of letters,' said he. 'How do you define the word "grotesque"?'

'Strange – remarkable,' I suggested.

He shook his head at my definition.

'There is surely something more than that,' said he; 'some underlying suggestion of the tragic and the terrible. If you cast your mind back to some of those narratives with which you have afflicted a long-suffering public, you will recognise how often the grotesque has deepened into the criminal. Think of that little affair of the red-headed men. That was grotesque enough in the outset, and yet it ended in a desperate attempt at robbery. Or, again, there was that most grotesque affair of the five orange pips, which led straight to a murderous conspiracy. The word puts me on the alert.'

'Have you it there?' I asked.

He read the telegram aloud.

'Have just had most incredible and grotesque experience. May I consult you? – Scott Eccles, Post Office, Charing Cross.'

'Man or woman?' I asked.

'Oh, man, of course. No woman would ever send a reply-paid telegram. She would have come.'

'Will you see him?'

'My dear Watson, you know how bored I have been since we locked up Colonel Carruthers. My mind is like a racing engine, tearing itself to pieces because it is not connected up with the work for which it was built. Life is commonplace, the papers are sterile; audacity and romance seem to have passed for ever from the criminal world. Can you ask me, then, whether I am ready to look into any new problem, however trivial it may prove? But here, unless I am mistaken, is our client.'

A measured step was heard upon the stairs, and a moment later a stout, tall, grey-whiskered and solemnly respectable person was ushered into the room. His life history was written in his heavy features and pompous manner. From his spats to his gold-rimmed spectacles he was a Conservative, a church-man, a good citizen, orthodox and conventional to the last degree. But some amazing experience had disturbed his native composure and left its traces in his bristling hair, his flushed, angry cheeks, and his flurried, excited manner. He plunged instantly into his business.

'I have had a most singular and unpleasant experience, Mr Holmes,' said he. 'Never in my life have I
been placed in such a situation. It is most improper –
most outrageous. I must insist upon some explanation.'
He swelled and puffed in his anger.

'Pray sit down, Mr Scott Eccles,' said Holmes in a
soothing voice. 'May I ask, in the first place, why you
came to me at all?'

'Well, sir, it did not appear to be a matter which
concerned the police, and yet, when you have heard
the facts, you must admit that I could not leave it
where it was. Private detectives are a class with whom
I have absolutely no sympathy, but none the less,
having heard your name – '

'Quite so. But, in the second place, why did you not
come at once?'

'What do you mean?'

Holmes glanced at his watch.

'It is a quarter-past two,' he said. 'Your telegram
was dispatched about one. But no one can glance at
your toilet and attire without seeing that your disturbance dates from the moment of your waking.'

Our client smoothed down his unbrushed hair and
felt his unshaven chin.

'You are right, Mr Holmes. I never gave a thought to
my toilet. I was only too glad to get out of such a house.
But I have been running round making enquiries before
I came to you. I went to the house agents, you know,
and they said that Mr Garcia's rent was paid up all right
and that everything was in order at Wisteria Lodge.'

'Come, come, sir,' said Holmes, laughing. 'You are
like my friend, Dr Watson, who has a bad habit of
telling his stories wrong end foremost. Please arrange
your thoughts and let me know, in their due sequence,

exactly what those events are which have sent you out unbrushed and unkempt, with dress boots and waistcoat buttoned awry, in search of advice and assistance.'

Our client looked down with a rueful face at his own unconventional appearance.

'I'm sure it must look very bad, Mr Holmes, and I am not aware that in my whole life such a thing has ever happened before. But I will tell you the whole queer business, and when I have done so you will admit, I am sure, that there has been enough to excuse me.'

But his narrative was nipped in the bud. There was a bustle outside, and Mrs Hudson opened the door to usher in two robust and official-looking individuals, one of whom was well known to us as Inspector Gregson of Scotland Yard, an energetic, gallant, and, within his limitations, a capable officer. He shook hands with Holmes and introduced his comrade as Inspector Baynes, of the Surrey Constabulary.

'We are hunting together, Mr Holmes, and our trail lay in this direction.' He turned his bulldog eyes upon our visitor. 'Are you Mr John Scott Eccles, of Popham House, Lee?'

'I am.'

'We have been following you about all the morning.'

'You traced him through the telegram, no doubt,' said Holmes.

'Exactly, Mr Holmes. We picked up the scent at Charing Cross Post Office and came on here.'

'But why do you follow me? What do you want?'

'We wish a statement, Mr Scott Eccles, as to the events which led up to the death last night of Mr Aloysius Garcia, of Wisteria Lodge, near Esher.'

Our client had sat up with staring eyes and every tinge of colour struck from his astonished face.

'Dead? Did you say he was dead?'

'Yes, sir, he is dead.'

'But how? An accident?'

'Murder, if ever there was one upon earth.'

'Good God! This is awful! You don't mean – you don't mean that I am suspected?'

'A letter of yours was found in the dead man's pocket, and we know by it that you had planned to pass last night at his house.'

'So I did.'

'Oh, you did, did you?'

Out came the official notebook.

'Wait a bit, Gregson,' said Sherlock Holmes. 'All you desire is a plain statement, is it not?'

'And it is my duty to warn Mr Scott Eccles that it may be used against him.'

'Mr Eccles was going to tell us about it when you entered the room. I think, Watson, a brandy and soda would do him no harm. Now, sir, I suggest that you take no notice of this addition to your audience, and that you proceed with your narrative exactly as you would have done had you never been interrupted.'

Our visitor had gulped off the brandy and the colour had returned to his face. With a dubious glance at the inspector's notebook, he plunged at once into his extraordinary statement.

'I am a bachelor,' said he, 'and being of a sociable turn I cultivate a large number of friends. Among these are the family of a retired brewer called Melville, living at Abermarle Mansion, Kensington. It was at his table that I met some weeks ago a young fellow named Garcia. He was, I understood, of Spanish descent and connected in some way with the Embassy. He spoke perfect English, was pleasing in his manners, and as good-looking a man as ever I saw in my life.

'In some way we struck up quite a friendship, this young fellow and I. He seemed to take a fancy to me from the first, and within two days of our meeting he came to see me at Lee. One thing led to another, and it ended in his inviting me out to spend a few days at his house, Wisteria Lodge, between Esher and Oxshott. Yesterday evening I went to Esher to fulfil this engagement.

'He had described his household to me before I went there. He lived with a faithful servant, a countryman of his own, who looked after all his needs. This fellow could speak English and did his housekeeping for him. Then there was a wonderful cook, he said, a half-breed whom he had picked up in his travels, who could serve an excellent dinner. I remember that he remarked what a queer household it was to find in the heart of Surrey, and that I agreed with him, though it has proved a good deal queerer than I thought.

'I drove to the place – about two miles on the south side of Esher. The house was a fair-sized one, standing back from the road, with a curving drive which was banked with high evergreen shrubs. It was an old, tumbledown building in a crazy state of disrepair. When the trap pulled up on the grass-grown drive in front of the blotched and weather-stained door, I had doubts as to my wisdom in visiting a man whom I knew so slightly. He opened the door himself, however, and greeted me with a great show of cordiality. I was handed over to the manservant, a melancholy, swarthy individual, who led the way, my bag in his hand, to my bedroom. The whole place was depressing. Our dinner was tête-á-tête, and though my host did his best to be entertaining, his thoughts seemed to continually wander, and he talked so vaguely and wildly that I could hardly understand him. He continually drummed his fingers on the table, gnawed his nails, and gave other signs of nervous impatience. The dinner itself was neither well served nor well cooked, and the gloomy presence of the taciturn servant did not help to enliven us. I can assure you that many times in the course of the evening I wished that I could invent some excuse which would take me back to Lee.

'One thing comes back to my memory which may have a bearing upon the business that you two gentlemen are investigating. I thought nothing of it at the time. Near the end of dinner a note was handed in by the servant. I noticed that after my host had read it he seemed even more distrait and strange than before. He gave up all pretence at conversation and sat, smoking endless cigarettes, lost in his own thoughts, but he made no remark as to the contents. About eleven I was glad to go to bed. Some time later Garcia looked in at my door – the room was dark at the time – and asked me if I had rung. I said that I had not. He apologised for having disturbed me so late, saying that it was nearly one o'clock. I dropped off after this and slept soundly all night.

'And now I come to the amazing part of my tale. When I woke it was broad daylight. I glanced at my watch, and the time was nearly nine. I had particularly asked to be called at eight, so I was very much astonished at this forgetfulness. I sprang up and rang for the servant. There was no response. I rang again and again, with the same result. Then I came to the conclusion that the bell was out of order. I huddled on my clothes and hurried downstairs in an exceedingly bad temper to order some hot water. You can imagine my surprise when I found that there was no one there. I shouted in the hall. There was no answer. Then I ran from room to room. All were deserted. My host had shown me which was his bedroom the night before, so I knocked at the door. No reply. I turned the handle and walked in. The room was empty, and the bed had never been slept in. He had gone with the rest. The foreign host, the foreign footman, the foreign cook, all had vanished in the night! That was the end of my visit to Wisteria Lodge.'

Sherlock Holmes was rubbing his hands and chuckling as he added this bizarre incident to his collection of strange episodes.

'Your experience is, so far as I know, perfectly unique,' said he. 'May I ask, sir, what you did then?'

'I was furious. My first idea was that I had been the victim of some absurd practical joke. I packed my things, banged the hall door behind me, and set off for Esher, with my bag in my hand. I called at Allan Brothers', the chief land agents in the village, and found that it was from this firm that the villa had been rented. It struck me that the whole proceeding could hardly be for the purpose of making a fool of me, and that the main object must be to get out of the rent. It is late in March, so quarter-day is at hand. But this theory would not work. The agent was obliged to me for my warning, but told me that the rent had been paid in advance. Then I made my way to town and called at the Spanish Embassy. The man was unknown there. After this I went to see Melville, at whose house I had first met Garcia, but I found that he really knew rather less about him than I did. Finally when I got your reply to my wire I came out to you, since I gather that you are a person who gives advice in difficult cases. But now, Mr Inspector, I understand, from what you said when you entered the room, that you can carry the story on, and that some tragedy has occurred. I can assure you that every word I have said is the truth, and that, outside of what I have told you, I know absolutely nothing about the fate of this man. My only desire is to help the law in every possible way.'

'I am sure of it, Mr Scott Eccles – I am sure of it,' said Inspector Gregson in a very amiable tone. 'I am bound to say that everything which you have said agrees very closely with the facts as they have come to our notice. For example, there was that note which arrived during dinner. Did you chance to observe what became of it?'

'Yes, I did. Garcia rolled it up and threw it into the fire.'

'What do you say to that, Mr Baynes?'

The country detective was a stout, puffy, red man, whose face was only redeemed from grossness by two extraordinarily bright eyes, almost hidden behind the heavy creases of cheek and brow. With a slow smile he drew a folded and discoloured scrap of paper from his pocket.

'It was a dog-grate, Mr Holmes, and he overpitched it. I picked this out unburned from the back of it.'

Holmes smiled his appreciation.

'You must have examined the house very carefully to find a single pellet of paper.'

'I did, Mr Holmes. It's my way. Shall I read it, Mr Gregson?'

The Londoner nodded.

'The note is written upon ordinary cream-laid paper

without watermark. It is a quarter-sheet. The paper is cut off in two snips with a short-bladed scissors. It has been folded over three times and sealed with purple wax, put on hurriedly and pressed down with some flat oval object. It is addressed to Mr Garcia, Wisteria Lodge. It says:

'Our own colours, green and white. Green open, white shut. Main stair, first corridor, seventh right, green baize. Godspeed.   D.

'It is a woman's writing, done with a sharp-pointed pen, but the address is either done with another pen or by someone else. It is thicker and bolder, as you see.'

'A very remarkable note,' said Holmes, glancing it over. 'I must compliment you, Mr Baynes, upon your attention to detail in your examination of it. A few trifling points might perhaps be added. The oval seal is undoubtedly a plain sleeve-link – what else is of such a shape? The scissors were bent nail scissors. Short as the two snips are, you can distinctly see the same slight curve in each.'

The country detective chuckled.

'I thought I had squeezed all the juice out of it, but I see there was a little over,' he said. 'I'm bound to say that I make nothing of the note except that there was something on hand, and that a woman, as usual, was at the bottom of it.'

Mr Scott Eccles had fidgeted in his seat during this conversation.

'I am glad you found the note, since it corroborates my story,' said he. 'But I beg to point out that I have not yet heard what has happened to Mr Garcia, nor what has become of his household.'

'As to Garcia,' said Gregson, 'that is easily answered. He was found dead this morning upon Oxshott Common, nearly a mile from his home. His head had been smashed to pulp by heavy blows of a sandbag or some such instrument, which had crushed rather than wounded. It is a lonely corner, and there is no house within a quarter of a mile of the spot. He had apparently been struck down first from behind, but his assailant had gone on beating him long after he was dead. It was a most furious assault. There are no footsteps nor any clue to the criminals.'

'Robbed?'

'No, there was no attempt at robbery.'

'This is very painful – very painful and terrible,' said Mr Scott Eccles in a querulous voice, 'but it is really uncommonly hard on me. I had nothing to do with my host going off upon a nocturnal excursion and meeting so sad an end. How do I come to be mixed up with the case?'

'Very simply, sir,' Inspector Baynes answered. 'The only document found in the pocket of the deceased was a letter from you saying that you would be with him on the night of his death. It was the envelope of this letter which gave us the dead man's name and address. It was after nine this morning when we reached his house and found neither you nor anyone else inside it. I wired to Mr Gregson to run you down in London while I examined Wisteria Lodge. Then I came into town, joined Mr Gregson, and here we are.'

'I think now,' said Gregson, rising, 'we had best put this matter into an official shape. You will come round with us to the station, Mr Scott Eccles, and let us have your statement in writing.'

'Certainly, I will come at once. But I retain your services, Mr Holmes. I desire you to spare no expense and no pains to get at the truth.'

My friend turned to the country inspector.

'I suppose that you have no objection to my collaborating with you, Mr Baynes?'

'Highly honoured, sir, I am sure.'

'You appear to have been very prompt and business-like in all that you have done. Was there any clue, may I ask, as to the exact hour that the man met his death?'

'He had been there since one o'clock. There was rain about that time, and his death had certainly been before the rain.'

'But that is perfectly impossible, Mr Baynes,' cried our client. 'His voice is unmistakable. I could swear to it that it was he who addressed me in my bedroom at that very hour.'

'Remarkable, but by no means impossible,' said Holmes, smiling.

'You have a clue?' asked Gregson.

'On the face of it the case is not a very complex one, though it certainly presents some novel and interesting features. A further knowledge of facts is necessary before I would venture to give a final and definite opinion. By the way, Mr Baynes, did you find anything remarkable besides this note in your examination of the house?'

The detective looked at my friend in a singular way.

'There were,' said he, 'one or two *very* remarkable things. Perhaps when I have finished at the police-station you would care to come out and give me your opinion of them.'

'I am entirely at your service,' said Sherlock Holmes,

ringing the bell. 'You will show these gentlemen out, Mrs Hudson, and kindly send the boy with this telegram. He is to pay a five-shilling reply.'

We sat for some time in silence after our visitors had left. Holmes smoked hard, with his brows drawn down over his keen eyes, and his head thrust forward in the eager way characteristic of the man.

'Well, Watson,' he asked, turning suddenly upon me, 'what do you make of it?'

'I can make nothing of this mystification of Scott Eccles.'

'But the crime?'

'Well, taken with the disappearance of the man's companions, I should say that they were in some way concerned in the murder and had fled from justice.'

'That is certainly a possible point of view. On the face of it you must admit, however, that it is very strange that his two servants should have been in a conspiracy against him and should have attacked him on the one night when he had a guest. They had him alone at their mercy every other night in the week.'

'Then why did they fly?'

'Quite so. Why did they fly? There is a big fact. Another big fact is the remarkable experience of our client, Scott Eccles. Now, my dear Watson, is it beyond the limits of human ingenuity to furnish an explanation which would cover both of these big facts? If it were one which would also admit of the mysterious note with its very curious phraseology, why, then it would be worth accepting as a temporary hypothesis. If the fresh facts which come to our knowledge all fit themselves into the scheme, then our hypothesis may gradually become a solution.'

'But what is our hypothesis?'

Holmes leaned back in his chair with half-closed eyes.

'You must admit, my dear Watson, that the idea of a joke is impossible. There were grave events afoot, as the sequel showed, and the coaxing of Scott Eccles to Wisteria Lodge had some connection with them.'

'But what possible connection?'

'Let us take it link by link. There is, on the face of it, something unnatural about this strange and sudden friendship between the young Spaniard and Scott Eccles. It was the former who forced the pace. He called upon Eccles at the other end of London on the very day after he first met him, and he kept in close touch with him until he got him down to Esher. Now, what did he want with Eccles? What could Eccles supply? I see no charm in the man. He is not particularly intelligent – not a man likely to be congenial to a quick-witted Latin. Why, then, was he picked out from all the other people whom Garcia met as particularly suited to his purpose? Has he any one outstanding quality? I say that he has. He is the very type of conventional British respectability, and the very man as a witness to impress another Briton. You saw yourself how neither of the inspectors dreamed of questioning his statement, extraordinary as it was.'

'But what was he to witness?'

'Nothing, as things turned out, but everything had they gone another way. That is how I read the matter.'

'I see, he might have proved an alibi.'

'Exactly, my dear Watson; he might have proved an alibi. We will suppose, for argument's sake, that the household of Wisteria Lodge are confederates in some design. The attempt, whatever it may be, is to come off, we will say, before one o'clock. By some juggling of the clocks it is quite possible that they may have got Scott Eccles to bed earlier than he thought, but in any case it is likely that when Garcia went out of his way to tell him that it was one it was really not more than twelve. If Garcia could do whatever he had to do and be back by the hour mentioned he had evidently a powerful reply to any accusation. Here was this irreproachable Englishman ready to swear in any court of law that the accused was in the house all the time. It was an insurance against the worst.'

'Yes, yes, I see that. But how about the disappearance of the others?'

'I have not all my facts yet, but I do not think there are any insuperable difficulties. Still, it is an error to argue in front of your data. You find yourself insensibly twisting them round to fit your theories.'

'And the message?'

'How did it run? "Our own colours, green and white." Sounds like racing. "Green open, white shut." That is clearly a signal. "Main stair, first corridor, seventh right, green baize." This is an assignation. We may find a jealous husband at the bottom of it all. It was clearly a dangerous quest. She would not have said "Godspeed" had it not been so. "D" – that should be a guide.'

'The man was a Spaniard. I suggest that "D" stands for Dolores, a common female name in Spain.'

'Good, Watson, very good – but quite inadmissible. A Spaniard would write to a Spaniard in Spanish. The writer of this note is certainly English. Well, we can only possess our soul in patience until this excellent inspector comes back for us. Meanwhile we can thank our lucky fate which has rescued us for a few short hours from the insufferable fatigues of idleness.'

An answer had arrived to Holmes's telegram before our Surrey officer had returned. Holmes read it and was about to place it in his notebook when he caught a glimpse of my expectant face. He tossed it across with a laugh.

'We are moving in exalted circles,' said he.

The telegram was a list of names and addresses:

Lord Harringby, The Dingle; Sir George Ffolliott, Oxshott Towers; Mr Hynes Hynes, J.P., Purdley Place; Mr James Baker Williams, Forton Old Hall; Mr Henderson, High Gable; Revd Joshua Stone, Nether Walsling.

'This is a very obvious way of limiting our field of operations,' said Holmes. 'No doubt Baynes, with his methodical mind, has already adopted some similar plan.'

'I don't quite understand.'

'Well, my dear fellow, we have already arrived at the conclusion that the message received by Garcia at dinner was an appointment or an assignation. Now, if the obvious reading of it is correct, and in order to keep the tryst one has to ascend a main stair and seek the seventh door in a corridor, it is perfectly clear that the house is a very large one. It is equally certain that this house cannot be more than a mile or two from Oxshott, since Garcia was walking in that direction and hoped, according to my reading of the facts, to be back in Wisteria Lodge in time to avail himself of an alibi, which would only be valid up to one o'clock. As the number of large houses close to Oxshott must be limited, I adopted the obvious method of sending to the agents mentioned by Scott Eccles and obtaining a list of them. Here they are in this telegram, and the other end of our tangled skein must lie among them.'

It was nearly six o'clock before we found ourselves in the pretty Surrey village of Esher, with Inspector Baynes as our companion.

Holmes and I had taken things for the night, and found comfortable quarters at the Bull. Finally we set out in the company of the detective on our visit to Wisteria Lodge. It was a cold, dark March evening, with a sharp wind and a fine rain beating upon our faces, a fit setting for the wild common over which our road passed and the tragic goal to which it led us.

2

The Tiger of San Pedro

A cold and melancholy walk of a couple of miles brought us to a high wooden gate, which opened into a gloomy avenue of chestnuts. The curved and shadowed drive led us to a low, dark house, pitch-black against a slate-coloured sky. From the front window upon the left of the door there peeped a glimmer of a feeble light.

'There's a constable in possession,' said Baynes. 'I'll knock at the window.' He stepped across the grass plot and tapped with his hand on the pane. Through the fogged glass I dimly saw a man spring up from a chair beside the fire, and heard a sharp cry from within the room. An instant later a white-faced, hard-breathing policeman had opened the door, the candle wavering in his trembling hand.

'What's the matter, Walters?' asked Baynes sharply.

The man mopped his forehead with his handkerchief and gave a long sigh of relief.

'I am glad you have come, sir. It has been a long evening, and I don't think my nerve is as good as it was.'

'Your nerve, Walters? I should not have thought you had a nerve in your body.'

'Well, sir, it's this lonely, silent house and the queer thing in the kitchen. Then when you tapped at the window I thought it had come again.'

'That what had come again?'

'The devil, sir, for all I know. It was at the window.'

'What was at the window, and when?'

'It was just about two hours ago. The light was just fading. I was sitting reading in the chair. I don't know what made me look up, but there was a face looking in at me through the lower pane. Lord, sir, what a face it was! I'll see it in my dreams.'

'Tut, tut, Walters. This is not talk for a police-constable.'

'I know, sir, I know; but it shook me, sir, and there's no use to deny it. It wasn't black, sir, nor was it white, nor any colour that I know, but a kind of queer shade like clay with a splash of milk in it. Then there was the size of it – it was twice yours, sir. And the look of it – the great staring goggle eyes, and the line of white teeth like a hungry beast. I tell you, sir, I couldn't move a finger, nor get my breath, till it whisked away and was gone. Out I ran and through the shrubbery, but thank God there was no one there.'

'If I didn't know you were a good man, Walters, I

should put a black mark against you for this. If it were the devil himself a constable on duty should never thank God that he could not lay his hands upon him. I suppose the whole thing is not a vision and a touch of nerves?'

'That, at least, is very easily settled,' said Holmes, lighting his little pocket lantern. 'Yes,' he reported, after a short examination of the grass bed, 'a number twelve shoe, I should say. If he was all on the same scale as his foot he must certainly have been a giant.'

'What became of him?'

'He seems to have broken through the shrubbery and made for the road.'

'Well,' said the inspector with a grave and thoughtful face, 'whoever he may have been, and whatever he may have wanted, he's gone for the present, and we have more immediate things to attend to. Now, Mr Holmes, with your permission, I will show you round the house.'

The various bedrooms and sitting-rooms had yielded nothing to a careful search. Apparently the tenants had brought little or nothing with them, and all the furniture down to the smallest details had been taken over with the house. A good deal of clothing with the stamp of Marx and Co., High Holborn, had been left behind. Telegraphic enquiries had been already made which showed that Marx knew nothing of his customer save that he was a good payer. Odds and ends, some pipes, a few novels, two of them in Spanish, an old-fashioned pin-fire revolver, and a guitar were amongst the personal property.

'Nothing in all this,' said Baynes, stalking, candle in hand, from room to room. 'But now, Mr Holmes, I invite your attention to the kitchen.'

It was a gloomy, high-ceilinged room at the back of

the house, with a straw litter in one corner, which served apparently as a bed for the cook. The table was piled with half-eaten dishes and dirty plates, the debris of last night's dinner.

'Look at this,' said Baynes. 'What do you make of it?'

He held up his candle before an extraordinary object which stood at the back of the dresser. It was so wrinkled and shrunken and withered that it was difficult to say what it might have been. One could but say that it was black and leathery and that it bore some resemblance to a dwarfish, human figure. At first, as I examined it, I thought that it was a mummified negro baby, and then it seemed a very twisted and ancient monkey. Finally I was left in doubt as to whether it was animal or human. A double band of white shells were strung round the centre of it.

'Very interesting – very interesting indeed!' said Holmes, peering at this sinister relic. 'Anything more?'

In silence Baynes led the way to the sink and held forward his candle. The limbs and body of some large white bird, torn savagely to pieces with the feathers still on, were littered all over it. Holmes pointed to the wattles on the severed head.

'A white cock,' said he. 'Most interesting! It is really a very curious case.'

But Mr Baynes had kept his most sinister exhibit to the last. From under the sink he drew a zinc pail which contained a quantity of blood. Then from the table he took a platter heaped with small pieces of charred bone.

'Something has been killed and something has been burned. We raked all these out of the fire. We had a doctor in this morning. He says that they are not human.'

Holmes smiled and rubbed his hands.

'I must congratulate you, Inspector, on handling so distinctive and instructive a case. Your powers, if I may say so without offence, seem superior to your opportunities.'

Inspector Baynes's small eyes twinkled with pleasure.

'You're right, Mr Holmes. We stagnate in the provinces. A case of this sort gives a man a chance, and I hope that I shall take it. What do you make of these bones?'

'A lamb, I should say, or a kid.'

'And the white cock?'

'Curious, Mr Baynes, very curious. I should say almost unique.'

'Yes, sir, there must have been some very strange people with some very strange ways in this house. One of them is dead. Did his companions follow him and kill him? If they did we should have them, for every port is watched. But my own views are different. Yes, sir, my own views are very different.'

'You have a theory then?'

'And I'll work it myself, Mr Holmes. It's only due to my own credit to do so. Your name is made, but I have still to make mine. I should be glad to be able to say afterwards that I had solved it without your help.'

Holmes laughed good-humouredly.

'Well, well, Inspector,' said he. 'Do you follow your path and I will follow mine. My results are always very much at your service if you care to apply to me for them. I think that I have seen all that I wish in this house, and that my time may be more profitably employed elsewhere. *Au revoir* and good luck!'

I could tell by numerous subtle signs, which might have been lost upon anyone but myself, that Holmes was on a hot scent. As impassive as ever to the casual observer, there were none the less a subdued eagerness and suggestion of tension in his brightened eyes and brisker manner which assured me that the game was afoot. After his habit he said nothing, and after mine I asked no questions. Sufficient for me to share the sport and lend my humble help to the capture without distracting that intent brain with needless interruption. All would come round to me in due time.

I waited, therefore – but to my ever-deepening disappointment I waited in vain. Day succeeded day, and my friend took no step forward. One morning he spent in town, and I learned from a casual reference that he had visited the British Museum. Save for this one excursion, he spent his days in long and often solitary walks, or in chatting with a number of village gossips whose acquaintance he had cultivated.

'I'm sure, Watson, a week in the country will be invaluable to you,' he remarked. 'It is very pleasant to see the first green shoots upon the hedges and the catkins on the hazels once again. With a spud, a tin box, and an elementary book on botany, there are instructive days to be spent.' He prowled about with this equipment himself, but it was a poor show of plants which he would bring back of an evening.

Occasionally in our rambles we came across Inspector Baynes. His fat, red face wreathed itself in smiles and his small eyes glittered as he greeted my companion. He said little about the case, but from that little we gathered that he also was not dissatisfied at the course of events. I must admit, however, that I was somewhat surprised when, some five days after the crime, I opened my morning paper to find in large letters:

'The Oxshott Mystery. A Solution. Arrest of Supposed Assassin.'

Holmes sprang in his chair as if he had been stung when I read the headlines.

'By Jove!' he cried. 'You don't mean that Baynes has got him?'

'Apparently,' said I as I read the following report:

'Great excitement was caused in Esher and the neighbouring district when it was learned late last night that an arrest had been effected in connection with the Oxshott murder. It will be remembered that Mr Garcia, of Wisteria Lodge, was found dead on Oxshott Common, his body showing signs of extreme violence, and that on the same night his servant and his cook fled, which appeared to show their participation in the crime. It was suggested, but never proved, that the deceased gentleman may have had valuables in the house, and that their abstraction was the motive of the crime. Every effort was made by Inspector Baynes, who has the case in hand, to ascertain the hiding place of the fugitives, and he had good reason to believe that they had not gone far but were lurking in some retreat which had been already prepared. It was certain from the first, however, that they would eventually be detected, as the cook, from the evidence of one or two tradespeople who have caught a glimpse of him through the window, was a man of most remarkable appearance – being a huge and hideous mulatto, with yellowish features of a pronounced negroid type. This man has been seen since the crime, for he was detected and pursued by Constable Walters on the same evening, when he had the audacity to revisit Wisteria Lodge. Inspector Baynes, considering that such a visit must have some purpose in view and was likely, therefore, to be repeated, abandoned the house but left an ambuscade in the shrubbery. The man walked into the trap and was captured last night after a struggle in which Constable Downing was badly bitten by the savage. We understand that when the prisoner is brought before the magistrates a remand will be applied for by the police, and that great developments are hoped from his capture.'

'Really we must see Baynes at once,' cried Holmes, picking up his hat. 'We will just catch him before he starts.' We hurried down the village street and found, as we had expected, that the inspector was just leaving his lodgings.

'You've seen the paper, Mr Holmes?' he asked, holding one out to us.

'Yes, Baynes, I've seen it. Pray don't think it a liberty if I give you a word of friendly warning.'

'Of warning, Mr Holmes?'

'I have looked into this case with some care, and I am not convinced that you are on the right lines. I don't want you to commit yourself too far unless you are sure.'

'You're very kind, Mr Holmes.'

'I assure you I speak for your good.'

It seemed to me that something like a wink quivered for an instant over one of Mr Baynes's tiny eyes.

'We agreed to work on our own lines, Mr Holmes. That's what I am doing.'

'Oh, very good,' said Holmes. 'Don't blame me.'

'No, sir; I believe you mean well by me. But we all

have our own systems, Mr Holmes. You have yours, and maybe I have mine.'

'Let us say no more about it.'

'You're welcome always to my news. This fellow is a perfect savage, as strong as a carthorse and as fierce as the devil. He chewed Downing's thumb nearly off before they could master him. He hardly speaks a word of English, and we can get nothing out of him but grunts.'

'And you think you have evidence that he murdered his late master?'

'I didn't say so, Mr Holmes; I didn't say so. We all have our little ways. You try yours and I will try mine. That's the agreement.'

Holmes shrugged his shoulders as we walked away together. 'I can't make the man out. He seems to be riding for a fall. Well, as he says, we must each try our own way and see what comes of it. But there's something in Inspector Baynes which I can't quite understand.'

'Just sit down in that chair, Watson,' said Sherlock Holmes when we had returned to our apartment at the Bull. 'I want to put you in touch with the situation, as I may need your help tonight. Let me show you the evolution of this case so far as I have been able to follow it. Simple as it has been in its leading features, it has none the less presented surprising difficulties in the way of an arrest. There are gaps in that direction which we have still to fill.

'We will go back to the note which was handed in to Garcia upon the evening of his death. We may put aside this idea of Baynes's that Garcia's servants were concerned in the matter. The proof of this lies in the fact that it was *he* who had arranged for the presence of

Scott Eccles, which could only have been done for the purpose of an alibi. It was Garcia, then, who had an enterprise, and apparently a criminal enterprise, in hand that night in the course of which he met his death. I say "criminal" because only a man with a criminal enterprise desires to establish an alibi. Who, then, is most likely to have taken his life? Surely the person against whom the criminal enterprise was directed. So far it seems to me that we are on safe ground.

'We can now see a reason for the disappearance of Garcia's household. They were *all* confederates in the same unknown crime. If it came off when Garcia returned, any possible suspicion would be warded off by the Englishman's evidence, and all would be well. But the attempt was a dangerous one, and if Garcia did *not* return by a certain hour it was probable that his own life had been sacrificed. It had been arranged, therefore, that in such a case his two subordinates were to make for some prearranged spot where they could escape investigation and be in a position afterwards to renew their attempt. That would fully explain the facts, would it not?'

The whole inexplicable tangle seemed to straighten out before me. I wondered, as I always did, how it had not been obvious to me before.

'But why should one servant return?'

'We can imagine that in the confusion of flight something precious, something which he could not bear to part with, had been left behind. That would explain his persistence, would it not?'

'Well, what is the next step?'

'The next step is the note received by Garcia at the dinner. It indicates a confederate at the other end.

Now, where was the other end? I have already shown you that it could only lie in some large house, and that the number of large houses is limited. My first days in this village were devoted to a series of walks in which in the intervals of my botanical researches I made a reconnaissance of all the large houses and an examination of the family history of the occupants. One house, and only one, riveted my attention. It is the famous old Jacobean grange of High Gable, one mile on the farther side of Oxshott, and less than half a mile from the scene of the tragedy. The other mansions belonged to prosaic and respectable people who live far aloof from romance. But Mr Henderson, of High Gable, was by all accounts a curious man to whom curious adventures might befall. I concentrated my attention, therefore, upon him and his household.

'A singular set of people, Watson – the man himself the most singular of them all. I managed to see him on a plausible pretext, but I seemed to read in his dark, deep-set, brooding eyes that he was perfectly aware of my true business. He is a man of fifty, strong, active, with iron-grey hair, great bunched black eyebrows, the step of a deer and the air of an emperor – a fierce, masterful man, with a red-hot spirit behind his parchment face. He is either a foreigner or has lived long in the tropics, for he is yellow and sapless, but tough as whipcord. His friend and secretary, Mr Lucas, is undoubtedly a foreigner, chocolate brown, wily, suave, and catlike, with a poisonous gentleness of speech. You see, Watson, we have come already upon two sets of foreigners – one at Wisteria Lodge and one at High Gable – so our gaps are beginning to close.

'These two men, close and confidential friends, are

the centre of the household; but there is one other person who for our immediate purpose may be even more important. Henderson has two children – girls of eleven and thirteen. Their governess is a Miss Burnet, an Englishwoman of forty or thereabouts. There is also one confidential manservant. This little group forms the real family, for they travel about together, and Henderson is a great traveller, always on the move. It is only within the last weeks that he has returned, after a year's absence, to High Gable. I may add that he is enormously rich, and whatever his whims may be he can very easily satisfy them. For the rest, his house is full of butlers, footmen, maid-servants, and the usual overfed, underworked staff of a large English country house.

'So much I learned partly from village gossip and partly from my own observation. There are no better instruments than discharged servants with a grievance, and I was lucky enough to find one. I call it luck, but it would not have come my way had I not been looking out for it. As Baynes remarks, we all have our systems. It was my system which enabled me to find John Warner, late gardener of High Gable, sacked in a moment of temper by his imperious employer. He in turn had friends among the indoor servants who unite in their fear and dislike of their master. So I had my key to the secrets of the establishment.

'Curious people, Watson! I don't pretend to understand it all yet, but very curious people anyway. It's a double-winged house, and the servants live on one side, the family on the other. There's no link between the two save for Henderson's own servant, who serves the family's meals. Everything is carried to a certain door, which forms the one connection. Governess and

420

children hardly go out at all, except into the garden. Henderson never by any chance walks alone. His dark secretary is like his shadow. The gossip among the servants is that their master is terribly afraid of something. "Sold his soul to the devil in exchange for money," says Warner, "and expects his creditor to come up and claim his own." Where they came from, or who they are, nobody has an idea. They are very violent. Twice Henderson has lashed at folk with his dog-whip, and only his long purse and heavy compensation have kept him out of the courts.

'Well, now, Watson, let us judge the situation by this new information. We may take it that the letter came out of this strange household and was an invitation to Garcia to carry out some attempt which had already been planned. Who wrote the note? It was someone within the citadel, and it was a woman. Who then but Miss Burnet, the governess? All our reasoning seems to point that way. At any rate, we may take it as a hypothesis and see what consequences it would entail. I may add that Miss Burnet's age and character make it certain that my first idea that there might be a love interest in our story is out of the question.

'If she wrote the note she was presumably the friend and confederate of Garcia. What, then, might she be expected to do if she heard of his death? If he met it in some nefarious enterprise her lips might be sealed. Still, in her heart, she must retain bitterness and hatred against those who had killed him and would presumably help so far as she could to have revenge upon them. Could we see her, then, and try to use her? That was my first thought. But now we come to a sinister fact. Miss Burnet has not been seen by any human eye since the night of the murder. From that evening she has utterly vanished. Is she alive? Has she perhaps met her end on the same night as the friend whom she had summoned? Or is she merely a prisoner? There is the point which we still have to decide.

'You will appreciate the difficulty of the situation, Watson. There is nothing upon which we can apply for a warrant. Our whole scheme might seem fantastic if laid before a magistrate. The woman's disappearance counts for nothing, since in that extraordinary household any member of it might be invisible for a week. And yet she may at the present moment be in danger of her life. All I can do is to watch the house and leave my agent, Warner, on guard at the gates. We can't let such a situation continue. If the law can do nothing we must take the risk ourselves.'

'What do you suggest?'

'I know which is her room. It is accessible from the top of an outhouse. My suggestion is that you and I go tonight and see if we can strike at the very heart of the mystery.'

It was not, I must confess, a very alluring prospect. The old house with its atmosphere of murder, the singular and formidable inhabitants, the unknown dangers of the approach, and the fact that we were putting ourselves legally in a false position all combined to damp my ardour. But there was something in the ice-cold reasoning of Holmes which made it impossible to shrink from any adventure which he might recommend. One knew that thus, and only thus, could a solution be found. I clasped his hand in silence, and the die was cast.

But it was not destined that our investigation should have so adventurous an ending. It was about five o'clock, and the shadows of the March evening were beginning to fall, when an excited rustic rushed into our room.

'They've gone, Mr Holmes. They went by the last train. The lady broke away, and I've got her in a cab downstairs.'

'Excellent, Warner!' cried Holmes, springing to his feet. 'Watson, the gaps are closing rapidly.'

In the cab was a woman, half-collapsed from nervous exhaustion. She bore upon her aquiline and emaciated face the traces of some recent tragedy. Her head hung listlessly upon her breast, but as she raised it and turned her dull eyes upon us I saw that her pupils were dark dots in the centre of the broad grey iris. She was drugged with opium.

'I watched at the gate, same as you advised, Mr Holmes,' said our emissary, the discharged gardener. 'When the carriage came out I followed it to the station. She was like one walking in her sleep, but when they tried to get her into the train she came to life and struggled. They pushed her into the carriage. She fought her way out again. I took her part, got her into a cab, and here we are. I shan't forget the face at the carriage window as I led her away. I'd have a short life if he had his way – the black-eyed, scowling, yellow devil.'

We carried her upstairs, laid her on the sofa, and a couple of cups of the strongest coffee soon cleared her brain from the mists of the drug. Baynes had been summoned by Holmes, and the situation rapidly explained to him.

'Why, sir, you've got me the very evidence I want,' said the inspector warmly, shaking my friend by the hand. 'I was on the same scent as you from the first.'

'What! You were after Henderson?'

'Why, Mr Holmes, when you were crawling in the shrubbery at High Gable I was up one of the trees in the plantation and saw you down below. It was just who would get his evidence first.'

'Then why did you arrest the mulatto?'

Baynes chuckled.

'I was sure Henderson, as he calls himself, felt that he was suspected, and that he would lie low and make no move so long as he thought he was in any danger. I arrested the wrong man to make him believe that our eyes were off him. I knew he would be likely to clear off then and give us a chance of getting at Miss Burnet.'

Holmes laid his hand upon the inspector's shoulder.

'You will rise high in your profession. You have instinct and intuition,' said he.

Baynes flushed with pleasure.

'I've had a plain-clothes man waiting at the station all the week. Wherever the High Gable folk go he will keep them in sight. But he must have been hard put to it when Miss Burnet broke away. However, your man picked her up, and it all ends well. We can't arrest without her evidence, that is clear, so the sooner we get a statement the better.'

'Every minute she gets stronger,' said Holmes, glancing at the governess. 'But tell me, Baynes, who is this man Henderson?'

'Henderson,' the inspector answered, 'is Don Murillo, once called the Tiger of San Pedro.'

The Tiger of San Pedro! The whole history of the man came back to me in a flash. He had made his name as the most lewd and bloodthirsty tyrant that had ever governed any country with a pretence to civilisation. Strong, fearless, and energetic, he had sufficient virtue to enable him to impose his odious vices upon a cowering people for ten or twelve years. His name was a terror through all Central America. At the end of that time there was a universal rising against him. But he was as cunning as he was cruel, and at the first whisper of coming trouble he had secretly conveyed his treasures aboard a ship which was manned by devoted adherents. It was an empty palace which was stormed by the insurgents next day. The dictator, his two children, his secretary, and his wealth had all escaped them. From that moment he had vanished from the world, and his identity had been a frequent subject for comment in the European Press.

'Yes, sir, Don Murillo, the Tiger of San Pedro,' said Baynes. 'If you look it up you will find that the San Pedro colours are green and white, same as in the note, Mr Holmes. Henderson he called himself, but I traced him back, Paris and Rome and Madrid to Barcelona, where his ship came in in 1886. They've been looking for him all the time for their revenge, but it is only now that they have begun to find him out.'

'They discovered him a year ago,' said Miss Burnet, who had sat up and was now intently following the conversation. 'Once already his life has been attempted, but some evil spirit shielded him. Now, again, it is the noble, chivalrous Garcia who has fallen, while the monster goes safe. But another will come, and yet another, until some day justice will be done; that is as certain as the rise of tomorrow's sun.' Her thin hands clenched, and her worn face blanched with the passion of her hatred.

'But how come you into this matter, Miss Burnet?' asked Holmes. 'How can an English lady join in such a murderous affair?'

'I join in it because there is no other way in the world by which justice can be gained. What does the law of England care for the rivers of blood shed years ago in San Pedro, or for the shipload of treasure which this man has stolen? To you they are like crimes committed in some other planet. But *we* know. We have learned the truth in sorrow and in suffering. To us there is no fiend in hell like Juan Murillo, and no peace in life while his victims still cry for vengeance.'

'No doubt,' said Holmes, 'he was as you say. I have heard that he was atrocious. But how are you affected?'

'I will tell you it all. This villain's policy was to murder, on one pretext or another, every man who showed such promise that he might in time come to be a dangerous rival. My husband – yes, my real name is Signora Victor Durando – was the San Pedro minister in London. He met me and married me there. A nobler man never lived upon earth. Unhappily, Murillo heard of his excellence, recalled him on some pretext, and had him shot. With a premonition of his fate he had refused to take me with him. His estates were confiscated, and I was left with a pittance and a broken heart.

'Then came the downfall of the tyrant. He escaped as you have just described. But the many whose lives he had ruined, whose nearest and dearest had suffered torture and death at his hands, would not let the matter rest. They banded themselves into a society which should never be dissolved until the work was done. It was my part after we had discovered in the transformed Henderson the fallen despot, to attach myself to his household and keep the others in touch with his movements. This I was able to do by securing the position of governess in his family. He little knew that the woman who faced him at every meal was the woman whose husband he had hurried at an hour's notice into eternity. I smiled on him, did my duty to his children, and bided my time. An attempt was made in Paris and failed. We zig-zagged swiftly here and there over Europe to throw off the pursuers and finally returned to this house, which he had taken upon his first arrival in England.

'But here also the ministers of justice were waiting. Knowing that he would return there, Garcia, who is the son of the former highest dignitary in San Pedro, was waiting with two trusty companions of humble station, all three fired with the same reasons for revenge. He could do little during the day, for Murillo took every precaution and never went out save with his satellite Lucas, or Lopez as he was known in the days of his greatness. At night, however, he slept alone, and the avenger might find him. On a certain evening, which had been prearranged, I sent my friend final instructions, for the man was forever on the alert and continually changed his room. I was to see that the doors were open and the signal of a green or white light in a window which faced the drive was to give notice if all was safe or if the attempt had better be postponed.

'But everything went wrong with us. In some way I had excited the suspicion of Lopez, the secretary. He crept up behind me and sprang upon me just as I had finished the note. He and his master dragged me to my room and held judgment upon me as a convicted traitress. Then and there they would have plunged their knives into me could they have seen how to escape the consequences of the deed. Finally, after much debate, they concluded that my murder was too dangerous. But they determined to get rid for ever of Garcia. They had gagged me, and Murillo twisted my arm round until I gave him the address. I swear that he might have twisted it off had I understood what it would mean to Garcia. Lopez addressed the note which I had written, sealed it with his sleeve-link, and sent it by the hand of the servant, José. How they murdered him I do not know, save that it was Murillo's hand who struck him down, for Lopez had remained to guard me. I believe he must have waited among the gorse bushes through which the path winds and struck him down as he passed. At first they were of a mind to let him enter the house and to kill him as a detected burglar; but they argued that if they were mixed up in an enquiry their own identity would at once be publicly disclosed and they would be open to further attacks. With the death of Garcia, the pursuit might cease, since such a death might frighten others from the task.

'All would now have been well for them had it not been for my knowledge of what they had done. I have no doubt that there were times when my life hung in the balance. I was confined to my room, terrorised by the most horrible threats, cruelly ill-used to break my spirit – see this stab on my shoulder and the bruises from end to end of my arms – and a gag was thrust into my mouth on the one occasion when I tried to call from the window. For five days this cruel imprisonment continued, with hardly enough food to hold body and soul together. This afternoon a good lunch was brought me, but the moment after I took it I knew that I had been drugged. In a sort of dream I remember being half-led, half-carried to the carriage; in the same state I was conveyed to the train. Only then, when the wheels were almost moving, did I suddenly realise that my liberty lay in my own hands.

I sprang out, they tried to drag me back, and had it not been for the help of this good man, who led me to the cab, I should never had broken away. Now, thank God, I am beyond their power for ever.'

We had all listened intently to this remarkable statement. It was Holmes who broke the silence.

'Our difficulties are not over,' he remarked, shaking his head. 'Our police work ends, but our legal work begins.'

'Exactly,' said I. 'A plausible lawyer could make it out as an act of self-defence. There may be a hundred crimes in the background, but it is only on this one that they can be tried.'

'Come, come,' said Baynes cheerily, 'I think better of the law than that. Self-defence is one thing. To entice a man in cold blood with the object of murdering him is another, whatever danger you may fear from him. No, no, we shall all be justified when we see the tenants of High Gable at the next Guildford Assizes.'

It is a matter of history, however, that a little time was still to elapse before the Tiger of San Pedro should meet with his deserts. Wily and bold, he and his companion threw their pursuer off their track by entering a lodging-house in Edmonton Street and leaving by the back-gate into Curzon Square. From that day they were seen no more in England. Some six months afterwards the Marquess of Montalva and Signor Rulli, his secretary, were both murdered in their rooms at the Hotel Escurial at Madrid. The crime was ascribed to Nihilism, and the murderers were never arrested. Inspector Baynes visited us at Baker Street with a printed description of the dark face of the secretary, and of the masterful features, the

429

magnetic black eyes, and the tufted brows of his master. We could not doubt that justice, if belated, had come at last.

'A chaotic case, my dear Watson,' said Holmes over an evening pipe. 'It will not be possible for you to present in that compact form which is dear to your heart. It covers two continents, concerns two groups of mysterious persons, and is further complicated by the highly respectable presence of our friend, Scott Eccles, whose inclusion shows me that the deceased Garcia had a scheming mind and a well-developed instinct of self-preservation. It is remarkable only for the fact that amid a perfect jungle of possibilities we, with our worthy collaborator, the inspector, have kept our close hold on the essentials and so been guided along the crooked and winding path. Is there any point which is not quite clear to you?'

'The object of the mulatto cook's return?'

'I think that the strange creature in the kitchen may account for it. The man was a primitive savage from the backwoods of San Pedro, and this was his fetish. When his companion and he had fled to some pre-arranged retreat – already occupied, no doubt, by a confederate – the companion had persuaded him to leave so compromising an article of furniture. But the mulatto's heart was with it, and he was driven back to it next day, when, on reconnoitring through the window, he found policeman Walters in possession. He waited three days longer, and then his piety or his superstition drove him to try once more. Inspector Baynes, who, with his usual astuteness, had minimised the incident before me, had really recognised its importance and had left a trap into which the creature walked. Any other point, Watson?'

'The torn bird, the pail of blood, the charred bones, all the mystery of that weird kitchen?'

Holmes smiled as he turned up an entry in his notebook.

'I spent a morning in the British Museum reading up on that and other points. Here is a quotation from Eckermann's *Voodooism and the Negroid Religions*:

'The true voodoo-worshipper attempts nothing of importance without certain sacrifices which are intended to propitiate his unclean gods. In extreme cases these rites take the form of human sacrifices followed by cannibalism. The more usual victims are a white cock, which is plucked in pieces alive, or a black goat, whose throat is cut and body burned.

'So you see our savage friend was very orthodox in his ritual. It is grotesque, Watson,' Holmes added, as he slowly fastened his notebook, 'but, as I have had occasion to remark, there is but one step from the grotesque to the horrible.'

15

The Cardboard Box

In choosing a few typical cases which illustrate the remarkable mental qualities of my friend, Sherlock Holmes, I have endeavoured, as far as possible, to select those which presented the minimum of sensationalism, while offering a fair field for his talents. It is, however, unfortunately impossible entirely to separate the sensational from the criminal, and a chronicler is left in the dilemma that he must either sacrifice details which are essential to his statement and so give a false impression of the problem, or he must use matter which chance, and not choice, has provided him with. With this short preface I shall turn to my notes of what proved to be a strange, though a peculiarly terrible, chain of events.

It was a blazing hot day in August. Baker Street was like an oven, and the glare of the sunlight upon the yellow brickwork of the house across the road was painful to the eye. It was hard to believe that these were the same walls which loomed so gloomily through the fogs of winter. Our blinds were half-drawn, and Holmes lay curled upon the sofa, reading and re-reading a letter which he had received by the morning post. For myself, my term of service in India had trained me to stand heat better than cold, and a thermometer at ninety was no hardship. But the morning paper was uninteresting. Parliament had risen. Everybody was out of town, and I yearned for the glades of the New Forest or the shingle of Southsea. A depleted bank account had caused me to postpone my holiday, and as to my companion, neither the country nor the sea presented the slightest attraction to him. He loved to lie in the very centre of five millions of people, with his filaments stretching out and running through them, responsive to every little rumour or suspicion of unsolved crime. Appreciation of nature found no place among his many gifts, and his only change was when he turned his mind from the evil-doer of the town to track down his brother of the country.

Finding that Holmes was too absorbed for conversation I had tossed aside the barren paper, and leaning back in my chair I fell into a brown study. Suddenly my companion's voice broke in upon my thoughts.

'You are right, Watson,' said he. 'It does seem a most preposterous way of settling a dispute.'

'Most preposterous!' I exclaimed, and then suddenly realising how he had echoed the inmost thought of my soul, I sat up in my chair and stared at him in blank amazement.

'What is this, Holmes?' I cried. 'This is beyond anything which I could have imagined.'

He laughed heartily at my perplexity.

'You remember,' said he, 'that some little time ago when I read you the passage in one of Poe's sketches in which a close reasoner follows the unspoken thoughts of his companion, you were inclined to treat the matter as a mere *tour-de-force* of the author. On my remarking that I was constantly in the habit of doing the same thing you expressed incredulity.'

'Oh, no!'

'Perhaps not with your tongue, my dear Watson,

433

but certainly with your eyebrows. So when I saw you throw down your paper and enter upon a train of thought, I was very happy to have the opportunity of reading it off, and eventually of breaking into it, as a proof that I had been *en rapport* with you.'

But I was still far from satisfied. 'In the example which you read to me,' said I, 'the reasoner drew his conclusions from the actions of the man whom he observed. If I remember right, he stumbled over a heap of stones, looked up at the stars, and so on. But I have been seated quietly in my chair, and what clues can I have given you?'

'You do yourself an injustice. The features are given to man as the means by which he shall express his emotions, and yours are faithful servants.'

'Do you mean to say that you read my train of thoughts from my features?'

'Your features and especially your eyes. Perhaps you cannot yourself recall how your reverie commenced?'

'No, I cannot.'

'Then I will tell you. After throwing down your paper, which was the action which drew my attention to you, you sat for half a minute with a vacant expression. Then your eyes fixed themselves upon your newly framed picture of General Gordon, and I saw by the alteration in your face that a train of thought had been started. But it did not lead very far. Your eyes flashed across to the unframed portrait of Henry Ward Beecher which stands upon the top of your books. Then you glanced up at the wall, and of course your meaning was obvious. You were thinking that if the portrait were framed it would just cover that bare space and correspond with Gordon's picture there.'

'You have followed me wonderfully!' I exclaimed.

'So far I could hardly have gone astray. But now your thoughts went back to Beecher, and you looked hard across as if you were studying the character in his features. Then your eyes ceased to pucker, but you continued to look across, and your face was thoughtful. You were recalling the incidents of Beecher's career. I was well aware that you could not do this without thinking of the mission which he undertook on behalf of the North at the time of the Civil War, for I remember your expressing your passionate indignation at the way in which he was received by the more turbulent of our people. You felt so strongly about it that I knew you could not think of Beecher without thinking of that also. When a moment later I saw your eyes wander away from the picture, I suspected that your mind had now turned to the Civil War, and when I observed that your lips set, your eyes sparkled, and your hands clenched I was positive that you were indeed thinking of the gallantry which was shown by both sides in that desperate struggle. But then, again, your face grew sadder, you shook your head. You were dwelling upon the sadness and horror and useless waste of life. Your hand stole towards your own old wound and a smile quivered on your lips, which showed me that the ridiculous side of this method of settling international questions had forced itself upon your mind. At this point I agreed with you that it was preposterous and was glad to find that all my deductions had been correct.'

'Absolutely!' said I. 'And now that you have explained it, I confess that I am as amazed as before.'

'It was very superficial, my dear Watson, I assure you. I should not have intruded it upon your attention had you not shown some incredulity the other day. But I have in my hands here a little problem which may prove to be more difficult of solution than my small essay in thought-reading. Have you observed in the paper a short paragraph referring to the remarkable contents of a packet sent through the post to Miss Cushing, of Cross Street, Croydon?'

'No, I saw nothing.'

'Ah! then you must have overlooked it. Just toss it over to me. Here it is, under the financial column. Perhaps you would be good enough to read it aloud.'

I picked up the paper which he had thrown back to me and read the paragraph indicated. It was headed, 'A Gruesome Packet'.

'Miss Susan Cushing, living at Cross Street, Croydon, has been made the victim of what must be regarded as a peculiarly revolting practical joke, unless some more sinister meaning should prove to be attached to the incident. At two o'clock yesterday afternoon a small packet, wrapped in brown paper, was handed in by the postman. A cardboard box was inside, which was filled with coarse salt. On emptying this, Miss Cushing was horrified to find two human ears, apparently quite freshly severed. The box had been sent by parcel post from Belfast upon the morning before. There is no indication as to the sender, and the matter is the more mysterious as Miss Cushing, who is a maiden lady of fifty, has led a most retired life, and has so few acquaintances or correspondents that it is a rare event for her to receive anything through the post. Some years ago, however, when she resided at Penge, she let apartments in her house to three young medical students, whom she was obliged to get rid of on account of their noisy and irregular habits. The police are of opinion that this outrage may have been perpetrated upon Miss Cushing by these youths, who owed her a grudge and who hoped to frighten her by sending her these relics of the dissecting-rooms. Some probability is lent to the theory by the fact that one of these students came from the north of Ireland, and, to the best of Miss Cushing's belief, from Belfast. In the meantime, the matter is being actively investigated, Mr Lestrade, one of the very smartest of our detective officers, being in charge of the case.'

'So much for the *Daily Chronicle*,' said Holmes as I finished reading. 'Now for our friend Lestrade. I had a note from him this morning, in which he says: "I think that this case is very much in your line. We have every hope of clearing the matter up, but we find a little difficulty in getting anything to work upon. We have, of course, wired to the Belfast post-office, but a large number of parcels were handed in upon that day, and they have no means of identifying this particular one, or of remembering the sender. The box is a half-pound box of honeydew tobacco and does not help us in any way. The medical student theory still appears to me to be the most feasible, but if you should have a few hours to spare I should be very happy to see you out here. I shall be either at the house or in the police-station all day."

'What say you, Watson? Can you rise superior to the heat and run down to Croydon with me on the off chance of a case for your annals?'

'I was longing for something to do.'

'You shall have it then. Ring for our boots and tell them to order a cab. I'll be back in a moment when I have changed my dressing-gown and filled my cigar-case.'

A shower of rain fell while we were in the train, and the heat was far less oppressive in Croydon than in town. Holmes had sent on a wire, so that Lestrade, as wiry, as dapper, and as ferret-like as ever, was waiting for us at the station. A walk of five minutes took us to Cross Street, where Miss Cushing resided.

It was a very long street of two-storey brick houses, neat and prim, with whitened stone steps and little groups of aproned women gossiping at the doors. Halfway down, Lestrade stopped and tapped at a door, which was opened by a small servant girl. Miss Cushing was sitting in the front room, into which we were ushered. She was a placid-faced woman, with large, gentle eyes, and grizzled hair curving down over her temples on each side. A worked antimacassar lay upon her lap and a basket of coloured silks stood upon a stool beside her.

'They are in the outhouse, those dreadful things,' said she as Lestrade entered. 'I wish that you would take them away altogether.'

'So I shall, Miss Cushing. I only kept them here until my friend, Mr Holmes, should have seen them in your presence.'

'Why in my presence, sir?'

'In case he wished to ask any questions.'

'What is the use of asking me questions when I tell you I know nothing whatever about it?'

'Quite so, madam,' said Holmes in his soothing way. 'I have no doubt that you have been annoyed more than enough already over this business.'

'Indeed I have, sir. I am a quiet woman and live a retired life. It is something new for me to see my name in the papers and to find the police in my house. I won't have those things in here, Mr Lestrade. If you wish to see them you must go to the outhouse.'

It was a small shed in the narrow garden which ran behind the house. Lestrade went in and brought out a yellow cardboard box, with a piece of brown paper and some string. There was a bench at the end of the path, and we all sat down while Homes examined, one by one, the articles which Lestrade had handed to him.

'The string is exceedingly interesting,' he remarked, holding it up to the light and sniffing at it. 'What do you make of this string, Lestrade?'

'It has been tarred.'

'Precisely. It is a piece of tarred twine. You have also, no doubt, remarked that Miss Cushing has cut the cord with a scissors, as can be seen by the double fray on each side. This is of importance.'

'I cannot see the importance,' said Lestrade.

'The importance lies in the fact that the knot is left intact, and that this knot is of a peculiar character.'

'It is very neatly tied. I had already made a note of that effect,' said Lestrade complacently.

'So much for the string, then,' said Holmes, smiling, 'now for the box wrapper. Brown paper, with a distinct smell of coffee. What, did you not observe it? I think there can be no doubt of it. Address printed in rather straggling characters: "Miss S. Cushing, Cross Street, Croydon". Done with a broad-pointed pen, probably a J, and with very inferior ink. The word "Croydon" has been originally spelled with an "i", which has been changed to "y". The parcel was directed, then, by a man – the printing is distinctly masculine – of limited education and unacquainted with the town of Croydon. So far, so good! The box is a yellow, half-pound honeydew box, with nothing distinctive save two thumb marks at the left bottom corner. It is filled with rough salt of the quality used for preserving hides and other of the coarser commercial purposes. And embedded in it are these very singular enclosures.'

He took out the two ears as he spoke, and laying a board across his knee he examined them minutely, while Lestrade and I, bending forward on each side of him, glanced alternately at these dreadful relics and at the thoughtful, eager face of our companion. Finally he returned them to the box once more and sat for a while in deep meditation.

'You have observed, of course,' said he at last, 'that the ears are not a pair.'

'Yes, I have noticed that. But if this were the practical joke of some students from the dissecting-rooms, it would be as easy for them to send two odd ears as a pair.'

'Precisely. But this is not a practical joke.'

'You are sure of it?'

'The presumption is strongly against it. Bodies in the dissecting-rooms are injected with preservative fluid. These ears bear no signs of this. They are fresh, too. They have been cut off with a blunt instrument, which would hardly happen if a student had done it. Again, carbolic or rectified spirits would be the preservatives which would suggest themselves to the medical mind, certainly not rough salt. I repeat that there is no practical joke here, but that we are investigating a serious crime.'

A vague thrill ran through me as I listened to my companion's words and saw the stern gravity which had hardened his features. This brutal preliminary seemed to shadow forth some strange and inexplicable horror in the background. Lestrade, however, shook his head like a man who is only half convinced.

'There are objections to the joke theory, no doubt,' said he, 'but there are much stronger reasons against the other. We know that this woman has led a most quiet and respectable life at Penge and here for the last twenty years. She has hardly been away from her home for a day during that time. Why on earth, then, should any criminal send her the proofs of his guilt, especially as, unless she is a most consummate actress, she understands quite as little of the matter as we do?'

'That is the problem which we have to solve,' Holmes answered, 'and for my part I shall set about it by presuming that my reasoning is correct, and that a double murder has been committed. One of these ears is a woman's, small, finely formed, and pierced for an earring. The other is a man's, sunburned, discoloured, and also pierced for an earring. These two people are presumably dead, or we should have heard their story before now. Today is Friday. The packet was posted on Thursday morning. The tragedy, then, occurred on Wednesday or Tuesday, or earlier. If the two people were murdered, who but their murderer would have sent this sign of his work to Miss Cushing? We may take it that the sender of the packet is the man whom we want. But he must have some strong reason for sending Miss Cushing this packet. What reason then? It must have been to tell her that the deed was done! or to pain her, perhaps. But in that case she knows who it is. Does she know? I doubt it. If she knew, why should she call the police in? She might have buried the ears, and no one would have been the wiser. That is what she would have done if she had wished to shield the criminal. But if she does not wish to shield him she would give his name. There is a tangle here which needs straightening out.' He had been talking in a high, quick voice, staring blankly up over the garden fence, but now he sprang briskly to his feet and walked towards the house.

'I have a few questions to ask Miss Cushing,' said he.

'In that case I may leave you here,' said Lestrade, 'for I have another small business on hand. I think that I have nothing further to learn from Miss Cushing. You will find me at the police-station.'

'We shall look in on our way to the train,' answered Holmes. A moment later he and I were back in the front room, where the impassive lady was still quietly working away at her antimacassar. She put it down on her lap as we entered and looked at us with her frank, searching blue eyes.

'I am convinced, sir,' she said, 'that this matter is a mistake, and that the parcel was never meant for me at all. I have said this several times to the gentleman from Scotland Yard, but he simply laughs at me. I have not an enemy in the world, as far as I know, so why should anyone play me such a trick?'

'I am coming to be of the same opinion, Miss Cushing,' said Holmes, taking a seat beside her. 'I think that it is more than probable . . . ' He paused, and I was surprised, on glancing round, to see that he was staring with singular intentness at the lady's profile. Surprise and satisfaction were both for an instant to be read upon his eager face, though when she glanced round to find out the cause of his silence he had become as demure as ever. I stared hard myself at her flat, grizzled hair, her trim cap, her little gilt earrings, her placid features; but I could see nothing which could account for my companion's evident excitement.

'There were one or two questions – '

'Oh, I am weary of questions!' cried Miss Cushing impatiently.

'You have two sisters, I believe.'

'How could you know that?'

'I observed the very instant that I entered the room that you have a portrait group of three ladies upon the mantelpiece, one of whom is undoubtedly yourself, while the others are so exceedingly like you that there could be no doubt of the relationship.'

'Yes, you are quite right. Those are my sisters, Sarah and Mary.'

'And here at my elbow is another portrait, taken at Liverpool, of your younger sister, in the company of a man who appears to be a steward by his uniform. I observe that she was unmarried at the time.'

'You are very quick at observing.'

'That is my trade.'

'Well, you are quite right. But she was married to Mr Browner a few days afterwards. He was on the South American line when that was taken, but he was so fond of her that he couldn't abide to leave her for so long, and he got into the Liverpool and London boats.'

'Ah, the *Conqueror*, perhaps?'

'No, the *May Day*, when last I heard. Jim came down here to see me once. That was before he broke the pledge; but afterwards he would always take drink when he was ashore, and a little drink would send him stark, staring mad. Ah! it was a bad day that ever he took a glass in his hand again. First he dropped me, then he quarrelled with Sarah, and now that Mary has stopped writing we don't know how things are going with them.'

It was evident that Miss Cushing had come upon a subject on which she felt very deeply. Like most people who lead a lonely life, she was shy at first, but ended by becoming extremely communicative. She told us many details about her brother-in-law the steward, and then wandering off on the subject of her former lodgers, the medical students, she gave us a long account of their delinquencies, with their names and those of their hospitals. Holmes listened attentively to everything, throwing in a question from time to time.

'About your second sister, Sarah,' said he. 'I wonder, since you are both maiden ladies, that you do not keep house together.'

'Ah! you don't know Sarah's temper or you would wonder no more. I tried it when I came to Croydon, and we kept on until about two months ago, when we had to part. I don't want to say a word against my own sister, but she was always meddlesome and hard to please, was Sarah.'

'You say that she quarrelled with your Liverpool relations.'

'Yes, and they were the best of friends at one time. Why, she went up there to live in order to be near them. And now she has no word hard enough for Jim Browner. The last six months that she was here she would speak of nothing but his drinking and his ways. He had caught her meddling, I suspect, and given her a bit of his mind, and that was the start of it.'

'Thank you, Miss Cushing,' said Holmes, rising and bowing. 'Your sister Sarah lives, I think you said, at New Street, Wallington? Goodbye, and I am very sorry that you should have been troubled over a case with which, as you say, you have nothing whatever to do.'

There was a cab passing as we came out, and Holmes hailed it.

'How far to Wallington?' he asked.

'Only about a mile, sir.'

'Very good. Jump in, Watson. We must strike while the iron is hot. Simple as the case is, there have been one or two very instructive details in connection with it. Just pull up at a telegraph-office as you pass, cabby.'

Holmes sent off a short wire and for the rest of the drive lay back in the cab, with his hat tilted over his nose to keep the sun from his face. Our driver pulled up at a house which was not unlike the one which we had just quitted. My companion ordered him to wait, and had his hand upon the knocker, when the door opened and a grave young gentleman in black, with a very shiny hat, appeared on the step.

'Is Miss Cushing at home?' asked Holmes.

'Miss Sarah Cushing is extremely ill,' said he. 'She has been suffering since yesterday from brain symptoms of great severity. As her medical adviser, I cannot possibly take the responsibility of allowing anyone to see her. I should recommend you to call again in ten days.' He drew on his gloves, closed the door, and marched off down the street.

'Well, if we can't we can't,' said Holmes, cheerfully.

'Perhaps she could not or would not have told you much.'

'I did not wish her to tell me anything. I only wanted to look at her. However, I think that I have got all that I want. Drive us to some decent hotel, cabby, where we may have some lunch, and afterwards we shall drop down upon friend Lestrade at the police-station.'

We had a pleasant little meal together, during which Holmes would talk about nothing but violins, narrating

445

with great exultation how he had purchased his own Stradivarius, which was worth at least five hundred guineas, at a Jew broker's in Tottenham Court Road for fifty-five shillings. This led him to Paganini, and we sat for an hour over a bottle of claret while he told me anecdote after anecdote of that extraordinary man. The afternoon was far advanced and the hot glare had softened into a mellow glow before we found ourselves at the police-station. Lestrade was waiting for us at the door.

'A telegram for you, Mr Holmes,' said he.

'Ha! It is the answer!' He tore it open, glanced his eyes over it, and crumpled it into his pocket. 'That's all right,' said he.

'Have you found out anything?'

'I have found out everything!'

'What!' Lestrade stared at him in amazement. 'You are joking.'

'I was never more serious in my life. A shocking crime has been committed, and I think I have now laid bare every detail of it.'

'And the criminal?'

Holmes scribbled a few words upon the back of one of his visiting cards and threw it over to Lestrade.

'That is the name,' he said. 'You cannot effect an arrest until tomorrow night at the earliest. I should prefer that you do not mention my name at all in connection with the case, as I choose to be only associated with those crimes which present some difficulty in their solution. Come on, Watson.' We strode off together to the station, leaving Lestrade still staring with a delighted face at the card which Holmes had thrown him.

* * *

'The case,' said Sherlock Holmes as we chatted over our cigars that night in our rooms at Baker Street, 'is one where, as in the investigations which you have chronicled under the names of "A Study in Scarlet" and of "The Sign of the Four", we have been compelled to reason backwards from effects to causes. I have written to Lestrade asking him to supply us with the details which are now wanting, and which he will only get after he has secured his man. That he may be safely trusted to do, for although he is absolutely devoid of reason, he is as tenacious as a bulldog when he once understands what he has to do, and indeed, it is just this tenacity which has brought him to the top at Scotland Yard.'

'Your case is not complete, then?' I asked.

'It is fairly complete in essentials. We know who the author of the revolting business is, although one of the victims still escapes us. Of course, you have formed your own conclusions.'

'I presume that this Jim Browner, the steward of a Liverpool boat, is the man whom you suspect?'

'Oh! it is more than a suspicion.'

'And yet I cannot see anything save very vague indications.'

'On the contrary, to my mind nothing could be more clear. Let me run over the principal steps. We approached the case, you remember, with an absolutely blank mind, which is always an advantage. We had formed no theories. We were simply there to observe and to draw inferences from our observations. What did we see first? A very placid and respectable lady, who seemed quite innocent of any secret, and a portrait which showed me that she had two younger sisters. It instantly flashed across my mind that the box might have been meant for one of these. I set the idea aside as one which could be disproved or confirmed at our leisure. Then we went to the garden, as you remember, and we saw the very singular contents of the little yellow box.

'The string was of the quality which is used by sail-makers aboard ship, and at once a whiff of the sea was perceptible in our investigation. When I observed that the knot was one which is popular with sailors, that the parcel had been posted at a port, and that the male ear was pierced for an earring which is so much more common among sailors than landsmen, I was quite certain that all the actors in the tragedy were to be found among our seafaring classes.

'When I came to examine the address of the packet I observed that it was to Miss S. Cushing. Now, the oldest sister would, of course, be Miss Cushing, and although her initial was "S" it might belong to one of the others as well. In that case we should have to commence our investigation from a fresh basis altogether. I therefore went into the house with the intention of clearing up this point. I was about to assure Miss Cushing that I was convinced that a mistake had been made when you may remember that I came suddenly to a stop. The fact was that I had just seen something which filled me with surprise and at the same time narrowed the field of our enquiry immensely.

'As a medical man, you are aware, Watson, that there is no part of the body which varies so much as the human ear. Each ear is as a rule quite distinctive and differs from all other ones. In last year's *Anthropological Journal* you will find two short monographs from my pen upon the subject. I had, therefore, examined the ears in the box with the eyes of an expert and had carefully noted their anatomical peculiarities. Imagine my surprise, then, when on looking at Miss Cushing I perceived that her ear corresponded exactly with the female ear which I had just inspected. The matter was entirely beyond coincidence. There was the same shortening of the pinna, the same broad curve of the upper lobe, the same convolution of the inner cartilage. In all essentials it was the same ear.

'In the first place, her sister's name was Sarah, and her address had until recently been the same, so that it was quite obvious how the mistake had occurred and for whom the packet was meant. Then we heard of this steward, married to the third sister, and learned that he had at one time been so intimate with Miss Sarah that she had actually gone up to Liverpool to be near the Browners, but a quarrel had afterwards divided them. This quarrel had put a stop to all communications for some months, so that if Browner had occasion to address a packet to Miss Sarah, he would undoubtedly have done so to her old address.

'And now the matter had begun to straighten itself out wonderfully. We had learned of the existence of this steward, an impulsive man, of strong passions – you remember that he threw up what must have been a very superior berth in order to be nearer to his wife – subject, too, to occasional fits of hard drinking. We had reason to believe that his wife had been murdered, and that a man – presumably a seafaring man – had been murdered at the same time. Jealousy, of course, at once suggests itself as the motive for the crime. And why should these proofs of the deed be sent to Miss Sarah Cushing? Probably because during her residence in Liverpool she had some hand in bringing about the events which led to the tragedy. You will observe that this line of boats call at Belfast, Dublin, and Waterford; so that, presuming that Browner had committed the deed and had embarked at once upon his steamer, the *May Day*, Belfast would be the first place at which he could post his terrible packet.

'A second solution was at this stage obviously possible, and although I thought it exceedingly unlikely, I was determined to elucidate it before going further. An unsuccessful lover might have killed Mr and Mrs Browner, and the male ear might have belonged to the husband. There were many grave objections to this theory, but it was conceivable. I therefore sent off a telegram to my friend Algar, of the Liverpool force, and asked him to find out if Mrs Browner were at home, and if Browner had departed in the *May Day*. Then we went on to Wallington to visit Miss Sarah.

'I was curious, in the first place, to see how far the family ear had been reproduced in her. Then, of course, she might give us very important information, but I was not sanguine that she would. She must have heard of the business the day before, since all Croydon was ringing with it, and she alone could have understood for whom the packet was meant. If she had been willing to help justice she would probably have communicated with the police already. However, it was clearly our duty to see her, so we went. We found that the news of the arrival of the packet – for her illness dated from that time – had such an effect upon her as to bring on brain fever. It was clearer than ever that she understood its full significance, but equally clear that we should have to wait some time for any assistance from her.

'However, we were really independent of her help. Our answers were waiting for us at the police-station, where I had directed Algar to send them. Nothing could be more conclusive. Mrs Browner's house had been closed for more than three days, and the neighbours were of opinion that she had gone south to see her relatives. It had been ascertained at the shipping offices that Browner had left aboard of the *May Day*, and I calculate that she is due in the Thames tomorrow night. When he arrives he will be met by the obtuse but resolute Lestrade, and I have no doubt that we shall have all our details filled in.'

Sherlock Holmes was not disappointed in his expectations. Two days later he received a bulky envelope, which contained a short note from the detective, and a typewritten document, which covered several pages of foolscap.

'Lestrade has got him all right,' said Holmes, glancing up at me. 'Perhaps it would interest you to hear what he says.

'MY DEAR MR HOLMES – In accordance with the scheme which we had formed in order to test our theories' ['the "we" is rather fine, Watson, is it not?'] 'I went down to the Albert Dock yesterday at 6 p.m., and boarded the S.S. *May Day*, belonging to the Liverpool, Dublin, and London Steam Packet Company. On enquiry, I found that there was a steward on board of the name of James Browner and that he had acted during the voyage in such an extraordinary manner that the captain had been compelled to relieve him of his duties. On descending to his berth, I found him seated upon a chest with his head sunk upon his hands, rocking himself to and fro. He is a big, powerful chap, clean-shaven, and very swarthy – something like Aldridge, who helped us in the bogus laundry affair. He jumped up when he heard my business, and I had my whistle to my lips to call a couple of river police, who were round the corner, but he seemed to have no heart in him, and he held out his hands quietly enough for the darbies. We brought him along to the cells, and his box as well, for we thought there might be something incriminating; but, bar a big sharp knife such as most sailors have, we got nothing for our trouble. However, we find that we shall want no more evidence, for on being brought before the inspector at the station he asked leave to make a statement, which was, of course, taken down, just as he made it, by our shorthand man. We had three copies typewritten, one of which I enclose. The affair proves, as I always thought it would, to be an extremely simple one, but I am obliged to you for assisting me in my investigation.

'With kind regards,

'Yours very truly,
G. LESTRADE.

'Hum! The investigation really was a very simple one,' remarked Holmes, 'but I don't think it struck him in that light when he first called us in. However, let us see what Jim Browner has to say for himself. This is his statement as made before Inspector Montgomery at the Shadwell Police Station, and it has the advantage of being verbatim.'

' "Have I anything to say? Yes, I have a deal to say. I have to make a clean breast of it all. You can hang me, or you can leave me alone. I don't care a plug which you do. I tell you I've not shut an eye in sleep since I did it, and I don't believe I ever will again until I get past all waking. Sometimes it's his face, but most generally it's hers. I'm never without one or the other before me. He looks frowning and black-like, but she has a kind o' surprise upon her face. Ay, the white lamb, she might well be surprised when she read death on a face that had seldom looked anything but love upon her before.

' "But it was Sarah's fault, and may the curse of a broken man put a blight on her and set the blood rotting in her veins! It's not that I want to clear myself. I know that I went back to drink, like the beast that I was. But she would have forgiven me; she would have stuck as close to me as a rope to a block if that woman had never darkened our door. For Sarah Cushing loved me – that's the root of the business – she loved me until all her love turned to poisonous hate when she knew that I thought more of my wife's footmark in the mud than I did of her whole body and soul.

' "There were three sisters altogether. The old one was just a good woman, the second was a devil, and the third was an angel. Sarah was thirty-three, and Mary was twenty-nine when I married. We were just as happy as the day was long when we set up house together, and in all Liverpool there was no better woman than my Mary. And then we asked Sarah up for a week, and the week grew into a month, and one thing led to another, until she was just one of ourselves.

' "I was blue ribbon at that time, and we were putting a little money by, and all was as bright as a new dollar. My God, whoever would have thought that it could have come to this? Whoever would have dreamed it?

' "I used to be home for the weekends very often, and sometimes if the ship were held back for cargo I would have a whole week at a time, and in this way I saw a deal of my sister-in-law, Sarah. She was a fine tall woman, black and quick and fierce, with a proud way of carrying her head, and a glint from her eye like a spark from a flint. But when little Mary was there I had never a thought of her, and that I swear as I hope for God's mercy.

' "It had seemed to me sometimes that she liked to be alone with me, or to coax me out for a walk with her, but I had never thought anything of that. But one evening my eyes were opened. I had come up from the ship and found my wife out, but Sarah at home. 'Where's Mary?' I asked. 'Oh, she has gone to pay some accounts.' I was impatient and paced up and down the room. 'Can't you be happy for five minutes without Mary, Jim?' says she. 'It's a bad compliment to me that you can't be contented with my society for so short a time.' 'That's all right, my lass,' said I, putting out my hand towards her in a kindly way, but she had it in both hers in an instant, and they burned as if they were in a fever. I looked into her eyes and I read it all there. There was no need for her to speak, nor for me either. I frowned and drew my hand away. Then she stood by my side in silence for a bit, and then put up her hand and patted me on the shoulder. 'Steady old Jim!' said she, and with a kind o' mocking laugh, she ran out of the room.

' "Well, from that time Sarah hated me with her whole heart and soul, and she is a woman who can hate, too. I was a fool to let her go on biding with us – a besotted fool – but I never said a word to Mary, for I knew it would grieve her. Things went on much as before, but after a time I began to find that there was a bit of a change in Mary herself. She had always been so trusting and so innocent, but now she became queer and suspicious, wanting to know where I had been and what I had been doing, and whom my letters were from, and what I had in my pockets, and a thousand such follies. Day by day she grew queerer and more irritable, and we had ceaseless rows about nothing. I was fairly puzzled by it all. Sarah avoided me now, but she and Mary were just inseparable. I can see now how she was plotting and scheming and poisoning my wife's mind against me, but I was such a blind beetle that I could not understand it at the time. Then I broke my blue ribbon and began to drink again, but I think I should not have done it if Mary had been the same as ever. She had some reason to be disgusted with me now, and the gap between us began to be wider and wider. And then this Alec Fairbairn chipped in, and things became a thousand times blacker.

' "It was to see Sarah that he came to my house first, but soon it was to see us, for he was a man with winning ways, and he made friends wherever he went. He was a dashing, swaggering chap, smart and curled, who had seen half the world and could talk of what he had seen. He was good company, I won't deny it, and he had wonderful polite ways with him for a sailor man, so that I think there must have been a time when he knew more of the poop than the forecastle. For a month he was in and out of my house, and never once did it cross my mind that harm might come of his soft, tricky ways. And then at last something made me suspect, and from that day my peace was gone for ever.

' "It was only a little thing, too. I had come into the parlour unexpected, and as I walked in at the door I saw a light of welcome on my wife's face. But as she saw who it was it faded again, and she turned away with a look of disappointment. That was enough for me. There was no one but Alec Fairbairn whose step she could have mistaken for mine. If I could have seen him then I should have killed him, for I have always been like a madman when my temper gets loose. Mary saw the devil's light in my eyes, and she ran forward with her hands on my sleeve. 'Don't, Jim, don't!' says she. 'Where's Sarah?' I asked. 'In the kitchen,' says she. 'Sarah,' says I as I went in, 'this man Fairbairn is never to darken my door again.' 'Why not?' says she. 'Because I order it.' 'Oh!' says she, 'if my friends are not good enough for this house, then I am not good enough for it either.' 'You can do what you like,' says I, 'but if Fairbairn shows his face here again I'll send you one of his ears for a keepsake.' She was frightened by my face, I think, for she never answered a word, and the same evening she left my house.

' "Well, I don't know now whether it was pure devilry on the part of this woman, or whether she thought that she could turn me against my wife by encouraging her to misbehave. Anyway, she took a house just two streets off and let lodgings to sailors. Fairbairn used to stay there, and Mary would go round to have tea with her sister and him. How often she went I don't know, but I followed her one day, and as I broke in at the door Fairbairn got away over the back garden wall, like the cowardly skunk that he was. I swore to my wife that I would kill her if I found her in his company again, and I led her back with me, sobbing and trembling, and as white as a piece of paper. There was no trace of love between us any longer. I could see that she hated me and feared me,

456

and when the thought of it drove me to drink, then she despised me as well.

' "Well, Sarah found that she could not make a living in Liverpool, so she went back, as I understand, to live with her sister in Croydon, and things jogged on much the same as ever at home. And then came this week and all the misery and ruin.

' "It was in this way. We had gone on the *May Day* for a round voyage of seven days, but a hogshead got loose and started one of our plates, so that we had to put back into port for twelve hours. I left the ship and came home, thinking what a surprise it would be for my wife, and hoping that maybe she would be glad to see me so soon. The thought was in my head as I turned into my own street, and at that moment a cab passed me, and there she was, sitting by the side of Fairbairn, the two chatting and laughing, with never a thought for me as I stood watching them from the footpath.

' "I tell you, and I give you my word for it, that from that moment I was not my own master, and it is all like a dim dream when I look back on it. I had been drinking hard of late, and the two things together fairly turned my brain. There's something throbbing in my head now, like a docker's hammer, but that morning I seemed to have all Niagara whizzing and buzzing in my ears.

' "Well, I took to my heels, and I ran after the cab. I had a heavy oak stick in my hand, and I tell you I saw red from the first; but as I ran I got cunning, too, and hung back a little to see them without being seen. They pulled up soon at the railway station. There was a good crowd round the booking-office, so I got quite close to them without being seen. They took tickets for

New Brighton. So did I, but I got in three carriages behind them. When we reached it they walked along the Parade, and I was never more than a hundred yards from them. At last I saw them hire a boat and start for a row, for it was a very hot day, and they thought, no doubt, that it would be cooler on the water.

' "It was just as if they had been given into my hands. There was a bit of a haze, and you could not see more than a few hundred yards. I hired a boat for myself, and I pulled after them. I could see the blur of their craft, but they were going nearly as fast as I, and they must have been a long mile from the shore before I caught them up. The haze was like a curtain all round us, and there were we three in the middle of it. My God, shall I ever forget their faces when they saw who was in the boat that was closing in upon them? She screamed out. He swore like a madman and jabbed at me with an oar, for he must have seen death in my eyes. I got past it and got one in with my stick that crushed his head like an egg. I would have spared her, perhaps, for all my madness, but she threw her arms round him, crying out to him, and calling him 'Alec'. I struck again, and she lay stretched beside him. I was like a wild beast then that had tasted blood. If Sarah had been there, by the Lord, she should have joined them. I pulled out my knife, and – well, there! I've said enough. It gave me a kind of savage joy when I thought how Sarah would feel when she had such signs as these of what her meddling had brought about. Then I tied the bodies into the boat, stove a plank, and stood by until they had sunk. I knew very well that the owner would think that they had lost their bearings in the haze, and had drifted off out to sea. I cleaned myself up, got back to land, and joined my ship without a soul having a suspicion of what had passed. That night I made up the packet for Sarah Cushing, and next day I sent it from Belfast.

' "There you have the whole truth of it. You can hang me, or do what you like with me, but you cannot punish me as I have been punished already. I cannot shut my eyes but I see those two faces staring at me – staring at me as they stared when my boat broke through the haze. I killed them quick, but they are killing me slow; and if I have another night of it I shall be either mad or dead before morning. You won't put me alone into a cell, sir? For pity's sake don't, and may you be treated in your day of agony as you treat me now."

'What is the meaning of it, Watson?' said Holmes solemnly as he laid down the paper. 'What object is served by this circle of misery and violence and fear? It must tend to some end, or else our universe is ruled by chance, which is unthinkable. But what end? There is the great standing perennial problem to which human reason is as far from an answer as ever.'

16

The Red Circle

I

'Well, Mrs Warren, I cannot see that you have any particular cause for uneasiness, nor do I understand why I, whose time is of some value, should interfere in the matter. I really have other things to engage me.' So spoke Sherlock Holmes, and turned back to the great scrapbook in which he was arranging and indexing some of his recent material.

But the landlady had the pertinacity and also the cunning of her sex. She held her ground firmly.

'You arranged an affair for a lodger of mine last year,' she said – 'Mr Fairdale Hobbs.'

'Ah, yes – a simple matter.'

'But he would never cease talking of it – your kindness, sir, and the way in which you brought light into the darkness. I remembered his words when I was in doubt and darkness myself. I know you could if you only would.'

Holmes was accessible upon the side of flattery, and also, to do him justice, upon the side of kindliness. The two forces made him lay down his gum-brush with a sigh of resignation and push back his chair.

'Well, well, Mrs Warren, let us hear about it, then. You don't object to tobacco, I take it? Thank you, Watson – the matches! You are uneasy, as I understand, because your new lodger remains in his rooms and you cannot see him. Why, bless you, Mrs Warren, if I were your lodger you often would not see me for weeks on end.'

'No doubt, sir; but this is different. It frightens me, Mr Holmes. I can't sleep for fright. To hear his quick step moving here and moving there from early morning to late at night, and yet never to catch so much as a glimpse of him – it's more than I can stand. My husband is as nervous over it as I am, but he is out at his work all day, while I get no rest from it. What is he hiding for? What has he done? Except for the girl, I am all alone in the house with him, and it's more than my nerves can stand.'

Holmes leaned forward and laid his long, thin fingers upon the woman's shoulder. He had an almost hypnotic power of soothing when he wished. The scared look faded from her eyes, and her agitated features smoothed into their usual commonplace. She sat down in the chair which he had indicated.

'If I take it up I must understand every detail,' said he. 'Take time to consider. The smallest point may be the most essential. You say that the man came ten days ago and paid you for a fortnight's board and lodging?'

'He asked my terms, sir. I said fifty shillings a week. There is a small sitting-room and bedroom, and all complete, at the top of the house.'

'Well?'

'He said, "I'll pay you five pounds a week if I can have it on my own terms." I'm a poor woman, sir, and Mr Warren earns little, and the money meant much to me. He took out a ten-pound note, and he held it out to me then and there. "You can have the same every fortnight for a long time to come if you keep the terms," he said. "If not, I'll have no more to do with you."

'What were the terms?'

'Well, sir, they were that he was to have a key of the house. That was all right. Lodgers often have them. Also, that he was to be left entirely to himself and never, upon any excuse, to be disturbed.'

'Nothing wonderful in that, surely?'

'Not in reason, sir. But this is out of all reason. He has been there for ten days, and neither Mr Warren, nor I, nor the girl has once set eyes upon him. We can hear that quick step of his pacing up and down, up and down, night, morning, and noon; but except on that first night he has never once gone out of the house.'

'Oh, he went out the first night, did he?'

'Yes, sir, and returned very late – after we were all in bed. He told me after he had taken the rooms that he would do so and asked me not to bar the door. I heard him come up the stair after midnight.'

'But his meals?'

'It was his particular direction that we should always, when he rang, leave his meal upon a chair, outside his door. Then he rings again when he has finished, and we take it down from the same chair. If he wants anything else he prints it on a slip of paper and leaves it.'

'Prints it?'

'Yes, sir; prints it in pencil. Just the word, nothing more. Here's the one I brought to show you – "SOAP". Here's another – "MATCH". This is one he left the first morning – "DAILY GAZETTE". I leave that paper with his breakfast every morning.'

'Dear me, Watson,' said Holmes, staring with great curiosity at the slips of foolscap which the landlady had handed to him, 'this is certainly a little unusual. Seclusion I can understand; but why print? Printing is a clumsy process. Why not write? What would it suggest, Watson?'

'That he desired to conceal his handwriting.'

'But why? What can it matter to him that his landlady should have a word of his writing? Still, it may be as you say. Then, again, why such laconic messages?'

'I cannot imagine.'

'It opens a pleasing field for intelligent speculation. The words are written with a broad-pointed, violet-tinted pencil of a not unusual pattern. You will observe that the paper is torn away at the side here after the printing was done, so that the "S" of "SOAP" is partly gone. Suggestive, Watson, is it not?'

'Of caution?'

'Exactly. There was evidently some mark, some thumbprint, something which might give a clue to the person's identity. Now, Mrs Warren, you say that the man was of middle size, dark, and bearded. What age would he be?'

'Youngish, sir – not over thirty.'

'Well, can you give me no further indications?'

'He spoke good English, sir, and yet I thought he was a foreigner by his accent.'

'And he was well dressed?'

'Very smartly dressed, sir – quite the gentleman. Dark clothes – nothing you would note.'

'He gave no name?'

'No, sir.'

'And has had no letters or callers?'

'None.'

'But surely you or the girl enter his room of a morning?'

'No, sir; he looks after himself entirely.'

'Dear me! that is certainly remarkable. What about his luggage?'

'He had one big brown bag with him – nothing else.'

'Well, we don't seem to have much material to help us. Do you say nothing has come out of that room – absolutely nothing?'

The landlady drew an envelope from her bag; from it she shook out two burnt matches and a cigarette-end upon the table.

'They were on his tray this morning. I brought them because I had heard that you can read great things out of small ones.'

Holmes shrugged his shoulders.

'There is nothing here,' said he. 'The matches have, of course, been used to light cigarettes. That is obvious from the shortness of the burnt end. Half the match is consumed in lighting a pipe or cigar. But, dear me! this cigarette stub is certainly remarkable. The gentleman was bearded and moustached, you say?'

'Yes, sir.'

'I don't understand that. I should say that only a clean-shaven man could have smoked this. Why, Watson, even your modest moustache would have been singed.'

'A holder?' I suggested.

'No, no; the end is matted. I suppose there could not be two people in your rooms, Mrs Warren?'

'No, sir. He eats so little that I often wonder it can keep life in one.'

'Well, I think we must wait for a little more material. After all, you have nothing to complain of. You have received your rent, and he is not a troublesome lodger, though he is certainly an unusual one. He pays you well, and if he chooses to lie concealed it is no direct business of yours. We have no excuse for an intrusion upon his privacy until we have some reason to think that there is a guilty reason for it. I've taken up the matter, and I won't lose sight of it. Report to me if anything fresh occurs, and rely upon my assistance if it should be needed.'

'There are certainly some points of interest in this case, Watson,' he remarked when the landlady had left us. 'It may, of course, be trivial – individual eccentricity; or it may be very much deeper than appears on the surface. The first thing that strikes one is the obvious possibility that the person now in the rooms may be entirely different from the one who engaged them.'

'Why should you think so?'

'Well, apart from this cigarette-end, was it not suggestive that the only time the lodger went out was immediately after his taking the rooms? He came back – or someone came back – when all witnesses were out of the way. We have no proof that the person who came back was the person who went out. Then, again, the man who took the rooms spoke English well. This other, however, prints "match" when it should have been "matches". I can imagine that the word was taken out of a dictionary, which would give the noun but not the plural. The laconic style may be to conceal the absence of knowledge of English. Yes, Watson, there are good reasons to suspect that there has been a substitution of lodgers.'

'But for what possible end?'

'Ah! there lies our problem. There is one rather obvious line of investigation.' He took down the great book in which, day by day, he filed the agony columns of the various London journals. 'Dear me!' said he, turning over the pages, 'what a chorus of groans, cries, and bleatings! What a rag-bag of singular happenings! But surely the most valuable hunting-ground that ever was given to a student of the unusual! This person is alone and cannot be approached by letter without a breach of that absolute secrecy which is desired. How is any news or any message to reach him from without? Obviously by advertisement through a newspaper. There seems no other way, and fortunately we need concern ourselves with the one paper only. Here are the *Daily Gazette* extracts of the last fortnight. "Lady with a black boa at Prince's Skating Club" – that we may pass. "Surely Jimmy will not break his mother's heart" – that appears to be irrelevant. "If the lady who fainted on Brixton bus" – she does not interest me. "Every day my heart longs – " Bleat, Watson – unmitigated bleat! Ah, this is a little more possible. Listen to this: "Be patient. Will find some sure means of communication. Meanwhile, this column. – G." That is two days after Mrs Warren's lodger arrived. It sounds plausible, does it not? The mysterious one could understand English, even if he could not print it. Let us see if we can pick up the trace again. Yes, here we are – three days later. "Am making successful arrangements. Patience and prudence. The clouds will pass. – G." Nothing for a week after that. Then comes something much more definite: "The path is clearing. If I find chance signal message remember code agreed – one A, two B, and so on. You will hear soon. – G." That was in yesterday's paper, and there is nothing in today's. It's all very appropriate to Mrs Warren's lodger. If we wait a little, Watson, I don't doubt that the affair will grow more intelligible.'

So it proved; for in the morning I found my friend standing on the hearthrug with his back to the fire and a smile of complete satisfaction upon his face.

'How's this, Watson?' he cried, picking up the paper from the table. ' "High red house with white stone facings. Third floor. Second window left. After dusk. – G." That is definite enough. I think after breakfast we must make a little reconnaissance of Mrs Warren's neighbourhood. Ah, Mrs Warren! what news do you bring us this morning?'

Our client had suddenly burst into the room with an explosive energy which told of some new and momentous development.

'It's a police matter, Mr Holmes!' she cried. 'I'll have no more of it! He shall pack out of there with his baggage. I would have gone straight up and told him so, only I thought it was but fair to you to take your opinion first. But I'm at the end of my patience, and when it comes to knocking my old man about – '

'Knocking Mr Warren about?'

'Using him roughly, anyway.'

'But who used him roughly?'

'Ah! that's what we want to know! It was this morning, sir. Mr Warren is a timekeeper at Morton and Waylight's, in Tottenham Court Road. He has to be out of the house before seven. Well, this morning he had not gone ten paces down the road when two men came up behind him, threw a coat over his head, and bundled him into a cab that was beside the kerb. They drove him an hour, and then opened the door and shot him out. He lay in the roadway so shaken in his wits that he never saw what became of the cab. When he picked himself up he found he was on Hampstead Heath; so he took a bus home, and there he lies now on his sofa, while I came straight round to tell you what had happened.'

'Most interesting,' said Holmes. 'Did he observe the appearance of these men – did he hear them talk?'

'No; he is clean dazed. He just knows that he was lifted up as if by magic and dropped as if by magic. Two at least were in it, and maybe three.'

'And you connect this attack with your lodger?'

'Well, we've lived there fifteen years and no such happenings ever came before. I've had enough of him. Money's not everything. I'll have him out of my house before the day is done.'

'Wait a bit, Mrs Warren. Do nothing rash. I begin to think that this affair may be very much more important than appeared at first sight. It is clear now that some danger is threatening your lodger. It is equally clear that his enemies, lying in wait for him near your door, mistook your husband for him in the foggy morning light. On discovering their mistake they released him. What they would have done had it not been a mistake, we can only conjecture.'

'Well, what am I to do, Mr Holmes?'

'I have a great fancy to see this lodger of yours, Mrs Warren.'

'I don't see how that is to be managed, unless you break in the door. I always hear him unlock it as I go down the stair after I leave the tray.'

'He has to take the tray in. Surely we could conceal ourselves and see him do it.'

The landlady thought for a moment.

'Well, sir, there's the boxroom opposite. I could arrange a looking-glass, maybe, and if you were behind the door – '

'Excellent!' said Holmes. 'When does he lunch?'

468

'About one, sir.'

'Then Dr Watson and I will come round in time. For the present, Mrs Warren, goodbye.'

At half-past twelve we found ourselves upon the steps of Mrs Warren's house – a high, thin, yellow-brick edifice in Great Orme Street, a narrow thorough-fare at the north-east side of the British Museum. Standing as it does near the corner of the street, it commands a view down Howe Street, with its more pretentious houses. Holmes pointed with a chuckle to one of these, a row of residential flats, which projected so that they could not fail to catch the eye.

'See, Watson!' said he. ' "High red house with stone facings." There is the signal station all right. We know the place, and we know the code; so surely our task should be simple. There's a "to let" card in that window. It is evidently an empty flat to which the confederate has access. Well, Mrs Warren, what now?'

'I have it all ready for you. If you will both come up and leave your boots below on the landing, I'll put you there now.'

It was an excellent hiding-place which she had arranged. The mirror was so placed that, seated in the dark, we could very plainly see the door opposite. We had hardly settled down in it, and Mrs Warren left us, when a distant tinkle announced that our mysterious neighbour had rung. Presently the landlady appeared with the tray, laid it down upon a chair beside the closed door, and then, treading heavily, departed. Crouching together in the angle of the door, we kept our eyes fixed upon the mirror. Suddenly, as the landlady's footsteps died away, there was the creak of a turning key, the handle revolved, and two thin hands darted out and lifted the tray from the chair. An instant later it was hurriedly replaced, and I caught a glimpse of a dark, beautiful, horrified face glaring at the narrow opening of the boxroom. Then the door crashed to, the key turned once more, and all was silence. Holmes twitched my sleeve, and together we stole down the stair.

'I will call again in the evening,' said he to the expectant landlady. 'I think, Watson, we can discuss this business better in our own quarters.'

'My surmise, as you saw, proved to be correct,' said he, speaking from the depths of his easy-chair. 'There has been a substitution of lodgers. What I did not foresee is that we should find a woman, and no ordinary woman, Watson.'

'She saw us.'

'Well, she saw something to alarm her. That is certain. The general sequence of events is pretty clear, is it not? A couple seek refuge in London from a very terrible and instant danger. The measure of that danger is the rigour of their precautions. The man, who has some work which he must do, desires to leave the woman in absolute safety while he does it. It is not an easy problem, but he solved it in an original fashion, and so effectively that her presence was not even known to the landlady who supplies her with food. The printed messages, as is now evident, were to prevent her sex being discovered by her writing. The man cannot come near the woman, or he will guide their enemies to her. Since he cannot communicate with her direct, he has recourse to the agony column of a paper. So far all is clear.'

'But what is at the root of it?'

'Ah, yes, Watson – severely practical, as usual! What is at the root of it all? Mrs Warren's whimsical problem enlarges somewhat and assumes a more sinister aspect as we proceed. This much we can say: that it is no ordinary love escapade. You saw the woman's face at the sign of danger. We have heard, too, of the attack upon the landlord, which was undoubtedly meant for the lodger. These alarms, and the desperate need for secrecy, argue that the matter is one of life or death. The attack upon Mr Warren further shows that the enemy, whoever they are, are themselves not aware of the substitution of the female lodger for the male. It is very curious and complex, Watson.'

'Why should you go further in it? What have you to gain from it?'

'What, indeed? It is art for art's sake, Watson. I suppose when you doctored you found yourself studying cases without thought of a fee?'

'For my education, Holmes.'

'Education never ends, Watson. It is a series of lessons with the greatest for the last. This is an instructive case. There is neither money nor credit in it, and yet one would wish to tidy it up. When dusk comes we should find ourselves one stage advanced in our investigation.'

When we returned to Mrs Warren's rooms, the gloom of a London winter evening had thickened into one grey curtain, a dead monotone of colour, broken only by the sharp yellow squares of the windows and the blurred haloes of the gas-lamps. As we peered from the darkened sitting-room of the lodging-house, one more dim light glimmered high up through the obscurity.

'Someone is moving in that room,' said Holmes in a whisper, his gaunt and eager face thrust forward to the windowpane. 'Yes, I can see his shadow. There he is again! He has a candle in his hand. Now he is peering across. He wants to be sure that she is on the lookout. Now he begins to flash. Take the message also, Watson, that we may check each other. A single flash – that is "A", surely. Now, then. How many did you make it? Twenty. So did I. That should mean "T". A T – that's intelligible enough. Another "T". Surely this is the beginning of a second word. Now, then – TENTA. Dead stop. That can't be all, Watson? ATTENTA gives no sense. Nor is it any better as three words – AT TEN TA, unless T.A. are a person's initials. There it goes again! What's that? ATTE – why, it is the same message over again. Curious, Watson, very curious. Now he is off once more! AT – why, he is repeating it for the third time. ATTENTA three times! How often will he repeat it? No, that seems to be the finish. He has withdrawn from the window. What do you make of it, Watson?'

'A cipher message, Holmes.'

My companion gave a sudden chuckle of comprehension. 'And not a very obscure cipher, Watson,' said he. 'Why, of course, it is Italian! The "A" means that it is addressed to a woman. "Beware! Beware! Beware!" How's that, Watson?'

'I believe you have hit it.'

'Not a doubt of it. It is a very urgent message, thrice repeated to make it more so. But beware of what? Wait a bit; he is coming to the window once more.'

Again we saw the dim silhouette of a crouching man and the whisk of the small flame across the window as the signals were renewed. They came more rapidly than before – so rapid that it was hard to follow them.

'PERICOLO – pericolo – eh, what's that, Watson?

"Danger", isn't it? Yes, by Jove, it's a danger signal. There he goes again! PERI. Halloa, what on earth – '

The light had suddenly gone out, the glimmering square of window had disappeared, and the third floor formed a dark band round the lofty building, with its tiers of shining casements. That last warning cry had been suddenly cut short. How, and by whom? The same thought occurred on the instant to us both. Holmes sprang up from where he crouched by the window.

'This is serious, Watson,' he cried. 'There is some devilry going forward! Why should such a message stop in such a way? I should put Scotland Yard in touch with this business – and yet, it is too pressing for us to leave.'

'Shall I go for the police?'

'We must define the situation a little more clearly. It may bear some more innocent interpretation. Come, Watson, let us go across ourselves and see what we can make of it.'

2

As we walked rapidly down Howe Street I glanced back at the building which we had left. There, dimly outlined at the top window, I could see the shadow of a head, a woman's head, gazing tensely, rigidly, out into the night, waiting with breathless suspense for the renewal of that interrupted message. At the doorway of the Howe Street flats a man, muffled in a cravat and greatcoat, was leaning against the railing. He started as the hall-light fell upon our faces.

'Holmes!' he cried.

'Why, Gregson!' said my companion as he shook hands with the Scotland Yard detective. 'Journeys end with lovers' meetings. What brings you here?'

'The same reasons that bring you, I expect,' said Gregson. 'How you got on to it I can't imagine.'

'Different threads, but leading up to the same tangle. I've been taking the signals.'

'Signals?'

'Yes, from that window. They broke off in the middle. We came over to see the reason. But since it is safe in your hands I see no object in continuing this business.'

'Wait a bit!' cried Gregson eagerly. 'I'll do you this justice, Mr Holmes, that I was never in a case yet that I didn't feel stronger for having you on my side. There's only the one exit to these flats, so we have him safe.'

'Who is he?'

'Well, well, we score over you for once, Mr Holmes. You must give us best this time.' He struck his stick sharply upon the ground, on which a cabman, his whip in his hand, sauntered over from a four-wheeler which stood on the far side of the street. 'May I introduce you to Mr Sherlock Holmes?' he said to the cabman. 'This is Mr Leverton, of Pinkerton's American Agency.'

'The hero of the Long Island cave mystery?' said Holmes. 'Sir, I am pleased to meet you.'

The American, a quiet, businesslike young man, with a clean-shaven, hatchet face, flushed up at the words of commendation. 'I am on the trail of my life now, Mr Holmes,' said he. 'If I can get Gorgiano – '

'What! Gorgiano of the Red Circle?'

'Oh, he has a European fame, has he? Well, we've learned all about him in America. We *know* he is at the

474

bottom of fifty murders, and yet we have nothing positive we can take him on. I tracked him over from New York, and I've been close to him for a week in London, waiting some excuse to get my hand on his collar. Mr Gregson and I ran him to ground in that big tenement house, and there's only one door, so he can't slip us. There's three folk come out since he went in, but I'll swear he wasn't one of them.'

'Mr Holmes talks of signals,' said Gregson. 'I expect, as usual, he knows a good deal that we don't.'

In a few clear words Holmes explained the situation as it had appeared to us. The American struck his hands together with vexation.

'He's on to us!' he cried.

'Why do you think so?'

'Well, it figures out that way, does it not? Here he is, sending out messages to an accomplice – there are several of his gang in London. Then suddenly, just as by your own account he was telling them that there was danger, he broke short off. What could it mean except that from the window he had suddenly either caught sight of us in the street, or in some way come to understand how close the danger was, and that he must act right away if he was to avoid it? What do you suggest, Mr Holmes?'

'That we go up at once and see for ourselves.'

'But we have no warrant for his arrest.'

'He is in unoccupied premises under suspicious circumstances,' said Gregson. 'That is good enough for the moment. When we have him by the heels we can see if New York can't help us to keep him. I'll take the responsibility of arresting him now.'

Our official detectives may blunder in the matter of intelligence, but never in that of courage. Gregson climbed the stair to arrest this desperate murderer with the same absolutely quiet and businesslike bearing with which he would have ascended the official staircase of Scotland Yard. The Pinkerton man had tried to push past him, but Gregson had firmly elbowed him back. London dangers were the privilege of the London force.

The door of the left-hand flat upon the third landing was standing ajar. Gregson pushed it open. Within all was absolute silence and darkness. I struck a match and lit the detective's lantern. As I did so, and as the flicker steadied into a flame, we all gave a gasp of surprise. On the deal boards of the carpetless floor there was outlined a fresh track of blood. The red steps pointed towards us and led away from an inner room, the door of which was closed. Gregson flung it open and held his light full blaze in front of him, while we all peered eagerly over his shoulders.

In the middle of the floor of the empty room was huddled the figure of an enormous man, his clean-shaven, swarthy face grotesquely horrible in its con-tortion and his head encircled by a ghastly crimson halo of blood, lying in a broad wet circle upon the white woodwork. His knees were drawn up, his hands thrown out in agony, and from the centre of his broad, brown, upturned throat there projected the white haft of a knife driven blade-deep into his body. Giant as he was, the man must have gone down like a poleaxed ox before that terrific blow. Beside his right hand a most formidable horn-handled, two-edged dagger lay upon the floor, and near it a black kid glove.

'By George! it's Black Gorgiano himself!' cried the American detective. 'Someone has got ahead of us this time.'

'Here is the candle in the window, Mr Holmes,' said Gregson. 'Why, whatever are you doing?'

Holmes had stepped across, had lit the candle, and was passing it backwards and forwards across the windowpanes. Then he peered into the darkness, blew the candle out, and threw it on the floor.

'I rather think that will be helpful,' said he. He came over and stood in deep thought while the two professionals were examining the body. 'You say that three people came out from the flat while you were waiting downstairs,' said he at last. 'Did you observe them closely?'

'Yes, I did.'

'Was there a fellow about thirty, black-bearded, dark, of middle size?'

'Yes; he was the last to pass me.'

'That is your man, I fancy. I can give you his description, and we have a very excellent outline of his footmark. That should be enough for you.'

'Not much, Mr Holmes, among the millions of London.'

'Perhaps not. That is why I thought it best to summon this lady to your aid.'

We all turned round at the words. There, framed in the doorway, was a tall and beautiful woman – the mysterious lodger of Bloomsbury. Slowly she advanced, her face pale and drawn with a frightful apprehension, her eyes fixed and staring, her terrified gaze riveted upon the dark figure on the floor.

'You have killed him!' she muttered. 'Oh, *Dio mio*, you have killed him!' Then I heard a sudden sharp intake of her breath, and she sprang into the air with a cry of joy. Round and round the room she danced, her hands clapping, her dark eyes gleaming with delighted wonder, and a thousand pretty Italian exclamations pouring from her lips. It was terrible and amazing to see such a woman so convulsed with joy at such a sight. Suddenly she stopped and gazed at us all with a questioning stare.

'But you! You are police, are you not? You have killed Giuseppe Gorgiano. Is it not so?'

'We are police, madam.'

She looked round into the shadows of the room.

'But where, then, is Gennaro?' she asked. 'He is my husband, Gennaro Lucca. I am Emilia Lucca, and we are both from New York. Where is Gennaro? He called me this moment from this window, and I ran with all my speed.'

'It was I who called,' said Holmes.

'You! How could you call?'

'Your cipher was not difficult, madam. Your presence here was desirable. I knew that I had only to flash "Vieni" and you would surely come.'

The beautiful Italian looked with awe at my companion.

'I do not understand how you know these things,' she said. 'Giuseppe Gorgiano – how did he – ' She paused, and then suddenly her face lit up with pride and delight. 'Now I see it! My Gennaro! My splendid, beautiful Gennaro, who has guarded me safe from all harm, he did it, with his own strong hand he killed the monster! Oh, Gennaro, how wonderful you are! What woman could ever be worthy of such a man?'

'Well, Mrs Lucca,' said the prosaic Gregson, laying his hand upon the lady's sleeve with as little sentiment as if she were a Notting Hill hooligan, 'I am not very clear yet who you are or what you are; but you've said enough to make it very clear that we shall want you at the Yard.'

'One moment, Gregson,' said Holmes. 'I rather fancy that this lady may be as anxious to give us information as we can be to get it. You understand, madam, that your husband will be arrested and tried for the death of the man who lies before us? What you say may be used in evidence. But if you think that he has acted from motives which are not criminal, and which he would wish to have known, then you cannot serve him better than by telling us the whole story.'

'Now that Gorgiano is dead we fear nothing,' said the lady. 'He was a devil and a monster, and there can be no judge in the world who would punish my husband for having killed him.'

'In that case,' said Holmes, 'my suggestion is that we lock this door, leave things as we found them, go with this lady to her room, and form our opinion after we have heard what it is that she has to say to us.'

Half an hour later we were seated, all four, in the small sitting-room of Signora Lucca, listening to her remarkable narrative of those sinister events, the ending of which we had chanced to witness. She spoke in rapid and fluent but very unconventional English, which, for the sake of clearness, I will make grammatical.

'I was born in Posilippo, near Naples,' said she, 'and was the daughter of Augusto Barelli, who was the chief lawyer and once the deputy of that part. Gennaro was in my father's employment, and I came to love him, as any woman must. He had neither money nor position – nothing but his beauty and strength and energy – so my father forbade the match. We fled together, were married at Bari, and sold my jewels to gain the money which would take us to America. This

479

was four years ago, and we have been in New York ever since.

'Fortune was very good to us at first. Gennaro was able to do a service to an Italian gentleman – he saved him from some ruffians in the place called the Bowery, and so made a powerful friend. His name was Tito Castalotte, and he was the senior partner of the great firm of Castalotte and Zamba, who are the chief fruit importers of New York. Signor Zamba is an invalid, and our new friend Castalotte has all power within the firm, which employs more than three hundred men. He took my husband into his employment, made him head of a department, and showed his goodwill towards him in every way. Signor Castalotte was a bachelor, and I believe that he felt as if Gennaro was his son, and both my husband and I loved him as if he were our father. We had taken and furnished a little house in Brooklyn, and our whole future seemed assured when that black cloud appeared which was soon to overspread our sky.

'One night, when Gennaro returned from his work, he brought a fellow-countryman back with him. His name was Gorgiano, and he had come also from Posilippo. He was a huge man, as you can testify, for you have looked upon his corpse. Not only was his body that of a giant but everything about him was grotesque, gigantic, and terrifying. His voice was like thunder in our little house. There was scarce room for the whirl of his great arms as he talked. His thoughts, his emotions, his passions, all were exaggerated and monstrous. He talked, or rather roared, with such energy that others could but sit and listen, cowed with the mighty stream of words. His eyes blazed at you and held you at his mercy. He was a terrible and wonderful man. I thank God that he is dead!

'He came again and again. Yet I was aware that Gennaro was no more happy than I was in his presence. My poor husband would sit pale and listless, listening to the endless raving upon politics and upon social questions which made up our visitor's conversation. Gennaro said nothing, but I, who knew him so well, could read in his face some emotion which I had never seen there before. At first I thought that it was dislike. And then, gradually, I understood that it was more than dislike. It was fear – a deep, secret, shrinking fear. That night – the night that I read his terror – I put my arms round him and I implored him by his love for me and by all that he held dear to hold nothing from me, and to tell me why this huge man overshadowed him so.

'He told me, and my own heart grew cold as ice as I listened. My poor Gennaro, in his wild and fiery days, when all the world seemed against him and his mind was driven half mad by the injustices of life, had joined a Neapolitan society, the Red Circle, which was allied to the old Carbonari. The oaths and secrets of this brotherhood were frightful, but once within its rule no escape was possible. When we had fled to America Gennaro thought that he had cast it all off for ever. What was his horror one evening to meet in the streets the very man who had initiated him in Naples, the giant Gorgiano, a man who had earned the name of "Death" in the south of Italy, for he was red to the elbow in murder! He had come to New York to avoid the Italian police, and he had already planted a branch of this dreadful society in his new home. All this Gennaro told me and showed me a summons which he had received that very day, a Red Circle drawn upon the head of it telling him that a lodge would be held upon a certain date, and that his presence at it was required and ordered.

'That was bad enough, but worse was to come. I had noticed for some time that when Gorgiano came to us, as he constantly did, in the evening, he spoke much to me; and even when his words were to my husband those terrible, glaring, wild-beast eyes of his were always turned upon me. One night his secret came out. I had awakened what he called "love" within him – the love of a brute – a savage. Gennaro had not yet returned when he came. He pushed his way in, seized me in his mighty arms, hugged me in his bear's embrace, covered me with kisses, and implored me to come away with him. I was struggling and screaming when Gennaro entered and attacked him. He struck Gennaro senseless and fled from the house which he was never more to enter. It was a deadly enemy that we made that night.

'A few days later came the meeting. Gennaro returned from it with a face which told me that something dreadful had occurred. It was worse than we could have imagined possible. The funds of the society were raised by blackmailing rich Italians and threatening them with violence should they refuse the money. It seems that Castalotte, our dear friend and benefactor, had been approached. He had refused to yield to threats, and he had handed the notices to the police. It was resolved now that such an example should be made of him as would prevent any other victim from rebelling. At the meeting it was arranged that he and his house should be blown up with dynamite. There was a drawing of lots as to who should carry out the deed. Gennaro saw our enemy's cruel face smiling at him as he dipped his hand in the bag. No doubt it had been prearranged in some fashion, for it was the fatal disc with the Red Circle upon it, the mandate for murder, which lay upon his palm. He was to kill his best friend, or he was to expose himself and me to the vengeance of his comrades. It was part of their fiendish system to punish those whom they feared or hated by injuring not only their own persons but those whom they loved, and it was the knowledge of this which hung as a terror over my poor Gennaro's head and drove him nearly crazy with apprehension.

'All that night we sat together, our arms round each other, each strengthening each for the troubles that lay before us. The very next evening had been fixed for the attempt. By midday my husband and I were on our way to London, but not before he had given our benefactor full warning of his danger, and had also left such information for the police as would safeguard his life for the future.

'The rest, gentlemen, you know for yourselves. We were sure that our enemies would be behind us like our own shadows. Gorgiano had his private reasons for vengeance, but in any case we knew how ruthless, cunning, and untiring he could be. Both Italy and America are full of stories of his dreadful powers. If ever they were exerted it would be now. My darling made use of the few clear days which our start had given us in arranging for a refuge for me in such a fashion that no possible danger could reach me. For his own part, he wished to be free that he might communicate both with the American and with the Italian police. I do not myself know where he lived, or how. All that I learned was through the columns of a newspaper. But once as I looked through my window, I saw two Italians watching the house, and I understood that in some way Gorgiano had found our retreat. Finally Gennaro told me, through the paper, that he would signal to me from a certain window, but when the signals came they were nothing but warnings, which were suddenly interrupted. It is very clear to me now that he knew Gorgiano to be close upon him, and that, thank God! he was ready for him when he came. And now, gentlemen, I would ask you whether we have anything to fear from the law, or whether any judge upon earth would condemn my Gennaro for what he has done?'

'Well, Mr Gregson,' said the American, looking across at the official, 'I don't know what your British point of view may be, but I guess that in New York this lady's husband will receive a pretty general vote of thanks.'

'She will have to come with me and see the chief,' Gregson answered. 'If what she says is corroborated, I do not think she or her husband has much to fear. But what I can't make head or tail of, Mr Holmes, is how on earth *you* got yourself mixed up in the matter.'

'Education, Gregson, education. Still seeking knowledge at the old university. Well, Watson, you have one more specimen of the tragic and grotesque to add to your collection. By the way, it is not eight o'clock, and a Wagner night at Covent Garden! If we hurry, we might be in time for the second act.'

17

The Bruce-Partington Plans

In the third week of November, in the year 1895, a dense yellow fog settled down upon London. From the Monday to the Thursday I doubt whether it was ever possible from our windows in Baker Street to see the loom of the opposite houses. The first day Holmes had spent in cross-indexing his huge book of references. The second and third had been patiently occupied upon a subject which he had recently made his hobby – the music of the Middle Ages. But when, for the fourth time, after pushing back our chairs from breakfast we saw the greasy, heavy brown swirl still drifting past us and condensing in oily drops upon the windowpanes, my comrade's impatient and active nature could endure this drab existence no longer. He paced restlessly about our sitting-room in a fever of suppressed energy, biting his nails, tapping the furniture, and chafing against inaction.

'Nothing of interest in the paper, Watson?' he said.

I was aware that by anything of interest, Holmes meant anything of criminal interest. There was the news of a revolution, of a possible war, and of an impending change of government; but these did not come within the horizon of my companion. I could see nothing recorded in the shape of crime which was not commonplace and futile. Holmes groaned and resumed his restless meanderings.

'The London criminal is certainly a dull fellow,' said

he in the querulous voice of the sportsman whose game has failed him. 'Look out of this window, Watson. See how the figures loom up, are dimly seen, and then blend once more into the cloud-bank. The thief or the murderer could roam London on such a day as the tiger does the jungle, unseen until he pounces, and then evident only to his victim.'

'There have,' said I, 'been numerous petty thefts.'

Holmes snorted his contempt.

'This great and sombre stage is set for something more worthy than that,' said he. 'It is fortunate for this community that I am not a criminal.'

'It is, indeed!' said I heartily.

'Suppose that I were Brooks or Woodhouse, or any of the fifty men who have good reason for taking my life, how long could I survive against my own pursuit? A summons, a bogus appointment, and all would be over. It is well they don't have days of fog in the Latin countries – the countries of assassination. By Jove! here comes something at last to break our dead monotony.'

It was the maid with a telegram. Holmes tore it open and burst out laughing.

'Well, well! What next?' said he. 'Brother Mycroft is coming round.'

'Why not?' I asked.

'Why not? It is as if you met a tramcar coming down a country lane. Mycroft has his rails and he runs on them. His Pall Mall lodgings, the Diogenes Club, Whitehall – that is his cycle. Once, and only once, he has been here. What upheaval can possibly have derailed him?'

'Does he not explain?'

Holmes handed me his brother's telegram.

Must see you over Cadogan West. Coming at once.
                                        MYCROFT.

'Cadogan West? I have heard the name.'

'It recalls nothing to my mind. But that Mycroft should break out in this erratic fashion! A planet might as well leave its orbit. By the way, do you know what Mycroft is?'

I had some vague recollection of an explanation at the time of the Adventure of the Greek Interpreter.

'You told me that he had some small office under the British government.'

Holmes chuckled.

'I did not know you quite so well in those days. One has to be discreet when one talks of high matters of state. You are right in thinking that he is under the British government. You would also be right in a sense if you said that occasionally he *is* the British government.'

'My dear Holmes!'

'I thought I might surprise you. Mycroft draws four hundred and fifty pounds a year, remains a subordinate, has no ambitions of any kind, will receive neither honour nor title, but remains the most indispensable man in the country.'

'But how?'

'Well, his position is unique. He has made it for himself. There has never been anything like it before, nor will be again. He has the tidiest and most orderly brain, with the greatest capacity for storing facts, of any man living. The same great powers which I have turned to the detection of crime he has used for this particular business. The conclusions of every department are passed to him, and he is the central exchange, the clearing-house, which makes out the balance. All other men are specialists, but his specialism is omniscience. We will suppose that a minister needs information as to a point which involves the Navy, India, Canada and the bimetallic question; he could get his separate advices from various departments upon each, but only Mycroft can focus them all, and say offhand how each factor would affect the other. They began by using him as a short-cut, a convenience; now he has made himself an essential. In that great brain of his everything is pigeonholed and can be handed out in an instant. Again and again his word has decided the national policy. He lives in it. He thinks of nothing else save when, as an intellectual exercise, he unbends if I call upon him and ask him to advise me on one of my little problems. But Jupiter is descending today. What on earth can it mean? Who is Cadogan West, and what is he to Mycroft?'

'I have it,' I cried, and plunged among the litter of papers upon the sofa. 'Yes, yes, here he is, sure enough! Cadogan West was the young man who was found dead on the Underground on Tuesday morning.'

Holmes sat up at attention, his pipe halfway to his lips.

'This must be serious, Watson. A death which has caused my brother to alter his habits can be no ordinary one. What in the world can he have to do with it? The case was featureless as I remember it. The young man had apparently fallen out of the train and killed himself. He had not been robbed, and there was no particular reason to suspect violence. Is that not so?'

'There has been an inquest,' said I, 'and a good many fresh facts have come out. Looked at more closely, I should certainly say that it was a curious case.'

'Judging by its effect upon my brother, I should think it must be a most extraordinary one.' He snuggled down in his armchair. 'Now, Watson, let us have the facts.'

'The man's name was Arthur Cadogan West. He was twenty-seven years of age, unmarried, and a clerk at Woolwich Arsenal.'

'Government employ. Behold the link with brother Mycroft!'

'He left Woolwich suddenly on Monday night. Was last seen by his fiancée, Miss Violet Westbury, whom he left abruptly in the fog about seven-thirty that evening. There was no quarrel between them and she can give no motive for his action. The next thing heard of him was when his dead body was discovered by a platelayer named Mason, just outside Aldgate Station on the Underground system in London.'

'When?'

'The body was found at six on the Tuesday morning. It was lying wide of the metals upon the left hand of the track as one goes eastward, at a point close to the station, where the line emerges from the tunnel in which it runs. The head was badly crushed – an injury which might well have been caused by a fall from the train. The body could only have come on the line in that way. Had it been carried down from any neighbouring street, it must have passed the station barriers, where a collector is always standing. This point seems absolutely certain.'

'Very good. The case is definite enough. The man, dead or alive, either fell or was precipitated from a train. So much is clear to me. Continue.'

'The trains which traverse the lines of rail beside which the body was found are those which run from west to east, some being purely Metropolitan, and some from Willesden and outlying junctions. It can be stated for certain that this young man, when he met his death, was travelling in this direction at some late hour of the night, but at what point he entered the train it is impossible to state.'

'His ticket, of course, would show that.'

'There was no ticket in his pockets.'

'No ticket! Dear me, Watson, this is really very singular. According to my experience it is not possible to reach the platform of a Metropolitan train without exhibiting one's ticket. Presumably, then, the young man had one. Was it taken from him in order to conceal the station from which he came? It is possible. Or did he drop it in the carriage? That is also possible. But the point is of curious interest. I understand that there was no sign of robbery?'

'Apparently not. There is a list here of his possessions. His purse contained two pounds fifteen. He had also a chequebook on the Woolwich branch of the Capital and Counties Bank. Through this his identity was established. There were also two dress-circle tickets for the Woolwich Theatre, dated for that very evening. Also a small packet of technical papers.'

Holmes gave an exclamation of satisfaction.

'There we have it at last, Watson! British government – Woolwich Arsenal – technical papers – brother Mycroft, the chain is complete. But here he comes, if I am not mistaken, to speak for himself.'

A moment later the tall and portly form of Mycroft Holmes was ushered into the room. Heavily built and massive, there was a suggestion of uncouth physical inertia in the figure, but above this unwieldy frame there was perched a head so masterful in its brow, so alert in its steel-grey, deep-set eyes, so firm in its lips, and so subtle in its play of expression, that after the first glance one forgot the gross body and remembered only the dominant mind.

At his heels came our old friend Lestrade, of Scotland Yard – thin and austere. The gravity of both their faces foretold some weighty quest. The detective shook hands without a word. Mycroft Holmes struggled out of his overcoat and subsided into an armchair.

'A most annoying business, Sherlock,' said he. 'I extremely dislike altering my habits, but the powers that be would take no denial. In the present state of Siam it is most awkward that I should be away from the office. But it is a real crisis. I have never seen the Prime Minister so upset. As to the Admiralty – it is buzzing like an overturned beehive. Have you read up the case?'

'We have just done so. What were the technical papers?'

'Ah, there's the point! Fortunately, it has not come out. The Press would be furious if it did. The papers which this wretched youth had in his pocket were the plans of the Bruce-Partington submarine.'

Mycroft Holmes spoke with a solemnity which showed his sense of the importance of the subject. His brother and I sat expectant.

'Surely you have heard of it? I thought everyone had heard of it.'

'Only as a name.'

'Its importance can hardly be exaggerated. It has been the most jealously guarded of all govern-ment secrets. You may take it from me that naval warfare becomes impossible within the radius of a

Bruce-Partington's operation. Two years ago a very large sum was smuggled through the Estimates and was expended in acquiring a monopoly of the invention. Every effort has been made to keep the secret. The plans, which are exceedingly intricate, comprising some thirty separate patents, each essential to the working of the whole, are kept in an elaborate safe in a confidential office adjoining the Arsenal, with burglar-proof doors and windows. Under no conceivable circumstances were the plans to be taken from the office. If the Chief Constructor of the Navy desired to consult them, even he was forced to go to the Woolwich office for the purpose. And yet here we find them in the pocket of a dead junior clerk in the heart of London. From an official point of view it's simply awful.'

'But you have recovered them?'

'No, Sherlock, no! That's the pinch. We have not. Ten papers were taken from Woolwich. There were seven in the pocket of Cadogan West. The three most essential are gone – stolen, vanished. You must drop everything, Sherlock. Never mind your usual petty puzzles of the police-court. It's a vital international problem that you have to solve. Why did Cadogan West take the papers, where are the missing ones, how did he die, how came his body where it was found, how can the evil be set right? Find an answer to all these questions, and you will have done good service for your country.'

'Why do you not solve it yourself, Mycroft? You can see as far as I.'

'Possibly, Sherlock. But it is a question of getting details. Give me your details, and from an armchair I will return you an excellent expert opinion. But to run here and run there, to cross-question railway guards, and lie on my face with a lens to my eye – it is not my *métier*. No, you are the one man who can clear the matter up. If you have a fancy to see your name in the next honours list – '

My friend smiled and shook his head.

'I play the game for the game's own sake,' said he. 'But the problem certainly presents some points of interest, and I shall be very pleased to look into it. Some more facts, please.'

'I have jotted down the more essential ones upon this sheet of paper, together with a few addresses which you will find of service. The actual official guardian of the papers is the famous government expert, Sir James Walter, whose decorations and sub-titles fill two lines of a book of reference. He has grown grey in the service, is a gentleman, a favoured guest in the most exalted houses, and, above all, a man whose patriotism is beyond suspicion. He is one of two who have a key of the safe. I may add that the papers were undoubtedly in the office during working hours on Monday, and that Sir James left for London about three o'clock taking his key with him. He was at the house of Admiral Sinclair at Barclay Square during the whole of the evening when this incident occurred.'

'Has the fact been verified?'

'Yes; his brother, Colonel Valentine Walter, has testified to his departure from Woolwich, and Admiral Sinclair to his arrival in London; so Sir James is no longer a direct factor in the problem.'

'Who was the other man with a key?'

'The senior clerk and draughtsman, Mr Sidney Johnson. He is a man of forty, married, with five children. He is a silent, morose man, but he has, on the whole, an excellent record in the public service. He is unpopular with his colleagues, but a hard worker. According to his own account, corroborated only by the word of his wife, he was at home the whole of Monday evening after office hours, and his key has never left the watch-chain upon which it hangs.'

'Tell us about Cadogan West.'

'He has been ten years in the service and has done good work. He has the reputation of being hot-headed and imperious, but a straight, honest man. We have nothing against him. He was next Sidney Johnson in the office. His duties brought him into daily, personal contact with the plans. No one else had the handling of them.'

'Who locked up the plans that night?'

'Mr Sidney Johnson, the senior clerk.'

'Well, it is surely perfectly clear who took them away. They are actually found upon the person of this junior clerk, Cadogan West. That seems final, does it not?'

'It does, Sherlock, and yet it leaves so much un-explained. In the first place, why did he take them?'

'I presume they were of value?'

'He could have got several thousands for them very easily.'

'Can you suggest any possible motive for taking the papers to London except to sell them?'

'No, I cannot.'

'Then we must take that as our working hypothesis. Young West took the papers. Now this could only be done by having a false key – '

'Several false keys. He had to open the building and the room.'

'He had, then, several false keys. He took the papers

to London to sell the secret, intending, no doubt, to have the plans themselves back in the safe next morning before they were missed. While in London on this treasonable mission he met his end.'

'How?'

'We will suppose that he was travelling back to Woolwich when he was killed and thrown out of the compartment.'

'Aldgate, where the body was found, is considerably past the station for London Bridge, which would be his route to Woolwich.'

'Many circumstances could be imagined under which he would pass London Bridge. There was someone in the carriage, for example, with whom he was having an absorbing interview. This interview led to a violent scene in which he lost his life. Possibly he tried to leave the carriage, fell out on the line, and so met his end. The other closed the door. There was a thick fog, and nothing could be seen.'

'No better explanation can be given with our present knowledge; and yet consider, Sherlock, how much you leave untouched. We will suppose, for argument's sake, that young Cadogan West *had* determined to convey these papers to London. He would naturally have made an appointment with the foreign agent and kept his evening clear. Instead of that he took two tickets for the theatre, escorted his fiancée halfway there, and then suddenly disappeared.'

'A blind,' said Lestrade, who had sat listening with some impatience to the conversation.

'A very singular one. That is objection number one. Objection number two: We will suppose that he reaches London and sees the foreign agent. He must bring back the papers before morning or the loss will be

495

discovered. He took away ten. Only seven were in his pocket. What had become of the other three? He certainly would not leave them of his own free will. Then, again, where is the price of his treason? One would have expected to find a large sum of money in his pocket.'

'It seems to me perfectly clear,' said Lestrade. 'I have no doubt at all as to what occurred. He took the papers to sell them. He saw the agent. They could not agree as to price. He started home again, but the agent went with him. In the train the agent murdered him, took the more essential papers, and threw his body from the carriage. That would account for everything, would it not?'

'Why had he no ticket?'

'The ticket would have shown which station was nearest the agent's house. Therefore he took it from the murdered man's pocket.'

'Good, Lestrade, very good,' said Holmes. 'Your theory holds together. But if this is true, then the case is at an end. On the one hand, the traitor is dead. On the other, the plans of the Bruce-Partington submarine are presumably already on the Continent. What is there for us to do?'

'To act, Sherlock – to act!' cried Mycroft, springing to his feet. 'All my instincts are against this explanation. Use your powers! Go to the scene of the crime! See the people concerned! Leave no stone unturned! In all your career you have never had so great a chance of serving your country.'

'Well, well!' said Holmes, shrugging his shoulders. 'Come, Watson! And you, Lestrade, could you favour us with your company for an hour or two? We will begin our investigation by a visit to Aldgate Station.

Goodbye, Mycroft. I shall let you have a report before evening, but I warn you in advance that you have little to expect.'

An hour later Holmes, Lestrade and I stood upon the Underground railroad at the point where it emerges from the tunnel immediately before Aldgate Station. A courteous red-faced old gentleman represented the railway company.

'This is where the young man's body lay,' said he, indicating a spot about three feet from the metals. 'It could not have fallen from above, for these, as you see, are all blank walls. Therefore, it could only have come from a train, and that train, so far as we can trace it, must have passed about midnight on Monday.'

'Have the carriages been examined for any sign of violence?'

'There are no such signs, and no ticket has been found.'

'No record of a door being found open?'

'None.'

'We have had some fresh evidence this morning,' said Lestrade. 'A passenger who passed Aldgate in an ordinary Metropolitan train about eleven-forty on Monday night declares that he heard a heavy thud, as of a body striking the line, just before the train reached the station. There was dense fog, however, and nothing could be seen. He made no report of it at the time. Why, whatever is the matter with Mr Holmes?'

My friend was standing with an expression of strained intensity upon his face, staring at the railway metals where they curved out of the tunnel. Aldgate is a junction, and there was a network of points. On these his eager, questioning eyes were fixed, and I saw on his keen, alert face that tightening of the lips, that quiver of the nostrils, and concentration of the heavy, tufted brows which I knew so well.

'Points,' he muttered; 'the points.'

'What of it? What do you mean?'

'I suppose there are no great number of points on a system such as this?'

'No; they are very few.'

'And a curve, too. Points, and a curve. By Jove! if it were only so.'

'What is it, Mr Holmes? Have you a clue?'

'An idea – an indication, no more. But the case certainly grows in interest. Unique, perfectly unique, and yet why not? I do not see any indications of bleeding on the line.'

'There were hardly any.'

'But I understand that there was a considerable wound.'

'The bone was crushed, but there was no great external injury.'

'And yet one would have expected some bleeding. Would it be possible for me to inspect the train which contained the passenger who heard the thud of a fall in the fog?'

'I fear not, Mr Holmes. The train has been broken up before now, and the carriages redistributed.'

'I can assure you, Mr Holmes,' said Lestrade, 'that every carriage has been carefully examined. I saw to it myself.'

It was one of my friend's most obvious weaknesses that he was impatient with less alert intelligences than his own.

'Very likely,' said he, turning away. 'As it happens, it was not the carriages which I desired to examine.

Watson, we have done all we can here. We need not trouble you any further, Mr Lestrade. I think our investigations must now carry us to Woolwich.'

At London Bridge, Holmes wrote a telegram to his brother, which he handed to me before dispatching it. It ran thus:

> See some light in the darkness, but it may possibly flicker out. Meanwhile, please send by messenger, to await return at Baker Street, a complete list of all foreign spies or international agents known to be in England, with full address. SHERLOCK

'That should be helpful, Watson,' he remarked as we took our seats in the Woolwich train. 'We certainly owe brother Mycroft a debt for having introduced us to what promises to be a really very remarkable case.'

His eager face still wore that expression of intense and high-strung energy, which showed me that some novel and suggestive circumstance had opened up a stimulating line of thought. See the foxhound with hanging ears and drooping tail as it lolls about the kennels, and compare it with the same hound as, with gleaming eyes and straining muscles, it runs upon a breast-high scent – such was the change in Holmes since the morning. He was a different man from the limp and lounging figure in the mouse-coloured dressing-gown who had prowled so restlessly only a few hours before round the fog-girt room.

'There is material here. There is scope,' said he. 'I am dull indeed not to have understood its possibilities.'

'Even now they are dark to me.'

'The end is dark to me also, but I have hold of one idea which may lead us far. The man met his death elsewhere, and his body was on the *roof* of a carriage.'

'On the roof!'

'Remarkable, is it not? But consider the facts. Is it a coincidence that it is found at the very point where the train pitches and sways as it comes round on the points? Is not that the place where an object upon the roof might be expected to fall off? The points would affect no object inside the train. Either the body fell from the roof, or a very curious coincidence has occurred. But now consider the question of the blood. Of course, there was no bleeding on the line if the body had bled elsewhere. Each fact is suggestive in itself. Together they have a cumulative force.'

'And the ticket, too!' I cried.

'Exactly. We could not explain the absence of a ticket. This would explain it. Everything fits together.'

'But suppose it were so, we are still as far as ever from unravelling the mystery of his death. Indeed, it becomes not simpler but stranger.'

'Perhaps,' said Holmes, thoughtfully, 'perhaps.' He relapsed into a silent reverie, which lasted until the slow train drew up at last in Woolwich Station. There he called a cab and drew Mycroft's paper from his pocket.

'We have quite a little round of afternoon calls to make,' said he. 'I think that Sir James Walter claims our first attention.'

The house of the famous official was a fine villa with green lawns stretching down to the Thames. As we reached it the fog was lifting, and a thin, watery sunshine was breaking through. A butler answered our ring.

'Sir James, sir!' said he with solemn face. 'Sir James died this morning.'

'Good heavens!' cried Holmes in amazement. 'How did he die?'

'Perhaps you would care to step in, sir, and see his brother, Colonel Valentine?'

'Yes, we had best do so.'

We were ushered into a dim-lit drawing-room, where an instant later we were joined by a very tall, handsome, light-bearded man of fifty, the younger brother of the dead scientist. His wild eyes, stained cheeks, and unkempt hair all spoke of the sudden blow which had fallen upon the household. He was hardly articulate as he spoke of it.

'It was this horrible scandal,' said he. 'My brother, Sir James, was a man of very sensitive honour, and he could not survive such an affair. It broke his heart. He was always so proud of the efficiency of his department, and this was a crushing blow.'

'We had hoped that he might have given us some indications which would have helped us to clear the matter up.'

'I assure you that it was all a mystery to him as it is to you and to all of us. He had already put all his knowledge at the disposal of the police. Naturally he had no doubt that Cadogan West was guilty. But all the rest was inconceivable.'

'You cannot throw any new light upon the affair?'

'I know nothing myself save what I have read or heard. I have no desire to be discourteous, but you can understand, Mr Holmes, that we are much disturbed at present, and I must ask you to hasten this interview to an end.'

'This is indeed an unexpected development,' said my friend when we had regained the cab. 'I wonder if the death was natural, or whether the poor old fellow killed himself! If the latter, may it be taken as some sign of self-reproach for duty neglected? We must leave that question to the future. Now we shall turn to the Cadogan Wests.'

A small but well-kept house in the outskirts of the town sheltered the bereaved mother. The old lady was too dazed with grief to be of any use to us, but at her side was a white-faced young lady, who introduced herself as Miss Violet Westbury, the fiancée of the dead man, and the last to see him upon that fatal night.

'I cannot explain it, Mr Holmes,' she said. 'I have not shut an eye since the tragedy, thinking, thinking, thinking, night and day, what the true meaning of it can be. Arthur was the most single-minded, chivalrous, patriotic man upon earth. He would have cut his right hand off before he would sell a state secret confided to his keeping. It is absurd, impossible, preposterous to anyone who knew him.'

'But the facts, Miss Westbury?'

'Yes, yes; I admit I cannot explain them.'

'Was he in any want of money?'

'No; his needs were very simple and his salary ample. He had saved a few hundreds, and we were to marry at the New Year.'

'No signs of any mental excitement? Come, Miss Westbury, be absolutely frank with us.'

The quick eye of my companion had noted some change in her manner. She coloured and hesitated.

'Yes,' she said at last, 'I had a feeling that there was something on his mind.'

'For long?'

'Only for the last week or so. He was thoughtful and worried. Once I pressed him about it. He admitted that there was something, and that it was concerned with his official life. "It is too serious for me to speak about, even to you," said he. I could get nothing more.'

Holmes looked grave.

'Go on, Miss Westbury. Even if it seems to tell against him, go on. We cannot say what it may lead to.'

'Indeed, I have nothing more to tell. Once or twice it seemed to me that he was on the point of telling me something. He spoke one evening of the importance of the secret, and I have some recollection that he said that no doubt foreign spies would pay a great deal to have it.'

My friend's face grew graver still.

'Anything else?'

'He said that we were slack about such matters – that it would be easy for a traitor to get the plans.'

'Was it only recently that he made such remarks?'

'Yes, quite recently.'

'Now tell us of that last evening.'

'We were to go to the theatre. The fog was so thick that a cab was useless. We walked, and our way took us close to the office. Suddenly he darted away into the fog.'

'Without a word?'

'He gave an exclamation; that was all. I waited but he never returned. Then I walked home. Next morning, after the office opened, they came to enquire. About twelve o'clock we heard the terrible news. Oh, Mr Holmes, if you could only, only save his honour! It was so much to him.'

Holmes shook his head sadly.

'Come, Watson,' said he, 'our ways lie elsewhere. Our next station must be the office from which the papers were taken.'

'It was black enough before against this young man, but our enquiries make it blacker,' he remarked as the cab lumbered off. 'His coming marriage gives a motive

503

for the crime. He naturally wanted money. The idea was in his head, since he spoke about it. He nearly made the girl an accomplice in the treason by telling her his plans. It is all very bad.'

'But surely, Holmes, character goes for something? Then, again, why should he leave the girl in the street and dart away to commit a felony?'

'Exactly! There are certainly objections. But it is a formidable case which they have to meet.'

Mr Sidney Johnson, the senior clerk, met us at the office and received us with that respect which my companion's card always commanded. He was a thin, gruff, bespectacled man of middle age, his cheeks haggard, and his hands twitching from the nervous strain to which he had been subjected.

'It is bad, Mr Holmes, very bad! Have you heard of the death of the chief?'

'We have just come from his house.'

'The place is disorganised. The chief dead, Cadogan West dead, our papers stolen. And yet, when we closed our door on Monday evening, we were as efficient an office as any in the government service. Good God, it's dreadful to think of! That West, of all men, should have done such a thing!'

'You are sure of his guilt, then?'

'I can see no other way out of it. And yet I would have trusted him as I trust myself.'

'At what hour was the office closed on Monday?'

'At five.'

'Did you close it?'

'I am always the last man out.'

'Where were the plans?'

'In that safe. I put them there myself.'

'Is there no watchman to the building?'

'There is, but he has other departments to look after as well. He is an old soldier and a most trustworthy man. He saw nothing that evening. Of course the fog was very thick.'

'Suppose that Cadogan West wished to make his way into the building after hours; he would need three keys, would he not, before he could reach the papers?'

'Yes, he would. The key of the outer door, the key of the office, and the key of the safe.'

'Only Sir James Walter and you had those keys?'

'I had no keys of the doors – only of the safe.'

'Was Sir James a man who was orderly in his habits?'

'Yes, I think he was. I know that so far as those three keys are concerned he kept them on the same ring. I have often seen them there.'

'And that ring went with him to London?'

'He said so.'

'And your key never left your possession?'

'Never.'

'Then West, if he is the culprit, must have had a duplicate. And yet none was found upon his body. One other point: if a clerk in this office desired to sell the plans, would it not be simpler to copy the plans for himself than to take the originals, as was actually done?'

'It would take considerable technical knowledge to copy the plans in an effective way.'

'But I suppose either Sir James, or you, or West had that technical knowledge?'

'No doubt we had, but I beg you won't try to drag me into the matter, Mr Holmes. What is the use of our speculating in this way when the original plans were actually found on West?'

'Well, it is certainly singular that he should run the risk of taking originals if he could safely have taken copies, which would have equally served his turn.'

'Singular, no doubt – and yet he did so.'

'Every enquiry in this case reveals something in-explicable. Now there are three papers still missing. They are, as I understand, the vital ones.'

'Yes, that is so.'

'Do you mean to say that anyone holding these three papers, and without the seven others, could construct a Bruce-Partington submarine?'

'I reported to that effect to the Admiralty. But today I have been over the drawings again, and I am not so sure of it. The double valves with the automatic self-adjusting slots are drawn in one of the papers which have been returned. Until the foreigners had invented that for themselves they could not make the boat. Of course they might soon get over the difficulty.'

'But the three missing drawings are the most important?'

'Undoubtedly.'

'I think, with your permission, I will now take a stroll round the premises. I do not recall any other question which I desired to ask.'

He examined the lock of the safe, the door of the room, and finally the iron shutters of the window. It was only when we were on the lawn outside that his interest was strongly excited. There was a laurel bush outside the window, and several of the branches bore signs of having been twisted or snapped. He examined them carefully with his lens, and then some dim and vague marks upon the earth beneath. Finally he asked the chief clerk to close the iron shutters, and he pointed out to me that they hardly met in the centre, and that it would be possible for anyone outside to see what was going on within the room.

'The indications are ruined by three days' delay. They may mean something or nothing. Well, Watson, I do not think that Woolwich can help us further. It is a small crop which we have gathered. Let us see if we can do better in London.'

Yet we added one more sheaf to our harvest before we left Woolwich Station. The clerk in the ticket-office was able to say with confidence that he saw Cadogan West – whom he knew well by sight – upon the Monday night, and that he went to London by the eight-fifteen to London Bridge. He was alone and took a single third-class ticket. The clerk was struck at the time by his excited and nervous manner. So shaky was he that he could hardly pick up his change, and the clerk had helped him with it. A reference to the timetable showed that the eight-fifteen was the first train which it was possible for West to take after he had left the lady about seven-thirty.

'Let us reconstruct, Watson,' said Holmes after half an hour of silence. 'I am not aware that in all our joint researches we have ever had a case which was more difficult to get at. Every fresh advance which we make only reveals a fresh ridge beyond. And yet we have surely made some appreciable progress.

'The effect of our enquiries at Woolwich has in the main been against young Cadogan West; but the indications at the window would lend themselves to a more favourable hypothesis. Let us suppose, for example, that he had been approached by some foreign agent. It might have been done under such pledges as would have prevented him from speaking of it, and yet would have affected his thoughts in the direction indicated by his remarks to his fiancée. Very good. We will now suppose that as he went to the theatre with the young lady he suddenly, in the fog, caught a glimpse of this same agent going in the direction of the office. He was an impetuous man, quick in his decisions. Everything gave way to his duty. He followed the man, reached the window, saw the abstraction of the documents, and pursued the thief. In this way we get over the objection that no one would take originals when he could make copies. This outsider had to take originals. So far it holds together.'

'What is the next step?'

'Then we come into difficulties. One would imagine that under such circumstances the first act of young Cadogan West would be to seize the villain and raise the alarm. Why did he not do so? Could it have been an official superior who took the papers? That would explain West's conduct. Or could the chief have given West the slip in the fog, and West started at once to London to head him off from his own rooms, presuming that he knew where the rooms were? The call must have been very pressing, since he left his girl standing in the fog and made no effort to communicate with her. Our scent runs cold here, and there is a vast gap between either hypothesis and the laying of West's body, with seven papers in his pocket, on the roof of a Metropolitan train. My instinct now is to work from the other end. If Mycroft has given us the list of addresses we may be able to pick our man and follow two tracks instead of one.'

Surely enough, a note awaited us at Baker Street. A government messenger had brought it post-haste. Holmes glanced at it and threw it over to me.

There are numerous small fry, but few who would handle so big an affair. The only men worth considering are Adolph Meyer, of 13 Great George Street, Westminster; Louis La Rothiere, of Campden Mansions, Notting Hill; and Hugo Oberstein, 13 Caulfield Gardens, Kensington. The latter was known to be in town on Monday and is now reported as having left. Glad to hear you have seen some light. The Cabinet awaits your final report with the utmost anxiety. Urgent representations have arrived from the very highest quarter. The whole force of the state is at your back if you should need it.

MYCROFT

'I'm afraid,' said Holmes, smiling, 'that all the queen's horses and all the queen's men cannot avail in this matter.' He had spread out his big map of London and leaned eagerly over it. 'Well, well,' said he presently with an exclamation of satisfaction, 'things are turning a little in our direction at last. Why, Watson, I do honestly believe that we are going to pull it off, after all.' He slapped me on the shoulder with a sudden burst of hilarity. 'I am going out now. It is only a reconnaissance. I will do nothing serious without my trusted comrade and biographer at my elbow. Do you stay here, and the odds are that you will see me again in an hour or two. If time hangs heavy get foolscap and a pen, and begin your narrative of how we saved the state.'

I felt some reflection of his elation in my own mind, for I knew well that he would not depart so far from his usual austerity of demeanour unless there was good cause for exultation. All the long November evening I waited, filled with impatience for his return. At last, shortly after nine o'clock, there arrived a messenger with a note:

Am dining at Goldini's Restaurant, Gloucester Road, Kensington. Please come at once and join me there. Bring with you a jemmy, a dark lantern, a chisel, and a revolver.   S.H.

It was a nice equipment for a respectable citizen to carry through the dim, fog-draped streets. I stowed them all discreetly away in my overcoat and drove straight to the address given. There sat my friend at a little round table near the door of the garish Italian restaurant.

'Have you had something to eat? Then join me in a coffee and curaçao. Try one of the proprietor's cigars. They are less poisonous than one would expect. Have you the tools?'

'They are here, in my overcoat.'

'Excellent. Let me give you a short sketch of what I have done, with some indication of what we are about to do. Now it must be evident to you, Watson, that this young man's body was *placed* on the roof of the train. That was clear from the instant that I determined the fact that it was from the roof, and not from a carriage, that he had fallen.'

'Could it not have been dropped from a bridge?'

'I should say it was impossible. If you examine the roofs you will find that they are slightly rounded, and there is no railing round them. Therefore, we can say for certain that young Cadogan West was placed on it.'

'How could he be placed there?'

'That was the question which we had to answer. There is only one possible way. You are aware that the Underground runs clear of tunnels at some points in the West End. I had a vague memory that as I have travelled by it I have occasionally seen windows just above my head. Now, suppose that a train halted under such a window, would there be any difficulty in laying a body upon the roof?'

'It seems most improbable.'

'We must fall back upon the old axiom that when all other contingencies fail, whatever remains, however improbable, must be the truth. Here all other contingencies *have* failed. When I found that the leading international agent, who had just left London, lived in a row of houses which abutted upon the Underground, I was so pleased that you were a little astonished at my sudden frivolity.'

'Oh, that was it, was it?'

'Yes, that was it. Mr Hugo Oberstein, of 13 Caulfield Gardens, had become my objective. I began my operations at Gloucester Road Station, where a very helpful official walked with me along the track and allowed me to satisfy myself not only that the back-stair windows of Caulfield Gardens open on the line, but the even more essential fact that, owing to the intersection of one of the larger railways, the Underground trains are frequently held motionless for some minutes at that very spot.'

'Splendid, Holmes! You have got it!'

'So far – so far, Watson. We advance, but the goal is afar. Well, having seen the back of Caulfield Gardens, I visited the front and satisfied myself that the bird was indeed flown. It is a considerable house, unfurnished, so far as I could judge, in the upper rooms. Oberstein lived there with a single valet, who was probably a confederate entirely in his confidence. We must bear in mind that Oberstein has gone to the Continent to dispose of his booty, but not with any idea of flight; for he had no reason to fear a warrant, and the idea of an amateur domiciliary visit would certainly never occur to him. Yet that is precisely what we are about to make.'

'Could we not get a warrant and legalise it?'

'Hardly on the evidence.'

'What can we hope to do?'

'We cannot tell what correspondence may be there.'

'I don't like it, Holmes.'

'My dear fellow, you shall keep watch in the street. I'll do the criminal part. It's not a time to stick at trifles. Think of Mycroft's note, of the Admiralty, the Cabinet, the exalted person who waits for news. We are bound to go.'

My answer was to rise from the table.

'You are right, Holmes. We are bound to go.'

He sprang up and shook me by the hand.

'I knew you would not shrink at the last,' said he, and for a moment I saw something in his eyes which was nearer to tenderness than I had ever seen. The next instant he was his masterful, practical self once more.

'It is nearly half a mile, but there is no hurry. Let us walk,' said he. 'Don't drop the instruments, I beg. Your arrest as a suspicious character would be a most unfortunate complication.'

Caulfield Gardens was one of those lines of flat-faced, pillared, and porticoed houses which are so prominent a product of the middle Victorian epoch in the West End of London. Next door there appeared to be a children's party, for the merry buzz of young voices and the clatter of a piano resounded through the night. The fog still hung about and screened us with its friendly shade. Holmes had lit his lantern and flashed it upon the massive door.

'This is a serious proposition,' said he. 'It is certainly bolted as well as locked. We would do better in the area. There is an excellent archway down yonder in case a too zealous policeman should intrude. Give me a hand, Watson, and I'll do the same for you.'

A minute later we were both in the area. Hardly had we reached the dark shadows before the step of the policeman was heard in the fog above. As its soft rhythm died away, Holmes set to work upon the lower door. I saw him stoop and strain until with a sharp crash it flew open. We sprang through into the dark passage, closing the area door behind us. Holmes let the way up the curving, uncarpeted stair. His little fan of yellow light shone upon a low window.

'Here we are, Watson – this must be the one.' He threw it open, and as he did so there was a low, harsh murmur, growing steadily into a loud roar as a train dashed past us in the darkness. Holmes swept his light along the window-sill. It was thickly coated with soot from the passing engines, but the black surface was blurred and rubbed in places.

'You can see where they rested the body. Halloa, Watson! what is this? There can be no doubt that it is a blood mark.' He was pointing to faint discolorations along the woodwork of the window. 'Here it is on the stone of the stair also. The demonstration is complete. Let us stay here until a train stops.'

We had not long to wait. The very next train roared from the tunnel as before, but slowed in the open, and then, with a creaking of brakes, pulled up immediately beneath us. It was not four feet from the window-ledge to the roof of the carriages. Holmes softly closed the window.

'So far we are justified,' said he. 'What do you think of it, Watson?'

'A masterpiece. You have never risen to a greater height.'

'I cannot agree with you there. From the moment that I conceived the idea of the body being upon the roof, which surely was not a very abstruse one, all the rest was inevitable. If it were not for the grave interests involved the affair up to this point would be insignificant. Our difficulties are still before us. But perhaps we may find something here which may help us.'

We had ascended the kitchen stair and entered the suite of rooms upon the first floor. One was a dining-room, severely furnished and containing nothing of interest. A second was a bedroom, which also drew blank. The remaining room appeared more promising, and my companion settled down to a systematic examination. It was littered with books and papers, and was evidently used as a study. Swiftly and methodically Holmes turned over the contents of drawer after drawer and cupboard after cupboard, but no gleam of success came to brighten his austere face. At the end of an hour he was no further than when he started.

'The cunning dog has covered his tracks,' said he. 'He has left nothing to incriminate him. His dangerous correspondence has been destroyed or removed. This is our last chance.'

It was a small tin cashbox which stood upon the writing-desk. Holmes pried it open with his chisel. Several rolls of paper were within, covered with figures and calculations, without any note to show to what they referred. The recurring words, 'water

THE BRUCE-PARTINGTON PLANS

pressure' and 'pressure to the square inch' suggested some possible relation to a submarine. Holmes tossed them all impatiently aside. There only remained an envelope with some small newspaper slips inside it. He shook them out on the table, and at once I saw by his eager face that his hopes had been raised.

'What's this, Watson? Eh? What's this? Record of a series of messages in the advertisements of a paper. *Daily Telegraph* agony column by the print and paper. Right-hand top corner of a page. No dates – but messages arrange themselves. This must be the first: "Hoped to hear sooner. Terms agreed to. Write fully to address given on card. Pierrot."

'Next comes: "Too complex for description. Must have full report. Stuff awaits you when goods delivered. Pierrot."

'Then comes: "Matter presses. Must withdraw offer unless contract completed. Make appointment by letter. Will confirm by advertisement. Pierrot."

'Finally: "Monday night after nine. Two taps. Only ourselves. Do not be so suspicious. Payment in hard cash when goods delivered. Pierrot."

'A fairly complete record, Watson! If we could only get at the man at the other end!' He sat lost in thought, tapping his fingers on the table. Finally he sprang to his feet.

'Well, perhaps it won't be so difficult, after all. There is nothing more to be done here, Watson. I think we might drive round to the offices of the *Daily Telegraph*, and so bring a good day's work to a conclusion.'

Mycroft Holmes and Lestrade had come round by appointment after breakfast next day and Sherlock

Holmes had recounted to them our proceedings of the day before. The professional shook his head over our confessed burglary.

'We can't do these things in the force, Mr Holmes,' said he. 'No wonder you get results that are beyond us. But some of these days you'll go too far, and you'll find yourself and your friend in trouble.'

'For England, home and beauty – eh, Watson? Martyrs on the altar of our country. But what do you think of it, Mycroft?'

'Excellent, Sherlock! Admirable! But what use will you make of it?'

Holmes picked up the *Daily Telegraph* which lay upon the table.

'Have you seen Pierrot's advertisement today?'

'What? Another one?'

'Yes, here it is: "Tonight. Same hour. Same place. Two taps. Most vitally important. Your own safety at stake. Pierrot."

'By George!' cried Lestrade. 'If he answers that we've got him!'

'That was my idea when I put it in. I think if you could both make it convenient to come with us about eight o'clock to Caulfield Gardens we might possibly get a little nearer to a solution.'

One of the most remarkable characteristics of Sherlock Holmes was his power of throwing his brain out of action and switching all his thoughts on to lighter things whenever he had convinced himself that he could no longer work to advantage. I remember that during the whole of that memorable day he lost himself in a monograph which he had undertaken upon the Polyphonic Motets of Lassus. For my own part I had none of this power of detachment, and the day, in consequence, appeared to be interminable. The great national importance of the issue, the suspense in high quarters, the direct nature of the experiment which we were trying – all combined to work upon my nerve. It was a relief to me when at last, after a light dinner, we set out upon our expedition. Lestrade and Mycroft met us by appointment at the outside of Gloucester Road Station. The area door of Oberstein's house had been left open the night before, and it was necessary for me, as Mycroft Holmes absolutely and indignantly declined to climb the railings, to pass in and open the hall door. By nine o'clock we were all seated in the study, waiting patently for our man.

An hour passed and yet another. When eleven struck, the measured beat of the great church clock seemed to sound the dirge of our hopes. Lestrade and Mycroft were fidgeting in their seats and looking twice a minute at their watches. Holmes sat silent and composed, his eyelids half shut, but every sense on the alert. He raised his head with a sudden jerk.

'He is coming,' said he.

There had been a furtive step past the door. Now it returned. We heard a shuffling sound outside, and then two sharp taps with the knocker. Holmes rose, motioning us to remain seated. The gas in the hall was a mere point of light. He opened the outer door, and then as a dark figure slipped past him he closed and fastened it. 'This way!' we heard him say, and a moment later our man stood before us. Holmes had followed him closely, and as the man turned with a cry of surprise and alarm he caught him by the collar and threw him back into the room. Before our prisoner had recovered his balance the door was shut and Holmes standing with his back against it. The man glared round him, staggered, and fell senseless upon the floor. With the shock, his broad-brimmed hat flew from his head, his cravat slipped down from his lips, and there were the long light beard and the soft, handsome delicate features of Colonel Valentine Walter.

Holmes gave a whistle of surprise.

'You can write me down an ass this time, Watson,' said he. 'This was not the bird that I was looking for.'

'Who is he?' asked Mycroft eagerly.

'The younger brother of the late Sir James Walter, the head of the Submarine Department. Yes; yes; I see the fall of the cards. He is coming to. I think that you had best leave his examination to me.'

We had carried the prostrate body to the sofa. Now our prisoner sat up, looked round him with a horror-stricken face, and passed his hand over his forehead, like one who cannot believe his own senses.

'What is this?' he asked. 'I came here to visit Mr Oberstein.'

'Everything is known, Colonel Walter,' said Holmes. 'How an English gentleman could behave in such a manner is beyond my comprehension. But your whole correspondence and relations with Oberstein are within our knowledge. So also are the circumstances connected with the death of young Cadogan West. Let me advise you to gain at least the small credit for repentance and confession, since there are still some details which we can only learn from your lips.'

The man groaned and sank his face in his hands. We waited, but he was silent.

'I can assure you,' said Holmes, 'that every essential is already known. We know that you were pressed for money; that you took an impress of the keys which your brother held; and that you entered into a correspondence with Oberstein, who answered your letters through the advertisement columns of the *Daily Telegraph*. We are aware that you went down to the office in the fog on Monday night, but that you were seen and followed by young Cadogan West, who had probably some previous reason to suspect you. He saw your theft, but could not give the alarm, as it was just possible that you were taking the papers to your brother in London. Leaving all his private concerns, like the good citizen that he was, he followed you closely in the fog and kept at your heels until you reached this very house. There he intervened, and then it was, Colonel Walter, that to treason you added the more terrible crime of murder.'

'I did not! I did not! Before God I swear that I did not!' cried our wretched prisoner.

'Tell us, then, how Cadogan West met his end before you laid him upon the roof of a railway carriage.'

'I will. I swear to you that I will. I did the rest. I confess it. It was just as you say. A Stock Exchange debt had to be paid. I needed the money badly. Oberstein offered me five thousand. It was to save myself from ruin. But as to murder, I am as innocent as you.'

'What happened, then?'

'He had his suspicions before, and he followed me as you describe. I never knew it until I was at the very door. It was thick fog, and one could not see three yards. I had given two taps and Oberstein had come to the door. The young man rushed up and demanded to know what we were about to do with the papers. Oberstein had a short life-preserver. He always carried it with him. As West forced his way after us into the house Oberstein struck him on the head. The blow was a fatal one. He was dead within five minutes. There he lay in the hall, and we were at our wit's end what to do. Then Oberstein had this idea about the trains which halted under his back window. But first he examined the papers which I had brought. He said that three of them were essential, and that he must keep them. "You cannot keep them," said I. "There will be a dreadful row at Woolwich if they are not returned." "I must keep them," said he, "for they are so technical that it is impossible in the time to make copies." "Then they must all go back together tonight," said I. He thought for a little, and then he cried out that he had it. "Three I will keep," said he. "The others we will stuff into the pocket of this young man. When he is found the whole business will assuredly be put to his account." I could see no other way out of it, so we did as he suggested. We waited half an hour at the window before a train stopped. It was so thick that nothing could be seen, and we had no difficulty in lowering West's body on to the train. That was the end of the matter so far as I was concerned.'

'And your brother?'

'He said nothing, but he had caught me once with his keys, and I think that he suspected. I read in his eyes that he suspected. As you know, he never held up his head again.'

There was silence in the room. It was broken by Mycroft Holmes.

'Can you not make reparation? It would ease your conscience, and possibly your punishment.'

'What reparation can I make?'

'Where is Oberstein with the papers?'

'I do not know.'

'Did he give you no address?'

'He said that letters to the Hôtel du Louvre, Paris, would eventually reach him.'

'Then reparation is still within your power,' said Sherlock Holmes.

'I will do anything I can. I owe this fellow no particular goodwill. He has been my ruin and my downfall.'

'Here are paper and pen. Sit at this desk and write to my dictation. Direct the envelope to the address given. That is right. Now the letter:

'DEAR SIR – With regard to our transaction, you will no doubt have observed by now that one essential detail is missing. I have a tracing which will make it complete. This has involved me in extra trouble, however, and I must ask you for a further advance of five hundred pounds. I will not trust it to the post, nor will I take anything but gold or notes. I would come to you abroad, but it would excite remark if I left the country at present. Therefore I shall expect to meet you in the smoking-room of the Charing Cross Hotel at noon on Saturday. Remember that only English notes, or gold, will be taken.

'That will do very well. I shall be very much surprised if it does not fetch our man.'

And it did! It is a matter of history – that secret history of a nation which is often so much more intimate and interesting than its public chronicles – that Oberstein, eager to complete the coup of his lifetime, came to the lure and was safely engulfed for fifteen years in a British prison. In his trunk were found the invaluable

Bruce-Partington plans, which he had put up for auction in all the naval centres of Europe.

Colonel Walter died in prison towards the end of the second year of his sentence. As to Holmes, he returned refreshed to his monograph upon the Polyphonic Motets of Lassus, which has since been printed for private circulation, and is said by experts to be the last word upon the subject. Some weeks afterwards I learned incidentally that my friend spent a day at Windsor, whence he returned with a remarkably fine emerald tiepin. When I asked him if he had bought it, he answered that it was a present from a certain gracious lady in whose interests he had once been fortunate enough to carry out a small commission. He said no more; but I fancy that I could guess at that lady's august name, and I have little doubt that the emerald pin will for ever recall to my friend's memory the adventure of the Bruce-Partington plans.

18

The Dying Detective

Mrs Hudson, the landlady of Sherlock Holmes, was a long-suffering woman. Not only was her first-floor flat invaded at all hours by throngs of singular and often undesirable characters, but her remarkable lodger showed an eccentricity and irregularity in his life which must have sorely tried her patience. His incredible untidiness, his addiction to music at strange hours, his occasional revolver practice within doors, his weird and often malodorous scientific experiments, and the atmosphere of violence and danger which hung around him made him the very worst tenant in London. On the other hand, his payments were princely. I have no doubt that the house might have been purchased at the price which Holmes paid for his rooms during the years that I was with him.

The landlady stood in the deepest awe of him and never dared to interfere with him, however outrageous his proceedings might seem. She was fond of him, too, for he had a remarkable gentleness and courtesy in his dealings with women. He disliked and distrusted the sex, but he was always a chivalrous opponent. Knowing how genuine was her regard for him, I listened earnestly to her story when she came to my rooms in the second year of my married life and told me of the sad condition to which my poor friend was reduced.

'He's dying, Dr Watson,' said she. 'For three days he has been sinking, and I doubt if he will last the day.

He would not let me get a doctor. This morning when I saw his bones sticking out of his face and his great bright eyes looking at me I could stand no more of it. "With your leave or without it, Mr Holmes, I am going for a doctor this very hour," said I. "Let it be Watson, then," said he. I wouldn't waste an hour in coming to him, sir, or you may not see him alive.'

I was horrified, for I had heard nothing of his illness. I need not say that I rushed for my coat and my hat. As we drove back I asked for the details.

'There is little I can tell you, sir. He has been working at a case down at Rotherhithe, in an alley near the river, and he has brought this illness back with him. He took to his bed on Wednesday afternoon and has never moved since. For these three days neither food nor drink has passed his lips.'

'Good God! Why did you not call in a doctor?'

'He wouldn't have it, sir. You know how masterful he is. I didn't dare to disobey him. But he's not long for this world, as you'll see for yourself the moment that you set eyes on him.'

He was indeed a deplorable spectacle. In the dim light of a foggy November day the sick-room was a gloomy spot, but it was that gaunt, wasted face staring at me from the bed which sent a chill to my heart. His eyes had the brightness of fever, there was a hectic flush upon either cheek, and dark crusts clung to his lips; the thin hands upon the coverlet twitched incessantly, his voice was croaking and spasmodic. He lay listlessly as I entered the room, but the sight of me brought a gleam of recognition to his eyes.

'Well, Watson, we seem to have fallen upon evil days,' said he in a feeble voice, but with something of his old carelessness of manner.

'My dear fellow!' I cried, approaching him.

'Stand back! Stand right back!' said he with the sharp imperiousness which I had associated only with moments of crisis. 'If you approach me, Watson, I shall order you out of the house.'

'But why?'

'Because it is my desire. Is that not enough?'

Yes, Mrs Hudson was right. He was more masterful than ever. It was pitiful, however, to see his exhaustion.

'I only wished to help,' I explained.

'Exactly! You will help best by doing what you are told.'

'Certainly, Holmes.'

He relaxed the austerity of his manner.

'You are not angry?' he asked, gasping for breath.

Poor devil, how could I be angry when I saw him lying in such a plight before me?

'It's for your own sake, Watson,' he croaked.

'For *my* sake?'

'I know what is the matter with me. It is a coolie disease from Sumatra – a thing that the Dutch know more about than we, though they have made little of it up to date. One thing only is certain. It is infallibly deadly, and it is horribly contagious.'

He spoke now with a feverish energy, the long hands twitching and jerking as he motioned me away.

'Contagious by touch, Watson – that's it, by touch. Keep your distance and all is well.'

'Good heavens, Holmes! Do you suppose that such a consideration weighs with me for an instant? It would not affect me in the case of a stranger. Do you imagine it would prevent me from doing my duty to so old a friend?'

Again I advanced, but he repulsed me with a look of furious anger.

'If you will stand there I will talk. If you do not you must leave the room.'

I have so deep a respect for the extraordinary qualities of Holmes that I have always deferred to his wishes, even when I least understood them. But now all my professional instincts were aroused. Let him be my master elsewhere, I at least was his in a sick-room.

'Holmes,' said I, 'you are not yourself. A sick man is but a child, and so I will treat you. Whether you like it or not, I will examine your symptoms and treat you for them.'

He looked at me with venomous eyes.

'If I am to have a doctor whether I will or not, let me at least have someone in whom I have confidence,' said he.

'Then you have none in me?'

'In your friendship, certainly. But facts are facts, Watson, and, after all, you are only a general practitioner with very limited experience and mediocre qualifications. It is painful to have to say these things, but you leave me no choice.'

I was bitterly hurt.

'Such a remark is unworthy of you, Holmes. It shows me very clearly the state of your own nerves. But if you have no confidence in me I would not intrude my services. Let me bring Sir Jasper Meek or Penrose Fisher, or any of the best men in London. But someone you *must* have, and that is final. If you think that I am going to stand here and see you die without either helping you myself or bringing anyone else to help you, then you have mistaken your man.'

'You mean well, Watson,' said the sick man

with something between a sob and a groan. 'Shall I demonstrate your own ignorance? What do you know, pray, of Tapanuli fever? What do you know of the black Formosa corruption?'

'I have never heard of either.'

'There are many problems of disease, many strange pathological possibilities, in the East, Watson.' He paused after each sentence to collect his failing strength. 'I have learned so much during some recent researches which have a medico-criminal aspect. It was in the course of them that I contracted this complaint. You can do nothing.'

'Possibly not. But I happen to know that Dr Ainstree, the greatest living authority upon tropical disease, is now in London. All remonstrance is useless, Holmes, I am going this instant to fetch him.' I turned resolutely to the door.

Never have I had such a shock! In an instant, with a tiger-spring, the dying man had intercepted me. I heard the sharp snap of a twisted key. The next moment he had staggered back to his bed, exhausted and panting after his one tremendous out-flame of energy.

'You won't take the key from me by force, Watson. I've got you, my friend. Here you are, and here you will stay until I will otherwise. But I'll humour you.' (All this in little gasps, with terrible struggles for breath between.) 'You've only my own good at heart. Of course I know that very well. You shall have your way, but give me time to get my strength. Not now, Watson, not now. It's four o'clock. At six you can go.'

'This is insanity, Holmes.'

'Only two hours, Watson. I promise you will go at six. Are you content to wait?'

'I seem to have no choice.'

'None in the world, Watson. Thank you, I need no help in arranging the clothes. You will please keep your distance. Now, Watson, there is one other condition that I would make. You will seek help, not from the man you mention, but from the one that I choose.'

'By all means.'

'The first three sensible words that you have uttered since you entered this room, Watson. You will find some books over there. I am somewhat exhausted; I wonder how a battery feels when it pours electricity into a non-conductor? At six, Watson, we resume our conversation.'

But it was destined to be resumed long before that hour, and in circumstances which gave me a shock hardly second to that caused by his spring to the door. I had stood for some minutes looking at the silent figure in the bed. His face was almost covered by the clothes and he appeared to be asleep. Then, unable to settle down to reading, I walked slowly round the room, examining the pictures of celebrated criminals with which every wall was adorned. Finally, in my aimless perambulation, I came to the mantelpiece. A litter of pipes, tobacco-pouches, syringes, penknives, revolver-cartridges, and other debris was scattered over it. In the midst of these was a small black and white ivory box with a sliding lid. It was a neat little thing, and I had stretched out my hand to examine it more closely when –

It was a dreadful cry that he gave – a yell which might have been heard down the street. My skin went cold and my hair bristled at that horrible scream. As I turned I caught a glimpse of a convulsed face and frantic eyes. I stood paralysed, with the little box in my hand.

'Put it down! Down, this instant, Watson – this

instant, I say!' His head sank back upon the pillow and he gave a deep sigh of relief as I replaced the box upon the mantelpiece. 'I hate to have my things touched, Watson. You know that I hate it. You fidget me beyond endurance. You, a doctor – you are enough to drive a patient into an asylum. Sit down, man, and let me have my rest!'

The incident left a most unpleasant impression upon my mind. The violent and causeless excitement, followed by this brutality of speech, so far removed from his usual suavity, showed me how deep was the disorganisation of his mind. Of all ruins, that of a noble mind is the most deplorable. I sat in silent dejection until the stipulated time had passed. He seemed to have been watching the clock as well as I, for it was hardly six before he began to talk with the same feverish animation as before.

'Now, Watson,' said he. 'Have you any change in your pocket?'

'Yes.'

'Any silver?'

'A good deal.'

'How many half-crowns?'

'I have five.'

'Ah, too few! Too few! How very unfortunate, Watson! However, such as they are you can put them in your watch pocket. And all the rest of your money in your left trouser pocket. Thank you. It will balance you so much better like that.'

This was raving insanity. He shuddered, and again made a sound between a cough and a sob.

'You will now light the gas, Watson, but you will be very careful that not for one instant shall it be more than half on. I implore you to be careful, Watson.

Thank you, that is excellent. No, you need not draw the blind. Now you will have the kindness to place some letters and papers upon this table within my reach. Thank you. Now some of that litter from the mantelpiece. Excellent, Watson! There is a sugar-tongs there. Kindly raise that small ivory box with its assistance. Place it here among the papers. Good! You can now go and fetch Mr Culverton Smith, of 13 Lower Burke Street.'

To tell the truth, my desire to fetch a doctor had somewhat weakened, for poor Holmes was so obviously delirious that it seemed dangerous to leave him. However, he was as eager now to consult the person named as he had been obstinate in refusing.

'I never heard the name,' said I.

'Possibly not, my good Watson. It may surprise you to know that the man upon earth who is best versed in this disease is not a medical man, but a planter. Mr Culverton Smith is a well-known resident of Sumatra, now visiting London. An outbreak of the disease upon his plantation, which was distant from medical aid, caused him to study it himself, with some rather far-reaching consequences. He is a very methodical person, and I did not desire you to start before six, because I was well aware that you would not find him in his study. If you could persuade him to come here and give us the benefit of his unique experience of this disease, the investigation of which has been his dearest hobby, I cannot doubt that he could help me.'

I give Holmes's remarks as a consecutive whole and will not attempt to indicate how they were interrupted by gaspings for breath and those clutchings of his hands which indicated the pain from which he was suffering. His appearance had changed for the worse during the few hours that I had been with him. Those hectic spots were more pronounced, the eyes shone more brightly out of darker hollows, and a cold sweat glimmered upon his brow. He still retained, however, the jaunty gallantry of his speech. To the last gasp he would always be the master.

'You will tell him exactly how you have left me,' said he. 'You will convey the very impression which is in your own mind – a dying man – a dying and delirious man. Indeed, I cannot think why the whole bed of the ocean is not one solid mass of oysters, so prolific the creatures seem. Ah, I am wandering! Strange how the brain controls the brain! What was I saying, Watson?'

'My directions for Mr Culverton Smith.'

'Ah, yes, I remember. My life depends upon it. Plead with him, Watson. There is no good feeling between us. His nephew, Watson – I had suspicions of foul play and I allowed him to see it. The boy died horribly. He has a grudge against me. You will soften him, Watson. Beg him, pray him, get him here by any means. He can save me – only he!'

'I will bring him in a cab, if I have to carry him down to it.'

'You will do nothing of the sort. You will persuade him to come. And then you will return in front of him. Make any excuse so as not to come with him. Don't forget, Watson. You won't fail me. You never did fail me. No doubt there are natural enemies which limit the increase of the creatures. You and I, Watson, we have done our part. Shall the world, then, be overrun by oysters? No, no; horrible! You'll convey all that is in your mind.'

I left him, full of the image of this magnificent

intellect babbling like a foolish child. He had handed me the key, and with a happy thought I took it with me lest he should lock himself in. Mrs Hudson was waiting, trembling and weeping, in the passage. Behind me as I passed from the flat I heard Holmes's high, thin voice in some delirious chant. Below, as I stood whistling for a cab, a man came on me through the fog.

'How is Mr Holmes, sir?' he asked.

It was an old acquaintance, Inspector Morton, of Scotland Yard, dressed in unofficial tweeds.

'He is very ill,' I answered.

He looked at me in a most singular fashion. Had it not been too fiendish, I could have imagined that the gleam of the fanlight showed exultation in his face.

'I heard some rumour of it,' said he.

The cab had driven up, and I left him.

Lower Burke Street proved to be a line of fine houses lying in the vague borderland between Notting Hill and Kensington. The particular one at which my cabman pulled up had an air of smug and demure respectability in its old-fashioned iron railings, its massive folding-door, and its shining brasswork. All was in keeping with a solemn butler who appeared framed in the pink radiance of a tinted electrical light behind him.

'Yes, Mr Culverton Smith is in. Dr Watson! Very good, sir, I will take up your card.'

My humble name and title did not appear to impress Mr Culverton Smith. Through the half-open door I heard a high, petulant, penetrating voice.

'Who is this person? What does he want? Dear me, Staples, how often have I said that I am not to be disturbed in my hours of study?'

There came a gentle flow of soothing explanation from the butler.

'Well, I won't see him, Staples. I can't have my work interrupted like this. I am not at home. Say so. Tell him to come in the morning if he really must see me.'

Again the gentle murmur.

'Well, well, give him that message. He can come in the morning, or he can stay away. My work must not be hindered.'

I thought of Holmes tossing upon his bed of sickness and counting the minutes, perhaps, until I could bring help to him. It was not a time to stand upon ceremony. His life depended upon my promptness. Before the apologetic butler had delivered his message I had pushed past him and was in the room.

With a shrill cry of anger a man rose from a reclining chair beside the fire. I saw a great yellow face, coarse-grained and greasy, with heavy double-chin, and two sullen, menacing grey eyes which glared at me from under tufted and sandy brows. A high bald head had a small velvet smoking-cap poised coquettishly upon one side of its pink curve. The skull was of enormous capacity, and yet as I looked down I saw to my amazement that the figure of the man was small and frail, twisted in the shoulders and back like one who has suffered from rickets in his childhood.

'What's this?' he cried in a high, screaming voice. 'What is the meaning of this intrusion? Didn't I send you word that I would see you tomorrow morning?'

'I am sorry,' said I, 'but the matter cannot be delayed. Mr Sherlock Holmes – '

The mention of my friend's name had an extra-ordinary effect upon the little man. The look of anger passed in an instant from his face. His features became tense and alert.

'Have you come from Holmes?' he asked.

'I have just left him.'

'What about Holmes? How is he?'

'He is desperately ill. That is why I have come.'

The man motioned me to a chair, and turned to resume his own. As he did so I caught a glimpse of his face in the mirror over the mantelpiece. I could have sworn that it was set in a malicious and abominable smile. Yet I persuaded myself that it must have been some nervous contraction which I had surprised, for he turned to me an instant later with genuine concern upon his features.

'I am sorry to hear this,' said he. 'I only know Mr Holmes through some business dealings which we have had, but I have every respect for his talents and his character. He is an amateur of crime, as I am of disease. For him the villain, for me the microbe. There are my prisons,' he continued, pointing to a row of bottles and jars which stood upon a side table. 'Among those gelatine cultivations some of the very worst offenders in the world are now doing time.'

'It was on account of your special knowledge that Mr Holmes desired to see you. He has a high opinion of you and thought that you were the one man in London who could help him.'

The little man started, and the jaunty smoking-cap slid to the floor.

'Why?' he asked. 'Why should Mr Holmes think that I could help him in his trouble?'

'Because of your knowledge of Eastern diseases.'

'But why should he think that this disease which he has contracted is Eastern?'

'Because, in some professional enquiry, he has been working among Chinese sailors down in the docks.'

Mr Culverton Smith smiled pleasantly and picked up his smoking-cap.

'Oh, that's it – is it?' said he. 'I trust the matter is not so grave as you suppose. How long has he been ill?'

'About three days.'

'Is he delirious?'

'Occasionally.'

'Tut, tut! This sounds serious. It would be inhuman not to answer his call. I very much resent any interruption to my work, Dr Watson, but this case is certainly exceptional. I will come with you at once.'

I remembered Holmes's injunction.

'I have another appointment,' said I.

'Very good. I will go alone. I have a note of Mr Holmes's address. You can rely upon my being there within half an hour at most.'

It was with a sinking heart that I re-entered Holmes's bedroom. For all that I knew the worst might have happened in my absence. To my enormous relief, he had improved greatly in the interval. His appearance was as ghastly as ever, but all trace of delirium had left him and he spoke in a feeble voice, it is true, but with even more than his usual crispness and lucidity.

'Well, did you see him, Watson?'

'Yes; he is coming.'

'Admirable, Watson! Admirable! You are the best of messengers.'

'He wished to return with me.'

'That would never do, Watson. That would be obviously impossible. Did he ask what ailed me?'

'I told him about the Chinese in the East End.'

'Exactly! Well, Watson, you have done all that a good friend could. You can now disappear from the scene.'

'I must wait and hear his opinion, Holmes.'

'Of course you must. But I have reasons to suppose that this opinion would be very much more frank and valuable if he imagines that we are alone. There is just room behind the head of my bed, Watson.'

'My dear Holmes!'

'I fear there is no alternative, Watson. The room does not lend itself to concealment, which is as well, as it is the less likely to arouse suspicion. But just there, Watson, I fancy that it could be done.' Suddenly he sat up with a rigid intentness upon his haggard face. 'There are the wheels, Watson. Quick, man, if you love me! And don't budge, whatever happens – whatever happens, do you hear? Don't speak! Don't move! Just listen with all your ears.' Then in an instant his sudden access of strength departed, and his masterful, purposeful talk droned away into the low, vague murmurings of a semi-delirious man.

From the hiding-place into which I had been so swiftly hustled I heard the footfalls upon the stair, with the opening and the closing of the bedroom door. Then, to my surprise, there came a long silence, broken only by the heavy breathings and gaspings of the sick man. I could imagine that our visitor was standing by the bedside and looking down at the sufferer. At last that strange hush was broken.

'Holmes!' he cried. 'Holmes!' in the insistent tone of one who awakens a sleeper. 'Can't you hear me, Holmes?' There was a rustling, as if he had shaken the sick man roughly by the shoulder.

'Is that you, Mr Smith?' Holmes whispered. 'I hardly dared hope that you would come.'

The other laughed.

'I should imagine not,' he said. 'And yet, you see, I am here. Coals of fire, Holmes – coals of fire!'

'It is very good of you – very noble of you. I appreciate your special knowledge.'

Our visitor sniggered.

'You do. You are, fortunately, the only man in London who does. Do you know what is the matter with you?'

'The same,' said Holmes.

'Ah! You recognise the symptoms?'

'Only too well.'

'Well, I shouldn't be surprised, Holmes. I shouldn't be surprised if it *were* the same. A bad lookout for you if it is. Poor Victor was a dead man on the fourth day – a strong, hearty young fellow. It was certainly, as you said, very surprising that he should have contracted an out-of-the-way Asiatic disease in the heart of London – a disease, too, of which I had made such a very special study. Singular coincidence, Holmes. Very smart of you to notice it, but rather uncharitable to suggest that it was cause and effect.'

'I knew that you did it.'

'Oh, you did, did you? Well, you couldn't prove it, anyhow. But what do you think of yourself spreading reports about me like that, and then crawling to me for help the moment you are in trouble? What sort of a game is that – eh?'

I heard the rasping, laboured breathing of the sick man. 'Give me the water!' he gasped.

'You're precious near your end, my friend, but I don't want you to go till I have had a word with you. That's why I give you water. There, don't slop it about! That's right. Can you understand what I say?'

Holmes groaned.

'Do what you can for me. Let bygones be bygones,' he whispered. 'I'll put the words out of my head – I swear I will. Only cure me, and I'll forget it.'

'Forget what?'

'Well, about Victor Savage's death. You as good as admitted just now that you had done it. I'll forget it.'

'You can forget it or remember it, just as you like. I don't see you in the witness box. Quite another shaped box, my good Holmes, I assure you. It matters nothing to me that you should know how my nephew died. It's not him we are talking about. It's you.'

'Yes, yes.'

'The fellow who came for me – I've forgotten his name – said that you contracted it down in the East End among the sailors.'

'I could only account for it so.'

'You are proud of your brains, Holmes, are you not? Think yourself smart, don't you? You came across someone who was smarter this time. Now cast your mind back, Holmes. Can you think of no other way you could have got this thing?'

'I can't think. My mind is gone. For Heaven's sake help me!'

'Yes, I will help you. I'll help you to understand just where you are and how you got there. I'd like you to know before you die.'

'Give me something to ease my pain.'

'Painful, is it? Yes, the coolies used to do some squealing towards the end. Takes you as cramp, I fancy.'

'Yes, yes; it is cramp.'

'Well, you can hear what I say, anyhow. Listen now! Can you remember any unusual incident in your life just about the time your symptoms began?'

'No, no; nothing.'

'Think again.'

'I'm too ill to think.'

'Well, then, I'll help you. Did anything come by post?'

'By post?'

'A box by chance?'

'I'm fainting – I'm gone!'

'Listen, Holmes!' There was a sound as if he was shaking the dying man, and it was all that I could do to hold myself quiet in my hiding-place. 'You must hear me. You *shall* hear me. Do you remember a box – an ivory box? It came on Wednesday. You opened it – do you remember?'

'Yes, yes, I opened it. There was a sharp spring inside it. Some joke – '

'It was no joke, as you will find to your cost. You fool, you would have it and you have got it. Who asked you to cross my path? If you had left me alone I would not have hurt you.'

'I remember,' Holmes gasped. 'The spring! It drew blood. This box – this on the table.'

'The very one, by George! And it may as well leave the room in my pocket. There goes your last shred of evidence. But you have the truth now, Holmes, and you can die with the knowledge that I killed you. You knew too much of the fate of Victor Savage, so I have sent you to share it. You are very near your end, Holmes. I will sit here and I will watch you die.'

Holmes's voice had sunk to an almost inaudible whisper.

'What is that?' said Smith. 'Turn up the gas? Ah, the shadows begin to fall, do they? Yes, I will turn it up, that I may see you the better.' He crossed the room and the light suddenly brightened. 'Is there any other little service that I can do you, my friend?'

'A match and a cigarette.'

I nearly called out in my joy and my amazement. He was speaking in his natural voice – a little weak, perhaps, but the very voice I knew. There was a long pause, and I felt that Culverton Smith was standing in silent amazement looking down at his companion.

'What's the meaning of this?' I heard him say at last in a dry, rasping tone.

'The best way of successfully acting a part is to be it,' said Holmes. 'I give you my word that for three days I have tasted neither food nor drink until you were good enough to pour me out that glass of water. But it is the tobacco which I find most irksome. Ah, here *are* some cigarettes.' I heard the striking of a match. 'That is very much better. Halloa! halloa! Do I hear the step of a friend?'

There were footfalls outside, the door opened, and Inspector Morton appeared.

'All is in order and this is your man,' said Holmes.

The officer gave the usual cautions.

'I arrest you on the charge of the murder of one Victor Savage,' he concluded.

'And you might add of the attempted murder of one Sherlock Holmes,' remarked my friend with a chuckle. 'To save an invalid trouble, Inspector, Mr Culverton Smith was good enough to give our signal by turning up the gas. By the way, the prisoner has a small box in the right-hand pocket of his coat which it would be as well to remove. Thank you. I would handle it gingerly if I were you. Put it down here. It may play its part in the trial.'

There was a sudden rush and a scuffle, followed by the clash of iron and a cry of pain.

'You'll only get yourself hurt,' said the inspector. 'Stand still, will you?' There was the click of the closing handcuffs.

'A nice trap!' cried the high, snarling voice. 'It will bring *you* into the dock, Holmes, not me. He asked me to come here to cure him. I was sorry for him and I came. Now he will pretend, no doubt, that I have said anything which he may invent which will corroborate his insane suspicions. You can lie as you like, Holmes. My word is always as good as yours.'

'Good heavens!' cried Holmes. 'I had totally forgotten him. My dear Watson, I owe you a thousand apologies. To think that I should have overlooked you! I need not introduce you to Mr Culverton Smith, since I understand that you met somewhat earlier in the evening. Have you the cab below? I will follow you when I am dressed, for I may be of some use at the station.'

'I never needed it more,' said Holmes as he refreshed himself with a glass of claret and some biscuits in the intervals of his toilet. 'However, as you know, my habits are irregular, and such a feat means less to me than to most men. It was very essential that I should impress Mrs Hudson with the reality of my condition, since she was to convey it to you, and you in turn to him. You won't be offended, Watson? You will realise that among your many talents dissimulation finds no place, and that if you had shared my secret you would never have been able to impress Smith with the urgent necessity of his presence, which was the vital point of the whole scheme. Knowing his vindictive nature, I was perfectly certain that he would come to look upon his handiwork.'

'But your appearance, Holmes – your ghastly face?'

'Three days of absolute fast does not improve one's beauty, Watson. For the rest, there is nothing which a sponge may not cure. With vaseline upon one's forehead, belladonna in one's eyes, rouge over the cheekbones, and crusts of beeswax round one's lips, a very satisfying effect can be produced. Malingering is a subject upon which I have sometimes thought of writing a monograph. A little occasional talk about half-crowns, oysters, or any other extraneous subject produces a pleasing effect of delirium.'

'But why would you not let me near you, since there was in truth no infection?'

'Can you ask, my dear Watson? Do you imagine that I have no respect for your medical talents? Could I fancy that your astute judgment would pass a dying man who, however weak, had no rise of pulse or temperature? At four yards, I could deceive you. If I failed to do so, who would bring my Smith within my grasp? No, Watson, I would not touch that box. You can just see if you look at it sideways where the sharp spring like a viper's tooth emerges as you open it. I dare say it was by some such device that poor Savage, who stood between this monster and a reversion, was done to death. My correspondence, however, is, as you know, a varied one, and I am somewhat upon my guard against any packages which reach me. It was clear to me, however, that by pretending that he had really succeeded in his design I might surprise a confession. That pretence I have carried out with the thoroughness of the true artist. Thank you, Watson, you must help me on with my coat. When we have finished at the police-station I think that something nutritious at Simpson's would not be out of place.'

19

The Disappearance of Lady Frances Carfax

'But why Turkish?' asked Mr Sherlock Holmes, gazing fixedly at my boots. I was reclining in a cane-backed chair at the moment, and my protruded feet had attracted his ever-active attention.

'English,' I answered in some surprise. 'I got them at Latimer's, in Oxford Street.'

Holmes smiled with an expression of weary patience.

'The bath!' he said; 'the bath! Why the relaxing and expensive Turkish rather than the invigorating home-made article?'

'Because for the last few days I have been feeling rheumatic and old. A Turkish bath is what we call an alterative in medicine – a fresh starting-point, a cleanser of the system.

'By the way, Holmes,' I added, 'I have no doubt the connection between my boots and a Turkish bath is a perfectly self-evident one to a logical mind, and yet I should be obliged to you if you would indicate it.'

'The train of reasoning is not very obscure, Watson,' said Holmes with a mischievous twinkle. 'It belongs to the same elementary class of deduction which I should illustrate if I were to ask you who shared your cab in your drive this morning.'

'I don't admit that a fresh illustration is an explanation,' said I with some asperity.

'Bravo, Watson! A very dignified and logical remonstrance. Let me see, what were the points?

Take the last one first – the cab. You observe that you have some splashes on the left sleeve and shoulder of your coat. Had you sat in the centre of a hansom you would probably have had no splashes, and if you had they would certainly have been symmetrical. Therefore it is clear that you sat at the side. Therefore it is equally clear that you had a companion.'

'That is very evident.'

'Absurdly commonplace, is it not?'

'But the boots and the bath?'

'Equally childish. You are in the habit of doing up your boots in a certain way. I see them on this occasion fastened with an elaborate double bow, which is not your usual method of tying them. You have, therefore, had them off. Who has tied them? A bootmaker – or the boy at the bath. It is unlikely that it is the bootmaker, since your boots are nearly new. Well, what remains? The bath. Absurd, is it not? But, for all that, the Turkish bath has served a purpose.'

'What is that?'

'You say that you have had it because you need a change. Let me suggest that you take one. How would Lausanne do, my dear Watson – first-class tickets and all expenses paid on a princely scale?'

'Splendid! But why?'

Holmes leaned back in his armchair and took his notebook from his pocket.

'One of the most dangerous classes in the world,' said he, 'is the drifting and friendless woman. She is the most harmless and often the most useful of mortals, but she is the inevitable inciter of crime in others. She is helpless. She is migratory. She has sufficient means to take her from country to country and from hotel to hotel. She is lost, as often as not, in a maze of obscure *pensions* and boarding houses. She is a stray chicken in a world of foxes. When she is gobbled up she is hardly missed. I much fear that some evil has come to the Lady Frances Carfax.'

I was relieved at this sudden descent from the general to the particular. Holmes consulted his notes.

'Lady Frances,' he continued, 'is the sole survivor of the direct family of the late Earl of Rufton. The estates went, as you may remember, in the male line. She was left with limited means, but with some very remarkable old Spanish jewellery of silver and curiously cut diamonds to which she was fondly attached – too attached, for she refused to leave them with her banker and always carried them about with her. A rather pathetic figure, the Lady Frances, a beautiful woman, still in fresh middle age, and yet, by a strange change, the last derelict of what only twenty years ago was a goodly fleet.'

'What has happened to her, then?'

'Ah, what has happened to the Lady Frances? Is she alive or dead? There is our problem. She is a lady of precise habits, and for four years it has been her invariable custom to write every second week to Miss Dobney, her old governess, who has long retired and lives in Camberwell. It is this Miss Dobney who has consulted me. Nearly five weeks have passed without a word. The last letter was from the Hôtel National at Lausanne. Lady Frances seems to have left there and given no address. The family are anxious, and as they are exceedingly wealthy no sum will be spared if we can clear the matter up.'

'Is Miss Dobney the only source of information? Surely she had other correspondents?'

'There is one correspondent who is a sure draw,

Watson. That is the bank. Single ladies must live, and their passbooks are compressed diaries. She banks at Silvester's. I have glanced over her account. The last cheque but one paid her bill at Lausanne, but it was a large one and probably left her with cash in hand. Only one cheque has been drawn since.'

'To whom, and where?'

'To Miss Marie Devine. There is nothing to show where the cheque was drawn. It was cashed at the Crédit Lyonnais at Montpellier less than three weeks ago. The sum was fifty pounds.'

'And who is Miss Marie Devine?'

'That also I have been able to discover. Miss Marie Devine was the maid of Lady Frances Carfax. Why she should have paid her this cheque we have not yet determined. I have no doubt, however, that your researches will soon clear the matter up.'

'*My* researches!'

'Hence the health-giving expedition to Lausanne. You know that I cannot possibly leave London while old Abrahams is in such mortal terror of his life. Besides, on general principles it is best that I should not leave the country. Scotland Yard feels lonely without me, and it causes an unhealthy excitement among the criminal classes. Go, then, my dear Watson, and if my humble counsel can ever be valued at so extravagant a rate as twopence a word, it waits your disposal night and day at the end of the Continental wire.'

Two days later found me at the Hôtel National at Lausanne, where I received every courtesy at the hands of M. Moser, the well-known manager. Lady Frances, as he informed me, had stayed there for several weeks. She had been much liked by all who met her. Her age was not more than forty. She was still handsome and bore every sign of having in her youth been a very lovely woman. M. Moser knew nothing of any valuable jewellery, but it had been remarked by the servants that the heavy trunk in the lady's bedroom was always scrupulously locked. Marie Devine, the maid, was as popular as her mistress. She was actually engaged to one of the head waiters in the hotel, and there was no difficulty in getting her address. It was 11 Rue de Trajan, Montpellier. All this I jotted down and felt that Holmes himself could not have been more adroit in collecting his facts.

Only one corner still remained in the shadow. No light which I possessed could clear up the cause for the lady's sudden departure. She was very happy at Lausanne. There was every reason to believe that she intended to remain for the season in her luxurious rooms overlooking the lake. And yet she had left at a single day's notice, which involved her in the useless payment of a week's rent. Only Jules Vibart, the lover of the maid, had any suggestion to offer. He connected the sudden departure with the visit to the hotel a day or two before of a tall, dark, bearded man. '*Un sauvage – un veritable sauvage!*' cried Jules Vibart. The man had rooms somewhere in the town. He had been seen talking earnestly to Madame on the promenade by the lake. Then he had called. She had refused to see him. He was English, but of his name there was no record. Madame had left the place immediately afterwards. Jules Vibart, and, what was of more importance, Jules Vibart's sweetheart, thought that this call and the departure were cause and effect. Only one thing Jules would not discuss. That was the reason why Marie had left her mistress. Of that he could or would say nothing. If I wished to know, I must go to Montpellier and ask her.

So ended the first chapter of my enquiry. The second was devoted to the place which Lady Frances Carfax had sought when she left Lausanne. Concerning this there had been some secrecy, which confirmed the idea that she had gone with the intention of throwing someone off her track. Otherwise why should not her luggage have been openly labelled for Baden? Both she and it reached the Rhenish spa by some circuitous route. This much I gathered from the manager of Cook's local office. So to Baden I went, after dispatching to Holmes an account of all my proceedings and receiving in reply a telegram of half-humorous commendation.

At Baden the track was not difficult to follow. Lady Frances had stayed at the Englischer Hof for a fortnight. While there she had made the acquaintance of a Dr Shlessinger and his wife, a missionary from South America. Like most lonely ladies, Lady Frances found her comfort and occupation in religion. Dr Shlessinger's remarkable personality, his wholehearted devotion, and the fact that he was recovering from a disease contracted in the exercise of his apostolic duties, affected her deeply. She had helped Mrs Shlessinger in the nursing of the convalescent saint. He spent his day, as the manager described it to me, upon a lounge-chair on the veranda, with an attendant lady upon either side of him. He was preparing a map of the Holy Land, with special reference to the kingdom of the Midianites, upon which he was writing a monograph. Finally, having improved much in health, he and his wife had returned to London, and Lady Frances had started thither in their company. This was just three weeks before, and the manager had heard nothing since. As to the maid, Marie, she had gone off some days beforehand in floods of tears, after informing the other maids that she was leaving service for ever. Dr Shlessinger had paid the bill of the whole party before his departure.

'By the way,' said the landlord in conclusion, 'you are not the only friend of Lady Frances Carfax who is enquiring after her just now. Only a week or so ago we had a man here upon the same errand.'

'Did he give a name?' I asked.

'None; but he was an Englishman, though of an unusual type.'

'A savage?' said I, linking my facts after the fashion of my illustrious friend.

'Exactly. That describes him very well. He is a bulky, bearded, sunburned fellow, who looks as if he would be more at home in a farmers' inn than in a fashionable hotel. A hard, fierce man, I should think, and one whom I should be sorry to offend.'

Already the mystery began to define itself, as figures grow clearer with the lifting of a fog. Here was this good and pious lady pursued from place to place by a sinister and unrelenting figure. She feared him, or she would not have fled from Lausanne. He had still followed. Sooner or later he would overtake her. Had he already overtaken her? Was *that* the secret of her continued silence? Could the good people who were her companions not screen her from his violence or his blackmail? What horrible purpose, what deep design, lay behind this long pursuit? There was the problem which I had to solve.

To Holmes I wrote showing how rapidly and surely I had got down to the roots of the matter. In reply I had a telegram asking for a description of Dr Shlessinger's left ear. Holmes's ideas of humour are strange and occasionally offensive, so I took no notice of his ill-timed jest – indeed, I had already reached Montpellier in my pursuit of the maid, Marie, before his message came.

I had no difficulty in finding the ex-servant and in learning all that she could tell me. She was a devoted creature, who had only left her mistress because she was sure that she was in good hands, and because her own approaching marriage made a separation inevitable in any case. Her mistress had, as she confessed with distress, shown some irritability of temper towards her during their stay in Baden, and had even questioned her once as if she had suspicions of her honesty, and this had made the parting easier than it would otherwise have been. Lady Frances had given her fifty pounds as a wedding-present. Like me, Marie viewed with deep distrust the stranger who had driven her mistress from Lausanne. With her own eyes she had seen him seize the lady's wrist with great violence on the public promenade by the lake. He was a fierce and terrible man. She believed that it was out of dread of him that Lady Frances had accepted the escort of the Shlessingers to London. She had never spoken to Marie about it, but many little signs had convinced the maid that her mistress lived in a state of continual nervous apprehension. So far she had got in her narrative, when suddenly she sprang from her chair and her face was convulsed with surprise and fear. 'See!' she cried. 'The miscreant follows still! There is the very man of whom I speak.'

Through the open sitting-room window I saw a huge, swarthy man with a bristling black beard walking slowly down the centre of the street and staring eagerly at the numbers of the houses. It was clear that, like myself, he was on the track of the maid. Acting upon the impulse of the moment, I rushed out and accosted him.

'You are an Englishman,' I said.

'What if I am?' he asked with a most villainous scowl.

'May I ask what your name is?'

'No, you may not,' said he with decision.

The situation was awkward, but the most direct way is often the best.

'Where is the Lady Frances Carfax?' I asked.

He stared at me with amazement.

'What have you done with her? Why have you pursued her? I insist upon an answer!' said I.

The fellow gave a bellow of anger and sprang upon me like a tiger. I have held my own in many a struggle, but the man had a grip of iron and the fury of a fiend. His hand was on my throat and my senses were nearly gone before an unshaven French *ouvrier* in a blue blouse darted out from a *cabaret* opposite, with a cudgel in his hand, and struck my assailant a sharp crack over the forearm, which made him leave go his hold. He stood for an instant fuming with rage and uncertain whether he should not renew his attack. Then, with a snarl of anger, he left me and entered the cottage from which I had just come. I turned to thank my preserver, who stood beside me in the roadway.

'Well, Watson,' said he, 'a very pretty hash you have made of it! I rather think you had better come back with me to London by the night express.'

An hour afterwards, Sherlock Holmes, in his usual garb and style, was seated in my private room at the hotel. His explanation of his sudden and opportune appearance was simplicity itself, for, finding that he could get away from London, he determined to head me off at the next obvious point of my travels. In the disguise of a working-man he had sat in the *cabaret* waiting for my appearance.

'And a singularly consistent investigation you have made, my dear Watson,' said he. 'I cannot at the moment recall any possible blunder which you have omitted. The total effect of your proceeding has been to give the alarm everywhere and yet to discover nothing.'

'Perhaps you would have done no better,' I answered bitterly.

'There is no "perhaps" about it. I *have* done better. Here is the Hon. Philip Green, who is a fellow-lodger with you in this hotel, and we may find him the starting-point for a more successful investigation.'

A card had come up on a salver, and it was followed by the same bearded ruffian who had attacked me in the street. He started when he saw me.

'What is this, Mr Holmes?' he asked. 'I had your note and I have come. But what has this man to do with the matter?'

'This is my old friend and associate, Dr Watson, who is helping us in this affair.'

The stranger held out a huge, sunburned hand, with a few words of apology.

'I hope I didn't harm you. When you accused me of hurting her I lost my grip of myself. Indeed, I'm not responsible in these days. My nerves are like live wires. But this situation is beyond me. What I want to know, in the first place, Mr Holmes, is, how in the world you came to hear of my existence at all.'

'I am in touch with Miss Dobney, Lady Frances's governess.'

'Old Susan Dobney with the mob cap! I remember her well.'

'And she remembers you. It was in the days before – before you found it better to go to South Africa.'

'Ah, I see you know my whole story. I need hide nothing from you. I swear to you, Mr Holmes, that there never was in this world a man who loved a woman with a more wholehearted love than I had for Frances. I was a wild youngster, I know – not worse than others of my class. But her mind was pure as snow. She could not bear a shadow of coarseness. So, when she came to hear of things that I had done, she would have no more to say to me. And yet she loved me – that is the wonder of it! – loved me well enough to remain single all her sainted days just for my sake alone. When the years had passed and I had made my money at Barberton I thought perhaps I could seek her out and soften her. I had heard that she was still unmarried. I found her at Lausanne and tried all I knew. She weakened, I think, but her will was strong, and when next I called she had left the town. I traced her to Baden, and then after a time heard that her maid was here. I'm a rough fellow, fresh from a rough life, and when Dr Watson spoke to me as he did I lost hold of myself for a moment. But for God's sake tell me what has become of the Lady Frances.'

'That is for us to find out,' said Sherlock Holmes with peculiar gravity. 'What is your London address, Mr Green?'

'The Langham Hotel will find me.'

'Then may I recommend that you return there and be on hand in case I should want you? I have no desire to encourage false hopes, but you may rest assured that all that can be done will be done for the safety of Lady

Frances. I can say no more for the instant. I will leave you this card so that you may be able to keep in touch with us. Now, Watson, if you will pack your bag I will cable to Mrs Hudson to make one of her best efforts for two hungry travellers at seven-thirty tomorrow.'

A telegram was awaiting us when we reached our Baker Street rooms, which Holmes read with an exclamation of interest and threw across to me. 'Jagged or torn,' was the message, and the place of origin, Baden.

'What is this?' I asked.

'It is everything,' Holmes answered. 'You may remember my seemingly irrelevant question as to this clerical gentleman's left ear. You did not answer it.'

'I had left Baden and could not enquire.'

'Exactly. For this reason I sent a duplicate to the manager of the Englischer Hof, whose answer lies here.'

'What does it show?'

'It shows, my dear Watson, that we are dealing with an exceptionally astute and dangerous man. The Revd Dr Shlessinger, missionary from South America, is none other than Holy Peters, one of the most unscrupulous rascals that Australia has ever evolved – and for a young country it has turned out some very finished types. His particular speciality is the beguiling of lonely ladies by playing upon their religious feelings, and his so-called wife, an Englishwoman named Fraser, is a worthy helpmate. The nature of his tactics suggested his identity to me, and this physical peculiarity – he was badly bitten in a saloon-fight at Adelaide in 1889 – confirmed my suspicion. This poor lady is in the hands of a most infernal couple, who will stick at nothing, Watson. That she is already dead is a very likely supposition. If not, she is undoubtedly in some sort of confinement and unable to write to Miss Dobney or her other friends. It is always possible that she never reached London, or that she has passed through it, but the former is improbable, as, with their system of registration, it is not easy for foreigners to play tricks with the Continental police; and the latter is also unlikely, as these rogues could not hope to find any other place where it would be as easy to keep a person under restraint. All my instincts tell me that she is in London, but as we have at present no possible means of telling where, we can only take the obvious steps, eat our dinner, and possess our souls in patience. Later in the evening I will stroll down and have a word with friend Lestrade at Scotland Yard.'

But neither the official police nor Holmes's own small but very efficient organisation sufficed to clear away the mystery. Amid the crowded millions of London the three persons we sought were as completely obliterated as if they had never lived. Advertisements were tried, and failed. Clues were followed, and led to nothing. Every criminal resort which Shlessinger might frequent was drawn in vain. His old associates were watched, but they kept clear of him. And then suddenly, after a week of helpless suspense, there came a flash of light. A silver-and-brilliant pendant of old Spanish design had been pawned at Bovington's, in Westminster Road. The pawner was a large, clean-shaven man of clerical appearance. His name and address were demonstrably false. The ear had escaped notice, but the description was surely that of Shlessinger.

Three times had our bearded friend from the Langham called for news – the third time within an hour of this fresh development. His clothes were getting looser on his great body. He seemed to be wilting away in his anxiety. 'If you will only give me something to do!' was his constant wail. At last Holmes could oblige him.

'He has begun to pawn the jewels. We should get him now.'

'But does this mean that any harm has befallen the Lady Frances?'

Holmes shook his head very gravely.

'Supposing that they have held her prisoner up to now, it is clear that they cannot let her loose without their own destruction. We must prepare for the worst.'

'What can I do?'

'These people do not know you by sight?'

'No.'

'It is possible that he will go to some other pawn-broker in the future. In that case, we must begin again. On the other hand, he has had a fair price and no questions asked, so if he is in need of ready money he will probably come back to Bovington's. I will give you a note to them, and they will let you wait in the shop. If the fellow comes you will follow him home. But no indiscretion, and, above all, no violence. I put you on your honour that you will take no step without my knowledge and consent.'

For two days the Hon. Philip Green (he was, I may mention, the son of the famous admiral of that name who commanded the Sea of Azof fleet in the Crimean War) brought us no news. On the evening of the third he rushed into our sitting-room, pale, trembling, with every muscle of his powerful frame quivering with excitement.

'We have him! We have him!' he cried.

He was incoherent in his agitation. Holmes soothed him with a few words and thrust him into an armchair.

'Come, now, give us the order of events,' said he.

'She came only an hour ago. It was the wife, this time, but the pendant she brought was the fellow of the other. She is a tall, pale woman, with ferret eyes.'

'That is the lady,' said Holmes.

'She left the office and I followed her. She walked up the Kennington Road, and I kept behind her. Presently she went into a shop. Mr Holmes, it was an undertaker's.'

My companion started. 'Well?' he asked in that vibrant voice which told of the fiery soul behind the cold grey face.

'She was talking to the woman behind the counter. I entered as well. "It is late," I heard her say, or words to that effect. The woman was excusing herself. "It should be there before now," she answered. "It took longer, being out of the ordinary." They both stopped and looked at me, so I asked some questions and then left the shop.'

'You did excellently well. What happened next?'

'The woman came out, but I had hid myself in a doorway. Her suspicions had been aroused, I think, for she looked round her. Then she called a cab and got in. I was lucky enough to get another and so to follow her. She got down at last at 36 Poultney Square, Brixton. I drove past, left my cab at the corner of the square, and watched the house.'

'Did you see anyone?'

'The windows were all in darkness save one on the lower floor. The blind was down, and I could not see in. I was standing there, wondering what I should do next, when a covered van drove up with two men in it.

They descended, took something out of the van, and carried it up the steps to the hall door. Mr Holmes, it was a coffin.'

'Ah!'

'For an instant I was on the point of rushing in. The door had been opened to admit the men and their burden. It was the woman who had opened it. But as I stood there she caught a glimpse of me, and I think that she recognised me. I saw her start, and she hastily closed the door. I remembered my promise to you, and here I am.'

'You have done excellent work,' said Holmes, scribbling a few words upon a half-sheet of paper. 'We can do nothing legal without a warrant, and you can serve the cause best by taking this note down to the authorities and getting one. There may be some difficulty, but I should think that the sale of the jewellery should be sufficient. Lestrade will see to all details.'

'But they may murder her in the meanwhile. What could the coffin mean, and for whom could it be but for her?'

'We will do all that can be done, Mr Green. Not a moment will be lost. Leave it in our hands. Now Watson,' he added as our client hurried away, 'he will set the regular forces on the move. We are, as usual, the irregulars, and we must take our own line of action. The situation strikes me as so desperate that the most extreme measures are justified. Not a moment is to be lost in getting to Poultney Square.'

'Let us try to reconstruct the situation,' said he as we drove swiftly past the Houses of Parliament and over Westminster Bridge. 'These villains have coaxed this unhappy lady to London, after first alienating her from her faithful maid. If she has written any letters they have been intercepted. Through some confederate they have engaged a furnished house. Once inside it, they have made her a prisoner, and they have become possessed of the valuable jewellery which has been their object from the first. Already they have begun to sell part of it, which seems safe enough to them, since they have no reason to think that anyone is interested in the lady's fate. When she is released she will, of course, denounce them. Therefore, she must not be released. But they cannot keep her under lock and key for ever. So murder is their only solution.'

'That seems very clear.'

'Now we will take another line of reasoning. When you follow two separate chains of thought, Watson, you will find some point of intersection which should approximate to the truth. We will start now, not from the lady but from the coffin, and argue backwards. That incident proves, I fear, beyond all doubt that the lady is dead. It points also to an orthodox burial with proper accompaniment of medical certificate and official sanction. Had the lady been obviously murdered, they would have buried her in a hole in the back garden. But here all is open and regular. What does this mean? Surely that they have done her to death in some way which has deceived the doctor and simulated a natural end – poisoning, perhaps. And yet how strange that they should ever let a doctor approach her unless he were a confederate, which is hardly a credible proposition.'

'Could they have forged a medical certificate?'

'Dangerous, Watson, very dangerous. No, I hardly see them doing that. Pull up, cabby! This is evidently the undertaker's, for we have just passed the pawn-broker's. Would you go in, Watson? Your appearance inspires confidence. Ask what hour the Poultney Square funeral takes place tomorrow.'

The woman in the shop answered me without hesitation that it was to be at eight o'clock in the morning. 'You see, Watson, no mystery; everything above board! In some way the legal forms have undoubtedly been complied with, and they think that they have little to fear. Well, there's nothing for it now but a direct frontal attack. Are you armed?'

'My stick!'

'Well, well, we shall be strong enough. "Thrice is he armed who hath his quarrel just." We simply can't afford to wait for the police or to keep within the four corners of the law. You can drive off, cabby. Now, Watson, we'll just take our luck together, as we have occasionally in the past.'

He had rung loudly at the door of a great dark house in the centre of Poultney Square. It was opened immediately, and the figure of a tall woman was outlined against the dim-lit hall.

'Well, what do you want?' she asked sharply, peering at us through the darkness.

'I want to speak to Dr Shlessinger,' said Holmes.

'There is no such person here,' she answered, and tried to close the door, but Holmes had jammed it with his foot.

'Well, I want to see the man who lives here, whatever he may call himself,' said Holmes firmly.

She hesitated. Then she threw open the door. 'Well, come in!' said she. 'My husband is not afraid to face any man in the world.' She closed the door behind us and showed us into a sitting-room on the right side of the hall, turning up the gas as she left us. 'Mr Peters will be with you in an instant,' she said.

Her words were literally true, for we had hardly time to look around the dusty and moth-eaten apartment in which we found ourselves before the door opened and a big, clean-shaven, bald-headed man stepped lightly into the room. He had a large red face, with pendulous cheeks, and a general air of superficial benevolence which was marred by a cruel, vicious mouth.

'There is surely some mistake here, gentlemen,' he said in an unctuous, make-everything-easy voice. 'I fancy that you have been misdirected. Possibly if you tried farther down the street – '

'That will do; we have no time to waste,' said my companion firmly. 'You are Henry Peters, of Adelaide, late the Revd Dr Shlessinger, of Baden and South America. I am as sure of that as that my own name is Sherlock Holmes.'

Peters, as I will now call him, started and stared hard at his formidable pursuer. 'I guess your name does not frighten me, Mr Holmes,' said he coolly. 'When a man's conscience is easy you can't rattle him. What is your business in my house?'

'I want to know what you have done with the Lady Frances Carfax, whom you brought away with you from Baden.'

'I'd be very glad if you could tell me where that lady may be,' Peters answered coolly. 'I've a bill against her for nearly a hundred pounds, and nothing to show for it but a couple of trumpery pendants that the dealer would hardly look at. She attached herself to Mrs Peters and me at Baden – it is a fact that I was using another name at the time – and she stuck on to us until we came to London. I paid her bill and her ticket. Once in London, she gave us the slip, and, as

I say, left these out-of-date jewels to pay her bills. You find her, Mr Holmes, and I'm your debtor.'

'I *mean* to find her,' said Sherlock Holmes. 'I'm going through this house till I do find her.'

'Where is your warrant?'

Holmes half drew a revolver from his pocket. 'This will have to serve till a better one comes.'

'Why, you're a common burglar.'

'So you might describe me,' said Holmes cheerfully. 'My companion is also a dangerous ruffian. And together we are going through your house.'

Our opponent opened the door.

'Fetch a policeman, Annie!' said he. There was a whisk of feminine skirts down the passage, and the hall door was opened and shut.

'Our time is limited, Watson,' said Holmes. 'If you try to stop us, Peters, you will most certainly get hurt. Where is that coffin which was brought into your house?'

'What do you want with the coffin? It is in use. There is a body in it.'

'I must see the body.'

'Never with my consent.'

'Then without it.' With a quick movement Holmes pushed the fellow to one side and passed into the hall. A door half opened stood immediately before us. We entered. It was the dining-room. On the table, under a half-lit chandelier, the coffin was lying. Holmes turned up the gas and raised the lid. Deep down in the recesses of the coffin lay an emaciated figure. The glare from the lights above beat down upon an aged and withered face. By no possible process of cruelty, starvation, or disease could this worn-out wreck be the still beautiful Lady Frances. Holmes's face showed his amazement, and also his relief.

'Thank God!' he muttered. 'It's someone else.'

'Ah, you've blundered badly for once, Mr Sherlock Holmes,' said Peters, who had followed us into the room.

'Who is the dead woman?'

'Well, if you really must know, she is an old nurse of my wife's, Rose Spender by name, whom we found in the Brixton Workhouse Infirmary. We brought her round here, called in Dr Horsom, of 13 Firbank Villas – mind you take the address, Mr Holmes – and had her carefully tended, as Christian folk should. On the third day she died – certificate says senile decay – but that's only the doctor's opinion, and of course you know better. We ordered her funeral to be carried out by Stimson and Co., of the Kennington Road, who will bury her at eight o'clock tomorrow morning. Can you pick any hole in that, Mr Holmes? You've made a silly blunder, and you may as well own up to it. I'd give something for a photograph of your gaping, staring face when you pulled aside that lid expecting to see the Lady Frances Carfax and only found a poor old woman of ninety.'

Holmes's expression was as impassive as ever under the jeers of his antagonist, but his clenched hands betrayed his acute annoyance.

'I am going through your house,' said he.

'Are you, though!' cried Peters as a woman's voice and heavy steps sounded in the passage. 'We'll soon see about that. This way, officers, if you please. These men have forced their way into my house, and I cannot get rid of them. Help me to put them out.'

A sergeant and a constable stood in the doorway. Holmes drew his card from his case.

'This is my name and address. This is my friend, Dr Watson.'

'Bless you, sir, we know you very well,' said the sergeant, 'but you can't stay here without a warrant.'

'Of course not. I quite understand that.'

'Arrest him!' cried Peters.

'We know where to lay our hands on this gentleman if he is wanted,' said the sergeant majestically, 'but you'll have to go, Mr Holmes.'

'Yes, Watson, we shall have to go.'

A minute later we were in the street once more. Holmes was as cool as ever, but I was hot with anger and humiliation. The sergeant had followed us.

'Sorry, Mr Holmes, but that's the law.'

'Exactly, Sergeant, you could not do otherwise.'

'I expect there was good reason for your presence there. If there is anything I can do – '

'It's a missing lady, Sergeant, and we think she is in that house. I expect a warrant presently.'

'Then I'll keep my eye on the parties, Mr Holmes. If anything comes along, I will surely let you know.'

It was only nine o'clock, and we were off full cry upon the trail at once. First we drove to Brixton Workhouse Infirmary, where we found that it was indeed the truth that a charitable couple had called some days before, that they had claimed an imbecile old woman as a former servant, and that they had obtained permission to take her away with them. No surprise was expressed at the news that she had since died.

The doctor was our next goal. He had been called in, had found the woman dying of pure senility, had actually seen her pass away, and had signed the certificate in due form. 'I assure you that everything was perfectly normal and there was no room for foul play in the matter,' said he. Nothing in the house had struck him as suspicious save that for people of their class it was remarkable that they should have no servant. So far and no further went the doctor.

Finally we found our way to Scotland Yard. There had been difficulties of procedure in regard to the warrant. Some delay was inevitable. The magistrate's signature might not be obtained until next morning. If Holmes would call about nine he could go down with Lestrade and see it acted upon. So ended the day, save that near midnight our friend, the sergeant, called to say that he had seen flickering lights here and there in the windows of the great dark house, but that no one had left it and none had entered. We could but pray for patience and wait for the morrow.

Sherlock Holmes was too irritable for conversation and too restless for sleep. I left him smoking hard, with his heavy, dark brows knotted together, and his long, nervous fingers tapping upon the arms of his chair, as he turned over in his mind every possible solution of the mystery. Several times in the course of the night I heard him prowling about the house. Finally, just after I had been called in the morning, he rushed into my room. He was in his dressing-gown, but his pale, hollow-eyed face told me that his night had been a sleepless one.

'What time was the funeral? Eight, was it not?' he asked eagerly. 'Well, it is seven-twenty now. Good heavens, Watson, what has become of any brains that God has given me? Quick, man, quick! It's life or death – a hundred chances on death to one on life. I'll never forgive myself, never, if we are too late!'

Five minutes had not passed before we were flying in a hansom down Baker Street. But even so it was twenty-five to eight as we passed Big Ben, and eight struck as we tore down the Brixton Road. But others were late as well as we. Ten minutes after the hour the hearse was still standing at the door of the house, and even as our foaming horse came to a halt the coffin, supported by three men, appeared on the threshold. Holmes darted forward and barred their way.

'Take it back!' he cried, laying his hand on the breast of the foremost. 'Take it back this instant!'

'What the devil do you mean? Once again I ask you, where is your warrant?' shouted the furious Peters, his big red face glaring over the farther end of the coffin.

'The warrant is on its way. The coffin shall remain in the house until it comes.'

The authority in Holmes's voice had its effect upon the bearers. Peters had suddenly vanished into the house, and they obeyed these new orders. 'Quick, Watson, quick! Here is a screwdriver!' he shouted as the coffin was replaced upon the table. 'Here's one for you, my man! A sovereign if the lid comes off in a minute! Ask no questions – work away! That's good! Another! And another! Now pull all together! It's giving! It's giving! Ah, that does it at last.'

With a united effort we tore off the coffin-lid. As we did so there came from the inside a stupefying and overpowering smell of chloroform. A body lay within, its head all wreathed in cotton-wool, which had been soaked in the narcotic. Holmes plucked it off and disclosed the statuesque face of a handsome and spiritual woman of middle age. In an instant he had passed his arm round the figure and raised her to a sitting position.

'Is she gone, Watson? Is there a spark left? Surely we are not too late!'

For half an hour it seemed that we were. What with actual suffocation, and what with the poisonous fumes of the chloroform, the Lady Frances seemed to have passed the last point of recall. And then, at last, with artificial respiration, with injected ether, and with every device that science could suggest, some flutter of life, some quiver of the eyelids, some dimming of a mirror, spoke of the slowly returning life. A cab had driven up, and Holmes, parting the blind, looked out at it. 'Here is Lestrade with his warrant,' said he. 'He will find that his birds have flown. And here,' he added as a heavy step hurried along the passage, 'is someone who has a better right to nurse this lady than we have. Good-morning, Mr Green; I think that the sooner we can move the Lady Frances the better. Meanwhile, the funeral may proceed, and the poor old woman who still lies in that coffin may go to her last resting-place alone.'

'Should you care to add the case to your annals, my dear Watson,' said Holmes that evening, 'it can only be as an example of that temporary eclipse to which even the best-balanced mind may be exposed. Such slips are common to all mortals, and the greatest is he who can recognise and repair them. To this modified credit I may, perhaps, make some claim. My night was haunted by the thought that somewhere a clue, a strange sentence, a curious observation, had come under my notice and had been too easily dismissed. Then, suddenly, in the grey of the morning, the words came back to me. It was the remark of the undertaker's wife, as reported by Philip Green. She had said, "It should be there before now. It took longer, being out of the ordinary." It was the coffin of which she spoke.

It had been out of the ordinary. That could only mean that it had been made to some special measurement. But why? Why? Then in an instant I remembered the deep sides, and the little wasted figure at the bottom. Why so large a coffin for so small a body? To leave room for another body. Both would be buried under the one certificate. It had all been so clear, if only my own sight had not been dimmed. At eight the Lady Frances would be buried. Our one chance was to stop the coffin before it left the house.

'It was a desperate chance that we might find her alive, but it *was* a chance, as the result showed. These people had never, to my knowledge, done a murder. They might shrink from actual violence at the last. They could bury her with no sign of how she met her end, and even if she were exhumed there was a chance for them. I hoped that such considerations might prevail with them. You can reconstruct the scene well enough. You saw the horrible den upstairs, where the poor lady had been kept so long. They rushed in and overpowered her with their chloroform, carried her down, poured more into the coffin to insure against her waking, and then screwed down the lid. A clever device, Watson. It is new to me in the annals of crime. If our ex-missionary friends escape the clutches of Lestrade, I shall expect to hear of some brilliant incidents in their future career.'

20

The Devil's Foot

In recording from time to time some of the curious experiences and interesting recollections which I associate with my long and intimate friendship with Mr Sherlock Holmes, I have continually been faced by difficulties caused by his own aversion to publicity. To his sombre and cynical spirit all popular applause was always abhorrent, and nothing amused him more at the end of a successful case than to hand over the actual exposure to some orthodox official, and to listen with a mocking smile to the general chorus of misplaced congratulation. It was indeed this attitude upon the part of my friend and certainly not any lack of interesting material which has caused me of late years to lay very few of my records before the public. My participation in some of his adventures was always a privilege which entailed discretion and reticence upon me.

It was, then, with considerable surprise that I received a telegram from Holmes last Tuesday – he has never been known to write where a telegram would serve – in the following terms:

Why not tell them of the Cornish horror – strangest case I have handled.

I have no idea what backward sweep of memory had brought the matter fresh to his mind, or what freak had caused him to desire that I should recount it; but I hasten, before another cancelling telegram may arrive, to hunt out the notes which give me the exact details of the case and to lay the narrative before my readers.

It was, then, in the spring of the year 1897 that Holmes's iron constitution showed some symptoms of giving way in the face of constant hard work of a most exacting kind, aggravated, perhaps, by occasional indiscretions of his own. In March of that year Dr Moore Agar, of Harley Street, whose dramatic introduction to Holmes I may some day recount, gave positive injunctions that the famous private agent lay aside all his cases and surrender himself to complete rest if he wished to avert an absolute breakdown. The state of his health was not a matter in which he himself took the faintest interest, for his mental detachment was absolute, but he was induced at last, on the threat of being permanently disqualified from work, to give himself a complete change of scene and air. Thus it was that in the early spring of that year we found ourselves together in a small cottage near Poldhu Bay, at the further extremity of the Cornish peninsula.

It was a singular spot, and one peculiarly well suited to the grim humour of my patient. From the windows of our little whitewashed house, which stood high upon a grassy headland, we looked down upon the whole sinister semicircle of Mounts Bay, that old death trap of sailing vessels, with its fringe of black cliffs and surge-swept reefs on which innumerable seamen have met their end. With a northerly breeze it lies placid and sheltered, inviting the storm-tossed craft to tack into it for rest and protection.

Then comes the sudden swirl round of the wind, the blistering gale from the south-west, the dragging anchor, the lee shore, and the last battle in the creaming breakers. The wise mariner stands far out from that evil place.

On the land side our surroundings were as sombre as on the sea. It was a country of rolling moors, lonely and dun-coloured, with an occasional church tower to mark the site of some old-world village. In every direction upon these moors there were traces of some vanished race which had passed utterly away, and left as its sole record strange monuments of stone, irregular mounds which contained the burned ashes of the dead, and curious earthworks which hinted at pre-historic strife. The glamour and mystery of the place, with its sinister atmosphere of forgotten nations, appealed to the imagination of my friend, and he spent much of his time in long walks and solitary meditations upon the moor. The ancient Cornish language had also arrested his attention, and he had, I remember, conceived the idea that it was akin to the Chaldean, and had been largely derived from the Phoenician traders in tin. He had received a consignment of books upon philology and was settling down to develop this thesis when suddenly, to my sorrow and to his unfeigned delight, we found ourselves, even in that land of dreams, plunged into a problem at our very doors which was more intense, more engrossing, and infinitely more mysterious than any of those which had driven us from London. Our simple life and peaceful, healthy routine were violently interrupted, and we were precipitated into the midst of a series of events which caused the utmost excitement not only in Cornwall but throughout the whole west of England. Many of my readers may retain some recollection of what was called at the time 'The Cornish Horror', though a most imperfect account of the matter reached the London Press. Now, after thirteen years, I will give the true details of this inconceivable affair to the public.

I have said that scattered towers marked the villages which dotted this part of Cornwall. The nearest of these was the hamlet of Tredannick Wollas, where the cottages of a couple of hundred inhabitants clustered round an ancient, moss-grown church. The vicar of the parish, Mr Roundhay, was something of an archaeologist, and as such Holmes had made his acquaintance. He was a middle-aged man, portly and affable, with a considerable fund of local lore. At his invitation we had taken tea at the vicarage and had come to know, also, Mr Mortimer Tregennis, an independent gentleman, who increased the clergyman's scanty resources by taking rooms in his large, straggling house. The vicar, being a bachelor, was glad to come to such an arrangement, though he had little in common with his lodger, who was a thin, dark, spectacled man, with a stoop which gave the impression of actual, physical deformity. I remember that during our short visit we found the vicar garrulous, but his lodger strangely reticent, a sad-faced, introspective man, sitting with averted eyes, brooding apparently upon his own affairs.

These were the two men who entered abruptly into our little sitting-room on Tuesday, March the 16th, shortly after our breakfast hour, as we were smoking together, preparatory to our daily excursion upon the moors.

'Mr Holmes,' said the vicar in an agitated voice, 'the most extraordinary and tragic affair has occurred during the night. It is the most unheard-of business. We can only regard it as a special Providence that you should chance to be here at the time, for in all England you are the one man we need.'

I glared at the intrusive vicar with no very friendly eyes; but Holmes took his pipe from his lips and sat up in his chair like an old hound who hears the view-halloa. He waved his hand to the sofa, and our palpitating visitor with his agitated companion sat side by side upon it. Mr Mortimer Tregennis was more self-contained than the clergyman, but the twitching of his thin hands and the brightness of his dark eyes showed that they shared a common emotion.

'Shall I speak or you?' he asked of the vicar.

'Well, as you seem to have made the discovery, whatever it may be, and the vicar to have had it second-hand, perhaps you had better do the speaking,' said Holmes.

I glanced at the hastily clad clergyman, with the formally dressed lodger seated beside him, and was amused at the surprise which Holmes's simple deduction had brought to their faces.

'Perhaps I had best say a few words first,' said the vicar, 'and then you can judge if you will listen to the details from Mr Tregennis, or whether we should not hasten at once to the scene of this mysterious affair. I may explain, then, that our friend here spent last evening in the company of his two brothers, Owen and George, and of his sister Brenda, at their house of Tredannick Wartha, which is near the old stone cross upon the moor. He left them shortly after ten o'clock, playing cards round the dining-room table, in excellent health and spirits. This morning, being an early riser, he walked in that direction before breakfast and was overtaken by the carriage of Dr Richards, who explained that he had just been sent for on a most urgent call to Tredannick Wartha. Mr Mortimer Tregennis naturally went with him. When he arrived at Tredannick Wartha he found an extraordinary state of things. His two brothers and his sister were seated round the table exactly as he had left them, the cards still spread in front of them and the candles burned down to their sockets. The sister lay back stone-dead in her chair, while the two brothers sat on each side of her laughing, shouting, and singing, the senses stricken clean out of them. All three of them, the dead woman and the two demented men, retained upon their faces an expression of the utmost horror – a convulsion of terror which was dreadful to look upon. There was no sign of the presence of anyone in the house, except Mrs Porter, the old cook and housekeeper, who declared that she had slept deeply and heard no sound during the night. Nothing had been stolen or disarranged, and there is absolutely no explanation of what the horror can be which has frightened a woman to death and two strong men out of their senses. There is the situation, Mr Holmes, in a nutshell, and if you can help us to clear it up you will have done a great work.'

I had hoped that in some way I could coax my companion back into the quiet which had been the object of our journey; but one glance at his intense face and contracted eyebrows told me how vain was now the expectation. He sat for some little time in silence, absorbed in the strange drama which had broken in upon our peace.

'I will look into this matter,' he said at last. 'On the face of it, it would appear to be a case of a very exceptional nature. Have you been there yourself, Mr Roundhay?'

'No, Mr Holmes. Mr Tregennis brought back the

account to the vicarage, and I at once hurried over with him to consult you.'

'How far is it to the house where this singular tragedy occurred?'

'About a mile inland.'

'Then we shall walk over together. But before we start I must ask you a few questions, Mr Mortimer Tregennis.'

The other had been silent all this time, but I had observed that his more controlled excitement was even greater than the obtrusive emotion of the clergyman. He sat with a pale, drawn face, his anxious gaze fixed upon Holmes, and his thin hands clasped convulsively together. His pale lips quivered as he listened to the dreadful experience which had befallen his family, and his dark eyes seemed to reflect something of the horror of the scene.

'Ask what you like, Mr Holmes,' said he eagerly. 'It is a bad thing to speak of, but I will answer you the truth.'

'Tell me about last night.'

'Well, Mr Holmes, I supped there, as the vicar has said, and my elder brother George proposed a game of whist afterwards. We sat down about nine o'clock. It was a quarter-past ten when I moved to go. I left them all round the table, as merry as could be.'

'Who let you out?'

'Mrs Porter had gone to bed, so I let myself out. I shut the hall door behind me. The window of the room in which they sat was closed, but the blind was not drawn down. There was no change in door or window this morning, or any reason to think that any stranger had been to the house. Yet there they sat, driven clean mad with terror, and Brenda lying dead of fright, with her head hanging over the arm of the chair. I'll never get the sight of that room out of my mind so long as I live.'

'The facts, as you state them, are certainly most remarkable,' said Holmes. 'I take it that you have no theory yourself which can in any way account for them?'

'It's devilish, Mr Holmes, devilish!' cried Mortimer Tregennis. 'It is not of this world. Something has come into that room which has dashed the light of reason from their minds. What human contrivance could do that?'

'I fear,' said Holmes, 'that if the matter is beyond humanity it is certainly beyond me. Yet we must exhaust all natural explanations before we fall back upon such a theory as this. As to yourself, Mr Tregennis, I take it you were divided in some way from your family, since they lived together and you had rooms apart?'

'That is so, Mr Holmes, though the matter is past and done with. We were a family of tin-miners at Redruth, but we sold our venture to a company, and so retired with enough to keep us. I won't deny that there was some feeling about the division of the money and it stood between us for a time, but it was all forgiven and forgotten, and we were the best of friends together.'

'Looking back at the evening which you spent together, does anything stand out in your memory as throwing any possible light upon the tragedy? Think carefully, Mr Tregennis, for any clue which can help me.'

'There is nothing at all, sir.'

'Your people were in their usual spirits?'

'Never better.'

'Were they nervous people? Did they ever show any apprehension of coming danger?'

'Nothing of the kind.'

'You have nothing to add then, which could assist me?'

Mortimer Tregennis considered earnestly for a moment.

'There is one thing occurs to me,' said he at last. 'As we sat at the table my back was to the window, and my brother George, he being my partner at cards, was facing it. I saw him once look hard over my shoulder, so I turned round and looked also. The blind was up and the window shut, but I could just make out the bushes on the lawn, and it seemed to me for a moment that I saw something moving among them. I couldn't even say if it was man or animal, but I just thought there was something there. When I asked him what he was looking at, he told me that he had the same feeling. That is all that I can say.'

'Did you not investigate?'

'No; the matter passed as unimportant.'

'You left them, then, without any premonition of evil?'

'None at all.'

'I am not clear how you came to hear the news so early this morning.'

'I am an early riser and generally take a walk before breakfast. This morning I had hardly started when the doctor in his carriage overtook me. He told me that old Mrs Porter had sent a boy down with an urgent message. I sprang in beside him and we drove on. When we got there we looked into that dreadful room. The candles and the fire must have burned out hours

577

before, and they had been sitting there in the dark until dawn had broken. The doctor said Brenda must have been dead at least six hours. There were no signs of violence. She just lay across the arm of the chair with that look on her face. George and Owen were singing snatches of songs and gibbering like two great apes. Oh, it was awful to see! I couldn't stand it, and the doctor was as white as a sheet. Indeed, he fell into a chair in a sort of faint, and we nearly had him on our hands as well.'

'Remarkable – most remarkable!' said Holmes, rising and taking his hat. 'I think, perhaps, we had better go down to Tredannick Wartha without further delay. I confess that I have seldom known a case which at first sight presented a more singular problem.'

Our proceedings of that first morning did little to advance the investigation. It was marked, however, at the outset by an incident which left the most sinister impression upon my mind. The approach to the spot at which the tragedy occurred is down a narrow, winding, country lane. While we made our way along it we heard the rattle of a carriage coming towards us and stood aside to let it pass. As it drove by us I caught a glimpse through the closed window of a horribly contorted, grinning face glaring out at us. Those staring eyes and gnashing teeth flashed past us like a dreadful vision.

'My brothers!' cried Mortimer Tregennis, white to his lips. 'They are taking them to Helston.'

We looked with horror after the black carriage, lumbering upon its way. Then we turned our steps towards this ill-omened house in which they had met their strange fate.

It was a large and bright dwelling, rather a villa than a cottage, with a considerable garden which was already, in that Cornish air, well filled with spring flowers. Towards this garden the window of the sitting-room fronted, and from it, according to Mortimer Tregennis, must have come that thing of evil which had by sheer horror in a single instant blasted their minds. Holmes walked slowly and thoughtfully among the flower-plots and along the path before we entered the porch. So absorbed was he in his thoughts, I remember, that he stumbled over the watering-pot, upset its contents, and deluged both our feet and the garden path. Inside the house we were met by the elderly Cornish housekeeper, Mrs Porter, who, with the aid of a young girl, looked after the wants of the family. She readily answered all Holmes's questions. She had heard nothing in the night. Her employers had all been in excellent spirits lately, and she had never known them more cheerful and prosperous. She had fainted with horror upon entering the room in the morning and seeing that dreadful company round the table. She had, when she recovered, thrown open the window to let the morning air in, and had run down to the lane, whence she sent a farm-lad for the doctor. The lady was on her bed upstairs if we cared to see her. It took four strong men to get the brothers into the asylum carriage. She would not herself stay in the house another day and was starting that very afternoon to rejoin her family at St Ives.

We ascended the stairs and viewed the body. Miss Brenda Tregennis had been a very beautiful girl, though now verging upon middle age. Her dark, clear-cut face was handsome, even in death, but there still lingered upon it something of that convulsion of horror which had been her last human emotion. From her bedroom we descended to the sitting-room, where this strange tragedy had actually occurred. The charred ashes of the overnight fire lay in the grate. On the table were the four guttered and burned-out candles, with the cards scattered over its surface. The chairs had been moved back against the walls, but all else was as it had been the night before. Holmes paced with light, swift steps about the room; he sat in the various chairs, drawing them up and reconstructing their positions. He tested how much of the garden was visible; he examined the floor, the ceiling, and the fireplace; but never once did I see that sudden brightening of his eyes and tightening of his lips which would have told me that he saw some gleam of light in this utter darkness.

'Why a fire?' he asked once. 'Had they always a fire in this small room on a spring evening?'

Mortimer Tregennis explained that the night was cold and damp. For that reason, after his arrival, the fire was lit. 'What are you going to do now, Mr Holmes?' he asked.

My friend smiled and laid his hand upon my arm. 'I think, Watson, that I shall resume that course of tobacco-poisoning which you have so often and so justly condemned,' said he. 'With your permission, gentlemen, we will now return to our cottage, for I am not aware that any new factor is likely to come to our notice here. I will turn the facts over in my mind, Mr Tregennis, and should anything occur to me I will certainly communicate with you and the vicar. In the meantime I wish you both good-morning.'

It was not until long after we were back in Poldhu Cottage that Holmes broke his complete and absorbed silence. He sat coiled in his armchair, his haggard and ascetic face hardly visible amid the blue swirl of his tobacco smoke, his black brows drawn down, his forehead contracted, his eyes vacant and far away. Finally he laid down his pipe and sprang to his feet.

'It won't do, Watson!' said he with a laugh. 'Let us walk along the cliffs together and search for flint arrows. We are more likely to find them than clues to this problem. To let the brain work without sufficient material is like racing an engine. It racks itself to pieces. The sea air, sunshine, and patience, Watson – all else will come.'

'Now, let us calmly define our position, Watson,' he continued as we skirted the cliffs together. 'Let us get a firm grip of the very little which we *do* know, so that when fresh facts arise we may be ready to fit them into their places. I take it, in the first place, that neither of us is prepared to admit diabolical intrusions into the affairs of men. Let us begin by ruling that entirely out of our minds. Very good. There remain three persons who have been grievously stricken by some conscious or unconscious human agency. That is firm ground. Now, when did this occur? Evidently, assuming his narrative to be true, it was immediately after Mr Mortimer Tregennis had left the room. That is a very important point. The presumption is that it was within a few minutes afterwards. The cards still lay upon the table. It was already past their usual hour for bed. Yet they had not changed their position or pushed back their chairs. I repeat, then, that the occurrence was immediately after his departure, and not later than eleven o'clock last night.

'Our next obvious step is to check, so far as we can, the movements of Mortimer Tregennis after he left the room. In this there is no difficulty, and they seem to be above suspicion. Knowing my methods as you do, you were, of course, conscious of the somewhat clumsy water-pot expedient by which I obtained a clearer impress of his foot than might otherwise have been possible. The wet, sandy path took it admirably. Last night was also wet, you will remember, and it was not difficult – having obtained a sample print – to pick out his track among others and to follow his movements. He appears to have walked away swiftly in the direction of the vicarage.

'If, then, Mortimer Tregennis disappeared from the scene, and yet some outside person affected the card-players, how can we reconstruct that person, and how was such an impression of horror conveyed? Mrs Porter may be eliminated. She is evidently harmless. Is there any evidence that someone crept up to the garden window and in some manner produced so terrific an effect that he drove those who saw it out of their senses? The only suggestion in this direction comes from Mortimer Tregennis himself, who says that his brother spoke about some movement in the garden. That is certainly remarkable, as the night was rainy, cloudy, and dark. Anyone who had the design to alarm these people would be compelled to place his very face against the glass before he could be seen. There is a three-foot flower-border outside this window, but no indication of a footmark. It is difficult to imagine, then, how an outsider could have made so terrible an impression upon the company, nor have we found any possible motive for so strange and elaborate an attempt. You perceive our difficulties, Watson?'

'They are only too clear,' I answered with conviction.

'And yet, with a little more material, we may prove

that they are not insurmountable,' said Holmes. 'I fancy that among your extensive archives, Watson, you may find some which were nearly as obscure. Meanwhile, we shall put the case aside until more accurate data are available, and devote the rest of our morning to the pursuit of neolithic man.'

I may have commented upon my friend's power of mental detachment, but never have I wondered at it more than upon that spring morning in Cornwall when for two hours he discoursed upon Celts, arrow-heads, and shards, as lightly as if no sinister mystery were waiting for his solution. It was not until we had returned in the afternoon to our cottage that we found a visitor awaiting us, who soon brought our minds back to the matter in hand. Neither of us needed to be told who that visitor was. The huge body, the craggy and deeply seamed face with the fierce eyes and hawklike nose, the grizzled hair which nearly brushed our cottage ceiling, the beard – golden at the fringes and white near the lips, save for the nicotine stain from his perpetual cigar – all these were as well known in London as in Africa, and could only be associated with the tremendous personality of Dr Leon Sterndale, the great lion-hunter and explorer.

We had heard of his presence in the district and had once or twice caught sight of his tall figure upon the moorland paths. He made no advances to us, how-ever, nor would we have dreamed of doing so to him, as it was well known that it was his love of seclusion which caused him to spend the greater part of the intervals between his journeys in a small bungalow buried in the lonely wood of Beauchamp Arriance. Here, amid his books and his maps, he lived an absolutely lonely life, attending to his own simple wants and paying little apparent heed to the affairs of his neighbours. It was a surprise to me, therefore, to hear him asking Holmes in an eager voice whether he had made any advance in his reconstruction of this mysterious episode. 'The county police are utterly at fault,' said he, 'but perhaps your wider experience has suggested some conceivable explanation. My only claim to being taken into your confidence is that during my many residences here I have come to know this family of Tregennis very well – indeed, upon my Cornish mother's side I could call them cousins – and their strange fate has naturally been a great shock to me. I may tell you that I had got as far as Plymouth upon my way to Africa, but the news reached me this morning, and I came straight back again to help in the enquiry.'

Holmes raised his eyebrows.

'Did you lose your boat through it?'

'I will take the next.'

'Dear me! that is friendship indeed.'

'I tell you they were relatives.'

'Quite so – cousins of your mother. Was your baggage aboard the ship?'

'Some of it, but the main part at the hotel.'

'I see. But surely this event could not have found its way into the Plymouth morning papers.'

'No, sir; I had a telegram.'

'Might I ask from whom?'

A shadow passed over the gaunt face of the explorer.

'You are very inquisitive, Mr Holmes.'

'It is my business.'

With an effort Dr Sterndale recovered his ruffled composure.

'I have no objection to telling you,' he said. 'It was

Mr Roundhay, the vicar, who sent me the telegram which recalled me.'

'Thank you,' said Holmes. 'I may say in answer to your original question that I have not cleared my mind entirely on the subject of this case, but that I have every hope of reaching some conclusion. It would be premature to say more.'

'Perhaps you would not mind telling me if your suspicions point in any particular direction?'

'No, I can hardly answer that.'

'Then I have wasted my time and need not prolong my visit.' The famous doctor strode out of our cottage in considerable ill-humour, and within five minutes Holmes had followed him. I saw him no more until the evening, when he returned with a slow step and haggard face which assured me that he had made no great progress with his investigation. He glanced at a telegram which awaited him and threw it into the grate.

'From the Plymouth hotel, Watson,' he said. 'I learned the name of it from the vicar, and I wired to make certain that Dr Leon Sterndale's account was true. It appears that he did indeed spend last night there, and that he has actually allowed some of his baggage to go on to Africa, while he returned to be present at this investigation. What do you make of that, Watson?'

'He is deeply interested.'

'Deeply interested – yes. There is a thread here which we have not yet grasped and which might lead us through the tangle. Cheer up, Watson, for I am very sure that our material has not yet all come to hand. When it does we may soon leave our difficulties behind us.'

Little did I think how soon the words of Holmes would be realised, or how strange and sinister would be that new development which opened up an entirely fresh line of investigation. I was shaving at my window in the morning when I heard the rattle of hoofs and, looking up, saw a dog-cart coming at a gallop down the road. It pulled up at our door, and our friend, the vicar, sprang from it and rushed up our garden path. Holmes was already dressed, and we hastened down to meet him.

Our visitor was so excited that he could hardly articulate, but at last in gasps and bursts his tragic story came out of him.

'We are devil-ridden, Mr Holmes! My poor parish is devil-ridden!' he cried. 'Satan himself is loose in it! We are given over into his hands!' He danced about in his agitation, a ludicrous object if it were not for his ashy face and startled eyes. Finally he shot out his terrible news.

'Mr Mortimer Tregennis died during the night, and with exactly the same symptoms as the rest of his family.'

Holmes sprang to his feet, all energy in an instant.

'Can you fit us both into your dog-cart?'

'Yes, I can.'

'Then, Watson, we will postpone our breakfast. Mr Roundhay, we are entirely at your disposal. Hurry – hurry, before things get disarranged.'

The lodger occupied two rooms at the vicarage, which were in an angle by themselves, the one above the other. Below was a large sitting-room; above, his bedroom. They looked out upon a croquet lawn which came up to the windows. We had arrived before the doctor or the police, so that everything was absolutely undisturbed. Let me describe exactly the scene as we saw it upon that misty March morning. It has left an impression which can never be effaced from my mind.

The atmosphere of the room was of a horrible and depressing stuffiness. The servant who had first entered had thrown up the window, or it would have been even more intolerable. This might partly be due to the fact that a lamp stood flaring and smoking on the centre table. Beside it sat the dead man, leaning back in his chair, his thin beard projecting, his spectacles pushed up on to his forehead, and his lean dark face turned towards the window and twisted into the same distortion of terror which had marked the features of his dead sister. His limbs were convulsed and his fingers contorted as though he had died in a very paroxysm of fear. He was fully clothed, though there were signs that his dressing had been done in a hurry. We had already learned that his bed had been slept in, and that the tragic end had come to him in the early morning.

One realised the red-hot energy which underlay Holmes's phlegmatic exterior when one saw the sudden change which came over him from the moment that he entered the fatal apartment. In an instant he was tense and alert, his eyes shining, his face set, his limbs quivering with eager activity. He was out on the lawn, in through the window, round the room, and up into the bedroom, for all the world like a dashing foxhound drawing a cover. In the bedroom he made a rapid cast around and ended by throwing open the window, which appeared to give him some fresh cause for excitement, for he leaned out of it with loud ejaculations of interest and delight. Then he rushed down the stair, out through the open window, threw himself upon his face on the lawn, sprang up and into the room once more, all with the energy of the hunter who is at the very heels of his quarry. The lamp, which was an ordinary standard, he examined with minute care, making certain measurements upon its bowl. He carefully scrutinised with his lens the talc shield which covered the top of the chimney and scraped off some ashes which adhered to its upper surface, putting some of them into an envelope, which he placed in his pocketbook. Finally, just as the doctor and the official police put in an appearance, he beckoned to the vicar and we all three went out upon the lawn.

'I am glad to say that my investigation has not been entirely barren,' he remarked. 'I cannot remain to discuss the matter with the police, but I should be exceedingly obliged, Mr Roundhay, if you would give the inspector my compliments and direct his attention to the bedroom window and to the sitting-room lamp. Each is suggestive, and together they are almost conclusive. If the police would desire further information I shall be happy to see any of them at the cottage. And now, Watson, I think that, perhaps, we shall be better employed elsewhere.'

It may be that the police resented the intrusion of an amateur, or that they imagined themselves to be upon some hopeful line of investigation; but it is certain that we heard nothing from them for the next two days. During this time Holmes spent some of his time smoking and dreaming in the cottage; but a greater portion in country walks which he undertook alone, returning after many hours without remark as to where he had been. One experiment served to show me the line of his investigation. He had bought a lamp which was the duplicate of the one which had burned in the room of Mortimer Tregennis on the morning of the tragedy. This he filled with the same oil as that used at the vicarage, and he carefully timed the period which it would take to be exhausted. Another experiment which he made was of a more unpleasant nature, and one which I am not likely ever to forget.

'You will remember, Watson,' he remarked one afternoon, 'that there is a single common point of resemblance in the varying reports which have reached us. This concerns the effect of the atmosphere of the room in each case upon those who had first entered it. You will recollect that Mortimer Tregennis, in describing the episode of his last visit to his brother's house, remarked that the doctor on entering the room fell into a chair? You had forgotten? Well I can answer for it that it was so. Now, you will remember also that Mrs Porter, the housekeeper, told us that she herself fainted upon entering the room and had afterwards opened the window. In the second case – that of Mortimer Tregennis himself – you cannot have forgotten the horrible stuffiness of the room when we arrived, though the servant had thrown open the window. That servant, I found upon enquiry, was so ill that she had gone to her bed. You will admit, Watson, that these facts are very suggestive. In each case there is evidence of a poisonous atmosphere. In each case, also, there is combustion going on in the room – in the one case a fire, in the other a lamp. The fire was needed, but the lamp was lit – as a comparison of the oil consumed will show – long after it was broad daylight. Why? Surely because there is some connection between three things – the burning, the stuffy atmosphere, and, finally, the madness or death of those unfortunate people. That is clear, is it not?'

'It would appear so.'

'At least we may accept it as a working hypothesis. We will suppose, then, that something was burned in each case which produced an atmosphere causing strange toxic effects. Very good. In the first instance – that of the Tregennis family – this substance was placed in the fire. Now the window was shut, but the fire would naturally carry fumes to some extent up the chimney. Hence one would expect the effects of the poison to be less than in the second case, where there was less escape for the vapour. The result seems to indicate that it was so, since in the first case only the woman, who had presumably the more sensitive organism, was killed, the others exhibiting that temporary or permanent lunacy which is evidently the first effect of the drug. In the second case the result was complete. The facts, therefore, seem to bear out the theory of a poison which worked by combustion.

'With this train of reasoning in my head I naturally looked about in Mortimer Tregennis's room to find some remains of this substance. The obvious place to look was the talc shelf or smoke-guard of the lamp. There, sure enough, I perceived a number of flaky ashes, and round the edges a fringe of brownish powder, which had not yet been consumed. Half of this I took, as you saw, and I placed it in an envelope.'

'Why half, Holmes?'

'It is not for me, my dear Watson, to stand in the way of the official police force. I leave them all the evidence which I found. The poison still remained upon the talc had they the wit to find it. Now, Watson, we will light our lamp; we will, however, take the precaution to open our window to avoid the premature decease of two deserving members of society, and you will seat yourself near that open window in an armchair unless, like a sensible man, you determine to have nothing to do with the affair. Oh, you will see it out, will you? I thought I knew my Watson. This chair I will place opposite yours, so that we may be the same distance from the poison and face to face. The door we will leave ajar. Each is now in a position to watch the other and to bring the experiment to an end should the symptoms seem alarming. Is that all clear? Well, then, I take our powder – or what remains of it – from the envelope, and I lay it above the burning lamp. So! Now, Watson, let us sit down and await developments.'

They were not long in coming. I had hardly settled in my chair before I was conscious of a thick, musky odour, subtle and nauseous. At the very first whiff of it my brain and my imagination were beyond all control. A thick, black cloud swirled before my eyes, and my mind told me that in this cloud, unseen as yet, but about to spring out upon my appalled senses, lurked all that was vaguely horrible, all that was monstrous and inconceivably wicked in the universe. Vague shapes swirled and swam amid the dark cloud-bank, each a menace and a warning of something coming, the advent of some unspeakable dweller upon the threshold, whose very shadow would blast my soul. A freezing horror took possession of me. I felt that my hair was rising, that my eyes were protruding, that my mouth was opened, and my tongue like leather. The turmoil within my brain was such that something must surely snap. I tried to scream and was vaguely aware of some hoarse croak which was my own voice, but distant and detached from myself. At the same moment, in some effort of escape, I broke through that cloud of despair and had a glimpse of Holmes's face, white, rigid, and drawn with horror – the very look which I had seen upon the features of the dead. It was that vision which gave me an instant of sanity and of strength. I dashed from my chair, threw my arms round Holmes, and together we lurched through the door, and an instant afterwards had thrown ourselves down upon the grass plot and were lying side by side, conscious only of the glorious sunshine which was bursting its way through the hellish cloud of terror which had girt us in. Slowly it rose from our souls like the mists from a landscape until peace and reason had returned, and we were sitting upon the grass, wiping our clammy foreheads, and looking with apprehension at each other to mark the last traces of that terrific experience which we had undergone.

'Upon my word, Watson!' said Holmes at last with an unsteady voice, 'I owe you both my thanks and an apology. It was an unjustifiable experiment even for one's self, and doubly so for a friend. I am really very sorry.'

'You know,' I answered with some emotion, for I have never seen so much of Holmes's heart before, 'that it is my greatest joy and privilege to help you.'

He relapsed at once into the half-humorous, half-cynical vein which was his habitual attitude to those about him. 'It would be superfluous to drive us mad, my dear Watson,' said he. 'A candid observer would certainly declare that we were so already before we embarked upon so wild an experiment. I confess that I never imagined that the effect could be so sudden and so severe.' He dashed into the cottage, and, reappearing with the burning lamp held at full arm's length, he threw it among a bank of brambles. 'We must give the room a little time to clear. I take it, Watson, that you have no longer a shadow of a doubt as to how these tragedies were produced?'

'None whatever.'

'But the cause remains as obscure as before. Come into the arbour here and let us discuss it together. That villainous stuff seems still to linger round my throat. I think we must admit that all the evidence points to this man, Mortimer Tregennis, having been the criminal in the first tragedy, though he was the victim in the second one. We must remember, in the first place, that there is some story of a family quarrel, followed by a reconciliation. How bitter that quarrel may have been, or how hollow the reconciliation we cannot tell. When I think of Mortimer Tregennis, with the foxy face and the small shrewd, beady eyes behind the spectacles, he is not a man whom I should judge to be of a particularly forgiving disposition. Well, in the next place, you will remember that this idea of someone moving in the garden, which took our attention for a moment from the real cause of the tragedy, emanated from him. He had a motive in misleading us. Finally, if he did not throw the substance into the fire at the moment of leaving the room, who did do so? The affair happened immediately after his departure. Had anyone else come in, the family would certainly have risen from the table. Besides, in peaceful Cornwall, visitors did not arrive after ten o'clock at night. We may take it, then, that all the evidence points to Mortimer Tregennis as the culprit.'

'Then his own death was suicide!'

'Well, Watson, it is on the face of it a not impossible supposition. The man who had the guilt upon his soul of having brought such a fate upon his own family might well be driven by remorse to inflict it upon himself. There are, however, some cogent reasons against it. Fortunately, there is one man in England who knows all about it, and I have made arrangements by which we shall hear the facts this afternoon from his own lips. Ah! he is a little before his time. Perhaps you would kindly step this way, Dr Leon Sterndale. We have been conducting a chemical experiment indoors which has left our little room hardly fit for the reception of so distinguished a visitor.'

I had heard the click of the garden gate, and now the majestic figure of the great African explorer appeared upon the path. He turned in some surprise towards the rustic arbour in which we sat.

'You sent for me, Mr Holmes. I had your note about an hour ago, and I have come, though I really do not know why I should obey your summons.'

'Perhaps we can clear the point up before we separate,' said Holmes. 'Meanwhile, I am much obliged to you for your courteous acquiescence. You will excuse this informal reception in the open air, but my friend Watson and I have nearly furnished an additional chapter to what the papers call the Cornish Horror, and we prefer a clear atmosphere for the present. Perhaps, since the matters which we have to discuss will affect you personally in a very intimate fashion, it is as well that we should talk where there can be no eavesdropping.'

The explorer took his cigar from his lips and gazed sternly at my companion.

'I am at a loss to know, sir,' he said, 'what you can have to speak about which affects me personally in a very intimate fashion.'

'The killing of Mortimer Tregennis,' said Holmes.

For a moment I wished that I were armed. Sterndale's fierce face turned to a dusky red, his eyes glared, and the knotted, passionate veins started out in his forehead, while he sprang forward with clenched hands towards my companion. Then he stopped, and with a violent effort he resumed a cold, rigid calmness, which was, perhaps, more suggestive of danger than his hot-headed outburst.

'I have lived so long among savages and beyond the law,' said he, 'that I have got into the way of being a law to myself. You would do well, Mr Holmes, not to forget it, for I have no desire to do you an injury.'

'Nor have I any desire to do you an injury, Dr Sterndale. Surely the clearest proof of it is that, knowing what I know, I have sent for you and not for the police.'

Sterndale sat down with a gasp, overawed for, perhaps, the first time in his adventurous life. There was a calm assurance of power in Holmes's manner which could not be withstood. Our visitor stammered for a moment, his great hands opening and shutting in his agitation.

'What do you mean?' he asked at last. 'If this is bluff upon your part, Mr Holmes, you have chosen a bad man for your experiment. Let us have no more beating about the bush. What *do* you mean?'

'I will tell you,' said Holmes, 'and the reason why I tell you is that I hope frankness may beget frankness. What my next step may be will depend entirely upon the nature of your own defence.'

'My defence?'

'Yes, sir.'

'My defence against what?'

'Against the charge of killing Mortimer Tregennis.'

Sterndale mopped his forehead with his handkerchief. 'Upon my word, you are getting on,' said he. 'Do all your successes depend upon this prodigious power of bluff?'

'The bluff,' said Holmes sternly, 'is upon your side, Dr Leon Sterndale, and not upon mine. As a proof I will tell you some of the facts upon which my conclusions are based. Of your return from Plymouth, allowing much of your property to go on to Africa, I will say nothing save that it first informed me that you were one of the factors which had to be taken into account in reconstructing this drama – '

'I came back – '

'I have heard your reasons and regard them as unconvincing and inadequate. We will pass that. You came down here to ask me whom I suspected. I refused to answer you. You then went to the vicarage, waited outside it for some time, and finally returned to your cottage.'

'How do you know that?'

'I followed you.'

'I saw no one.'

'That is what you may expect to see when I follow you. You spent a restless night at your cottage, and you formed certain plans, which in the early morning you proceeded to put into execution. Leaving your door just as day was breaking, you filled your pocket with some reddish gravel that was lying heaped beside your gate.'

Sterndale gave a violent start and looked at Holmes in amazement.

'You then walked swiftly for the mile which separated you from the vicarage. You were wearing,

I may remark, the same pair of ribbed tennis shoes which are at the present moment upon your feet. At the vicarage you passed through the orchard and the side hedge, coming out under the window of the lodger Tregennis. It was now daylight, but the household was not yet stirring. You drew some of the gravel from your pocket, and you threw it up at the window above you.'

Sterndale sprang to his feet.

'I believe that you are the devil himself!' he cried.

Holmes smiled at the compliment. 'It took two, or possibly three, handfuls before the lodger came to the window. You beckoned him to come down. He dressed hurriedly and descended to his sitting-room. You entered by the window. There was an interview – a short one – during which you walked up and down the room. Then you passed out and closed the window, standing on the lawn outside smoking a cigar and watching what occurred. Finally, after the death of Tregennis, you withdrew as you had come. Now, Dr Sterndale, how do you justify such conduct, and what were the motives for your actions? If you prevaricate or trifle with me, I give you my assurance that the matter will pass out of my hands for ever.'

Our visitor's face had turned ashen grey as he listened to the words of his accuser. Now he sat for some time in thought with his face sunk in his hands. Then with a sudden impulsive gesture he plucked a photograph from his breast-pocket and threw it on the rustic table before us.

'That is why I have done it,' said he.

It showed the bust and face of a very beautiful woman. Holmes stooped over it.

'Brenda Tregennis,' said he.

'Yes, Brenda Tregennis,' repeated our visitor. 'For

years I have loved her. For years she has loved me. There is the secret of that Cornish seclusion which people have marvelled at. It has brought me close to the one thing on earth that was dear to me. I could not marry her, for I have a wife who has left me for years and yet whom, by the deplorable laws of England, I could not divorce. For years Brenda waited. For years I waited. And this is what we have waited for.' A terrible sob shook his great frame, and he clutched his throat under his brindled beard. Then with an effort he mastered himself and spoke on.

'The vicar knew. He was in our confidence. He would tell you that she was an angel upon earth. That was why he telegraphed to me and I returned. What was my baggage or Africa to me when I learned that such a fate had come upon my darling? There you have the missing clue to my action, Mr Holmes.'

'Proceed,' said my friend.

Dr Sterndale drew from his pocket a paper packet and laid it upon the table. On the outside was written '*Radix pedis diaboli*' with a red poison label beneath it. He pushed it towards me. 'I understand that you are a doctor, sir. Have you ever heard of this preparation?'

'Devil's-foot root! No, I have never heard of it.'

'It is no reflection upon your professional know-ledge,' said he, 'for I believe that, save for one sample in a laboratory at Buda, there is no other specimen in Europe. It has not yet found its way either into the pharmacopoeia or into the literature of toxicology. The root is shaped like a foot, half human, half goatlike; hence the fanciful name given by a botanical missionary. It is used as an ordeal poison by the medicine-men in certain districts of west Africa and is kept as a secret among them. This particular specimen

I obtained under very extraordinary circumstances in the Ubangi country.' He opened the paper as he spoke and disclosed a heap of reddish-brown, snuff-like powder.

'Well, sir?' asked Holmes sternly.

'I am about to tell you, Mr Holmes, all that actually occurred, for you already know so much that it is clearly to my interest that you should know all. I have already explained the relationship in which I stood to the Tregennis family. For the sake of the sister I was friendly with the brothers. There was a family quarrel about money which estranged this man Mortimer, but it was supposed to be made up, and I afterwards met him as I did the others. He was a sly, subtle, scheming man, and several things arose which gave me a suspicion of him, but I had no cause for any positive quarrel.

'One day, only a couple of weeks ago, he came down to my cottage and I showed him some of my African curiosities. Among other things I exhibited this powder, and I told him of its strange properties, how it stimulates those brain centres which control the emotion of fear, and how either madness or death is the fate of the unhappy native who is subjected to the ordeal by the priest of his tribe. I told him also how powerless European science would be to detect it. How he took it I cannot say, for I never left the room, but there is no doubt that it was then, while I was opening cabinets and stooping to boxes, that he managed to abstract some of the devil's-foot root. I well remember how he plied me with questions as to the amount and the time that was needed for its effect, but I little dreamed that he could have a personal reason for asking.

'I thought no more of the matter until the vicar's telegram reached me at Plymouth. This villain had thought that I would be at sea before the news could reach me, and that I should be lost for years in Africa. But I returned at once. Of course, I could not listen to the details without feeling assured that my poison had been used. I came round to see you on the chance that some other explanation had suggested itself to you. But there could be none. I was convinced that Mortimer Tregennis was the murderer; that for the sake of money, and with the idea, perhaps, that if the other members of his family were all insane he would be the sole guardian of their joint property, he had used the devil's-foot powder upon them, driven two of them out of their senses, and killed his sister Brenda, the one human being whom I have ever loved or who has ever loved me. There was his crime; what was to be his punishment?

'Should I appeal to the law? Where were my proofs? I knew that the facts were true, but could I help to make a jury of countrymen believe so fantastic a story? I might or I might not. But I could not afford to fail. My soul cried out for revenge. I have said to you once before, Mr Holmes, that I have spent much of my life outside the law, and that I have come at last to be a law to myself. So it was even now. I determined that the fate which he had given to others should be shared by himself. Either that or I would do justice upon him with my own hand. In all England there can be no man who sets less value upon his own life than I do at the present moment.

'Now I have told you all. You have yourself supplied the rest. I did, as you say, after a restless night, set off early from my cottage. I foresaw the difficulty of arousing him, so I gathered some gravel from the pile which you have mentioned, and I used it to throw up to his window. He came down and admitted me through the window of the sitting-room. I laid his offence before him. I told him that I had come both as judge and executioner. The wretch sank into a chair, paralysed at the sight of my revolver. I lit the lamp, put the powder above it, and stood outside the window, ready to carry out my threat to shoot him should he try to leave the room. In five minutes he died. My God! how he died! But my heart was flint, for he endured nothing which my innocent darling had not felt before him. There is my story, Mr Holmes. Perhaps, if you loved a woman, you would have done as much yourself. At any rate, I am in your hands. You can take what steps you like. As I have already said, there is no man living who can fear death less than I do.'

Holmes sat for some little time in silence.

'What were your plans?' he asked at last.

'I had intended to bury myself in central Africa. My work there is but half finished.'

'Go and do the other half,' said Holmes. 'I, at least, am not prepared to prevent you.'

Dr Sterndale raised his giant figure, bowed gravely, and walked from the arbour. Holmes lit his pipe and handed me his pouch.

'Some fumes which are not poisonous would be a welcome change,' said he. 'I think you must agree, Watson, that it is not a case in which we are called upon to interfere. Our investigation has been independent, and our action shall be so also. You would not denounce the man?'

'Certainly not,' I answered.

'I have never loved, Watson, but if I did and if the

woman I loved had met such an end, I might act even as our lawless lion-hunter has done. Who knows? Well, Watson, I will not offend your intelligence by explaining what is obvious. The gravel upon the window-sill was, of course, the starting-point of my research. It was unlike anything in the vicarage garden. Only when my attention had been drawn to Dr Sterndale and his cottage did I find its counterpart. The lamp shining in broad daylight and the remains of powder upon the shield were successive links in a fairly obvious chain. And now, my dear Watson, I think we may dismiss the matter from our minds and go back with a clear conscience to the study of those Chaldean roots which are surely to be traced in the Cornish branch of the great Celtic speech.'

21

His Last Bow

An Epilogue of Sherlock Holmes

It was nine o'clock at night upon the second of August – the most terrible August in the history of the world. One might have thought already that God's curse hung heavy over a degenerate world, for there was an awesome hush and a feeling of vague expectancy in the sultry and stagnant air. The sun had long set, but one blood-red gash like an open wound lay low in the distant west. Above, the stars were shining brightly, and below, the lights of the shipping glimmered in the bay. The two famous Germans stood beside the stone parapet of the garden walk, with the long, low, heavily gabled house behind them, and they looked down upon the broad sweep of the beach at the foot of the great chalk cliff in which Von Bork, like some wandering eagle, had perched himself four years before. They stood with their heads close together, talking in low, confidential tones. From below the two glowing ends of their cigars might have been the smouldering eyes of some malignant fiend looking down in the darkness.

A remarkable man this Von Bork – a man who could hardly be matched among all the devoted agents of the Kaiser. It was his talents which had first recommended him for the English mission, the most important mission of all, but since he had taken it over those talents had become more and more manifest to the half-dozen people in the world who were really in touch with the truth. One of these was his present companion, Baron Von Herling, the chief secretary of the legation, whose huge one-hundred-horsepower Benz car was blocking the country lane as it waited to waft its owner back to London.

'So far as I can judge the trend of events, you will probably be back in Berlin within the week,' the secretary was saying. 'When you get there, my dear Von Bork, I think you will be surprised at the welcome you will receive. I happen to know what is thought in the highest quarters of your work in this country.' He was a huge man, the secretary, deep, broad, and tall, with a slow, heavy fashion of speech which had been his main asset in his political career.

Von Bork laughed.

'They are not very hard to deceive,' he remarked. 'A more docile, simple folk could not be imagined.'

'I don't know about that,' said the other thoughtfully. 'They have strange limits and one must learn to observe them. It is that surface simplicity of theirs which makes a trap for the stranger. One's first impression is that they are entirely soft. Then one comes suddenly upon something very hard, and you know that you have reached the limit and must adapt yourself to the fact. They have, for example, their insular conventions which simply *must* be observed.'

'Meaning "good form" and that sort of thing?' Von Bork sighed as one who had suffered much.

'Meaning British prejudice in all its queer manifestations. As an example I may quote one of my own worst blunders – I can afford to talk of my blunders, for you know my work well enough to be aware of my successes. It was on my first arrival. I was invited to a weekend gathering at the country house of a cabinet minister. The conversation was amazingly indiscreet.'

Von Bork nodded. 'I've been there,' said he dryly.

'Exactly. Well, I naturally sent a résumé of the information to Berlin. Unfortunately our good chancellor is a little heavy-handed in these matters, and he transmitted a remark which showed that he was aware of what had been said. This, of course, took the trail straight up to me. You've no idea the harm that it did me. There was nothing soft about our British hosts on that occasion, I can assure you. I was two years living it down. Now you, with this sporting pose of yours – '

'No, no, don't call it a pose. A pose is an artificial thing. This is quite natural. I am a born sportsman. I enjoy it.'

'Well, that makes it the more effective. You yacht against them, you hunt with them, you play polo, you match them in every game, your four-in-hand takes the prize at Olympia. I have even heard that you go the length of boxing with the young officers. What is the result? Nobody takes you seriously. You are a "good old sport", "quite a decent fellow for a German", a hard-drinking, nightclub, knock-about-town, devil-may-care young fellow. And all the time this quiet country house of yours is the centre of half the mischief in England, and the sporting squire the most astute secret-service man in Europe. Genius, my dear Von Bork – genius!'

'You flatter me, Baron. But certainly I may claim my four years in this country have not been unproductive. I've never shown you my little store. Would you mind stepping in for a moment?'

The door of the study opened straight on to the terrace. Von Bork pushed it back, and, leading the way, he clicked the switch of the electric light. He then closed the door behind the bulky form which followed him and carefully adjusted the heavy curtain over the latticed window. Only when all these precautions had been taken and tested did he turn his sunburned aquiline face to his guest.

'Some of my papers have gone,' said he. 'When my wife and the household left yesterday for Flushing they took the less important with them. I must, of course, claim the protection of the Embassy for the others.'

'Your name has already been filed as one of the personal suite. There will be no difficulties for you or your baggage. Of course, it is just possible that we may not have to go. England may leave France to her fate. We are sure that there is no binding treaty between them.'

'And Belgium?'

'Yes, and Belgium, too.'

Von Bork shook his head. 'I don't see how that could be. There is a definite treaty there. She could never recover from such a humiliation.'

'She would at least have peace for the moment.'

'But her honour?'

'Tut, my dear sir, we live in a utilitarian age. Honour is a mediaeval conception. Besides, England is not ready. It is an inconceivable thing, but even our special war tax of fifty million, which one would think made our purpose as clear as if we had advertised it on the front page of *The Times*, has not roused these people from their slumbers. Here and there one hears a question. It is my business to find an answer. Here and there also there is an irritation. It is my business to soothe it. But I can assure you that so far as the essentials go – the storage of munitions, the preparation for submarine attack, the arrangements for making high explosives – nothing is prepared. How, then, can England come in, especially when we have stirred her up such a devil's brew of Irish civil war, window-breaking Furies, and God knows what to keep her thoughts at home.'

'She must think of her future.'

'Ah, that is another matter. I fancy that in the future we have our own very definite plans about England, and that your information will be very vital to us. It is today or tomorrow with Mr John Bull. If he prefers today we are perfectly ready. If it is tomorrow we shall be more ready still. I should think they would be wiser to fight with allies than without them, but that is their own affair. This week is their week of destiny. But you were speaking of your papers.' He sat in the armchair with the light shining upon his broad bald head, while he puffed sedately at his cigar.

The large oak-panelled, book-lined room had a curtain hung in the farther corner. When this was drawn it disclosed a large, brass-bound safe. Von Bork detached a small key from his watch-chain, and after some considerable manipulation of the lock he swung open the heavy door.

'Look!' said he, standing clear, with a wave of his hand.

The light shone vividly into the opened safe, and the secretary of the embassy gazed with an absorbed interest at the rows of stuffed pigeon-holes with which it was furnished. Each pigeon-hole had its label, and his eyes as he glanced along them read a long series of such titles as 'Fords', 'Harbour-defences', 'Aero-planes', 'Ireland', 'Egypt', 'Portsmouth forts', 'The

Channel', 'Rosythe', and a score of others. Each compartment was bristling with papers and plans.

'Colossal!' said the secretary. Putting down his cigar he softly clapped his fat hands.

'And all in four years, Baron. Not such a bad show for the hard-drinking, hard-riding country squire. But the gem of my collection is coming and there is the setting all ready for it.' He pointed to a space over which 'Naval Signals' was printed.

'But you have a good dossier there already.'

'Out of date and waste paper. The Admiralty in some way got the alarm and every code has been changed. It was a blow, Baron – the worst setback in my whole campaign. But thanks to my chequebook and the good Altamont all will be well tonight.'

The Baron looked at his watch and gave a guttural exclamation of disappointment.

'Well, I really can wait no longer. You can imagine that things are moving at present in Carlton Terrace and that we have all to be at our posts. I had hoped to be able to bring news of your great coup. Did Altamont name no hour?'

Von Bork pushed over a telegram.

Will come without fail tonight and bring new sparking plugs.   ALTAMONT.

'Sparking plugs, eh?'

'You see he poses as a motor expert and I keep a full garage. In our code everything likely to come up is named after some spare part. If he talks of a radiator it is a battleship, of an oil pump a cruiser, and so on. Sparking plugs are naval signals.'

'From Portsmouth at midday,' said the secretary,

examining the superscription. 'By the way, what do you give him?'

'Five hundred pounds for this particular job. Of course he has a salary as well.'

'The greedy rogue. They are useful, these traitors, but I grudge them their blood money.'

'I grudge Altamont nothing. He is a wonderful worker. If I pay him well, at least he delivers the goods, to use his own phrase. Besides, he is not a traitor. I assure you that our most pan-Germanic Junker is a sucking dove in his feelings towards England as compared with a real bitter Irish-American.'

'Oh, an Irish-American?'

'If you heard him talk you would not doubt it. Sometimes I assure you I can hardly understand him. He seems to have declared war on the King's English as well as on the English king. Must you really go? He may be here any moment.'

'No. I'm sorry, but I have already overstayed my time. We shall expect you early tomorrow, and when you get that signal book through the little door on the Duke of York's steps you can put a triumphant finis to your record in England. What! Tokay!' He indicated a heavily sealed dust-covered bottle which stood with two high glasses upon a salver.

'May I offer you a glass before your journey?'

'No, thanks. But it looks like revelry.'

'Altamont has a nice taste in wines, and he took a fancy to my Tokay. He is a touchy fellow and needs humouring in small things. I have to study him, I assure you.' They had strolled out on to the terrace again, and along it to the further end where at a touch from the Baron's chauffeur the great car shivered and chuckled. 'Those are the lights of Harwich, I suppose,' said the secretary, pulling on his dust coat. 'How still and peaceful it all seems. There may be other lights within the week, and the English coast a less tranquil place! The heavens, too, may not be quite so peaceful if all that the good Zeppelin promises us comes true. By the way, who is that?'

Only one window showed a light behind them; in it there stood a lamp, and beside it, seated at a table, was a dear old ruddy-faced woman in a country cap. She was bending over her knitting and stopping occasionally to stroke a large black cat upon a stool beside her.

'That is Martha, the only servant I have left.'

The secretary chuckled.

'She might almost personify Britannia,' said he, 'with her complete self-absorption and general air of comfortable somnolence. Well, *au revoir*, Von Bork!' With a final wave of his hand he sprang into the car, and a moment later the two golden cones from the headlights shot forward through the darkness. The secretary lay back in the cushions of the luxurious limousine, with his thoughts so full of the impending European tragedy that he hardly observed that as his car swung round the village street it nearly passed over a little Ford coming in the opposite direction.

Von Bork walked slowly back to the study when the last gleams of the motor lamps had faded into the distance. As he passed he observed that his old housekeeper had put out her lamp and retired. It was a new experience to him, the silence and darkness of his widespread house, for his family and household had been a large one. It was a relief to him, however, to think that they were all in safety and that, but for that one old woman who had lingered in the kitchen, he had the whole place to himself. There was a good deal of tidying up to do inside his study and he set himself to do it until his keen, handsome face was flushed with the heat of the burning papers. A leather valise stood beside his table, and into this he began to pack very neatly and systematically the precious contents of his safe. He had hardly got started with the work, however, when his quick ears caught the sounds of a distant car. Instantly he gave an exclamation of satisfaction, strapped up the valise, shut the safe, locked it, and hurried out on to the terrace. He was just in time to see the lights of a small car come to a halt at the gate. A passenger sprang out of it and advanced swiftly towards him, while the chauffeur, a heavily built, elderly man with a grey moustache, settled down like one who resigns himself to a long vigil.

'Well?' asked Von Bork eagerly, running forward to meet his visitor.

For answer the man waved a small brown-paper parcel triumphantly above his head.

'You can give me the glad hand tonight, mister,' he cried. 'I'm bringing home the bacon at last.'

'The signals?'

'Same as I said in my cable. Every last one of them, semaphore, lamp code, Marconi – a copy, mind you, not the original. That was too dangerous. But it's the real goods, and you can lay to that.' He slapped the German upon the shoulder with a rough familiarity from which the other winced.

'Come in,' he said. 'I'm all alone in the house. I was only waiting for this. Of course a copy is better than the original. If an original were missing they would change the whole thing. You think it's all safe about the copy?'

The Irish-American had entered the study and stretched his long limbs from the armchair. He was a tall, gaunt man of sixty, with clear-cut features and a small goatee beard which gave him a general resemblance to the caricatures of Uncle Sam. A half-smoked, sodden cigar hung from the corner of his mouth, and as he sat down he struck a match and relit it. 'Making ready for a move?' he remarked as he looked round him. 'Say, mister,' he added, as his eyes fell upon the safe from which the curtain was now removed, 'you don't tell me you keep your papers in that?'

'Why not?'

'Gosh, in a wide-open contraption like that! And they reckon you to be some spy. Why, a Yankee crook would be into that with a can-opener. If I'd known that any letter of mine was goin' to lie loose in a thing like that I'd have been a mug to write to you at all.'

'It would puzzle any crook to force that safe,' Von Bork answered. 'You won't cut that metal with any tool.'

'But the lock?'

'No, it's a double combination lock. You know what that is?'

'Search me,' said the American.

'Well, you need a word as well as a set of figures before you can get the lock to work.' He rose and showed a double-radiating disc round the keyhole. 'This outer one is for the letters, the inner one for the figures.'

'Well, well, that's fine.'

'So it's not quite as simple as you thought. It was four years ago that I had it made, and what do you think I chose for the word and figures?'

'It's beyond me.'

'Well, I chose August for the word, and 1914 for the figures, and here we are.'

The American's face showed his surprise and admiration.

'My, but that was smart! You had it down to a fine thing.'

'Yes, a few of us even then could have guessed the date. Here it is, and I'm shutting down tomorrow morning.'

'Well, I guess you'll have to fix me up also. I'm not staying in this gol-darned country all on my lonesome. In a week or less, from what I see, John Bull will be on his hind legs and fair ramping. I'd rather watch him from over the water.'

'But you're an American citizen?'

'Well, so was Jack James an American citizen, but he's doing time in Portland all the same. It cuts no ice with a British copper to tell him you're an American citizen. "It's British law and order over here," says he. By the way, mister, talking of Jack James, it seems to me you don't do much to cover your men.'

'What do you mean?' Von Bork asked sharply.

'Well, you are their employer, ain't you? It's up to you to see that they don't fall down. But they do fall down, and when did you ever pick them up? There's James – '

'It was James's own fault. You know that yourself. He was too self-willed for the job.'

'James was a bonehead – I give you that. Then there was Hollis.'

'The man was mad.'

'Well, he went a bit woozy towards the end. It's enough to make a man bug-house when he has to play a part from morning to night with a hundred guys all

613

ready to set the coppers wise to him. But now there is Steiner – '

Von Bork started violently, and his ruddy face turned a shade paler.

'What about Steiner?'

'Well, they've got him, that's all. They raided his store last night, and he and his papers are all in Portsmouth gaol. You'll go off and he, poor devil, will have to stand the racket, and lucky if he gets off with his life. That's why I want to get over the water as soon as you do.'

Von Bork was a strong, self-contained man, but it was easy to see that the news had shaken him.

'How could they have got on to Steiner?' he muttered. 'That's the worst blow yet.'

'Well, you nearly had a worse one, for I believe they are not far off me.'

'You don't mean that!'

'Sure thing. My landlady down Fratton way had some enquiries, and when I heard of it I guessed it was time for me to hustle. But what I want to know, mister, is how the coppers know these things? Steiner is the fifth man you've lost since I signed on with you, and I know the name of the sixth if I don't get a move on. How do you explain it, and ain't you ashamed to see your men go down like this?'

Von Bork flushed crimson.

'How dare you speak in such a way!'

'If I didn't dare things, mister, I wouldn't be in your service. But I'll tell you straight what is in my mind. I've heard that with you German politicians when an agent has done his work you are not sorry to see him put away.'

Von Bork sprang to his feet.

'Do you dare to suggest that I have given away my own agents!'

'I don't stand for that, mister, but there's a stool pigeon or a cross somewhere, and it's up to you to find out where it is. Anyhow I am taking no more chances. It's me for little Holland, and the sooner the better.'

Von Bork had mastered his anger.

'We have been allies too long to quarrel now at the very hour of victory,' he said. 'You've done splendid work and taken risks, and I can't forget it. By all means go to Holland, and you can get a boat from Rotterdam to New York. No other line will be safe a week from now. I'll take that book and pack it with the rest.'

The American held the small parcel in his hand, but made no motion to give it up.

'What about the dough?' he asked.

'The what?'

'The boodle. The reward. The £500. The gunner turned damned nasty at the last, and I had to square him with an extra hundred dollars or it would have been nitsky for you and me. "Nothin' doin'!" says he, and he meant it, too, but the last hundred did it. It's cost me two hundred pound from first to last, so it isn't likely I'd give it up without gettin' my wad.'

Von Bork smiled with some bitterness. 'You don't seem to have a very high opinion of my honour,' said he, 'you want the money before you give up the book.'

'Well, mister, it is a business proposition.'

'All right. Have your way.' He sat down at the table and scribbled a cheque, which he tore from the book, but he refrained from handing it to his companion. 'After all, since we are to be on such terms, Mr Altamont,' said he, 'I don't see why I should trust you

any more than you trust me. Do you understand?'
he added, looking back over his shoulder at the
American. 'There's the cheque upon the table. I claim
the right to examine that parcel before you pick the
money up.'

The American passed it over without a word. Von
Bork undid a winding of string and two wrappers of
paper. Then he sat gazing for a moment in silent
amazement at a small blue book which lay before him.
Across the cover was printed in golden letters *Practical
Handbook of Bee Culture*. Only for one instant did the
master spy glare at this strangely irrelevant inscription.
The next he was gripped at the back of his neck by a
grasp of iron, and a chloroformed sponge was held in
front of his writhing face.

'Another glass, Watson!' said Mr Sherlock Holmes as
he extended the bottle of Imperial Tokay.

The thick-set chauffeur, who had seated himself by
the table, pushed forward his glass with some eagerness.

'It is a good wine, Holmes.'

'A remarkable wine, Watson. Our friend upon the
sofa has assured me that it is from Franz Josef's special
cellar at the Schoenbrunn Palace. Might I trouble you
to open the window, for chloroform vapour does not
help the palate.'

The safe was ajar, and Holmes standing in front of it
was removing dossier after dossier, swiftly examining
each, and then packing it neatly in Von Bork's valise.
The German lay upon the sofa sleeping stertorously
with a strap round his upper arms and another round
his legs.

'We need not hurry ourselves, Watson. We are safe
from interruption. Would you mind touching the bell?

There is no one in the house except old Martha, who has played her part to admiration. I got her the situation here when first I took the matter up. Ah, Martha, you will be glad to hear that all is well.'

The pleasant old lady had appeared in the doorway. She curtseyed with a smile to Mr Holmes, but glanced with some apprehension at the figure upon the sofa.

'It is all right, Martha. He has not been hurt at all.'

'I am glad of that, Mr Holmes. According to his lights he has been a kind master. He wanted me to go with his wife to Germany yesterday, but that would hardly have suited your plans, would it, sir?'

'No, indeed, Martha. So long as you were here I was easy in my mind. We waited some time for your signal tonight.'

'It was the secretary, sir.'

'I know. His car passed ours.'

'I thought he would never go. I knew that it would not suit your plans, sir, to find him here.'

'No, indeed. Well, it only meant that we waited half an hour or so until I saw your lamp go out and knew that the coast was clear. You can report to me tomorrow in London, Martha, at Claridge's Hotel.'

'Very good, sir.'

'I suppose you have everything ready to leave.'

'Yes, sir. He posted seven letters today. I have the addresses as usual.'

'Very good, Martha. I will look into them tomorrow. Good-night. These papers,' he continued as the old lady vanished, 'are not of very great importance, for, of course, the information which they represent has been sent off long ago to the German government. These are the originals which could not safely be got out of the country.'

'Then they are of no use.'

'I should not go so far as to say that, Watson. They will at least show our people what is known and what is not. I may say that a good many of these papers have come through me, and I need not add are thoroughly untrustworthy. It would brighten my declining years to see a German cruiser navigating the Solent according to the minefield plans which I have furnished. But you, Watson' – he stopped his work and took his old friend by the shoulders – 'I've hardly seen you in the light yet. How have the years used you? You look the same blithe boy as ever.'

'I feel twenty years younger, Holmes. I have seldom felt so happy as when I got your wire asking me to meet you at Harwich with the car. But you, Holmes – you have changed very little – save for that horrible goatee.'

'These are the sacrifices one makes for one's country, Watson,' said Holmes, pulling at his little tuft. 'Tomorrow it will be but a dreadful memory. With my hair cut and a few other superficial changes I shall no doubt reappear at Claridge's tomorrow as I was before this American stunt – I beg your pardon, Watson, my well of English seems to be permanently defiled – before this American job came my way.'

'But you have retired, Holmes. We heard of you as living the life of a hermit among your bees and your books in a small farm upon the South Downs.'

'Exactly, Watson. Here is the fruit of my leisured ease, the *magnum opus* of my latter years!' He picked up the volume from the table and read out the whole title, *Practical Handbook of Bee Culture, with Some Observations upon the Segregation of the Queen.* 'Alone I did it. Behold the fruit of pensive nights and laborious days when I watched the little working gangs as once I watched the criminal world of London.'

'But how did you get to work again?'

'Ah, I have often marvelled at it myself. The Foreign Minister alone I could have withstood, but when the Premier also deigned to visit my humble roof – ! The fact is, Watson, that this gentleman upon the sofa was a bit too good for our people. He was in a class by himself. Things were going wrong, and no one could understand why they were going wrong. Agents were suspected or even caught, but there was evidence of some strong and secret central force. It was absolutely necessary to expose it. Strong pressure was brought upon me to look into the matter. It has cost me two years, Watson, but they have not been devoid of excitement. When I say that I started my pilgrimage at Chicago, graduated in an Irish secret society at Buffalo, gave serious trouble to the constabulary at Skibbereen, and so eventually caught the eye of a subordinate agent of Von Bork, who recommended me as a likely man, you will realise that the matter was complex. Since then I have been honoured by his confidence, which has not prevented most of his plans going subtly wrong and five of his best agents being in prison. I watched them, Watson, and I picked them as they ripened. Well, sir, I hope that you are none the worse!'

The last remark was addressed to Von Bork himself, who after much gasping and blinking had lain quietly listening to Holmes's statement. He broke out now into a furious stream of German invective, his face convulsed with passion. Holmes continued his swift investigation of documents while his prisoner cursed and swore.

'Though unmusical, German is the most expressive

of all languages,' he observed when Von Bork had stopped from pure exhaustion. 'Hullo! Hullo!' he added as he looked hard at the corner of a tracing before putting it in the box. 'This should put another bird in the cage. I had no idea that the paymaster was such a rascal, though I have long had an eye upon him. Mister Von Bork, you have a great deal to answer for.'

The prisoner had raised himself with some difficulty upon the sofa and was staring with a strange mixture of amazement and hatred at his captor.

'I shall get level with you, Altamont,' he said, speaking with slow deliberation. 'If it takes me all my life I shall get level with you!'

'The old sweet song,' said Holmes. 'How often have I heard it in days gone by. It was a favourite ditty of the late lamented Professor Moriarty. Colonel Sebastian Moran has also been known to warble it. And yet I live and keep bees upon the South Downs.'

'Curse you, you double traitor!' cried the German, straining against his bonds and glaring murder from his furious eyes.

'No, no, it is not so bad as that,' said Holmes, smiling. 'As my speech surely shows you, Mr Altamont of Chicago had no existence in fact. I used him and he is gone.'

'Then who are you?'

'It is really immaterial who I am, but since the matter seems to interest you, Mr Von Bork, I may say that this is not my first acquaintance with the members of your family. I have done a good deal of business in Germany in the past and my name is probably familiar to you.'

'I would wish to know it,' said the Prussian grimly.

'It was I who brought about the separation between

Irene Adler and the late King of Bohemia when your cousin Heinrich was the Imperial Envoy. It was I also who saved from murder, by the Nihilist Klopman, Count Von und Zu Grafenstein, who was your mother's elder brother. It was I – '

Von Bork sat up in amazement.

'There is only one man,' he cried.

'Exactly,' said Holmes.

Von Bork groaned and sank back on the sofa. 'And most of that information came through you,' he cried. 'What is it worth? What have I done? It is my ruin for ever!'

'It is certainly a little untrustworthy,' said Holmes. 'It will require some checking and you have little time to check it. Your admiral may find the new guns rather larger than he expects, and the cruisers perhaps a trifle faster.'

Von Bork clutched at his own throat in despair.

'There are a good many other points of detail which will, no doubt, come to light in good time. But you have one quality which is very rare in a German, Mr Von Bork: you are a sportsman and you will bear me no ill-will when you realise that you, who have outwitted so many other people, have at last been outwitted yourself. After all, you have done your best for your country, and I have done my best for mine, and what could be more natural? Besides,' he added, not unkindly, as he laid his hand upon the shoulder of the prostrate man, 'it is better than to fall before some ignoble foe. These papers are now ready, Watson. If you will help me with our prisoner, I think that we may get started for London at once.'

It was no easy task to move Von Bork, for he was a strong and a desperate man. Finally, holding either arm, the two friends walked him very slowly down the garden walk which he had trod with such proud confidence when he received the congratulations of the famous diplomatist only a few hours before. After a short, final struggle he was hoisted, still bound hand and foot, into the spare seat of the little car. His precious valise was wedged in beside him.

'I trust that you are as comfortable as circumstances permit,' said Holmes when the final arrangements were made. 'Should I be guilty of a liberty if I lit a cigar and placed it between your lips?'

But all amenities were wasted upon the angry German.

'I suppose you realise, Mr Sherlock Holmes,' said he, 'that if your government bears you out in this treatment it becomes an act of war.'

'What about your government and all this treatment?' said Holmes, tapping the valise.

'You are a private individual. You have no warrant for my arrest. The whole proceeding is absolutely illegal and outrageous.'

'Absolutely,' said Holmes.

'Kidnapping a German subject.'

'And stealing his private papers.'

'Well, you realise your position, you and your accomplice here. If I were to shout for help as we pass through the village – '

'My dear sir, if you did anything so foolish you would probably enlarge the two limited titles of our village inns by giving us "The Dangling Prussian" as a signpost. The Englishman is a patient creature, but at present his temper is a little inflamed, and it would be as well not to try him too far. No, Mr Von Bork, you will go with us in a quiet, sensible fashion to Scotland

Yard, whence you can send for your friend, Baron Von Herling, and see if even now you may not fill that place which he has reserved for you in the ambassadorial suite. As to you, Watson, you are joining up with your old service, as I understand, so London won't be out of your way. Stand with me here upon the terrace, for it may be the last quiet talk that we shall ever have.'

The two friends chatted in intimate converse for a few minutes, recalling once again the days of the past, while their prisoner vainly wriggled to undo the bonds that held him. As they turned to the car Holmes pointed back to the moonlit sea and shook a thoughtful head.

'There's an east wind coming, Watson.'

'I think not, Holmes. It is very warm.'

'Good old Watson! You are the one fixed point in a changing age. There's an east wind coming all the same, such a wind as never blew on England yet. It will be cold and bitter, Watson, and a good many of us may wither before its blast. But it's God's own wind none the less, and a cleaner, better, stronger land will lie in the sunshine when the storm has cleared. Start her up, Watson, for it's time that we were on our way. I have a cheque for five hundred pounds which should be cashed early, for the drawer is quite capable of stopping it if he can.'

Afterword

The story so far: author Arthur Conan Doyle, tired of his charismatic detective creation Sherlock Holmes, killed him off in a story called 'The Final Problem', in which he tumbled to his death locked in combat with his arch enemy Professor Moriarty, the Napoleon of Crime, down the Reichenbach Falls in Switzerland. The reading public were aghast; Conan Doyle was delighted, for he now felt free to concentrate his efforts on what he considered his worthier literary works, his historical novels. He didn't want to be known just as 'the Sherlock man'. Time passed and then the author lit upon the plot for 'a real creeper' of a story featuring a phantom hound which roamed the moors of Devon bringing death to the members of the Baskerville family. In constructing this novel, he realised that he needed a detective hero to resolve the mystery. Common sense informed him that it would be silly to invent a new detective character when he had already created the world's greatest sleuth. So reluctantly he revived Sherlock Holmes for his novel *The Hound of the Baskervilles*, stating quite categorically that this adventure had taken place before the Reichenbach incident.

Now read on.

The reappearance of Mr Sherlock Holmes of Baker Street in *The Hound of the Baskervilles* gave readers and in particular publishers the hope that the detective would return permanently, that Doyle could be persuaded to drag the fellow from his watery grave and set him upon a new series of adventures. The author was approached by several eager publishers with this in mind and when the New York publisher of *Collier's* magazine offered him four thousand dollars per story he accepted.

No doubt it was the money that finally persuaded Doyle to resume the Holmes saga, but it was also the case that in 1903 the author was a different man from the one who had pushed Holmes over the Reichenbach Falls some ten years earlier. The intervening years had seen Doyle's stature, as both a literary and public figure, grow. He had written a wide range of novels and stories as well as plays and poetry and had actively become involved in the Boer War (1889–1902) and had written a history of this conflict and a pamphlet vindicating the actions of the British Army. He had also been knighted in 1902. So now Sir Arthur Conan Doyle was an experienced, well respected and successful man who no longer feared being obscured by the shadow of his detective creation. He had stretched his writing wings and had become an establishment figure. No doubt, he now felt that the readers would recognise Sherlock Holmes as only one of his many literary creations.

It now seems that Holmes's return was inevitable. Although originally Doyle claimed that his death was final and that he had been killed at the Reichenbach Falls, the author admitted later in life, in an article in the *Strand* in 1927, that 'no coroner had ever pronounced upon the body'. While Dr Watson may have believed that Holmes was dead, there was no eyewitness account of what had transpired at that fateful encounter between Holmes and Professor Moriarty. Could it be that deep down in his heart Doyle knew that he had not said his final goodbye to Sherlock Holmes? Consciously or subconsciously Doyle had left the door open for the detective's return and now, ten years on, the time seemed right.

Collier's magazine left the number of stories up to Doyle at first – it was to be no fewer than six, preferably at least eight and ideally twelve. The publisher hoped that some of the stories would feature American settings or contain aspects of particular relevance and interest to readers in the States. The new series would also appear in the *Strand* magazine in Britain. Despite the fact that originally Doyle had considered writing eight new stories, thus fulfilling his contract with *Collier's*, in the end he created thirteen new stories for *The Return*.

In a strange way, now that he had signed the contract to write a fresh series of Holmes's adventures, Doyle relished the challenge and dismissed the fears of those who doubted that he could capture the brilliance of the earlier tales – his mother included. Having set to work, he wrote to her, 'I don't think you need have any fears about Sherlock. I am not conscious of any failing powers, and my work is no less conscientious than of old . . . I have done no Sherlock Holmes stories for seven or eight years and I do not see why I should not have another go at them.'

It is true that Doyle was not approaching this collection of tales with the same eager, youthful, innovative fervour that he possessed when penning *The Adventures*; but now he was a more practised, experienced and professional writer.

Doyle's confidence that he could, like a practised magician, bring Holmes back to life by sleight of hand may have been boosted by his brother-in-law

E. W. Hornung, who carried out a similar resuscitation act successfully on his own character, Raffles, the gentleman thief. (Indeed it has been suggested by the noted Sherlockian/Doylean author Richard Lancelyn Green that there are echoes of the Raffles stories in several of the tales in *The Return*, especially 'Charles Augustus Milverton', which resembles the Raffles adventure 'The Wrong House'.)

Enthused by the task, Doyle wrote to his mother: ' . . . I have finished the first [story], "The Adventure of the Empty House". The plot, by the way, was given to me by Jean [Jean Leckie, who was to become his wife. They married in 1907], and it is a rare good one. You will think that Holmes was never dead, and that he is now very much alive.'

The focus of this first story, 'The Empty House', which provided the link between *The Memoirs* and *The Return*, is to explain what really happened at the Reichenbach Falls, to explain away Doyle's 'rash act', as he referred to it. The murder mystery involving the death of Ronald Adair is really secondary to the re-establishment of Holmes back in London, back in his Baker Street rooms, back with Watson and back on the case. The fact that neither the details of Holmes's escape from the supposed watery grave, nor his three-year absence from England are entirely convincing does not matter at all. The main thing for readers then, as now, is that Holmes is back. And by the end of the story, with Holmes and Watson in the cosy Baker Street sitting-room, it is as though he has not been away. (We are told that Holmes's brother, Mycroft, alone knew of Holmes's survival and kept on the Baker Street rooms in readiness for his eventual return.) The detective reassures his readers in the closing moments of 'The Empty House' by stating, 'Mr Sherlock Holmes is free to devote his life to examining those interesting little problems which the complex life of London so plentifully presents.'

The tone and scope of this first story is reflected throughout the collection, where often dramatic set pieces take the place of the reasoning process that had been a strong feature of the earlier collections. Doyle's writing always had a strong visual – almost cinematic – quality, and never more so than in *The Return*, which is crowded with vivid, indelible images. In 'The Empty House', for example, the scene of Watson's fainting on seeing his old friend reveal himself by removing his fantastic disguise as an old bookseller, and the silhouette of Holmes against the blinds of 221B as Moran aims his deadly air-gun are powerful vignettes. *The Return* is crammed with such moments: Jonas Oldacre bursting out of his hiding-place on hearing the shouts of 'Fire' in 'The Norwood Builder'; the sinister stick figure drawings which carried deadly warnings and Holmes clapping a pistol to the villain's head in 'The Dancing Men'; the eerily silent and mysterious bearded cyclist in 'The Solitary Cyclist'; the murdered man transfixed to the wall by a harpoon in 'Black Peter'; the shooting of the vile blackmailer in 'Charles Augustus Milverton'; and Watson's rude morning awakening, the brutal murder of Sir Eustace Brackenstall and Holmes clambering on the mantelpiece to scrutinise the bell-rope in 'The Abbey Grange' are clear examples of this. There are more.

If it is true that the flashes of detective brilliance are not as frequent in this collection, they are certainly still there. Holmes's deduction concerning the wine glasses and the bees-wing in 'The Abbey Grange', for example, is masterful and as brilliant as anything found in the earlier stories. However, it has to be admitted that these moments are more isolated than before. This was a point raised in an article by the editor of the American publication, *The Bookman*, in February 1905 in which he both praised and criticised the last story in the collection, 'The Second Stain'. After stating that he thought it was a good story, he added: 'but it is open to criticism that unlike the tales of the *Adventures* and *Memoirs*, it does not convince you of Holmes's superior powers of analytical reasoning. In the old stories you were put in the possession of the facts. Here you must take them for granted.'

Doyle responded to criticisms like these with a weary shrug. In a letter written around this time he said: 'You will appreciate more fully now my intense disinclination to continue these stories which has caused me to resist all entreaty for so many years. It is *impossible* to prevent a certain sameness and want of freshness. The most one can do is to try to produce such stories that if they had come first and the others second, they would then have seemed fresh and good.'

Doyle had a point. Critics were treating this series as though the previous two collections were flawless, which was far from the truth. Of course, also in the intervening years other writers had been busy creating their own brilliant detectives and where Holmes had once stood alone, he now had many rivals and a certain familiarity had crept in.

However, it is interesting to note that when Doyle came to compose a list of the twelve best Sherlock Holmes stories for a competition in the *Strand* in 1926 (excluding those from *The Casebook* which had not yet been published in book form) a third of the number were from *The Return*: 'The Dancing Men' was placed third on account of 'originality of plot'; 'The Empty House' was placed sixth because it explained the 'alleged death of Sherlock Holmes and introduced such a villain as Colonel Sebastian Moran'; 'The Second Stain' came eighth because it dealt 'with diplomacy and intrigue'; and 'The Priory School' was placed tenth, 'if only for the dramatic moment when Holmes points his finger at the Duke'.

The stories in the series were the last to be illustrated by Sidney Paget (who died soon afterwards) and this adds to the sense of their being of the finest vintage. They were also the first to be illustrated by Frederic Dorr Steele in *Collier's* magazine. The image of Holmes he presented in the superb drawings and coloured covers was based on the actor William Gillette, who had played the detective numerous times on the stage. He was, if you like, the Basil Rathbone or Jeremy Brett of his age.

Time lends us a clearer perspective on things and we can now judge the stories with more equanimity. As with *The Adventures* and *The Memoirs*, the quality of the plots and the inventiveness varies from tale to tale, but they are none the less great stories and all criticism pales before them. The character of this great fictional detective and his loyal chronicler shine like diamonds in a fog. The stage is filled with a cast of clients and villains who are vibrant and memorable. They are the fine vintage wine of Sherlockiana and I'm sure you will enjoy them.

His Last Bow – Some Reminiscences of Sherlock Holmes

Despite its title, *His Last Bow* is the penultimate collection of Sherlock Holmes stories, first published in 1917. However there is a sense of finality about this collection, underlined by Watson's Preface, which gives details of Holmes's retirement, 'in a small farm upon the Downs, five miles from Eastbourne'.

After the first set of post-Reichenbach stories appeared in book form as *The Return of Sherlock Holmes* in 1904, Doyle wrote only intermittently about his detective hero. The stories in *His Last Bow* were written over the period 1908–17 – just seven stories in nine years, which was a far cry from the early days when Doyle created all twelve stories in *The Adventures* within a year. The reason for this is not just that the author was growing old and had more calls upon his time; he also really had lost interest in Holmes and only when a clever idea came to him or he felt he needed to earn some extra money would he turn towards Baker Street once more.

It has been noted by many critics that almost all the pre-Reichenbach stories are of the finest vintage, while the post-Reichenbach material is more variable. This, to some extent, is true, but nevertheless each Holmes collection contains its own particular felicities and *His Last Bow* is no exception. Doylean scholar Owen Dudley Edwards has observed that this volume continued the movement begun in *The Return* towards literature for its own sake. In other words these are not merely detective stories but human dramas in which Sherlock Holmes has a pivotal role. Holmes has more work to do than detection and he is called upon by his creator to reflect a wider and increasingly less contained and ordered world. This culminates in the final story, 'His Last Bow', which takes place on the eve of the First World War, in 'the most terrible August in the history of the world'. Soon all the certainties of Holmes's Victorian and Edwardian world would be destroyed, consumed in the flames of war. It is fitting then that this should be the last time we see Holmes and Watson together – and what a memorable and touching moment it is, with the two friends chatting in intimate converse as the sun rises from the sea:

> 'There's an east wind coming, Watson.'
> 'I think not, Holmes, it is very warm.'
> 'Good old Watson. You are the one fixed point in a changing age.'

Doyle knew it was inappropriate to feature Holmes in this changing age, the new world forged out of conflict. Holmes and Watson were creatures of the past, of the world of horse-drawn cabs, gas lighting and telegrams. There was no real place for them in the modern world of aeroplanes, the cinema, motor cars (although one features in 'His Last Bow') and radio.

The other stories in this collection are a lively bunch featuring a clutch of intriguing villains, including Culverton Smith, whose plot to kill Sherlock Holmes almost succeeds, Dr Shlessinger (aka Holy Peters), who preys on the lonely Lady Frances Carfax, Black Gorgiano, the vicious leader of the Red Circle, and Don Juan Murrillo, the cruel dictator known as the Tiger of San Pedro. It is also in this volume we encounter Holmes's brother for the last time. In 'The Bruce-Partington Plans', we discover that the detective's heavyweight sibling not only works for the British government but 'occasionally he *is* the British government'.

While it is true to say that Doyle is always variable in his skill at plotting, as he was at the very beginning with *The Adventures*, he is always bang on target in portraying the relationship between Holmes and Watson. It towers over the plots and adds that indefinable extra to these fine stories which gives them the timeless quality that appeals to each succeeding generation.

Bibliography

Doyle, Arthur Conan, *Memories and Adventures*, Greenhill Books (reprint), 1988

Edwards, Owen Dudley, *The Quest for Sherlock Holmes*, Mainstream Publishing, 1983

Stashower, Daniel, *Teller of Tales: The Life of Arthur Conan Doyle*, Henry Holt, 1999

Riley, Dick and McAllister, Pam, *The Bedside, Bathtub and Armchair Companion to Sherlock Holmes*, 1999

Klinger, Leslie S., editor, *The New Annotated Sherlock Holmes*, Volumes 1 & 2, Norton, 2004

Biography

Arthur Conan Doyle was born in Edinburgh in 1859. After a rigorous Jesuit education he trained to become a doctor at Edinburgh University. Eventually he set up in medical practice in Southsea, and during the quiet periods between patients, he turned his hand to writing. Although Sherlock Holmes was Doyle's greatest creation, he believed that his historical novels, such as *Micah Clarke* and *The White Company*, were of greater literary quality. He also created the irascible Professor Challenger in *The Lost World* and the comic French soldier Brigadier Gerard. Doyle was knighted in 1902. Towards the end of his life he devoted much of his time to his belief in Spiritualism, using his writings as a means of providing funds to support his activities in this field. He died in 1930.